FROZEN STIFF

"Ryan mixes science and great storytelling in this cozy series . . . The forensic details ring true and add substance to this fast-paced and funny mystery. Good plotting and relationship drama keep the mystery rolling, while Mattie's humorous take on life provides many comedic moments."
—*Romantic Times Book Reviews*

"[Mattie's] competence as a former ER nurse, plus a quirky supporting cast, makes the series intriguing. Ryan has a good eye for forensic and medical detail, and Mattie gets to be the woman of the hour in her third outing."
—*Library Journal*

"Absorbing . . . Ryan smoothly blends humor, distinctive characters, and authentic forensic detail."
—*Publishers Weekly*

SCARED STIFF

"An appealing series on multiple fronts: the forensic details will interest Patricia Cornwell readers, though the tone here is lighter, while the often slapstick humor and the blossoming romance between Mattie and Hurley will draw Evanovich fans who don't object to the cozier mood."
—*Booklist*

"Ryan's sharp second mystery . . . shows growing skill at mixing humor with CSI-style crime."
—*Publishers Weekly*

WORKING STIFF

"Sassy, sexy, and suspenseful, Annelise Ryan knocks 'em dead in her wry and original *Working Stiff*."
—Carolyn Hart, author of *Dare to Die*

"Move over, Stephanie Plum. Make way for Mattie Winston, the funniest deputy coroner to cut up a corpse since, well, ever. I loved every minute I spent with her in this sharp and sassy debut mystery."
—Laura Levine, author of *Killer Cruise*

"Mattie Winston, RN, wasn't looking for excitement when she became a morgue assistant—quite the contrary—but she got plenty and so will readers who won't be able to put this book down."
—Leslie Meier, author of *Mother's Day Murder*

"*Working Stiff* has it all: suspense, laughter, a spicy dash of romance—and a heroine who's guaranteed to walk off with your heart. Mattie Winston is an unforgettable character who has me begging for a sequel. Annelise Ryan, are you listening?"
—Tess Gerritsen, *New York Times* bestselling author of *The Keepsake*

"Mattie is klutzy and endearing, and there are plenty of laugh-out-loud moments . . . her foibles are still fun and entertaining."
—*Romantic Times Book Reviews*

"Ryan, the psuedonym of a Wisconsin emergency nurse, brings her professional expertise to her crisp debut . . . Mattie wisecracks her way through an increasingly complex plot."
—*Publishers Weekly*

Books by Annelise Ryan

WORKING STIFF

SCARED STIFF

FROZEN STIFF

LUCKY STIFF (coming soon)

Published by Kensington Publishing Corporation

Frozen Stiff

Annelise Ryan

KENSINGTON BOOKS
http://www.kensingtonbooks.com

KENSINGTON BOOKS are published by

Kensington Publishing Corp.
119 West 40th Street
New York, NY 10018

All Kensington titles, imprints and distributed lines are available at special quantity discounts for bulk purchases for sales promotion, premiums, fund-raising, educational or institutional use.

Special book excerpts or customized printings can also be created to fit specific needs. For details, write or phone the office of the Kensington Special Sales Manager: Kensington Publishing Corp., 119 West 40th Street, New York, NY 10018. Attn. Special Sales Department. Phone: 1-800-221-2647.

Kensington and the K logo Reg. U.S. Pat. & TM Off.

ISBN-13: 978-0-7582-3457-5
ISBN-10: 0-7582-3457-0

First Hardcover Printing: September 2011
First Mass Market Printing: August 2012

10 9 8 7 6 5 4 3 2 1

Printed in the United States of America

For Scott, who has always been my "best man."

Acknowledgments

As always, a hearty thanks to my editor, Peter Senftleben, and my agent, Jamie Brenner, for your continued support and faith in me. I'm truly grateful to have you on my team. And hugs to my family and friends . . . I couldn't do it without your love and support.

Finally, a warm thanks to all the readers who have gotten to know Mattie and the other denizens of Sorenson, particularly those of you who have taken the time to write to me. Know that you are appreciated.

Chapter 1

Death is never pretty and this one is no exception. But the victim, whose face is largely untouched by the violence that killed her, is exceptionally beautiful: a tiny, well-shaped nose, huge blue eyes, auburn hair, pouty lips, and porcelain skin with nary a blemish. She falls short of perfection however, because her lips have a deep bluish tinge to them and much of that pale coloring comes from a lack of circulation. People tend to change colors once they're dead, especially when they're lying on top of snow like this woman is.

I hang around dead people a lot these days. My name is Mattie Winston and I work as a deputy coroner here in the small Wisconsin town of Sorenson. I've lived here all my life and before my current job I worked in the local hospital: five years as an ER nurse and seven in the OR. As a result, I know a goodly portion of the people who live in town, but this woman's face is unfamiliar to me. I'm certain I'd remember her if I'd ever seen her before because she is striking, even in death. This makes me suspect she's an out-of-towner, and the fact that Junior Feller—one of the two uniformed cops standing beside me and a Sorenson lifer like me—doesn't recognize her affirms this belief. I suppose it's possible our victim is simply new to the area, but I doubt it. If a woman this beautiful had moved to town it would have hit the gossip mill in record time and worried wives would be out in force with their husbands, keeping a watchful eye. Plus the victim isn't dressed like the average Sorensonian. Her tiny, petite frame is covered with knit black slacks, a form-fitting, lime-green jacket, and high-heeled leather boots. The clothes look like impractical, expensive, designer duds, whereas most of the locals tend to favor clodhopper boots, down-filled coats, furry trapper hats with earflaps, and layers of long underwear that make it look like the town is populated by descendants of the Michelin Man.

"I'd venture to say the cause of death is obvious," says Ron Colbert, the second uniformed cop. He makes this pronouncement with great authority, as if it's some brilliant investigative deduction despite the fact that we can all see a knife buried in the left side of the victim's chest. Colbert is new on the force—I met him for the first time a few weeks ago at the scene of another homicide—and like most rookies, he seems both eager and naïve, though my assumption of naïveté may be due to the fact that he looks like he's twelve years old thanks to his small stature and a zit in the middle of his forehead that looks like a third eye. It was Colbert who discovered the body as he was driving along the road: the bright splash of green on top of the fresh, white snow caught his attention. No doubt it was a bit of a rush for him since the most exciting calls our cops typically get are for teenaged marauders who are out cow tipping and snipe hunting, or an illegally parked tractor at one of the town's bars.

Deaths of any sort aren't all that common here in Sorenson—Wisconsinites tend to be a hardy bunch as our winters weaned out the weak gene pool decades ago. Homicides are even rarer, and as such they are often the highlight of a cop's career. Colbert must feel as if he hit the jackpot by running across two of them in a matter of weeks, so his eagerness is easy to understand.

I shift my focus from the corpse to take in my surroundings. The body is lying on the edge of a large, harvested cornfield blanketed with six inches of fresh snow that fell during the night. The morning sun glistens on the snow's surface, making it sparkle like a bed of diamonds. It's an isolated spot; there are fields all around us, the nearest house is half a mile away, and the road beside the body is hardly a main thoroughfare though the plows have already been through. All in all it combines to make for a picturesque setting. Given that it's the Friday before Thanksgiving, this slice of pastoral serenity triggers thoughts of traveling o'er the fields to Grandmother's house . . . until I remember the corpsicle.

I look back at the body site and note how clumps of snow cast aside by the plow have rolled down the shoulder's edge and into the bordering field, settling atop the small drifts like little snowman turds. The clumps are all around us, but there are none on the body. That, along with the blood-smeared path punched through the snowbank piled up on the shoulder, tells me our victim was dumped here after the plow came through.

I say so and Izzy, who is busy taking pictures of the scene, nods his agreement.

Izzy, whose full name is Izthak Rybarceski, is the county Medical Examiner as well as my boss, my friend, my neighbor, my landlord, and the anti-me. He is barely five feet tall with dark skin and hair—most of which circles his balding head like a friar fringe—whereas I clock in at six feet, and my fair skin, blond hair, and size twelve feet earned me the nickname Yeti in high school. Our only commonalities are a shared fondness for men, our tendency to grow insulation all year long like bears readying for hibernation, and our knowledge of internal anatomy.

I've only been at this job since early October. Izzy offered it to me a couple of months after I caught one of my hospital coworkers in an OR having a face-to-face meeting with a surgeon's one-eyed trouser snake. Unfortunately that surgeon was my husband, David Winston. In order to escape the painful reminders and curious stares, I fled both my job and my marriage. Izzy was kind enough to let me stay in the small cottage he has behind his house and it provided me with somewhere to hide while I licked my wounds. My new home is charming and cozy, and I'm forever grateful to Izzy for allowing me to move into it. But because Izzy has been my neighbor for several years, the cottage does have one major drawback: it's a stone's throw away from my marital home.

After a couple of months of isolation and self-pity, I emerged in need of money and a job. Given that the next nearest hospital is over an hour away and my main talent is my ability to look at blood and guts without puking or fainting, I feared I'd end up dressed in a trash-bag overcoat living under a bridge, or worse . . . with my mother. But Izzy rescued me once again by offering me a job as his assistant and nowadays I'm in the business of dissecting lives in every sense of the word.

I find my new career highly interesting on many levels, not the least of which is Steve Hurley, the primary homicide detective with the Sorenson Police Department. Unfortunately, I can't help but notice that he's the one thing missing from the scene before me now.

"Is Hurley coming?" I ask no one in particular.

"He had to go to Madison yesterday to testify in a trial and spent the night there," Junior says. "He called just a bit ago to say he had just gotten back and would be here soon." As if on cue, we hear the sound of a car approaching.

I look toward the road and recognize the car as Hurley's. My heart skips a beat, something that seems to happen whenever Hurley is around. His black hair, intense blue eyes, and sit-on-my-lap thighs always get me revved up, but I've been working extra hard to rein in my hormones. That's because, lately, Hurley has been oddly distant whenever we're together: courteous and professional, but also strangely detached. It's a puzzling change given that we've shared a couple of heated kisses in the not-so-distant past and I'm afraid I know the reason for it.

I watch him now as he parks behind my car, climbs out, and scans the road. When I see him shake his head in dismay, I think I know why: the macadam is damp, but otherwise clear. What little snow the plows left on the road has melted beneath the morning sun, effectively obliterating any tire-track evidence we might have been able to collect.

"Too bad the plow came through," Hurley hollers down to us, verifying my suspicion.

"It may not be all bad," I yell back. "It looks like the body was dumped here and knowing when the plow came through may help us figure out when."

Unfortunately the killer's trail down to the body has been smeared, smudged, and kicked apart enough that there are no usable boot prints to identify, damage I suspect may have been done intentionally. All may not be lost, however. Incidental evidence, like a fallen hair or fiber, could have been dropped along the path. Keenly aware of this possibility, everyone who has arrived on the scene has been careful to blaze their own trail to the body rather than contaminate the existing one.

After Junior points out the path the rest of us have followed, Hurley makes his way down to us and the body. I try to catch his eye to gauge today's level of temperament toward me, but his attention is focused solely on the surrounding area until he reaches our little group. Then his gaze shifts to the victim.

He stops dead in his tracks and the rosy color the cold has stamped on his cheeks drains away with frightening rapidity, leaving him nearly as pale as our corpse. As a nurse I've seen that happen plenty of times before, usually right before someone faints and does a face-plant on the floor.

I edge a bit closer to Hurley just in case. I harbor no illusions about my ability to catch him—he is well over six feet tall and sturdily built. But I figure if he does start to go down I can at least shove him hard enough to keep him from falling into our crime scene.

"Are you okay?" I ask him.

The others turn to look at him but he ignores us for several beats as he stares at the body. "Not really," he says finally, cutting his eyes back toward the neighboring field. He covers his mouth with one hand and his Adam's apple bounces as he swallows hard. "I'm feeling a bit off this morning. Must be something I ate."

The others in the group all shift a step away from Hurley, no doubt because they're afraid of getting ralphed on. I, on the other hand, move closer. I overcame my aversion to gross bodily excretions very early in my nursing career and it's going to take more than the threat of a little early morning barf to keep me away from a man who I've discovered can curl my toes with one kiss.

"I think I'm going to call someone else in for this one," Hurley says. He turns and backtracks along the trail he came in on, allowing me a few moments to surreptitiously admire his backside. Along the way he takes out his cell phone and punches in a number, but by the time he gets an answer he is too far away for me to hear the conversation. When he reaches the road, he hangs up and turns back to us.

"Bob Richmond is going to take this one," he hollers. "He should be here in about ten minutes. I'm heading home to bed."

This is bad news for me on several fronts. Bob Richmond is a grizzled old detective who is basically retired, though he occasionally fills in when needed. He's cranky, impatient, and built like the Pillsbury Dough Boy—and that's before you stuff him into a down-filled winter jacket. Plus, he's not Hurley, and as far as I'm concerned, that's his biggest fault.

Crestfallen, I watch as Hurley climbs into his car and pulls away without so much as a wave or a second glance. Once again I'm left feeling slighted and snubbed, and I have no idea why. Actually, that's not true; I do have a suspicion. A few weeks ago, while riding in the back of an ambulance with Hurley, fearing he was mortally wounded, I whispered in his ear that I might be falling in love with him. He was more or less unconscious at the time so I didn't think he heard me, but now I'm not so sure.

Swallowing down my frustration, I turn my attention back to our victim and try to push thoughts of Hurley from my mind, which is like trying not to breathe. Izzy has finished taking his pictures and we squat down on either side of the corpse to begin our field processing. The body is cold and rigid but I'm not sure if it's from the weather, rigor mortis, or a mix of the two. If she's frozen it will make it more difficult for us to determine a time of death since none of the usual indicators—stage of rigor, body temperature, and lividity—will be of much help. I'm getting a sinking feeling that nothing about this case is going to be easy.

As Izzy and I process the body—looking for surface evidence, bagging the hands, and rolling her over to place a sheet beneath her—Ron Colbert and Junior carefully examine the surrounding snow. About fifteen minutes into our efforts we hear another car engine approach and an old-model, blue sedan covered with patches of rust and primer rumbles around the curve.

I haven't seen Bob Richmond in a few years and he's even bigger now than he was then. I guess his weight at well over four hundred pounds, and as I watch him struggle out of his car and waddle toward us, the words, "Bring me Solo and the Wookie," come to mind. By the time he reaches the crest of the snow berm above us, he's so winded, all he can do is stand there for a minute and gasp for breath, his ragged exhalations creating giant cumulus clouds as they hit the cold morning air.

"Anyone . . . know . . . who she is?" he manages, staring down at the corpse.

We all shake our heads.

"Any trace?"

Izzy fields this one. "Nothing obvious yet. It looks like she was killed somewhere else and dumped here. We've got a trail in the snow but it's too messed up to be useful for prints."

"TOD?" Richmond asks.

Izzy shrugs. "At this point there's no way to know when she was killed. And since she may be frozen to some degree, I'm not sure how accurate a range I'll be able to give you later on."

Richmond nods and then looks over at me, staring with a curious expression. "Do I know you?"

"Mattie Winston. I'm a deputy coroner."

He looks confused and shakes his head, as if he's trying to get his hamster back on its wheel. "Since when?"

"Since a few weeks ago."

"What were you before that?"

"I worked as a nurse at Mercy Hospital."

His assumes an *aha* expression and nods. "You worked in the operating room, right?"

"For the past few years, yes. Before that I worked in the ER."

"I think you were working when I had my bunions removed."

I was, so I nod but say nothing. Most of what I remember about his case is how hard we struggled to move him off the OR table, but I figure mentioning that might not be the best way to start getting reacquainted.

"So how did you end up doing this?" he says, gesturing toward the dead woman.

Izzy and Junior exchange a look and then go back to their respective jobs with renewed intensity. They already know the sordid details, as does most of the town. Colbert, being new here, does not, but I can tell from the way he's eyeing the other two men that he caught their look and knows there's something juicy behind it.

"It's a long story," I tell Richmond, hoping he'll take the hint. But judging from the bemused expression on his face, all I've done is pique his interest.

"Aren't you married to a surgeon or something like that?" Richmond asks.

"Sort of," I say vaguely.

"Sort of?" he snorts. "You're sort of married? Isn't that like being a little bit pregnant?"

"We're separated," I tell him, trying to color my comment with an *as if it's any of your business* tone. "I'm filing for divorce."

"Is that right?" The curious tone of his voice tells me he's clearly unimpressed with my attempt to shut him down. "That's a darned shame. What went wrong?"

I find it hard to believe Richmond doesn't already know.

Gossip in our town flows faster than an arterial bleed, and the fallout from the breakup of my marriage was some of the biggest news to hit in a long time, given that it was reminiscent of the Lewinsky-Clinton debacle and tied to a couple of murders.

"Where the hell have you been, Richmond?" I ask irritably. "Living in a cave?"

"Wait," he says, his eyes narrowing. "Are you the one who was involved with that nurse who was murdered? Wasn't she boffing your husband or something?"

"Or something," I say irritably.

"So *you're* the one who got Steve Hurley stabbed."

I glare at him. "You make it sound like I stabbed him myself."

Richmond arches his brows at me as if to say, *Well, did you?*

"He was in the wrong place at the wrong time," I say. "That's all."

"Great. That's just great," Richmond says with a hugely dramatic sigh. "No wonder Hurley handed you off to me. Am I going to have to be looking over my shoulder every few seconds to make sure someone isn't coming after me with a deadly weapon?"

"We can only hope," I mutter under my breath. I turn my back to him and see that Izzy and the uniformed cops are hopping from one foot to the other, clapping their arms around themselves to try to keep warm. Richmond, who would be amply insulated if he was standing stark naked, appears immune to the cold. I'm pretty comfortable myself, mostly because I'm so hot under the collar.

Izzy says, "Hey, Bob, is it okay if we wrap this one up and take her in?"

Richmond doesn't answer right away and I suspect it's his passive-aggressive way of exerting his authority. "She was a

looker, wasn't she?" he observes. Everyone nods. "And nobody here recognizes her?" We all shake our heads. "So
probably not from around here," he concludes. "Yeah, go
ahead and take her in. When are you planning to post her?"

Izzy says, "Probably this afternoon. Depends on how
cold she is."

"Too bad you don't have a person-sized microwave,"
Richmond says. "We could put her in on defrost mode." He
laughs while we stare at him, and when he realizes his joke
has fallen flat he clears his throat and says, "Yeah, go ahead
and load her up."

"Do you want to call for transport or should I?" Izzy asks.

Richmond looks back toward the road with a puzzled expression and I groan, knowing what's coming next. Because
Izzy's legs are half the length of mine and his car is an old,
restored Impala with a bench front seat, every time I ride
with him I feel like one of those giant pretzels you can buy
in a mall kiosk. Today, to avoid the contortions, Izzy rode
with me to the scene in my recently acquired car—a shiny,
midnight blue, slightly used hearse.

"The transport is here already," Richmond says.

"That's not the transport," I explain, hearing the cops
snort behind me. "It's my personal vehicle."

"What do you mean your *personal vehicle?*"

"Just what I said. What part of it don't you understand?"

Richmond raises an eyebrow. "You're telling me you
drive a hearse? All the time?"

"Yeah. You got a problem with that?"

"It's rather pathetic, don't you think?"

I feel like telling him that being large enough to require a
backup beeper is pathetic, too, but I don't.

"If you're going to drive around in a hearse, why not use
it as one?" Richmond asks.

"Don't need to," I toss out. "These days you can buy

those little scented trees with the smell of decomp already in them."

We glare at one another for several seconds until Richmond mutters a "Hmph," and waddles off, dialing a number into his cell phone.

I've had the hearse for a few weeks now. After totaling my regular car—which was actually David's car according to the insurance and financing paperwork—I was left looking for a new vehicle I could afford on my own. The hearse was the only thing I could find. Though I wasn't too pleased with it initially, it's kind of grown on me. And my dog, Hoover, loves it. It's full of all kinds of interesting smells that can keep him occupied for hours.

Izzy and I get back to the job at hand, wrapping the woman's body in our sheet. The protruding knife makes the task a little challenging, though not as much as one might expect given the victim's endowments. Then, with some help from the uniforms, we slide her into a body bag, again taking care not to dislodge the murder weapon.

When we're done, Izzy takes out his wallet, hands me some money, and says, "Drive to Gerhardt's home improvement store, pick up some plastic buckets and trowels, and bring them back here. We'll need to collect the surface snow from the trail, and from beneath and around her body so we can look for trace evidence. I'll stay here and see that she gets to the morgue."

I nod and trudge my way back to the road, taking care to follow the same trail we made when we arrived on the scene. Since Richmond's car is parked behind mine I have to walk past it to get to my hearse. He is standing behind his driver's side door, which is open, leaning on it as he talks on his cell phone. I glance in at the car's interior and see that the passenger side floor is littered nearly seat high with wrappers and fast-food bags.

As I open the door to my hearse, Richmond ends his call, snapping his cell phone closed. "Funeral home will be here in fifteen," he yells down to the group by the body. Then he turns his attention on me. "Hey, Mattie?"

"What?"

"Do you know what you're doing with this job or do I have to stay here until you come back so I can watch you collect the evidence?"

I don't know if it's his attitude that's pissing me off or the fact that Hurley isn't here, but whichever it is, I'm definitely not feeling the love. I sense that he's eager to leave so I tell him, "I think you better stick around. I've never done snow evidence before."

He rolls his eyes and sighs. "Make it fast then," he grumbles. "And bring me back something to eat, would you?"

I scowl at him and try to think of a witty retort, but nothing comes to mind. Then, as I'm pulling away, an idea hits me. If I make a quick stop at home to let Hoover out for a break, maybe I can bring Richmond back a yellow Sno-Cone.

Chapter 2

As if the day hasn't gotten off to a bad enough start, when I arrive at the home improvement store, I see my brother-in-law, Lucien Colter, browsing the aisle straight ahead of me. I'm not a big fan of Lucien's. Though he seems to be a good husband to my sister, Desi, and a good father to their two kids, Ethan and Erika, he's utterly lacking in class and about as subtle as a baboon's ass. Lucien is a defense lawyer—and a highly successful one at that. I suspect his annoying persona and rumpled, unkempt look make a lot of people dismiss him, thinking he's a doofus or an incompetent. But to do so is a mistake. Dismissing Lucien is like partnering up with Dick Cheney for a hunting trip.

As far as I know, Lucien is faithful to my sister, but every conversation I have with him is heavily laden with crass sexual innuendo that leaves me feeling like I need a shower. So when I see him now, the first thing I do is look for a place to hide. I turn to my left and try to dart past a display of lightbulbs, only to have my foot slide on a melted pool of water from the snow I've tracked in. I grab the closest shelf to catch my balance and briefly think I've avoided disaster. Then the entire thing gives way, crashing down on top of the two shelves below it, clattering loudly as they collide. The tinkling sound of breaking glass fills the air as hundreds of lightbulbs are crushed beneath the shelves' weight.

Next thing I know, I'm sitting in the middle of an ocean of glass shards and tiny cardboard containers. I hear a huge collective gasp as everyone in the store within a mile radius of me turns to look to see what the commotion is about. One of the store clerks rushes toward me: a tall, skinny kid with a terminal case of acne.

"Holy crap, lady!" the kid says, his eyes hugely round. A plastic name badge pinned to his red vest says his name is Daniel. "You took down the whole display. *That's* going to cost you."

Since I expected the first words out of his mouth to be concern for my welfare, I'm momentarily stymied by this comment, enough so that I momentarily forget how I ended up in this predicament to begin with. Then I'm reminded when I hear Lucien's voice holler out.

"Mattiekins!"

I look over my shoulder to find Lucien standing behind me, his blue eyes sparkling with barely contained amusement, his strawberry-blond hair slicked back with enough grease to lube a fleet of cars. He's dressed in his usual worn and wrinkled suit—so threadbare it shines—and his pale blue shirt has a large mustard stain on the front of it. He helps me up, the two of us crunching bits of glass beneath our feet, and then he gives me a too-tight hug, his way of copping an easy feel. I squirm loose and push him away from me.

"Hello, Lucien. Fancy meeting you here."

"I stopped by to pick up a new snowblower. The old one went tits up."

I hear a few more gasps in the crowd milling around us and I'm not sure if it's disgust over Lucien's crass language, or mourning cries for a dead snowblower—an extended family member if you want to live through a winter in Wisconsin.

One of the men in the crowd yells out, "Hey, buddy, take my advice and get the Toro 1800. I cleared an entire acre of drive in one hour with that thing in the winter of oh-eight."

Another guy pipes up and says, "Hell, no, go with Craftsman. It threw that heavy wet snow we had last year a good twenty-five feet or more."

Within seconds, a rousing, chest-puffing debate ensues among the men in the group. Snowblowers are a measure of macho in Wisconsin and after any hefty snowfall you can find men on every block metaphorically unzipping and comparing blade size, horsepower, stages, and throw capacity. Any guy using a shovel is assumed to have gonads the size of a squirrel's.

The pimply-faced clerk is joined by another red-vested dweeb wearing a badge with the name Dick on it. "Jesus Christ, lady, what the hell is wrong with you?" Dick says, living up to his name. "You're going to have to pay for this, you know."

"Look, I'm sorry," I tell him. "My foot slipped in some water and I—"

"Clearly these shelves weren't constructed safely," Lucien jumps in.

Dick shoots him a give-me-a-break look and rolls his eyes.

Lucien quickly counters by whipping out a bent business card that still bears perforation marks along the edges, advertising the fact that it was printed on a personal computer. "This," he says, waving one hand over the scene as he hands the card to Dick with the other, "is obvious negligence. Not to mention the fact that you don't have any nonslip rugs in place. I'm a lawyer and my client here has been seriously traumatized by her injuries. Hell, her pain and suffering alone must be worth a good hundred thousand or so. Who's in charge here?"

Dick's red face pales. "I . . . he . . . I'll call the store manager," he says, grabbing a walkie-talkie clipped to his belt.

A heavyset woman off to my left drops to the floor and yells out, "Oh, no! The floor is wet here, too. I think I've twisted my knee. Can I have one of your cards?" she asks Lucien.

As other people in the crowd start taking a closer look at the floor beneath them, Dick scurries off at a panicked clip toward the front desk.

"Thanks, I think," I tell Lucien.

"Anything for you, Sweet Cheeks," he says. "And I know just how you can pay me back," he adds with a lecherous wink.

My cell phone rings and I take it out, grateful I won't have to hear the specifics of Lucien's payment plan. He leans over and sneaks a peek at the face of the phone to see who is calling and smiles when Hurley's name pops up.

"Ooh, a call from that hot detective," he says, wiggling his eyebrows. "Are you two bumping fuzzies yet?"

"Hardly," I say, still bristling over Hurley's distant attitude of late. "I think I scared him off by using the 'L' word back when I thought he might be dying."

"You told him you're a lesbian?" Lucien says loud enough for everyone to hear. "Are you?" he adds, looking intrigued.

Someone in the surrounding crowd yells out, "Hey, lawyer guy, can I have a card, too?" followed by a chorus of "Me

too, me too, me too." I'm saved from any further Lucien humil-
iations as a swarm of people close in and I gingerly pick my
way out of the lightbulb debris pile to answer Hurley's call.

"Hey, what's up, Hurley? Are you feeling better?"

"I'm fine."

I glance back and see Lucien completely surrounded by
potential clients looking to make a buck the good old American way—by suing someone. So I take advantage of his dis-
traction and disappear down a nearby aisle. "Are you sure?"
I say to Hurley. "You were looking pretty peaked the last
time I saw you, like maybe you're coming down with something. 'Tis the season, you know. Did you get a flu shot?"

"My health is fine," Hurley says. "Where are you?"

I tell him where I am and why, leaving out the details
about the lightbulb display.

"I need to talk to you," he says. "Can you come over to
my place later?"

An invite to the inner sanctum! My day is starting to look
better. I've never been inside Hurley's house, though I did
some snooping a while back and found out where he lives.
The fact that he hasn't invited me over has left me wondering if he has something to hide, or if I was reading a little too
much into the few full-body ogles and curl-my-toes kisses
we've shared thus far.

"Sure," I tell him, trying not to sound as eager as I am. "I
have to help Izzy post that body we found this morning, so it
will probably be five or later before I can get there."

"That's fine."

"Okay. I'll see you then."

I end the call before he has a chance to change his mind.
At first I'm pretty excited about the invite, hoping Hurley
wants to talk about our future relationship. But then I recall
the recent change in his attitude and wonder if I'm fooling
myself. In my experience, most men's understanding of

commitment is limited to mental institutions and beer brand loyalty. Maybe Hurley's planning to hit me with the let's-just-be-friends discussion, or the oops-I-meant-to-tell-you-I'm-married discussion, or the I-thought-you-knew-I-was-gay discussion.

My cell phone rings and when I see it's Hurley calling me back, panic rears its ugly head. *Damn, he's changed his mind already.*

I wince as I answer, bracing myself for the blow. "Hello?"

"I thought you might want my address," Hurley says. "Unless you somehow know where I live already."

Busted!

I consider trying to lie my way out of it by saying something like, *Oh yeah, silly me. I guess that would help.* But I don't. "Hey, Hurley, it's a small town. And you're not the only one with investigative resources, you know."

"Good," he says. "I plan to take full advantage of your resources." Before I can respond to that he adds, "See you later," and hangs up.

I'm left standing next to the nuts and bolts display feeling edgy and oddly titillated. I can think of several "resources" I possess that I'd love to let Hurley take advantage of, but I'm pretty sure that isn't what he meant. Whatever his meaning, my curiosity is definitely aroused. As are several other parts of my body.

Chapter 3

I make it out of the store without any further gropes from Lucien or attacks from the red-vested meanies, and arrive back at the body dump site about ten minutes later. Richmond is still there, wedged behind his steering wheel, his car showing a definite tilt toward the driver's side. As I haul my buckets and trowels out of the back of the hearse, he rolls down his window and hollers out to me, "Did you get me something to eat?"

"Sorry," I say, flashing him a fake smile. "The closest thing they had to anything edible at the hardware store was a package of tulip bulbs."

"Shit," I hear him mutter. The window goes back up and his door opens. I hear a series of grunts and groans as he tries to climb out of the car, and I consider offering him my jack to make it easier. Instead I leave him to his struggles and make my way back down to the body dump site. By the time I get there Richmond is standing by the snow berm above us, talking on his cell phone.

The body has been removed and though Izzy and Junior are gone, Ron Colbert is still here, standing guard over the site and trying to stay warm—newbies always get the dreck work.

I hand him a couple of buckets and a trowel. "I think all we need is the top, skim layer," I tell him. "If you can start collecting the surface snow from here up to the berm along the killer's trail, I'll do the body site."

Colbert nods and the two of us go about collecting our samples like two kids at the beach digging for clams. Fortunately the snow is the light, powdery kind so it's not difficult to collect, or very heavy once we do. By the time we're done, we have eight buckets of snow to haul up to my car.

As I grab two of them and slog my way along the circuitous trail back to the road, another car drives up. Richmond approaches the driver, hands over some money, and takes a pizza in return.

"Are you kidding me?" I say as the car drives off. "You ordered a pizza to be delivered out here?"

"Jealous?" he says, setting the box on the hood of his car and opening it.

As the smells of melted mozzarella, pepperoni, and sausage waft my way, I find that I am. I haven't had breakfast and it's now almost lunchtime. And that pizza is making my mouth water.

"A little," I confess.

"Then have a slice."

I consider his offer, arguing with myself that I should refuse simply to make a point. But it seems like biting off my nose to spite my face, or biting off some pizza to spite my hips. In the end, my stomach can't resist the smell and I toss my buckets into the back of the hearse and head back to Richmond's car. Colbert, who has deposited his buckets next to Richmond's car for now, has already swiped a slice for himself without asking, a severe breach of rookie etiquette. If looks could kill, Colbert would be as dead as our victim, judging from the expression on Richmond's face.

"Find anything?" Richmond asks as I take my first bite, giving my taste buds a mini orgasm.

Colbert and I both shake our heads. Once I've swallowed I say, "Nothing obvious, but once we get back to the lab, who knows?"

"Wouldn't count on it," Richmond grumbles. "The frigging criminals are getting way too smart these days. They watch all those forensic shows on TV and it's like giving 'em a primer on how to commit the perfect crime."

I finish scarfing down my slice of pizza ahead of Colbert and eye what's left in the box. But Richmond has a go-ahead-make-my-day look on his face that tells me he's shared all he's going to.

"We have four more buckets of snow to bring up," I tell him. "Want to give us a hand?"

He shoves a half-eaten slice of pizza in his mouth and lets it hang there while he claps his hands.

"Very funny," I grumble.

He shrugs and takes the slice out of his mouth, tearing off a large bite as he does so. "I'm here in a supervisory capacity only," he mumbles around a mouthful of pizza.

"Come on," I urge. "The exercise will do you good."

Judging from the look Richmond gives me, the word *exercise* is akin to the Antichrist. His smug laziness pisses me off, but rather than show it, I shrug to feign indifference and turn like I'm going back down to the crime scene. Then I accidentally on purpose nudge the pizza box, causing it to slide off the hood of the car. I make a half-assed attempt to catch it, ensuring that it tips upside down, dumping its contents onto the road.

"Oops," I say. "Sorry about that."

"Goddammittohell!" Richmond slurs past another mouthful of pizza. With a grunt and a groan he bends down and starts picking the slices up from the ground, placing them back in the box. If I think I've saved him from himself, I quickly realize otherwise as I watch him flick some gravel off one of the slices and then proceed to eat it.

Muttering to myself, I head back to the body site and trudge two more buckets up, passing Colbert along the way. I wait for him to bring the final two up and place them in the back of the hearse.

"Thanks, I appreciate the help," I say loudly for Richmond's benefit. I slam the tailgate door closed and glare at Richmond, who is still stone-picking his slices. "I'm ready to head back to the morgue," I tell him.

"I'm not," he says, shoving more pizza into his maw of a mouth.

"Guess I'll see you back there then."

He shakes his head at me and swallows down his food. "I should go with you, to ensure the chain of evidence."

"As a deputy coroner, I can do that alone. But if you want to come with me, you better do it now because, ready or not, I'm leaving." I climb in my car, start the engine, and have the satisfaction of seeing Richmond's face flush nearly purple as he grabs his pizza box, throws it into the passenger seat of his car, and then dashes—if that lumbering gait can be called a dash—to the driver's side of the car. As he squeezes in behind the steering wheel his car dips heavily to one side, and as I pull out I see him start his car with one hand as he shoves another piece of pizza into his mouth with the other.

Chapter 4

Richmond follows me back to the morgue, steering with one hand while he shovels food into his mouth with the other. I want to be disgusted by him, but truth is, I'm envious. My love affair with food rivals his, and his who-gives-a-shit attitude about his physique is one I wish I could adopt. Maintaining my weight has always been a battle, and lately it's become more like a war. Just being within breathing distance of food makes me gain.

Plus I have a theory about weight ups and downs. I'm convinced there are set amounts of fat that exist in the universe, as well as within every little microcosm of society, be it a work group, or a family, or a set of friends. Like other forms of mass, fat can't just disappear, and it tries to maintain a state of equilibrium. So if one person in a given microcosm loses weight, someone else in the same group has to gain. It's the basic physics of fat and, unfortunately, my little niche of the universe seems to be populated with a bunch of persistent, consistent losers who keep trying to shift their share of the fat onto me. If I ever figure out who they are, I'm going to start spiking their meals with Ensure.

I realize then that I should be nicer to Richmond. Since he's now within my circle of acquaintances, he may be the only thing keeping the local animal advocates groups from thinking I need to be pushed back into the ocean. Well, that and the fact that there's no ocean within a thousand miles of here.

By the time I pull into the morgue garage, some of the snow in my buckets has started to melt and the weight of them seems to have tripled. I struggle to lug two of them inside and then commandeer Izzy and our lab assistant, Arnie, to help with the rest. Richmond, who followed me inside with the first batch, stands by watching as the rest of us do all the work. We store the buckets in a utility room where Arnie will oversee the straining of the resultant water to look for trace evidence.

After taking off my coat and boots, I change into scrubs and make my way into the autopsy area, where I find our victim already laid out on one of the tables. Someone, Izzy I assume, has removed her body bag and plastic shroud, leaving her exposed to the room air so she can thaw out. As I look at her, I'm struck once again by how lovely she is, even in death.

Within minutes Izzy joins me, followed by Richmond, who has managed to dig up a jelly doughnut from somewhere. I watch as he bites into the pastry on one end and a huge glob of strawberry jam oozes out the other, landing on his shirtfront.

"Sorry, there's no food allowed in here," Izzy tells him.

Richmond shrugs, crams the rest of the doughnut into his mouth, scrapes the jelly from his shirt with a finger, and then shoves that in his mouth, too, leaving a huge, red stain on the shirt. It reminds me of the frozen smear of blood on the victim's chest and I turn to look at it. The blood doesn't look frosted anymore, leading me to think it may have thawed, but it is still mostly solidified from clotting.

"Mind if I watch?" says a male voice.

I look up and see Colbert has joined the fray.

"The chief said I could since I've never seen an autopsy before."

Izzy and I exchange looks. One's first autopsy is always a dicey experience and about half of the people who watch them either recycle their last meal or pass out. Sometimes they do both.

Izzy says, "Sure, but stand over there by the chair and if you start to feel light-headed, sit down immediately. If you think you're going to puke, the bathroom is right down the hall."

Colbert nods his understanding and waves away Izzy's concerns. "I'll be fine," he says.

Izzy walks over to the X-ray viewer and slides a film onto it. After studying it a minute, he frowns and says, "The knife pierced her left ventricle, which should have caused fibrillation and instantaneous death. But if it had, there should have been very little blood loss since her heart wasn't beating and the knife would have served as a tamponade. Clearly that's not the case, which makes me think there's another stab wound under all that blood."

Izzy and I don special goggles and turn on an overhead black light, and then carefully start washing away the clotted blood. The resultant maroon-colored water makes its way into channels that run the length of the stretcher and empty into a sieved drain that will collect any trace particles that might be in the water. After a minute or so of this, a second stab wound is revealed nearer the center of the victim's chest. "I'm betting that one hit the aorta," Izzy says. "That's why she bled out."

One of the overhead fluorescent bulbs flickers off, then on again, and in the resultant flash something catches my eye.

"I see something sticking out of the blood here," I say, picking up a pair of forceps. "It looks like a hair." I grab the end I can see with my instrument and tug. It comes free with a little resistance, revealing a short, black hair about an inch and a half in length. "I don't see any root," I say, examining the ends closely. "So no DNA."

Izzy holds out an envelope for me and I drop the hair inside. "It still may help narrow down suspects," he says.

Richmond snorts. "If we ever get any. It would help if we knew who she was. The fact that no one locally has been reported missing confirms my suspicion that she's not from around here."

The door to the autopsy room opens and a young lad dressed like an early twentieth-century newsboy walks in.

"Hey, Cass," Izzy says.

I do a double take and remove my goggles. This isn't the first time I've been surprised by Cass Zigler's appearance. In addition to being our file clerk-slash-secretary-slash-receptionist, she also spends time acting with our local thespian group. As a result, she often tries out her characters by dressing and playing the parts at work. I've never seen Cass as Cass, and I'm not sure I'd recognize her if I ran into her on the street.

"Cass?" Richmond says, his eyebrows arched. "You're a woman?"

"Not today. Today I'm Henry," she says, adopting a cockney accent and dropping the *H* on the name. "I'm your local newsboy, which seems appropriate at the moment because Alison Miller is out front asking if she can come back and get some information on your latest victim."

Alison Miller is Sorenson's ace reporter and photographer, and she and I share a long, and recently turbulent history. I've known her since high school and over the past month or so she has also been my chief competition for Hurley's affections. Fortunately she seems to have given up on this latest pursuit. When Hurley was injured and on his way to the OR drugged up on morphine with Alison at his side, he kept mumbling my name. Alison didn't take it very well and as a result she has quit hound-dogging Hurley and speaking to me.

"Let her come back," Izzy tells Cass. "Maybe she can help us identify our victim."

"What are you going to do?" Richmond says as Cass leaves the room. "Put a dead woman's picture in the paper?"

"No," Izzy says with an admirable degree of patience. "But the handle on this knife is quite unique and a picture of it might give us some leads. As might a picture of this tattoo on her ankle," he adds, pushing one of the woman's trouser legs up and revealing a colorful butterfly.

Not one to tolerate a public reprimand very well, Richmond tries to save pride by going on the offensive. "You have cross-dressers working your front desk?" he says, shaking his head with dismay. "What the hell is this office coming to, anyway?"

Colbert gives Richmond a wary look and does a little sidestep, as if to separate himself from the other man's insanity.

"Cass isn't a cross-dresser," Izzy says, his voice tight. "But if she was I would still hire her, as long as she did her job."

Richmond clucks his tongue and shakes his head woefully. "What a fine impression she must make on the public."

Since most of our "public" is dead on arrival, I'm with Izzy; I don't see what the big deal is. I start to say so but Izzy speaks before I can.

"Cass is an actor," he says. "And I see no harm in letting her practice some of her roles while she's working."

"An actor," Richmond harrumphs. "*That* explains a lot."

"Yes, an actor," Izzy repeats. His eyes have narrowed and I can tell he's starting to lose his patience. "She works with the same thespian group my partner, Dom, does. He's an actor, too. And gay. As am I. Do you have a problem with any of that?"

Despite the fact that Izzy is shorter than most twelve-year-olds and you could fit at least three of him into Richmond's mass, he looks quite intimidating. The two men have a little stare down—quite literally down, in Richmond's case since Izzy is only chest high to him—before the bigger man backs off.

"No," Richmond mutters finally, looking down at his feet. "No problem."

A long, tension-filled moment follows, during which I can hear water dripping from the faucet in one of the sinks. Everyone finally breathes again when Alison breezes into the room, her ubiquitous camera hanging around her neck. She glares briefly in my direction, then dismisses me and addresses Izzy.

"Whatcha got?" she asks. She walks toward the table, stopping when she's about a foot away. "Oh, my," she says, paling. "That's Callie Dunkirk."

"You know her?" Izzy says.

"Know her? Hell, I want to *be* her," Alison says. Then she winces and adds, "Well, except for the dead part."

"Are you sure it's her?" Izzy asks.

"Oh yeah," Alison says with a definitive nod. "I'd know her anywhere. Aside from her obvious physical attributes, the woman is . . . was one of the best investigative reporters in Chicago. She used to do a beat for the *Trib,* but about a year ago she got hired by that TV news show, *Behind the Scenes*. What is she doing up here?"

"We have no idea," Izzy says. "Until you got here, we didn't even know who she was."

Alison's eyes grow wide. "She must have been on to something big, something that got her killed."

"We don't know that," I caution. "For all we know she might have been just traveling through town, or meeting a boyfriend, or maybe she has family up here."

Alison shakes her head vehemently, her eyes bright with excitement. "Nope, she was here for a story. I just know it. All I have to do is figure out what it was."

"That might not be a wise avenue to pursue," Richmond says.

Alison turns to look at him and blinks her eyes several times. "Bob Richmond? I thought you were retired?"

He shrugs. "I still do some part-time stuff."

"Where's Hurley?" Alison asks, looking over at me.

"Sick. A stomach bug or something," I tell her, despite my knowledge to the contrary. "Richmond is going to handle this one."

Alison turns back to Richmond. "You might want to be careful yourself then," she tells him. "People who work with Mattie have an uncanny way of ending up injured or dead."

Chapter 5

I manage to bite my tongue and not snap back at Alison's snide comment. I'm assisted in this incredible show of restraint by Izzy, who wisely shoos Alison from the autopsy room and asks her to wait in the lobby or the library until we have the murder weapon removed.

It turns out that Callie's body isn't frozen but it is in full rigor—making it likely that the time of death was actually hours before we found her. Izzy carefully documents the wound trajectories and when that's done, he removes the knife. It's a wicked-looking thing, just over nine inches in length with a five-inch blade. There's a small nick in the blade near the hasp, and the handle, which appears to be ivory, has a dragon carved into it. After taking his own pictures and cleaning the blood off the knife, Izzy sets it in a tray in preparation for Alison's pictures.

When we open Callie up we discover that Izzy's guess about the cause of death is correct. The knife pierced both her aorta and her left ventricle. Eventually the first wound alone would have been fatal as it caused massive bleeding. Since the second wound would have stopped the heart, the amount of blood lost suggests that some time elapsed between the two wounds, making me wonder if the woman was alive and aware she was dying during the interval.

The remainder of the autopsy is relatively uneventful. Colbert does himself proud by managing to not only stay upright throughout the entire thing, but also asking intelligent, thoughtful questions about our findings, which other than the knife wounds and the single hair, consist mainly of some tiny metallic-looking globs we find entangled in Callie's hair. The metal pieces will need to be packaged and taken to the Madison crime lab where they can analyze them using energy dispersive X-ray spectroscopy. We also discover that Callie had caps on her teeth and breast implants, both of which will make it easier to confirm Alison's tentative ID.

I let Izzy deal with Alison and the knife photography, and after cleaning up the autopsy room, I change into my regular clothes, and head home. I'm eager to get to Hurley's place but need to stop by my own first to let my dog, Hoover, out for a break.

I've had Hoover for all of three weeks. I found him— filthy, frightened, and emaciated—hovering beside a grocery store Dumpster. Judging from his coloring, his ears, and the shape of his head, I'm guessing he's part yellow Lab or golden retriever. Judging from the way he inhales food, I suspect the other part is vacuum cleaner, hence his name.

So far Hoover has proven to be gentle, friendly, and quite smart. He has already mastered the come, sit, and stay commands, and he and my cat, Rubbish, entertain themselves quite nicely when I'm gone. Hoover's only negative is his predilection for eating the crotch out of any panties I leave lying around, a habit made even more annoying by the fact that I just committed a lot of money to a major underwear upgrade.

Hoover greets me now as he always does, with a happy yip and a wagging tail. This makes him the best companion and roommate I've ever had. My husband, David, never greeted me with that much enthusiasm, not even on our first anniversary when I met him at the door wearing nothing but some well-placed dollops of whipped cream.

After letting Hoover outside to do his business, I reward his devotion by indulging him in a few minutes of belly scratching. My cat, Rubbish, watches this with a look of disdain. Though he has tolerated the addition of a dog to our household, I sense there are times when he's not happy about having to share my attentions. And he seems to be all about self-expression, often making his displeasure known by barfing up a hairball on my bed, or taking a dump just outside the litter box rather than in it.

Once the animals are fed, watered, scratched, and otherwise attended to, I spend a little time on myself. I take a quick shower and wash my hair to get rid of the lingering smells of death, decay, and formaldehyde. Then I don some peach-colored, lace-trimmed undies that have fortunately evaded Hoover's teeth, and a matching bra. In case things go well at Hurley's tonight, I want to be ready and look my best. I then try on several different outfits and study each one carefully in the mirror, trying to find the one that hides my flaws the best. This involves checking out the rear view as well as the front, as the wrong combination of slacks and top makes my butt look as wide as a house. I finally settle on a pair of forgiving gray slacks and a long, loose-fitting, baby-blue sweater with a cowl-neck collar.

After blow-drying my hair and taming the more cantankerous strands with a curling iron, I put on some makeup. Deeming the result as good as it's going to get, I hop in the hearse and head for Hurley's house. My heart is racing with anticipation, wondering what he wants to talk about, wondering what the night will bring, and wondering how far I'm willing to let him go if things should progress along those lines. Even though David and I have been physically separated for several months, I'm technically still married. Consequently I'm not willing to go for the home run with Hurley yet, though I'm open to letting him run the bases if the mood strikes.

Of course, that's the optimist in me talking. My darker, more pessimistic side is still worried that Hurley might be planning to dump me because I uttered the "L" word. I've learned over the years that when it comes to men, emotions are like antimatter. Say anything that matters to them and they'll obliterate you. So I need to keep my shields at the ready tonight in case Hurley hits me with a barrage of anti-emotion photon torpedoes.

Thanks to the end of daylight savings time, the day has turned dark already even though it's only a little after five. Despite the shortened day, streetlights reflecting off the snow give the town a cozy ambience. I pull onto Hurley's street, park the hearse in front of his house, and take a moment to check out the neighborhood. It's an older area of town with towering oaks and well-preserved homes, most of which are close to a century in age. This is no cookie-cutter neighborhood either; the variety of styles among the houses is eclectic. Towering Victorians are sprinkled amidst Cape Cods, Italianates, Craftsmans, and Tudors.

Hurley's house is one of the Craftsmans in the neighborhood and the front porch, with its tapered stone columns, reflects that. The door is a classic fit for the style: a heavy wooden affair with dentil molding and a stained-glass window at the top. I'm about to push the doorbell when the door opens.

"Come on in," Hurley says. He looks past me to the curb, sees the hearse, and shakes his head. "You might as well have flashing neon signs on that thing, as subtle as it is."

"Hey, you helped me pick it out so no fair dissing it now."

"I know, I know. It's a sound vehicle and given the price you didn't have much of a choice. It's just not very . . . aesthetically pleasing."

I step into a foyer with beautiful wood wainscoting and dark, hardwood floors. There is a stairway on the left leading to the second floor, bordered by a rail and newel post that are both done in a classic Arts and Crafts design. Straight ahead is a hallway that ends in a kitchen; to my right is a living room. There is a delicious, spicy smell in the air that makes my stomach growl. Then I realize that the only thing I've eaten today is the one slice of pizza Richmond was willing to share.

As Hurley closes the door behind me, I undo my coat and shrug it off my shoulders. He takes it and hangs it in a coat closet beneath the stairs.

"Have you eaten?" Hurley asks me.

"Not since lunch. Something smells really good. Did you cook?"

"I did. Homemade lasagna and garlic bread, but it's not quite ready."

Hurley's sexy quotient has just leaped several notches. A man that looks as good as he does, kisses as good as he does, and cooks, too . . . hell, that's hitting the bell at the top of the carnival high striker game to me, especially since my idea of a home prepared meal is when I eat my food off of a real plate instead of the to-go container it came in.

"How about a glass of wine?" he offers.

I nod, thinking this is a good sign. Maybe he wants to get me relaxed and a little loose so we can pursue our relationship further. Then I think maybe he just wants to get me relaxed so I won't freak out when he dumps me.

I follow him out to the kitchen, where he unearths a bottle of pinot noir and two wineglasses. He puts the glasses on the table, which is already set with simple white dishes, and as he uncorks the wine bottle, I settle into one of the chairs and decide to try to put an end to my daylong suspense.

"So what is it you wanted to talk to me about?"

His eyes shift briefly to me, then back to the task at hand. There is a moment of silence as he finishes pouring and takes the seat across from me. Then he completely ignores my question by asking one of his own. "How did things go at the scene this morning after I left?"

"It went fine. So what is it you wanted to talk to me about?"

"Have you identified the victim yet?"

"Yes," I say with an exasperated sigh. "She's some reporter from Chicago. Now can you please tell me what it is you—"

"She's not *some reporter,*" he snaps, clearly irritated. "Her name is Callie Dunkirk."

I stare at him and after a few seconds I realize my mouth is hanging open, so I shut it. He holds my gaze the entire time, waiting. "You knew her," I say finally, realizing now why he acted the way he did when he first saw the body. He nods. "How?"

"We dated for a while."

I'm stymied, not only by the revelation that Hurley once dated the victim, but by the fact that he dated someone that gorgeous. Then I realize how stupid it is to be jealous of a dead woman. I'm starting to get an inkling of why he wanted to see me and it isn't making me happy. I have a sinking feeling that putting on my fancy underwear was a big waste of time. "How long ago?" I ask.

He shrugs and finally tears his eyes from mine, looking up at the ceiling instead. "It's been about a year and a half since we split up."

"Is that why you didn't want to take the case, because you knew her?"

"That's one reason."

"And the other?"

He hesitates and I can tell that whatever is coming next won't be good. "Before I tell you, I need you to promise me something."

"What?"

"You have to promise me that you'll keep what I'm about to tell you to yourself for the time being."

I consider this, figuring he's going to reveal some juicy tidbit of potential gossip. While gossip is a hot commodity in a small town like ours, one that can often be traded back and forth like money, I've spent most of my adult life working in a hospital, where confidentiality and privacy are absolutes. Thanks to HIPAA—a law that makes it easier to get your hands on top-secret government documents than medical information on a patient—I'm used to knowing the juicy stuff and not being able to share it. That's okay with me. It's the "being in the know" part that I value the most.

"Yeah, I promise," I tell Hurley.

He sucks in a deep breath and winces, as if bracing himself for a blow. Then he delivers one to me.

"I'm pretty sure that knife you found in her chest is mine."

Chapter 6

I stare slack-jawed at Hurley, stunned.

"Say something," he says, looking worried.

"You tricked me," is all I can manage.

"How so?"

"You made me promise to keep whatever you told me to myself but you didn't tell me it was going to be evidence in an ongoing case."

"I didn't kill her."

"I don't believe you did," I tell him, though at the moment I'm too confused to know if that's true or not. "That's not the point. By asking me to keep this under wraps you're asking me to compromise my investigation, *and* my job. Not to mention the possible legal ramifications. Christ, Hurley, what the hell were you thinking?"

"That I need your help."

"At the cost of my reputation and job?" I yell at him. I'm angry, not only because of the compromising position he's put me in, but because I know now that the matter he wanted to discuss with me has nothing at all to do with our future relationship, which at this point I fear may take place with both of us behind bars.

"You're upset."

"Of course I'm upset. You . . . you . . . argh!" I push back from the table, stand up, and start pacing.

"Mattie, answer me honestly. Do you think I could murder someone?"

I shoot him a glaring glance and keep pacing, but say nothing. The truth is I don't really know him well enough to answer. My gut—and perhaps a few untrustworthy nether regions of my body—are making me lean toward no, but my mind is cautioning me to think things through.

Hurley sighs, gets up from the table, and positions himself in front of me, forcing me to stop. He grabs my shoulders and holds me tight. "Mattie, look at me."

I do, and those piercing blue eyes of his calm me.

"Think about things a minute. Why would I tell you about any of this if I did it? Why would I take myself off the case if I did it? I mean, wouldn't it be easier for me to run the primary investigation so I could hide any incriminating evidence that turned up?"

He has a point.

"I need you to believe in me," he says, looking deep into my eyes. "I'm out on a very shaky limb here. I'm not sure what's going on yet but I promise you I didn't kill Callie. I'm going to need someone on the inside to help me, and right now you're the only person I trust."

I suppose I should be flattered, but at the moment I'm too confused and frightened.

"Will you help me?" he pleads.

I shrug his hands from my shoulders and return to the table. I grab my wineglass, slug back several big gulps, and drop into my chair.

"What do you want me to do?" I ask him.

"I need you to keep me posted on the results of the investigation. I'm going to be doing my own, of course, but I want to keep it under the radar."

"Tell me about the knife."

"It's one my father gave me years ago, before he died. I kept it in my boat outside. I checked this morning after I came back from the site and it's gone."

"Are you sure the knife is yours?"

He shrugs. "I can't be one-hundred-percent sure, but I'm at about ninety-nine. It's a pretty unique piece with a carved ivory handle. My father bought it over in Vietnam when he was in the service there. The man he bought it from was a villager who carved it himself. Supposedly it's the only one of its kind."

"Can you describe it in more detail for me?"

"Sure. It's about nine inches in length. There is a small nick in the blade just below the hasp. And the figure carved into the handle is a dragon."

"That's it," I tell him. "Show me where you kept it."

Hurley nods, picks up his wineglass, and heads for a door across the kitchen. Determined to keep my wits about me, I leave my own wine on the table and follow him. We enter a two-car garage that contains no vehicles and has been done over as some kind of workshop with a large table in the middle of the room and workbenches lining the perimeter walls. Hanging above and stored below the work areas are many sizes, shapes, and colors of sheet metal, and a variety of tools. The walls are insulated though unfinished, and a heater in the ceiling blows warm air onto my shoulders.

"What is all this?" I ask.

"It's my workshop. I dabble in metalwork on my off time, creating the occasional artsy piece, like wall hangings and some jewelry." He walks over to a side table, opens a drawer, and pulls out a small square of folded paper. He sets it on the workbench and carefully unfolds it, revealing a pair of fili-greed earrings that look like elongated silver lace doilies. "Stuff like this," he says, handing the earrings to me.

"These are beautiful," I say, holding them up to the light. "I had no idea you did anything like this."

"I don't do a lot of the small stuff anymore. Mostly I do bigger items, like that thing over there." He points to a piece leaning against the wall. It's a large rectangular chunk of varicolored metal strips woven together like a rug.

"What do you do with what you make?"

"I sell most of it, at flea markets mainly."

I try to give the earrings back to him but he pushes my hand away. "Keep them," he says.

"Are you trying to bribe me?"

"Absolutely." He smiles at me and adds, "The color suits you. Please take them."

"Okay, thanks." I remove the pierced earrings I'm wear-ing, fold them up inside the paper on the workbench, and put the whole thing in the pocket of my slacks. I then slip the new ones, which are done in a French hook style, through my ears.

"What do you think?" I ask him when I'm done. I turn my head from side to side to show off the earrings.

Hurley doesn't answer right away. He looks at the ear-rings and smiles, then his eyes shift to my hair, my face, my throat . . . his gaze softening as he goes. Then, as if someone flipped a switch, his smile disappears and he turns away. "They look great," he says, his voice catching slightly. Hur-ley's signals lately are about as clear as a broken traffic light and I can feel my level of frustration grow another notch. "I'm glad they found a good home."

There is an awkward moment as Hurley rearranges some tools on the center worktable that were just fine where they were and I try to figure out what the hell just happened. While I love the fact that Hurley has just given me jewelry, I can't help but wonder if I'll need Daniel Webster to defend me in the near future.

Hurley has left the earring drawer open and after glancing inside it, where I see neat little rows of folded paper envelopes that I assume hold more pieces of jewelry, I close it. The sound seems to shake Hurley loose and he walks over and opens a door in the far wall. "Come on out here," he says. "My boat is parked alongside the garage."

I follow him outside into the cold night air and there, hidden beneath a tarplike cover, is a small jon boat atop a trailer. He pulls the tarp off near the back of the boat and says, "I kept the knife in this little cubby here, beneath the seat."

I look where he's pointing and see a hollowed-out area under a metal seat that spans the width of the boat. "When's the last time you know it was there?"

"The last time I had the boat out, which was in mid-September."

"Are you sure you didn't just misplace it? Maybe you stuck it somewhere else and don't remember doing it."

"I thought of that," he says. "Even though I can't imagine why I would have taken it out of the boat, I spent a good part of today looking in every logical place as well as a few illogical ones. I can't find it anywhere."

"You need to tell Richmond."

Hurley's jaw clenches, the muscles in his cheeks twitching. "I can't, Mattie. Not yet anyway. Don't you see? Someone took my knife from my boat—a unique and distinctive knife, no less—and used it to kill someone I was once close to. I think I'm being set up."

I shiver, though I'm not sure if it's because of the cold or his words. "By whom? And why?"

"I don't know. That's why I need your help. That's why I want you to share any evidence you find with me." He rakes a hand through his hair as he speaks, and as I watch it fall back into place I remember the short, black hair we found in Callie's wound. I consider telling him about it but something makes me hold back. I'm not ready to share everything with him, at least not yet.

"You're putting me in a very difficult position, Hurley."

"I know that. Believe me, if I could think of a better way to handle this, I'd do it. But I can't. I'm up the proverbial creek with no paddle *and* I'm taking on water. Please, Mattie, I need you."

This final plea both heats my loins and melts my heart. As I look into the blue depths of his eyes, I realize I'm helpless to refuse him even though it may mean the premature death of my new career. My gut is screaming at me that it would be a huge mistake to agree to what he's asking of me, yet my heart is whispering, *Go for it*.

And go for it I do, though I decide to keep back a little something for myself, just in case. "I'll help you for now," I tell him, "but only if we can get back inside. It's freezing out here."

"Of course," he says, flashing me a relieved smile.

With a hand at the small of my back, he steers me back inside. I can feel the heat of his touch radiating through my sweater, and it makes me shiver again.

"I'm sorry, Mattie. I shouldn't have kept you outside so long without a coat."

"I'm fine," I tell him. "I got a little chill but I'll shake it off in a minute."

"Dinner will be ready soon," he says as we enter the kitchen. "That should warm you up, but you can use this in the meantime." He grabs a heavy flannel shirt off a hook by the door and drapes it over my shoulders. I thank him and pull it close, catching a whiff of a scent from it that is distinctly Hurley, something spicy, masculine, and a little bit dangerous. It sends my hormones into overdrive and suddenly I'm not the least bit cold anymore.

"I'd like to wash up before we eat. Where's your bathroom?"

Hurley directs me to a room at the top of the stairs and leaves me to find my way while he checks the lasagna in the oven.

The bathroom, which is done in blue and white tile with a hexagon tile floor, is small but sparkling clean, a surprising find in a bachelor pad. At first I fear it is too clean, but I finally find what I want when I snoop inside the medicine cabinet. There on the bottom shelf is a hairbrush. I remove the folded paper from my pocket and take the earrings out of it, dumping them loose into my other pocket. Then I carefully remove several hairs from the brush, place them on the paper, and fold it back up. After slipping it back into the pocket it came from, I flush the toilet, wash my hands, and head back to the kitchen.

I settle into the same chair I had before, just as Hurley sets a bubbling, delicious-smelling pan of lasagna on the table. A basket full of garlic bread is beside my plate and the heady aromas make me feel like I've died and gone to heaven. I'm practically drooling as Hurley cuts a generous square of lasagna from the pan and sets it on my plate. But just as I pick up my fork, my cell phone rings. I curse under my breath when I see that the caller ID says it's Izzy, which most likely means work for me.

"Hello, Izzy," I answer. "What's up?"

"There's been a death over at the hospital in the ER. EMS brought in an elderly gentleman with a cardiac history as a PNB."

PNB is medical speak for a pulseless nonbreather, meaning the patient was already dead when EMS found him. And given that he's now my patient, it's safe to assume that the efforts to revive him were unsuccessful.

"It sounds like your basic coronary," Izzy goes on, "but we still need to examine the patient, review the chart, and obtain a history. It should be pretty straightforward, and given your nursing background, I think it will be a good one for you to do for your first solo. Are you up for it?"

The delicious smells of garlic, mozzarella, and tomato sauce are making my stomach rumble, which makes me want to tell Izzy no. But I owe him on many levels, not the least of which is his giving me this job when I so desperately needed it.

"Sure," I tell him.

"Fabulous," Izzy says, and I can't help but smile at his choice of words. Even though he is openly gay, Izzy doesn't broadcast his proclivities much. But every once in a while he does or says something that screams gay to me. The way he says the word *fabulous* is one of those things. "How soon can you be there?"

"I'll head over now," I say, looking longingly first at the lasagna, then Hurley.

"Call me if you have any questions."

"Will do."

I end the call and give Hurley a woeful look. "I have to head over to the hospital to look into a death they had in the ER."

I'm hoping he'll look disappointed, or at the least, chagrined, but instead he looks contentedly resigned and says, "I understand. It's part of the job. We can have dinner some other time."

Easy for him to say. It seems like every time we try to get together in a nonwork-related way, somebody dies. I feel like I'm trying to date the Grim Reaper. And to make matters worse, I detect a distinct lack of conviction in Hurley's voice that makes me nervous.

I scarf down two quick bites of the lasagna, which tastes utterly divine, and then take a bite of garlic bread. When I've swallowed I tell him, "This is heaven. You're a very good cook."

He beams at me. "Thanks. How about I fix you a little to-go container and you can take some of it with you?"

"That would be fabulous," I tell him, echoing Izzy. I watch as he quickly packs up a meal of lasagna and garlic bread in a plastic container, giving it, some napkins, and a fork to me when he's done. It's a sweetly domestic scene and it's easy for me to imagine a lifetime of such moments with him. It fortifies my faith in the future of our relationship . . . until I remember that he's been implicated in a nasty murder and solicited my cooperation with a secret investigation.

"Thanks," I say, carrying my food out to the foyer and setting it on the lowest step of the staircase. He retrieves my coat from the closet while I take off the shirt he gave me and drape it over the newel post. Then he holds the coat for me so I can slip it on. After he settles it onto my shoulders, he turns me around to face him. Our eyes lock for a pregnant pause and I brace myself for the kiss I hope is coming.

Except it doesn't. All he does is smile and say, "Thanks for everything."

He hands me my to-go container and steers me out the door. I stumble off the porch in a state of mind-numbing confusion, climb into the hearse, and pull away.

As I head for the hospital, my mind scrambles to make sense of this change in Hurley's behavior. Damn men anyway! On the one hand they can be so easy to read. Speak to the small brain and they'll say or do anything. But their big brains function so differently from women's that it's like dealing with someone from another planet, maybe even another whole solar system.

The hell with him, I decide. Screw him, David, and all the other men in the world who possess the ability to manipulate my hormones and complicate my life. I mean really, why do I need a man in my life anyway? To fix things around the house? Clearly not, since David is about as inept at those things as a man could be and I can always hire a handyman. For sex? Well, that part is nice but there are plenty of other ways to find satisfaction, maybe even the aforesaid handyman. Children? Thanks to sperm banks and recent advances in modern reproductive science, I don't need a man for that either.

The more I think about it, the more convinced I become that I'm on to something. The whole idea of giving up men is oddly liberating; it makes me feel giddy and determined. By the time I reach the hospital, I've made up my mind. It's time to reevaluate my life, reexamine my goals, and focus on myself without any men in the picture. I am Mattie renewed, version two-point-oh, the latest and greatest release.

After parking the hearse, I open my to-go container and chomp down on a slice of buttery garlic bread. The delicious mix of soft, yeasty, still-warm bread, tangy garlic, and fresh butter is enough to make my toes curl with delight.

Damn, but Hurley can cook! Maybe it's too soon to give up on him altogether. I mean we have shared a few kisses that were hot enough to be a threat to global warming, and it was me he kept asking for when he was drugged up in the hospital. Surely all that meant something, didn't it?

I realize how desperately I want to believe in Hurley—to believe in *me* and Hurley—and already I'm rethinking my antiman dogma.

Way to go, Mattie, I mumble aloud. *It took you, what, all of two minutes to fall off your fanatical feminist pedestal?*

But I can't help myself. The more I think about it, the more convinced I become that Hurley feels something for me. The question is what? I'm pretty certain he feels some level of attraction, but is it enough? Did I scare him away? Given his current situation, is it possible he's just leading me on? Stringing me along to make me a happy follower so he can further his own agenda?

It's clear I'm not going to get any answers tonight so I shove the thoughts to the back of my mind and get out of the car, dragging my pedestal and the sad remnants of my membership card in the feminists' club along with me. Fortunately I have a death to look into, something I find much easier to deal with than men.

Chapter 7

After popping a couple of Tic-Tacs to mask my garlic breath, I make my way into the ER at a little after six. The waiting room is fairly crowded and as I scan the occupants with a habitual eye toward triage, I don't see anyone who looks critically ill, just miserable. Most of the folks are coughing, sneezing, and snotting all over the furniture and one another, ensuring the sharing and survival of whatever nasty little virus is dominating this year's flu season.

The gal behind the registration desk recognizes me and buzzes me into the back patient care area, where things are hopping. Every bed is full. I hear some poor soul barfing up his toenails in one room, and the screams of a miserable child in another. The nurses are all running about in a carefully choreographed dance of controlled chaos. I know from my own years working here that the arrival of the PNB most likely turned what might have been a merely busy shift into one that is now a mad and desperate scramble to catch up.

I make my way to the nurse's desk, where I see Ricky

"Rickets" Masterson standing in front of a full rack of charts. ER nurses have a habit of referring to patients not by their name, but by their bed number and diagnosis. So instead of John Doe, Bob Jones, and Susan Smith you get the Pancreatitis in Room Four, the Bowel Obstruction in Room Two, and the Bitch-On-Wheels Hypochondriac in Room Six. Several years ago when I worked in the ER, a bunch of us decided to make up nicknames for ourselves that were both close to our real names and to a disease or disorder. As a result, Ricky became Rickets, faring a whole lot better than my good friend, Phyllis, who is now referred to as Syph for short.

"Hey, Rickets, are you the charge nurse tonight?"

He shakes his head. "Nope, Lupus is," he says, referring to a nurse named Lucy. "But she's tied up at the moment with a Five-Year-Old Head Lac in Room Four who is trying out for a role in the next *Exorcist* movie. You here for the PNB in Room Two?"

"I am."

He hands me a clipboard containing the code sheets—a written summary of what happened during the attempts to resuscitate.

"Has the family been notified?" I ask.

"There's a daughter who apparently found him and called it in. She was here when he first arrived but I don't know if she's still here or not. Check with Constance." Constance, who was hired after the nicknaming session, has remained just Constance, probably a good thing since her last name is Pate and I'm pretty sure she'd be known as Constipation by now.

"Do you know where she is?"

Rickets gives me an apologetic look and shakes his head. "Sorry, it's been a zoo here tonight."

"Can you log me on to a computer so I can review the PNB's chart?"

"Sure." Rickets gets me into the computerized charting program and then leaves me to my own devices. After grabbing a notepad and pen, I glance at the data at the bottom of the code sheet and write down the man's name—Harold Minniver—and his age, which is seventy-two. Next I look up his chart on the computer and start taking notes. A scan of his medication list shows that he was on several heart drugs as well as one for high blood pressure, and his medical history includes a three-vessel heart bypass surgery five years ago. So far so good, I think, since these facts make the likelihood his death is attributable to some type of cardiac event that much higher. I switch to the nurse's narrative section but there is nothing entered there yet. This isn't too surprising; charting sometimes takes a backseat to actual care when things get hectic. Stuff gets written down as it's done, but sometimes the notes are scribbled on whatever's handy— paper towels, the bedsheets, the palm of a hand—and then entered into the computer chart later. A quick scan of the code sheets tells me that Constance was the primary on the case, so I'll have to wait to talk to her before I can get a thorough history of the night's events.

I move into a section of the chart that contains documentation by Mr. Minniver's primary physician. Here I see that the patient underwent a cardiac catheterization just two weeks ago following an episode of chest pain. Curious, I click on the tab that takes me to the cardiologist's notes and feel my hopes for a quick resolution sink faster than the blood count on a hemorrhaging patient: the cath showed no blockage of any sort, meaning Minniver most likely died of something other than a heart attack.

Since the nurses are all still busy and I have yet to see

Constance appear, I head for the room holding Mr. Minniver's body. He is lying on a stretcher with a sheet across his pelvis and various tubes sticking out of his body. There is an IV in each arm, a breathing tube protruding from his mouth, and a urinary catheter snaking out from beneath the sheet. His chest is covered with little stickers from the cardiac monitors and the EKG machine, and there are also two large pads—one on his upper right chest area and one on the lower left—that are connected to the defibrillator. His skin is cold to the touch and reddish-blue in color, and I can see the edges of a darker purple hue indicative of lividity beginning to form along his back. His hair, which is sparse, white, and short, is sticking up in little tufts along the sides of his head. The top of his head is bald.

The door to the room opens and Constance comes in accompanied by another nurse I don't recognize. "Hey, Mattie. Sorry to keep you waiting but the place has been crazy busy tonight."

"No problem."

"This is Karen Alcott," Constance says, nodding toward the other nurse. "I'm orienting her and I can tell you it's been a trial by fire tonight. Karen, this is Mattie Winston. She used to work here but these days she's with the ME's office."

"Nice to meet you," Karen says, looking thoughtful. Then she adds, "Are you the nurse I heard about who was involved with the nipple incident?"

I nod and quickly turn my attention back to Constance. "What can you tell me about Mr. Minniver?"

"Not a whole lot. The EMTs said his daughter found him slumped behind the wheel of his car in his garage. He was already pulseless when they found him and the daughter didn't do any CPR. By the time he got here he was straight line on the monitor but we worked on him for about twenty minutes anyway, mainly for the daughter's sake. We're guessing he developed chest pain or some other serious symptom and tried to drive himself to the hospital but collapsed before he could. His daughter says he has a cardiac history so we're guessing he had a heart attack."

"Is his daughter still here?"

Constance nods. "Her name is Patricia Nottingham. I just left her upstairs outside the chapel. She's making phone calls."

"I'll head up there to talk to her."

"Can I disconnect this stuff and take him to the morgue?" Constance asks, nodding toward the dead man. "We could use the bed."

"Not yet. There are some things I need to look into. Let me talk to the daughter first."

Constance sighs. "Okay, let me know."

I leave the room, grab my notepad and pen, and head for the second floor where the chapel is located. There is only one person outside in the hall, a fiftyish-looking woman who is pacing and talking on a cell phone. I hang back, watching her for a moment. Her face is drawn and tearstained, and her voice is hoarse, though I'm unsure if that's its natural state or if it became that way from crying. She sees me and seems to sense that I'm waiting on her because she tells the person on the phone, "There's someone here. Let me call you back."

I put on my best sympathetic smile and approach her. "Ms. Nottingham? I'm Mattie Winston. I'm with the Medical Examiner's office."

"Oh?" she says, looking confused. Then I see dawning on her face and her expression turns grim. She repeats herself, but with a much more serious tone. "Oh."

"I'm very sorry for your loss," I tell her, reciting the standard, wholly inadequate line.

She nods.

"Can we sit down for a minute? I'd like to talk to you about your father."

Again she nods and after looking around for a chair and finding none in the hallway, she heads toward the chapel. I follow her inside and we settle into the last of three pews on the left side of the room, leaving the two pews in front of us and the three on the right open.

"I understand you were the one who found your father?"

"Yes," she says, wincing with the memory. "He was in his car, out in the garage."

"Where in his car was he?"

"Behind the wheel, in the driver's seat."

"Were the keys in the ignition?"

"Yes."

"Was the car running when you found him?"

"No."

"Was the garage door open or closed?"

"Closed."

I reach out and put a hand on her shoulder. "I know this isn't easy for you, but can you describe what he looked like when you found him?"

She takes a deep breath and slowly lets it out. "He was slumped down in the seat. He looked . . . well . . ." Tears well in her eyes and she glances toward the ceiling, trying to regain her composure.

"Was he breathing?" I ask.

She shakes her head.

"Did you check for a pulse?"

"I did," she says. "But I couldn't feel one. I tried to shake him, thinking he might be asleep or something because he looked so pink."

"Pink?"

"Yeah," she says, sniffling. "His color was very pink, almost red. You know, ruddy looking."

Ruddy coloring is unusual and it makes me wonder if Mr. Minniver might have tried to commit suicide. Carbon monoxide poisoning typically causes a cherry-red color in the skin and if he was in his car with the garage door closed, carbon monoxide poisoning seems like a possibility.

"Ms. Nottingham, I know you said your father had his keys in the ignition but did you happen to notice whether or not the ignition was turned on?"

Her brow furrows as she thinks about this. "I don't think so," she says finally, "because the engine wasn't running."

I realize the engine might have been running and the car simply ran out of gas before he was found, but I don't say so. I'm pretty certain she has no idea what position the ignition was in. "Did you notice any unusual smells in the garage?" I ask. She furrows her forehead, looking confused, so I elaborate. "Like a strong odor of exhaust?"

She thinks a minute and then says, "No, I don't think so."

"I understand your dad had a history of heart problems?"

"He did, but he had that bypass surgery they do and he's been doing pretty well since then. In fact, he was checked out by his cardiologist just two weeks ago and they said his heart looked great."

This confirms what I read in his chart.

"What happened?" she asks, her voice hitching slightly. She dabs at the tears in her eyes with a worn-looking tissue she has crumpled in one hand. "Was it a stroke or something? I know he was pretty stressed out about some lawsuit he has going on with his neighbor. Could that have led to a stroke?"

"I don't really know," I tell her, unwilling to share my suicide theory yet. "We'll need to do an autopsy."

She pulls back from me. "You're going to cut him open?" she says, looking horrified.

"It sounds much worse than it is. An autopsy is a professional, scientific, and dignified process. It's not much different than having surgery at the hospital," I say, knowing it's a lie. While an autopsy *is* a professional and scientific process, there is nothing even remotely dignified about flaying someone open, removing all their organs, and turning their face inside out so you can saw part of their skull off and pop their brain out.

She shudders and hugs herself. "I suppose if you have to, you have to," she says. "Is this going to delay the funeral arrangements?"

"It shouldn't. We'll do the autopsy tomorrow and hopefully we'll have some answers by the afternoon. Most likely his body will be released the next day. Have you contacted a funeral home yet?"

She shakes her head. "No, but I think Dad had some kind of preburial plan with the Johnson Funeral Home. They did my mom when she died."

I jot down the name of the funeral home and then say, "There's one other thing I'd like to ask you. I want to go by your dad's house and take a look at the car and the garage. I'd like to do that tonight, if it's okay with you."

She shrugs, blows her nose in what's left of her tissue, and then digs in her purse. She hands me a single key on its own key ring and says, "There's a carriage-style light mounted next to the front door and the top of it opens so you can change the bulb. Dad usually kept a key taped to the inside of the lid. But take this one in case it's not there. The house was still open when I left and I don't know if the cops locked the place up when they were done. I don't want to go back there tonight."

"I'll make sure it's locked," I tell her. "How can I reach you later?"

She gives me her home address and her cell phone number, which I write down. In exchange, I hand her a card for the ME's office and tell her we'll be in touch, but that she can call anytime she wants to.

I leave her in the chapel and head back down to the ER, calling Izzy on my cell phone as I go. When he answers I fill him in on what I've discovered so far.

"So I'm thinking this might be a suicide and the cause of death could be carbon monoxide poisoning," I conclude. "I'm going to go by his house and check out the scene tonight but I'm thinking we're going to have to post him."

"I agree," Izzy says. "That's an excellent catch. Do you need me to come in and help you with anything tonight?"

"No, I think I'll be fine. I'll call Johnson Funeral Home and have them transport the body, then I'll check out Minniver's house."

"Holler at me if you need any help."

"Thanks, Izzy." I disconnect the call and make another one to the funeral home. They give me an ETA of twenty minutes, so I settle back in at the ER desk and look at Mr. Minniver's chart again so I can get his home address.

That's when I get my second big shock of the day.

Chapter 8

I'm stunned to discover that Mr. Minniver's house is right behind Hurley's. When I look at the times on Minniver's chart, I realize that he was found and brought to the hospital just before I arrived at Hurley's place for dinner.

I make a call to the police station and it's answered by Heidi Cronen, the dispatcher on duty. "Hey, Mattie, what's up?" she asks.

"I need to take a look inside the house of Harold Minniver, the man who was found dead in his car earlier this evening. Are any of the officers still there?"

"Hold on, let me check." She puts me on hold for half a minute, then comes back on and says, "They've already locked the place up."

"I have a key," I tell her. "But I'd like to have one of the officers who was on scene meet me there and go through the place with me."

She puts me on hold for another thirty seconds. "Ron

Colbert said he can meet you there in five if you want," she says when she comes back on.

"I need to get Minniver's body back to the morgue first. Can you tell him to meet me there in an hour instead?"

"Will do."

I hang up and start filling out all the paperwork necessary for processing Minniver's body but I'm quickly distracted. The ER is not an easy place to focus at times, and tonight proves no exception. Within minutes two ambulances pull up and the ER staff starts jockeying beds, trying to find a place to put the latest victims. As the EMTs wheel their respective patients into the main part of the ER, two things become apparent: the victims are hunters, and they are royally pissed off at one another. The first fact is obvious from their dress. Both men are wearing insulated bib overalls made out of a camouflage fabric. I'm guessing hunters wear this get-up so the deer won't see them as easily, but over the top of the camouflage both men are wearing vests and earflap hats—standard hunting fare—done in a blaze orange so bright it's likely visible from Mars. Despite this precaution, every year a couple of hunters are shot—supposedly by mistake—because some yahoo thinks deer have blaze-orange fur.

Here in Wisconsin we've learned to adapt to this idiocy because hunting is as much a rite of passage as growing pubic hair. In fact, I know a hunter or two who thinks the act of killing an innocent animal is what *gives* you pubic hair. During deer hunting season the air is filled with the sound of gunshots, the roads are riddled with carcasses of fleeing, frightened deer, and girlfriends and housewives everywhere are holding hunting widow parties—all-female get-togethers that often involve recipe sharing, chick-flick marathons, and frank discussions of everything from sex to what to pack in the kids' school lunches. Deer hunting season is as much of a holiday as Thanksgiving and since the two often overlap, it's not unusual to see people taking the entire last half of November off from their jobs, or schools that provide "teacher days" because they know many of their students will be missing from class.

That the two hunters entering the ER are pissed at one another is obvious because they are trading obscenities. The red flush in their cheeks tells me their blood pressures are reaching Mt. Vesuvius levels as torrents of their alcohol-laden breath waft through the air, quickly permeating the entire department.

The first guy, who is heavyset, bearded, and has a blood-soaked dressing wrapped around his right foot, is screaming and wagging a finger at the second man. "You shot me, you frigging asshole! You tried to kill me and don't you deny it. I knew you were pissed about that stock tip I gave you. I just knew it."

The second man, who is lean, tall, and has a neck like a giraffe, is grimacing in pain. His left leg is splinted from foot to hip and I can see dressings covering a large protuberance in his lower leg—an open tib-fib fracture. He glares back at the other man, and through gritted teeth says, "It was an accident, you fucking moron."

"The hell it was," grumbles the first guy. "You tried to kill me!" Seeing that he now has a larger, newer audience, he raises his voice several decibels, points to Giraffe Guy, and yells, "This fucker tried to kill me!"

Several state troopers have arrived with this entourage and I see one of them roll his eyes and shake his head. After a quick game of musical beds, the two hunters are finally ensconced in their separate rooms, each with a trooper close by to babysit. The eye-rolling trooper, a twenty-plus-year veteran named Hans Volger, enters the nurse's station and drops into a chair with an exhausted sigh.

"Rough night?" I ask him.

"Ya, you betcha," he says, tagging himself as a hardcore Norwegian. "Always is during hunting season. And these two drunken yahoos take the cake. Get this . . . the tall guy decided he didn't want to risk scaring off the deer by climbing down from his tree stand to take a dump. So what does he do? He drops his drawers, squats over the edge of the stand with his bare ass in the breeze, and tries to squeeze one out. Except the idiot lost his balance, fell ass backward, and broke his leg. Unfortunately he grabbed at his rifle when he felt himself falling, and he accidentally fired off a shot as he went down. The bullet went through the floor of another tree stand and hit the second guy in the foot." He shakes his head. "I'll bet all the deer out there are still laughing."

My funeral home transport arrives and I see that it's the twin sisters from Johnson's: Cassandra and Katherine, who go by the nicknames Cass and Kit. Their parents, who established the funeral home over thirty years ago, have always had a twisted sense of humor and it was never more apparent than when they named their daughters. The girls seem to have taken to their nicknames and the family business to a surprising degree. Not only are they both very involved in the day-to-day work, they both look the part with Morticia-like skin, builds, and hair.

After bidding Hans adieu, I take the twins into Minniver's room and assist them as they wrap him up, strap him up, and load him into their transport vehicle, which looks more like a soccer mom's minivan. I head out to my hearse and follow the funeral home car to the morgue.

Other than weighing Minniver on the huge floor scale in our take-in area, I leave all the rest of the processing for morning. After the sisters help me place Minniver's body in the fridge for the night, I finish my paperwork and leave.

Five minutes later I am in front of Minniver's house expecting to see a yellow-taped crime scene area, but the place looks like every other house on the street. As I pull into Minniver's driveway to park, a squad car pulls in behind me. I watch in my rearview mirror as Ron Colbert climbs out, and then I grab my evidence kit and get out to greet him.

"How come there's no crime scene tape here?" I ask him.

"Wasn't aware there was a crime," Colbert says with a shrug. "They said the guy had a heart attack."

"They who?"

He thinks a minute, scowling. "His daughter told us he had a cardiac history. And the EMTs said it looked like a heart attack."

"Looked like doesn't mean it is. And in this case, it probably isn't. The guy's heart was given a clean bill of health recently. Don't you guys typically preserve a scene until you know the cause of death?"

Colbert looks abashed, but then he brightens. "Well, we did lock the place up after the ambulance left so no one could get inside."

"No one without a key," I say, dangling the one Minniver's daughter gave me in front of his face. "Plus he kept a spare one hidden." I lead the way to the front porch, feeling my stomach knot when I see that the top to the porch light is open. Sure enough, there is no key there. "Interesting," I say.

"What?" Colbert asks.

"His spare key is gone. His daughter said he kept it taped to the underside of this lid," I explain, pointing at the light fixture. "We might need to dust that lid for fingerprints."

Colbert frowns again and asks, "Are you saying you think there's something fishy with this guy's death?"

"I think he may have committed suicide," I tell him, filling him in on what I've learned. "I want to take a look at his car to see if it was running. Your guys didn't take the keys out of the ignition or anything like that, did you?"

Colbert blushes and looks guilty as hell, making my hopes sink. "I don't know, to be honest. Let's go take a look."

I unlock the front door with the key Patricia gave me and step inside. It's a tidy Cape Cod furnished with comfortable-looking, mismatched pieces. Several lamps that were left turned on lend the interior a warm glow. I see an ashtray on a table at one end of the couch and inside it is an intricately carved pipe. The air smells of apple-scented tobacco, a scent that triggers a vague memory in my mind of a tall, brown-haired, pipe-smoking, smiling man I think is my father. But since my father left my mother when I was five, I can't be sure. My visual memories aren't nearly as vivid as the olfactory ones and whenever I've asked my mother what my father looked like, her response has always been "Like the devil himself."

"Should we glove up?" Colbert says, trying, I imagine, to make up for the lack of protocol earlier. I nod, set down my evidence case, open it, and remove two pairs of gloves: one pair for me and one pair for Colbert. I also take out two pairs of booties, which we stretch on over our shoes.

I take my camera out and turn it on as Colbert leads the way. After taking a few shots of the living room, I follow Colbert toward the kitchen. There we find a plate of partially eaten food on the table bearing the remnants of Minniver's last meal: baked macaroni and cheese, broccoli, ham, and a glass of what looks like iced tea. His fork, still holding a few bits of macaroni in its tines, is on the floor beneath the table. I snap pictures of all of it as well as a few shots of the room.

From there Colbert heads to the garage, which is just off the kitchen. Parked inside is Harold Minniver's car, a Toyota Rav4. I head around to the driver's side door, which is still open, snapping pictures as I step over several ripped-open, empty packages: debris left from the EMT's efforts. Harold's keys are still in the ignition but it is not turned on. After taking a picture of it, I reach in and flip the ignition over. The car starts up without hesitation.

"The gas tank is full," I tell Colbert, watching as the needle rises to the top and then taking a picture of the gauge. I'm not sure if I'm overdoing it with the picture thing, but since this is the first scene I've been to without Izzy, I want to err on the side of caution. "It looks like he never started the car, that he died right after getting in. The food on the table and the fork on the floor make me think that whatever happened to him, happened while he was eating. He dropped his fork, headed for the garage, and died before he could get his car started." I turn and look at Colbert. "His daughter told me she found him slumped behind the wheel and that the car wasn't running. It wasn't running when you guys got here, was it?"

Colbert shakes his head. "No. That much I'm sure of."

"So much for my suicide theory then," I mutter. I turn the engine off, bag & tag the keys, and hand them to Colbert. Then I take some pictures of the garage interior.

"So we have another incident of foul play?" Colbert says, his eyes huge with eager excitement as he watches me. You got to love that about new cops; murder and mayhem to them is like a freezer full of Ben & Jerry's to me.

"Not necessarily," I say, dashing his hopes. "There are plenty of other natural causes that might have killed him."

"Like what?"

"Like a blood clot in his lung, or a ruptured brain aneurysm."

"So you'll be able to tell what it was when you do the autopsy?"

"Hopefully, though sometimes we don't find an immediate cause of death."

"What do you do when that happens?"

"Run toxicology tests, look at the blood work, reexamine

the scene . . . but in this case I'm betting that we'll find something physical. There really isn't anything to suggest foul play."

"What about that key you said was missing?"

I frown at that. The missing key does bother me, but even so, I doubt it's very significant. I say so to Colbert but then caveat my statement by adding, "But just to be thorough, we should get someone to come out and dust the light for prints."

Colbert gets on his phone and calls into the office to arrange for an evidence tech to come out. While we're waiting, we look through the rest of the house but nothing else looks out of place. When the evidence tech arrives, we watch as he dusts the light cap, but the surface of the cap is pebbled and he tells us he's not likely to pull anything off it because of the texture. His prediction proves true and he's gone a few minutes later. Colbert and I prepare to follow suit but a niggling thought makes me head back to the kitchen. After rummaging through some of Minniver's drawers, I find some plastic baggies and collect what is left of his last meal. I pour a sample of his drink into an evidence vial from my scene kit, and then I put his fork and empty plate into a paper bag, sealing it all with evidence tape.

After locking the house, I head back to the morgue with Colbert following me. He watches as I log in the evidence, looking thoughtful, and I wonder if he's mulling over the possible ramifications of screwing up a crime scene.

As soon as Colbert leaves I head for the library, which serves double duty as my makeshift office, to finish my paperwork.

Just as I'm about to shut down the computer for the night, I take one last look at my notes and see where I jotted down Minniver's daughter's comment about her father being involved in a lawsuit of some sort with a neighbor. At the time she said it, I hadn't yet made the connection between Minniver's address and Hurley's. A strange tingle runs down my spine as I consider the possibilities, but even as I do, I dismiss the idea as ludicrous. It has to be a coincidence. There is no way Hurley could be involved in this death, too. Is there?

My hand hovers over the mouse, ready to click on SHUT DOWN, but I hesitate. Thirty seconds later my curiosity gets the better of me. I launch the Internet browser and click on the Wisconsin Circuit Court site. I type in Minniver's name and only one case pops up. When I click on the link and see the name of the defendant, my heart sinks. It's Steven Hurley.

Chapter 9

I spend the night tossing and turning, unable to sleep as I ponder the significance of Harold Minniver's death and the lawsuit he had against Hurley. Is it merely coincidence that two people who were close to Hurley are now dead? I debate how much information to share with Hurley and what to tell Izzy and Bob Richmond. I want to give Hurley a chance, but what if I'm protecting a dirty cop, a clever killer disguised as a gorgeous, tight-assed hunk of man-meat?

The next morning I take Hoover outside to do his thing before taking my shower. As I watch him make yellow snow I'm reminded of Bob Richmond and wonder how diligent the man is going to be in his investigation. I've gotten kind of used to Hurley's way of doing things and despite the fact that I sometimes overstep my bounds when it comes to investigating things, Hurley has been not only tolerant but supportive. I suspect Richmond isn't going to be quite as accommodating, which will make doing my own investigation for Hurley much more difficult.

Hoover and I head back inside, and after stripping off my flannel jammies, I'm standing naked waiting for the shower water to heat up when my cell phone rings. Thinking it's Izzy with a death call, I groan. But when I look at the caller ID I see it's Hurley. The idea of talking to Hurley while I'm stark raving naked makes me start to sweat despite the frigid temps outside.

I grab the phone, flip it open, and utter a cheery "Good morning!"

"Hardly," Hurley snaps. "Did you know about Minniver?"

This isn't the greeting I was expecting and I'm struck dumb for a moment. That's enough for Hurley to figure things out.

"You did, didn't you?"

"He was the case I was called out on last night when I was at your house," I admit. "I didn't know he was your neighbor until after I got to the hospital."

"Why didn't you tell me about him? Why is there crime scene tape at his house? And why am I finding all this out from my neighbors instead of you?"

"Whoa, slow down, would you?"

"I can't slow down, Mattie. People around me are turning up dead with frightening frequency lately and it's making me a tad anxious."

"Understandable," I say slowly.

Hurley lets forth with a weighty sigh. "You're not starting to have doubts about me, are you? Because I'm counting on you, and if you're withholding information from me, I'm thinking we've got a problem."

"Minniver was more than just your neighbor, wasn't he?"

He doesn't answer right away and while I'm waiting, I reach over and turn off the shower.

"We had some disagreements recently," Hurley says finally. "He didn't like where I put my fence, claiming it encroached on his property. He has . . . had some old survey map from twenty years ago that shows a different property line than what my survey shows. So he's suing me."

"Not anymore," I toss out.

Hurley groans. "What did he die of?"

"I don't know," I say honestly. "My first thought was that he had a heart attack but after reviewing his medical record I think that's unlikely. Right now I have no idea what killed him. We're going to post him this morning."

"Do you suspect something other than natural causes?"

"Not necessarily. While it's unlikely that his heart was the cause, he could have had a stroke, or thrown a blood clot, or blown an aneurysm. There are a ton of natural causes in a man his age that are plausible. Hopefully we'll be able to narrow it down once we've done the autopsy."

"I want to be there when you do it."

My heart skips a beat. There is nothing I like more than having Hurley around, even when it occurs over a dead body. But . . .

"I don't think that's a good idea," I say. "Clearly you've got some connections to this man other than the typical neighborly one. Given the other . . . situation, I think it might be wiser if you distanced yourself from the investigation."

"But that just makes me look guilty."

"Are you?"

This time the silence stretches out for what seems like a full minute or more, long enough that I start to wonder if he's disconnected the call. I'm about to call his name to see if he's still on the line when he says, "What do you think, Mattie? Do you think I went off the deep end and killed both my ex-girlfriend and my neighbor?"

The term "ex-girlfriend" rankles me, particularly when I realize I'm still naked. It just feels wrong to be nude and discussing an ex-lover with someone I have a current interest in. Plus, I'm reminded of how lovely and tiny and petite she was, and as I survey my own body in the mirror, I'm reminded of my many faults, not the least of which are the bingo wings I can see developing on my upper arms. Fortunately I'm spared visualizing anything below the waist since the mirror is mounted too high.

"I don't think you killed anyone, Hurley, but I want to hear you tell me," I say finally. "I need to hear it, from your lips to my ears."

"I didn't kill them, Mattie. I swear it. But I'm starting to get a very bad feeling about all of this."

Well, that makes two of us. "I'll call you after the autopsy is done, okay?" I say, hedging for now. I'm hoping that once I have a definitive cause of death for Harold Minniver, things will be clearer in my mind. "But there's no way you should be there. It's just too . . . too . . . dicey. I think you should continue with your case of the blue flu."

"I suppose you're right," Hurley admits, and while I'm tempted to breathe a sigh of relief, his quick capitulation leaves me suspicious. It doesn't help that he hangs up before I can utter another word. I stare at my phone a minute, wondering what to do.

Once I'm showered, dressed, and blown dry, I gather up the hair I collected from Hurley's bathroom, hop into my hearse, and head out. When I arrive at the office, I find it empty of any living souls, though there are now two dead ones in our morgue fridge. I check the fax machine and find a reply from a hospital in Chicago verifying that the numbers on the breast implants we sent them were surgically implanted in a patient named Callie Dunkirk, confirming our presumptive identity.

As I'm walking the fax report to Izzy's desk, I hear the door to the garage area open. A minute later Arnie, our lab tech and resident conspiracy theorist, appears. Despite his casual dress, John Lennon glasses, and ponytailed hair, all of which make him look more like a Woodstock survivor than a scientist, he's a whip-smart and very talented evidence tech.

"You're here early," he says when he sees me.

"I had my first solo last night and thought I'd come in to prep the body."

"Wow," he says, looking suitably impressed. "Izzy let you out on your own already?" The way he says it you'd think I was a serial murderer who'd just been paroled.

"He did," I say, "though it appeared at first blush to be a pretty basic case. It was a PNB the EMTs brought into the hospital. The guy had a cardiac history so it was assumed that was the cause of death."

"And you found something to make you think otherwise?" Arnie looks intrigued. He loves unraveling mysteries and he's suspicious by nature. Both qualities, combined with his faith in science, make him excellent at his job.

"I did, though it might have been some other natural cause." Arnie looks crestfallen. "I guess we'll find out soon enough."

"How much prep did you do last night?"

"Just the weight and the basic intake paperwork. I didn't do the vitreous samples . . . I hate those." Obtaining vitreous samples requires sticking a needle into the dead person's eye and withdrawing a sample of fluid. It gives me the heebie-jeebies. When I worked as an OR nurse, I never did the eye cases if I could help it. Eyes creep me out.

"No problem," Arnie says with a shrug. "How about we do the X-rays together and then I'll collect the vitreous samples while you develop the film."

"That would be great. Thanks."

I get the X-ray processor turned on and warmed up while Arnie fetches Harold Minniver's body from the fridge. After hoisting Minniver, still inside his body bag, onto the X-ray table, we shoot head-to-toe pictures of him. Then we put him back on the stretcher and wheel him into the autopsy room, where Arnie does the eye thing while I retreat to the dark room.

When I'm finished and carry the X-rays into the autopsy room, I see that Arnie has opened Minniver's body bag but has only started with the vitreous samples. "Have you gone over any of the evidence from Callie Dunkirk yet?" I ask him, turning my back and hanging the films on a wall-mounted viewer.

"I typed the blood from her wound," Arnie says. I shudder as I hear the faint squishy squeak of a needle entering an eyeball. "I also looked for fingerprints on the knife that killed her but the carved surface of the handle isn't very conducive to retaining them. I found a very small partial and sent it to Madison but I don't know if it will be enough. And those metal fragments we found in her hair? Turned out those are lead bits, most likely from soldering."

I'd forgotten about the metal bits and as soon as Arnie says this, I recall Hurley's workshop, where I saw both an acetylene torch and a soldering iron. I hadn't made the connection when I was there last night; I was too distracted by Hurley's presence. But I'm making it now and it seems a little too coincidental. The earrings Hurley gave me are still in my ears and my lobes feel hot all of a sudden.

"I also examined that hair we found in the congealed blood of the wound," Arnie says.

This is the direction I wanted the discussion to go so I shake off my sense of dread and try to focus on my original plan.

"What, exactly, do you look for when you examine hair evidence?" I ask, trying to sound only mildly curious. Arnie loves talking about his work and he takes great pride in what he does. So I'm hoping for a basic rundown of hair as trace evidence to give me some idea of what to look for if I compare Hurley's hair to the one found on Callie, assuming I can do so on the sly. But I forgot how extreme and varied Arnie's interests are, and he gives me a whole lot more than the basics.

"You'd be amazed at the things you can learn from hair," he starts. "Hair evidence has figured quite prominently in some very high-profile cases throughout history. For instance, an analysis of hairs from Napoleon's body revealed that he may have died of arsenic poisoning. Hairs that were connected to the anthrax mailing several years ago were analyzed with the hope they would implicate a scientist named Bruce Ivins at Fort Detrick in Maryland who was the primary suspect, but they weren't a match. The scientist then committed suicide, leaving that hair evidence as one of the biggest puzzles in the case."

Arnie pauses a second and a twinkle appears in his eye, letting me know the best is yet to come.

"On a more abstract level there is a rumor that hair samples collected in the Pacific Northwest prove the existence of a Big Foot type creature."

Ah yes, my distant relatives.

"And there are some who believe that redheads are actually alien-human hybrids."

Realizing that Arnie has now donned his foil hat, I try to steer him back on track. "I'd love to have you show me how you do hair analysis. I need to learn and it sounds like you really know your stuff."

"Sure." He brightens and stands a little straighter, puffing his narrow chest out so that he resembles a bird. If only Hurley were so easy. Arnie glances at his wristwatch and says, "We probably have time to do a quickie now if you want, before Izzy comes in."

As the double entendre hits him, his face turns Day-Glo red and his glasses start to fog over.

"A quickie it is then," I say, smiling.

For once, Arnie is speechless. His mouth opens and closes a few times, and he stammers out a few unintelligible syllables before turning away. He spends a moment zipping the body bag closed and cleaning his glasses off. By the time he's done, he seems to have recovered. "Come on up to my lab," he says, "and I'll give you a crash course on hair analysis."

"I'll meet you there in a minute. I need to make a quick trip to the ladies' room first." This is a lie but I need to fetch Hurley's hair from my purse and I don't want Arnie to know that. I scoot back to the library, take the paper-wrapped hair from my purse, and shove it into my pocket. As I dawdle long enough to equal a bathroom trip, I brace myself for what lies ahead, wondering if I'm about to commit career suicide.

Chapter 10

A rnie's lab area is located on the second floor of the building and is accessible only with a key card. As I make my way up the stairs, I ponder the potential implications of what I'm hoping to do. What if the hair I have matches the one found on Callie's body? Where do I go from there? Can I believe Hurley? Can I trust him? Or am I letting my hormones get the better of me?

Arnie's lab is an amazing demonstration of efficiency and order. The room looks smaller than it is because it's jampacked. Across the room from the entrance is Arnie's small desk, which sits perpendicular to the storage cabinets lining the far end of the left-hand wall. The right-hand wall contains a long, equipment-covered counter full of machines, microscopes, analyzers, and other lab paraphernalia, with more storage cabinets mounted overhead. I find Arnie standing near the middle of this counter and he waves me over.

"This is a comparison microscope," he says, pointing to

the device in front of him, which looks like two microscopes joined at the hip with a double eyepiece centered between them. "It allows you to examine two objects side by side to look for differences and commonalities. For instance, I could have compared the hair we found on Callie's body to one of her own hairs to try to determine if it was hers or the killer's. I didn't, because the evidential hair is coarse and black and hers are fine and auburn so the sources are obviously different. If the evidential hair wasn't a human hair—it is, and I'll explain how I know that in a second—I can look for a match in one of my reference books, or examine it next to sample references for different animal species: dogs, cats, horses, cows, etcetera, until I can determine what it came from. While an animal hair might not point directly to a given suspect, it can be useful in placing someone at a crime scene."

He pauses, reaches up, and plucks a hair from his own head, wincing as he does. I'm not sure if he's grimacing because of pain, or if it's because his own hair is rapidly thinning on top, a fact I suspect he compensates for with his ponytail.

He cuts a segment of the hair and puts it on top of a glass slide. "We typically fix hairs as a wet mount using a drop of glycerin," he explains, and after grabbing a nearby bottle, he unscrews its top and uses the attached eyedropper to apply a drop of a clear, viscous liquid to the hair. Then he places a cover slip atop the mount, causing the glycerin to spread over the entire sample. He positions the prepped slide on the bed of a nearby single stage microscope and turns its light on. After removing his glasses and positioning them atop his head, he looks through the eyepiece and adjusts the focus. When he's done he steps back and says, "First let me give you a crash course on hair structure. Take a look."

I bend down and peer through the scope.

"You're looking at the hair magnified one hundred times. You should be able to see three basic layers. The outer layer is called the cuticle—that's the part that looks like overlapping fish scales. It tells me what species the hair came from because each animal has a slightly different pattern. The dark line through the center of the hair shaft is the medulla, and between it and the cuticle is the cortex, which is where you'll find tiny cells that contain whatever pigment colors the hair. How that pigment is distributed can vary from person to person and can sometimes be useful in matching a hair to a particular owner."

I stand up and blink several times to adjust my focus. "You need a root to get DNA from a hair, right?"

"Yes, you do. But there is a lot of information you can get without the root. You can compare a hair to known samples for similarities. You can tell if a hair was cut off or pulled out, whether it's human or animal in origin, and, if it is human, you can usually tell if it's Negroid or Caucasian and where on the body it came from. Age might be discernible to some degree since infant hair is typically finer, but that can be a little iffy. With the right equipment you can also map out a dateline of exposure to certain poisons and elements by analyzing the hair shaft in small increments. But while we can compare color, structure, source, and length to determine if a given hair is consistent with a known sample, without a root it's not as distinct an identifier as say a fingerprint or DNA."

He walks over to a cabinet, opens a drawer, and removes a small cardboard box labeled with Callie Dunkirk's name. Inside the box is a paper envelope with a slide in it. "This," he says, proffering the slide, "is the hair from Callie Dunkirk's wound." He carefully removes the slide from the paper envelope and positions it on the left stage of the comparison microscope. He then switches the slide that holds his own hair to the right stage of the scope. After peering through the binocular eyepiece and making some minor adjustments to the focus, he stands aside and gestures for me to step in. "Take a look."

It takes me all of a second to determine the differences between the two hairs. They look nothing alike; not only is the evidentiary hair thicker and darker overall, its medulla is thicker, too. Plus the scale patterns on the two hairs are noticeably different.

The phone in Arnie's lab rings and I pull away from the microscope as he answers it. He listens for a few seconds and then mouths *Izzy* to me. I assume Izzy is awaiting my assistance with the autopsy on Harold Minniver, so I nod my understanding and start to head downstairs to the autopsy suite. I manage two steps before Arnie stops me by snapping his fingers and waving me back. I wait, curious, as he listens, muttering only the occasional "Uh-huh" or "Hmm . . ." into his end. A couple of times he shoots a glance at me and then quickly looks away in a manner that suggests I am the topic under discussion. But since I can't hear the other end of the conversation I don't know if I'm right or if Arnold Paranoianegger is starting to rub off on me.

Arnie finally manages to say, "I'll take care of it," just before he hangs up. "Izzy said to expect him in a half hour or so," he tells me.

"What was the rest of that conversation about?"

Arnie hesitates just long enough to make me even more suspicious. Well, that and the fact that he not only won't look me in the face, he won't even look at my boobs, something he does like an unconscious tic whenever we're together for any length of time. "There's some emergency meeting in Madison today that Izzy wants me to attend so he can get caught up on stuff here," he says, busying himself replacing the evidence slide in its envelope and box.

"What kind of meeting?" I push.

He shrugs as he puts the slide box back on the shelf and then he continues his cleanup by taking apart the slide he put together with his own hair. "I'm sure it's just boring business stuff," he says. "Administrative crap."

I narrow my eyes at him. "You were listening for an awful long time."

Arnie smiles but he still won't look at me. "Wow, attractive, smart, *and* you have a suspicious mind. I like that in a woman."

I'm pretty sure Arnie likes just about anything in a woman so I'm not swayed by his flattery. "You're avoiding the question."

"Was there a question in there?"

"An implied one," I say irritably. "You pick up on the subtlest of nuances all the time so don't try to pretend you didn't pick up on mine."

Arnie glances at his watch. "Ooh, look at the time." He slips out of his lab coat and grabs his parka. "I gotta run. I'll catch ya later, okay?"

He has to push past me in order to get out of the room and I'm tempted to stop him, something I could do easily enough based solely on size. The walkway is narrow and I've got several inches on Arnie in all directions. But just as I'm about to assume my Wonder Woman bullet-proof-bracelet stance, I remember that I have another agenda, one that would be best served by Arnie's departure.

So I let him go and as soon as he's gone, I slip Hurley's hair from my slacks pocket and prepare it on a slide using glycerin the way Arnie did. I position it on the right-hand side of the comparison scope and then retrieve the evidence hair removed from Callie Dunkirk's wound and position it on the left-hand side.

As I look through the scope, I hold my breath in anticipation for a few seconds. Then I blow it out in a frustrated sigh and mutter, "Crap." The two hairs are identical in color, width, and structure, meaning that the hair stuck in the dried blood in Callie's wound is a match to Hurley's.

Chapter 11

I carefully replace the evidence hair, take apart my prepped slide, and then head for the closest bathroom, where I dispose of the glass slide and the cover slip and flush Hurley's hair down the toilet. There are plenty more where it came from and for now I don't want to have it anywhere near me. My next big decision is whether or not to tell Hurley what I did and that his hair is a match to the one retrieved from Callie's body. Fortunately I need to get everything ready for the autopsy on Harold Minniver, a series of tasks that will give me plenty of time to procrastinate while I try to make a decision.

Izzy arrives as predicted and within the hour he has made the initial Y-incision, done the rib-cracking, and begun the organ removal on Mr. Minniver for examination and dissection. The heart and lungs come out first and, as I originally suspected, there is no external evidence of any acute trauma or disease to any of these organs.

But as I weigh each one and remove small samples from

them to store for later reference, I detect an odd, faint odor I've never smelled before. There's only me and Izzy in the room and I'm pretty sure it isn't coming from one of us. I sniff the containers used to store the organ samples, thinking maybe the chemicals in there have changed, but they smell the same as they always have, and distinctly different from the other odor.

I shrug it off until Izzy removes Harold's stomach and opens it to examine the contents. As expected, we find food remnants inside that match what he had on the plate that was on the table at his house. The usual sour smells of stomach acid and partially digested food waft up, but underlying it I detect the strange odor again, much stronger this time.

"What is that smell?" I ask Izzy.

"Stomach contents," he says.

"No, it's a different odor. I smelled it before when I sampled the lungs and it's even stronger now with the stomach contents. It smells like burnt, rancid nuts or something."

Izzy halts his dissection of the intestines, sets down his scalpel, and gives me a curious look. "Would you describe it as a bitter almond smell?" he asks.

I take another whiff. "I guess," I say with a shrug. "Is that what it smells like to you?"

"I can't smell it. But if it's what I think it is, only twenty-five to fifty percent of the population *can* smell it and most of those are women."

I've either heard or read this claim somewhere before and realize what Izzy is thinking. "You mean cyanide," I say.

"I do," Izzy says, sounding mildly excited. "It makes sense given the history and the symptoms you provided. Cyanide poisoning mimics carbon monoxide poisoning by causing the same cherry-red color in the blood and skin."

We both stand in silence for a moment, staring down at

Mr. Minniver's cut-open, emptied body, which looks like a macabre dugout canoe. Izzy finally breaks the silence.

"If that's what this is, it's a brilliant catch, Mattie. It could have easily escaped detection if not for your nose. Though it does complicate things for us since I doubt Mr. Minniver ingested cyanide on purpose and that means our hoped-for natural cause of death has just become a homicide."

We pause in the midst of our autopsy while Izzy degloves and turns on an extra exhaust fan. He then makes a phone call to the police station to report that Minniver's death might be a homicide. Once he's hung up, he dons a new pair of gloves and tells me, "Bob Richmond will be here shortly. Apparently Hurley is still feeling a bit under the weather."

I nod, trying to keep the guilt I feel from showing on my face. In the past Izzy has read me with a clarity that I find disturbing and I'm hoping now won't be another one of those times, or at least if he does see something in my expression he will interpret it as my disappointment over the fact that Hurley won't be coming.

Richmond shows up twenty minutes later, just as we're getting ready to open Minniver's skull, and as he enters the autopsy room a faint scent of frying oil wafts in with him, offering us a brief reprieve from the less savory chemical and bodily smells that typically permeate our air. Richmond is wearing a white shirt and blue tie, the former stained with what looks like a big glob of ketchup. Of course, given that Richmond is a homicide detective, it could be something else.

"Way to ruin a Saturday afternoon," Richmond grumbles.

"I'm guessing this fellow feels the same way," I say, gesturing toward Minniver's body.

Richmond has the good sense to look embarrassed for all of five seconds but it's long enough for Izzy to turn on the bone saw and drown out any further comment for the time being.

"So what makes you think this guy is a homicide?" Richmond says when Izzy finishes cutting through the skull and sets the bone saw aside. "And what's the cause of death?"

"Well," Izzy says, "there's no evidence of any natural cause of death so far and Mattie detected the scent of bitter almonds when we were dissecting his organs. While it's still an educated guess at this point, the smell combined with our other findings make me suspect the man was poisoned with cyanide. We'll know for sure once the lab tests are done."

"Cyanide?" Richmond scoffs. "Seriously? Or has someone been reading too many mystery novels lately?" He makes a pointed look in my direction.

"I'm very serious," Izzy says, scowling. I'm beginning to suspect he likes Richmond about as much as I do. "I don't joke about evidence."

Richmond makes a face but doesn't pursue his doubting Thomas attitude. Instead he asks, "Any idea how the cyanide might have gotten into his system?"

"The odor was strongest in his stomach so I'm guessing he ingested it," Izzy says.

I nod my agreement. "I went through his house last night with Colbert. We found a half-eaten meal on the table. It looks like whatever happened to him did so during his dinner."

"I don't suppose you collected any of the food," Richmond says, casting a doubtful look my way.

"As a matter of fact, I did," I say, trying not to look or sound too smug.

Richmond grunts and I take it for his version of grudging approval. "Is the guy married?" he asks.

"No, he's a widower. He has a daughter named Patricia Nottingham who lives across town."

"Does he have a shitload of money?"

I shrug, as does Izzy. "I doubt it, based on the way he was living," I say, "but even if he was rich, the daughter doesn't strike me as the killer type."

Richmond looks amused. "Considering that Hurley was nearly done in thanks to your supposed ability to recognize a killer, you'll understand why I might want to reserve judgment for now."

If looks could kill, Richmond would be heaped on one of the autopsy tables right now, assuming we could find a skid loader to hoist him onto it.

"Poisoning is typically a pretty personal method of killing someone," Richmond goes on, ignoring my glare. "Know of anyone else in his life who was close to him?"

Izzy and I both shake our heads. I stop glaring at Richmond and turn away so he can't see the expression on my face. Richmond might be irritating and semiretired, but I've heard that he's also a decent detective and that means he's good at reading people. I don't want to give him any opportunities to read me.

"We just got this case last evening," Izzy explains in our defense. "The gentleman was brought into the ER as a PNB and had a cardiac history. We thought initially is was a natural death."

"But there's no indication his heart was the cause?" Richmond asks.

Izzy shakes his head. "Nope, absolutely none." He gestures toward the partially dissected brain on his side of the table. "And this was the last place I had to look for an alternate cause. There is no evidence at all at this point that any natural disease process led to this man's death."

Richmond frowns. "How soon can you confirm the cyanide theory?"

"We have a rapid test we can do here. If it's positive it will be enough combined with the history and symptomology we've obtained for me to make a presumptive call. But the rapid test can give false positive results on rare occasions, so to get a definitive answer I'll have to send samples off to Madison for testing. It will take a couple of days to get those results."

A grumbling sound emanates from Richmond and I'm not sure if he's vocalizing something, or if it's just his stomach rumbling. "So how long is this rapid test gonna take?" he asks.

"Give me five minutes and I'll have an answer for you." Izzy takes a sample of the stomach contents and leaves the autopsy room. Richmond is right on his heels, leaving me alone with Minniver's body. I look at him lying there, his body flayed open, his scalp turned inside out and pulled down over his face, his brain pan empty. It reminds me of what I said to his daughter, about how an autopsy is a dignified process, much like a surgery. I can't help but wonder what she would think if she knew the reality.

I finish collecting and labeling my samples and both Izzy and Richmond return just as I'm finishing.

"The rapid test was positive," Izzy announces.

Richmond nods. "I had dispatch call this Nottingham woman. She's at home so I'm going to go over there and talk with her, see what I can dredge up. You want to come along to let her know the results?" Richmond asks Izzy. "I already delivered a death notice to the Dunkirk woman's family this weekend and I don't relish having to do it again."

"I'll do it," I offer. When Izzy shoots me a surprised look I add, "Well, I spoke with the daughter last night so I already have a rapport with her. Plus it *is* part of my job description."

"Is it something you're comfortable doing?" Izzy asks.

I shrug. "Those kinds of discussions are never comfortable, but I've done it enough times as a nurse that I'm used to it."

Izzy nods and says, "Okay then. I'll close up Mr. Minniver here and finish the paperwork."

Richmond blows out a huge sigh that fills the air with the faint scent of fried onions. I can't tell if he's miffed that I'll be going with him or not. "How soon can you be ready to go?" he asks me.

"Give me half an hour or so."

Richmond glances at his watch. "You have an hour," he says. "Meet me at the station at two o'clock and we'll ride over to the daughter's house together." He starts to leave but then turns back. "And we're taking my car," he adds pointedly. "I'm not showing up there with a frigging hearse in tow."

"Fine," I say, trying to sound cheerful. Though I'm not looking forward to having to spend time with Richmond, in order to keep tabs on the investigation and determine the degree of Hurley's involvement, I feel like I should be in on as much of it as possible. So I need to stay on Richmond's good side.

As Richmond turns to leave, he delivers a parting speech. "I'll get some guys to search Minniver's house and look into his life more thoroughly to see what else we can find out about him. But I'm telling you, poisoning is personal. I'm betting we don't have to look far."

I spend another few minutes helping Izzy and then head for the shower to get cleaned up. By the time I'm done I've got twenty-five minutes to spare and the police station is only a one-minute walk away, so I decide to use the extra time by doing a bit of research. I head for the library computer where a quick search of cyanide reveals all kinds of intriguing information, including the fact that it is often used in metallurgy work and electroplating.

This revelation sends a chill down my spine as I once again recall Hurley's garage workshop and his metalwork hobby. Then I hear Richmond's voice in my head, warning me that poisoning is personal. So far, all the fingers in this case are pointing firmly at Hurley.

As guilt over not telling Izzy what I know washes over me, I reach a decision and head for his office.

Chapter 12

My good intentions are thwarted by two things. The first is the fact that I can't find Izzy in either his office or the autopsy room. The second is a call on my cell phone.

At first I think it might be Richmond but when I look at the caller ID, I see it's Hurley. I hesitate, debating for a few seconds, before I take the call.

"Hello?"

"Mattie, it's me."

"Hey, what's up?"

"That's what I need to be asking you. There're a bunch of cops swarming around Minniver's house, so I'm guessing you found something on the autopsy."

"Yes, we did. We just finished up. In fact, I was about to call you," I lie. I head back to the library and shut myself inside, glancing around to make sure no one is close by to overhear me.

"So what did you find?" Hurley prods. I hesitate just long enough for him to deduce that the news isn't good. "Damn, it's something bad, isn't it? Is it something else that points to me?" He sounds both worried and angry. "It is, isn't it? Come on, tell me, Mattie. I need to know what the hell I'm dealing with here. Give it to me, would ya?"

"I will if you'll stop fretting for a moment," I manage when he pauses long enough to take a breath.

"Sorry," he mutters. "It's just that I feel like I'm operating in a vacuum here. You're the only person I can talk to right now."

The faint hint of desperation in his voice leaves me feeling guilty for doubting him. Even though I have no idea where in his house he is, or even if he's in his house, in my mind's eye I see him pacing back and forth in his kitchen, running his fingers through that thick shock of blue-black hair, worry creases crinkling the corners of his eyes. And rather than feeling empathy for the man, I find myself turned on. The idea of Hurley rendered helpless and vulnerable is oddly stimulating. After shaking off my mental images and cursing the fact that my libido seems to surge like a tsunami whenever Hurley's involved, I drop my informational bomb.

"It isn't confirmed yet but it looks like Harold Minniver was poisoned."

"Poisoned? That's typically pretty personal." *Echoes of Bob Richmond.* "What was he poisoned with?"

I feel an odd reluctance to say anything, as if the answer is a piece of spinach stuck in Hurley's teeth, or a booger hanging from his nose. "We think it was cyanide."

A long silence stretches between us and though I'm tempted to break it, I wait, curious to see what Hurley will say next.

"Shit," he says finally. He sounds sad, dejected, and defeated. "That's not good. I have a supply of potassium cyanide in my garage. I use it in my metalwork."

I squeeze my eyes closed and wince. Only now do I realize how much I was hoping to hear him say he didn't have any of the stuff.

"Mattie, are you still there?"

I open my eyes. "I'm here. Sorry, I was just thinking things through."

"It's all rather damning, isn't it?"

"It is, and there's more," I say, reaching a potentially disastrous decision. I tell him about the hair we found in Callie's wound, the one I took from his bathroom, and my subsequent examination of the two. When I'm finished talking, the line between us crackles with an awkward silence. Only because I can hear him breathing do I know he hasn't hung up on me.

"You're angry with me," I say, fearing he'll hate the fact that I did the hair comparison behind his back.

"On the contrary, I'm impressed. You need to have an open mind and be unbiased in things like this. But I *am* a little bothered by the fact that you didn't tell me what you were doing ahead of time. I would have gladly provided you with a hair sample to compare if you'd asked for one. The fact that you didn't makes me think you don't trust me."

His comment irritates me. "Well, the evidence against you *is* rather damning," I snap. "And I haven't known you all that long, Hurley. You're asking me to put my reputation and my job on the line for you and I need to be sure I'm making the right decision. If you don't like the way I'm doing things, feel free to enlist someone else."

"No, wait," he says quickly, sounding panicked. "I'm sorry, and you're right. It's not fair to ask you to trust me based on my word alone." He pauses and curses under his breath. "Please, I . . . I need you, Mattie."

His plea melts my lingering resistance, which to be honest wasn't much to begin with. Even though the evidence all seems to point toward him, my gut still tells me he's innocent. And I've learned to trust my gut for the most part, at least when it comes to matters not of the heart. Problem is, Hurley sort of overlaps the professional and romantic parts of my life.

"Fine," I tell him. "I'll help you. Where do we go from here?"

"I don't know." I can hear the exasperation in his voice. "I realize things don't look very good for me but I swear to you, I had nothing to do with Harold's death or Callie's. But it's becoming clear to me that someone wants it to look like I did."

"Okay, so who would do something like that?"

"My best guess is it's someone who wants to see me suffer, someone who's bearing a serious grudge against me."

"*Very* serious," I say. "I mean, this goes way beyond your typical payback."

"I've been a cop for a long time. I've made a few enemies."

"Any idea which one this might be?"

He lets out a heavy sigh. "The only one I can think of who hates me that much is Quinton Dilles, the asshole who cost me my job in Chicago. His wife was murdered and when I caught the case, I fingered him for it early on. But my efforts to prove it pissed him off and the guy is very rich and very well connected. He complained to some very important people about the way I was harassing him and the next thing I know, I'm given the option of taking a position investigating computer crimes, or quitting. So I quit and a month or so later, the new detective on the case dug up some very incriminating evidence and Dilles was arrested. His trial ended last month."

"What was the outcome?"

"Dilles was found guilty and sentenced to life in prison. He's in the Stateville Correctional Center down by Joliet."

"So you weren't the one who actually arrested him?"

"No, but Dilles has made it clear that he blames me for shining the spotlight on him in the first place. To be honest, I think the guy believed he was going to be acquitted. He's always had a privileged, I'm-special-and-nothing-can-touch-me attitude because of his wealth and position in the community. So I'm sure his conviction and sentence came as something of a surprise to him."

"Were you there? At the trial, I mean?"

"Not the whole thing, but I was there for the verdict and I have to admit it felt redeeming to see that bastard put behind bars."

"I'm sure it did. But if Dilles is in prison, he can't be the one out there trying to frame you."

"No, not him directly anyway. But the man does have some powerful resources and money at his disposal. It wouldn't be that hard for him to hire someone on the outside to do his dirty work."

"It might be worth looking into."

"It's a long shot, but yes, I suppose it would. Listen, I'm going to take a few personal days from work. I'll tell them I need to have some medical tests done. Richmond can take up the slack and that will free me up to do some investigating on my own. There are some people I want to see but I'd like you to function as my front man and do most of the actual talking. It will seem less official that way and besides, you have a knack for getting things out of people. For some reason they open up to you."

"Hey, what can I say? I'm charming."

"Hmm, yes, you are," he says.

The subtle shift in his tone makes something in my nether regions shift. A montage of mildly X-rated images flits through my mind with me and Hurley as the stars.

"Can you get off call tomorrow?" Hurley asks. "I'd like

you to go down to Chicago with me to talk to Callie's family and coworkers, to see what we can find out."

Mention of the stunningly beautiful woman Hurley used to date quashes my mental pornado. "I'll have to talk to Izzy," I tell him. "But I don't think it will be a problem given the hours I've put in this weekend."

"Good. Let's plan to meet at the Milwaukee airport tomorrow morning at nine."

"We're flying to Chicago?" I say, thinking maybe Hurley killed those people after all because clearly he's lost his mind.

"No, but we're not driving down there in that hearse of yours either. I'll meet you at the airport. You can park the hearse there and we'll go the rest of the way in my car."

"Look, I know you don't want to be seen in the hearse and that's fine, but why don't we just drive your car from here?"

"Because I don't want us to be seen together." I'm about to take offense at that when he adds, "At least not yet. Until I can figure out what's going on I don't want to compromise you any more than I already have."

I can think of any number of ways I'd like Hurley to compromise me, but I refrain from saying so.

"So here's what we're going to do," he says, and then I listen as he outlines a series of steps that make me feel like the starring role in a spy movie. It all seems rather exciting and Mata Hari-ish until he finishes with a warning.

"Watch your back, Mattie. Maybe I'm being paranoid, but there are just too many coincidences happening here. And until I know exactly what's going on and who's behind it all, anyone involved with me or the investigation might be in danger."

I disconnect the call and head for Izzy's office again. This time he's there, bent over his desk reading reports, a stack of papers and charts on either side of him.

I knock lightly on the door frame. "Can I ask a favor?"

"Shoot," he says without looking up.

"Any chance I can be off call tomorrow? I'd like to make a trip down to Chicago to do some early Christmas shopping."

He looks up at me, clearly amused, probably because he knows I love shopping about as much as I would love having someone rip out my toenails. "Sure, go for it. I think a little retail therapy will do you some good."

Shopping might be therapeutic for some women, but it only aggravates me most of the time. I grocery shop out of necessity, but I try to get in and out as quickly as possible. Even that becomes frustrating at times because the local grocer likes to rearrange the store just when I've memorized where everything is. And don't even get me started on the nightmare that is clothes shopping. Until someone opens up a Sasquatch boutique for women like me with long legs, baboon arms, and ample bosoms, who wear shoes big enough to house not only the Old Woman and all her kids but five other families, clothes shopping will always be a task I loathe.

Since Izzy knows all this, I have to wonder why he's smiling. Is he simply amused by the idea of me shopping? Or does he suspect that I'm lying to him for some reason? I again consider telling him about Hurley, but something holds me back. One more day, I promise myself. Just enough time to gather a few more tidbits of information.

Chapter 13

I find Bob Richmond in the break room of the police station finishing off the remains of a sub sandwich. Apparently he's changed his shirt because the stained white one has been replaced with a light blue one that looks a bit worn but is at least clean.

"You need to give me your cell number," I tell him. He does so, rattling the number off between bites. After I enter it into my cell phone, I say, "You ready to go?"

He nods, shoves the last of his sandwich in his mouth, and groans as he pushes himself away from the table and out of his chair. He moves like a man in his eighties.

"You know, if you keep eating like that you're going to keel over of a heart attack before you hit fifty," I tell him.

He swallows what he has in his mouth and shoots me a dirty look. I brace myself for what's coming, cursing my inability to turn off the nurse in me, but to my surprise, Richmond's expression softens.

"For your information, I'm fifty-three," he says. Then he

shakes his head woefully. "Look, I know my weight is un-healthy and I know the only way to control it is by not eating, but damned if I can help myself. No matter how much I eat, I never feel full. I've been fat my entire life and I'm too old to change now."

"You're never too old to change," I say, feeling a sudden and unexpected empathy for him. I know exactly how he feels. "You just need someone to help you come up with a rigidly controlled diet and a regular exercise program." I say this with great authority, knowing I don't practice what I preach. As far as I'm concerned, the basic four food groups are ice cream, chocolate, fried foods, and sweets. And when it comes to any type of regular exercise program, forget it. I get all ambitious when I gain a pound or twenty and start di-eting and exercising with total devotion. But it never lasts. As soon as I shed the weight, or at least most of it—I seem to regain a few pounds every year and my weight has been slowly but steadily creeping upward—I go right back to my slothful, fattening habits. And the older I get, the harder it is to shed those extra pounds. I used to be able to do it with a couple of weeks of serious dieting and exercise. Now it takes a couple of *months* of near starvation and exercise, and frankly, I often don't have the stick-to-itiveness to get through it.

Bob says, "I joined that exercise place over on Houghton Street last month but I only went once. Everyone in there is all fit and skinny and shit. I hate it."

"You just need a buddy to go with you, someone else who isn't perfect, so you don't feel alone."

He considers this, eyes me up and down, and says, "Would you go with me?"

"Me?" I squeak, both appalled and a bit offended at the idea that I'm the first person he would think of for an imper-fect partner.

"I'd pay for your membership."

"Thanks, Bob, but I don't think so."

"See, you're embarrassed to be seen with me. Admit it."

"No, that's not it at all," I say, wondering if it's true. "I'm just not very good at keeping a regular schedule."

Richmond shrugs. "I'm basically retired so I'm pretty flexible. We can fit the workouts into your schedule."

I open my mouth to protest but hesitate because I'm not sure what other excuses I have. Plus, I don't want to alienate Richmond too much right now because I need him to share his findings with me.

Richmond gives me a look of disgust. "So all that crap you just handed me about being healthy and eating healthy . . . that was just talk?" He shakes his head, looking disappointed. "I had you pegged as a stand-up person, someone with integrity. Clearly I was wrong. You're as judgmental as the rest of them."

"I'm not judging you; I'm just giving you my opinion as a nurse."

"Bull. You're just like everyone else. Admit it. The only reason you won't go with me is because you're embarrassed to be seen with me."

"I am not."

He gives me a disbelieving look. "Okay, you just keep telling yourself that."

"Fine," I snap. "I'll go with you to the stupid gym for a while. But you're paying for my membership."

"I already told you I would." He smiles and I think I see a hint of smugness there. I suspect I've just been played and played well, and I mentally kick myself. "We can talk about it some more later on," he adds. "Let's get this other nasty business out of the way first."

He heads for the parking lot and I follow, listening to him whistle. *Smug bastard*. When we get to his car, I go around to the passenger side and open the door. That's when I remember that Richmond has the contents of a small garbage Dumpster on the floor of his front seat.

"Oh, sorry about that," he says. "Hold on a sec and I'll clean it out." He comes around and starts grabbing handfuls of empty fast-food containers, but with no trash bags or garbage cans anywhere close by, he has nowhere to put them. So he tosses them into the backseat.

"If we're seriously going to do this gym thing, that shit's going to stop right now," I say, nodding toward the empty containers. "No more of that greasy fast-food stuff."

For a second Richmond gives me a woeful expression, as if he just lost a very close friend.

"I mean it, Bob. If you're going to keep eating like that, there's no point to all of this."

"Fine," he says with a resigned sigh. He finishes tossing the trash into the back and brushes a few crumbs off the front seat before gesturing for me to get in.

The inside of the car smells like a mall food court and my stomach growls hungrily. I momentarily fantasize about eating a Sbarro's pepperoni and cheese Stromboli followed by a Cinnabon classic bun smothered with extra cream cheese frosting. I can practically taste the food and it's all I can do not to tell Richmond we should head for the nearest mall and go crazy one last time. But I contain myself, force the images away, and focus on the task at hand.

I decide to take advantage of our recent bonding by pumping Richmond for information along the way to Patricia Nottingham's house. But I have to be quick since Nottingham's house is only a couple of minutes away.

"Anything new on the Callie Dunkirk case?" I ask as soon as we're under way.

"I talked with Dunkirk's mother and sister over the phone to deliver the bad news but they didn't have much insight to offer. I may have some guys down in Chicago take another run at them in a day or two, after they've had a little more time to grieve. I also talked to some of her coworkers at the TV station to see if she was working on anything that might have been dangerous, but I got nothing there, either. Apparently our Miss Dunkirk wasn't a very sharing person. She liked to keep things to herself.

"So at this point we got nothing. We don't know where she was killed, we don't know why she was up here or where her car is, and we don't have so much as a guess as to who killed her, or why." He sighs and shakes his head. "I hate investigations like this."

Hearing the frustration in his voice, I can't help but wonder how angry he would be if he knew what I was keeping from him, and how quickly he'd be on Hurley as a result. Though I typically revel in being the keeper of secrets, at the moment I'm not relishing my position at all. It makes me feel like I'm walking on glass shards, gingerly taking a step at a time, knowing that a single misstep might lead to painful, irreparable damage.

As we pull onto Patricia Nottingham's street, it's obvious she is not only expecting us, but anxious for our arrival because she has the front door open when Richmond parks at the curb. She watches us closely as we get out of the car, no doubt searching for clues.

I smile at her as we climb the porch stairs. "Hi, Patricia. This is Detective Bob Richmond." She acknowledges the introduction with a nod. "Here is your key back," I say, handing it to her. "Thank you for letting me borrow it."

She takes it and stuffs it inside her pants pocket. "Did you do the autopsy?"

"Let's go inside and talk," Richmond says.

Patricia waves us through the door and points to the left toward the living room. Richmond eyes the two delicate, antique chairs in the room and wisely takes a seat on the couch.

I settle into one of the chairs, and Patricia takes the other one.

"You found something, didn't you?" she asks, leaning forward eagerly, her eyes bouncing back and forth between me and Richmond before they finally settle on me.

"We did," I say. I glance over at Richmond, unsure how much he wants me to reveal this soon, and he gives me a subtle nod. "It appears your father may have been poisoned."

Patricia rears back, looking confused. "Poisoned? You mean like food poisoning?"

"Not exactly, no," I say, shooting another glance Richmond's way. He is studying Patricia intently and when he does nothing to interrupt or stop me, I continue. "It appears he was poisoned with cyanide."

"Cyanide? How on earth could that happen?"

"Most likely someone slipped it into his food or drink," Richmond says.

Patricia turns and looks at him, her expression horrified and even more befuddled. If she is in any way involved with this, she's putting on a damned good show. "Why would anyone want to poison him?" she asks.

Richmond says, "You tell me."

Patricia narrows her eyes at him. "Are you suggesting that *I* poisoned him?" The fierce look on her face makes that seem more possible than it did a moment ago. "I loved my father," she says, her eyes welling with tears. "Yes, he was a cantankerous old coot at times, and yes, he could be as stubborn as a mule, but he is . . . was my father. He's the only family I have left. And now he's gone."

She squeezes her eyes closed and tears course down her face. Richmond and I exchange looks and he shrugs.

"What sort of financial situation was your father in?" Richmond asks. I can tell Patricia is rankled by the question even though Richmond's tone is less accusatory than before.

"Did he have life insurance? A retirement plan? And who is his beneficiary?"

I wince, knowing this line of questioning is only going to incense Patricia even more. There is a spark in her eye, and I brace myself for the storm to come. But her next words are surprisingly calm and measured.

"Yes, I am my father's sole beneficiary. As I just told you, I'm his only surviving family member. He has—had a small pension. I'm not sure how much it is, but it's been enough for him to live on because his house is paid off. He was hardly wealthy and as far as life insurance goes, he had one policy that I know of, a small one for twenty-five thousand dollars that he said he got to cover his burial expenses."

She pauses, gets up and grabs a tissue from a box on an end table, and blows her nose. Then she looks at Richmond and says, "I am a widow. My husband died a little over five years ago but when he was younger he developed a software company that he sold for a very tidy sum. I am quite well off, thank you, and have no need for my father's money, or anyone else's. Anything else you'd like to know?"

The question comes out with an underlying tone of bitterness. She and Richmond engage in a twenty second stare-off before Richmond says, "Yes, there is. Can you think of anyone who had a grudge or problem with your father? Anyone who would benefit from his death? Anyone who might want revenge for some reason?"

She thinks a moment, starts to shake her head, and then stops. "Well, there was one thing but it was kind of silly really," she says, looking sheepish. "My father had a property dispute going on with one of his neighbors and was planning to take him to court."

I hold my breath and utter a silent prayer that she won't continue, but she does.

"And since this neighbor is a cop, Dad was convinced the

guy would get special treatment because he'd have an in with the courts. Dad kept ranting on about how he'd never get a fair trial, how it was all part of some bigger conspiracy to stomp on the little guys, and how the city's bourgeois government was just some secret cabal determined to screw him over." She pauses, shrugs, and gives us an embarrassed smile. "Dad could be pretty blunt and vocal at times. I know he and this neighbor were involved in a couple of shouting matches, so who knows?"

I feel my stomach knot up. When I look over at Richmond, I'm hoping to see indifference on his face and a quick dismissal of Patricia's idea. But instead I see keen interest.

"Do you know this neighbor's name?" Richmond asks.

Patricia nods and with a flash of frightening clarity, I know what's coming next. "I believe his name is Hurley," she says. "Steve Hurley."

Chapter 14

Though I expect Bob Richmond to discuss Patricia's revelations during our short ride back to the station, he doesn't get a chance. His cell phone rings and after answering the call and grunting a couple of times, he says, "Okay, be right there," and hangs up.

He looks over at me and says, "They found Callie Dunkirk's car."

"Where?"

"It was left parked on a side street, ironically not far from where this Minniver guy lived. I'm heading over to check it out now and my guys have called Izzy to meet us there since the car might also be the murder site. Want to come along?"

I swallow hard, realizing that if Callie's car is near Minniver's house, it's also near Hurley's. "Sure," I say.

A few minutes later we pull up on the scene, which is on a side street a couple of blocks down from Minniver's house. There are two cop cars on site, one behind a silver sedan parked against the curb, and the other idling with its lights flashing in the traffic lane beside it. A police evidence tech, a guy named Jonas, is standing beside the silver sedan, waiting. Also standing nearby are two uniformed cops: Ron Colbert and Alan Nielsen.

Richmond slides his car in front of the lit-up cruiser and shifts it into park. He opens his door to get out but it takes several attempts and a lot of groaning before he makes it.

"Is it locked?" he asks the cops as we approach.

Colbert and Nielsen both nod and then Nielsen raises his hand, which is holding a Slim Jim. "We're ready to open it whenever you say so. Looks like the keys are in it, along with her purse."

Thank goodness we live in a small town where most of the people are honest. In a large city, I doubt a parked car containing visible keys and a purse would last very long.

"Did you dust the handles yet?" Richmond asks.

"Yep, looks like they were all wiped clean," Jonas says.

"Okay, then, go ahead and open her up."

Nielsen deftly slides the Slim Jim down inside the driver side door and after a few seconds of finagling, he pops the lock. Jonas hands around a box of gloves and I take a pair and put them on. Richmond pulls out a pair, too, but when he tries to pull one on over his huge hand, it tears. "Cheap crap," he mutters, ripping the tattered glove off. He walks over to his own car, unlocks the trunk, and grabs some gloves from a box he has stashed inside.

I hear the rumble of a familiar car engine behind me and when I look I see Izzy's Impala turn the corner. He pulls in along the curb behind the parked cruiser and gets out, carrying his scene kit.

"You're just in time, Doc," Richmond says.

Izzy walks up and sets his kit down on the street beside

the just-unlocked door. He dons some gloves and then carefully opens the driver side door. We all peer inside, looking for signs of blood pools, drops, or splatter, anything that might indicate that this is where Callie Dunkirk was killed. But the car appears to be clean.

"I don't see any evidence to indicate she was stabbed in here," Izzy says. We all take a step back as Izzy removes his gloves, stuffs them in his pocket, and picks up his scene kit. "I'll leave the rest to you fellows," he says.

Jonas moves in with a small, battery-operated, hand-held vacuum and starts running it over the driver's seat and floor.

Izzy looks over at Richmond and me. "How did it go with Minniver's daughter?"

"Okay," I say with a shrug. "She took it well, considering."

"Did she have any ideas on who might have wanted to poison her father?"

Richmond snorts. "Yeah, she thinks it might have been Steve Hurley." He says this with obvious derision, making it clear what he thinks of the idea.

"Hurley?" Izzy echoes. "Where did that come from?"

"Apparently Hurley is a neighbor," I explain, "and there was some kind of property line dispute between him and this Minniver guy. Frankly, the whole idea of a cop or anyone, for that matter, killing someone over something so petty seems pretty absurd to me."

"Yeah, I have to agree," Richmond says. "Though Hurley is kind of an unknown quantity in these parts. He's still pretty new here."

"I've worked a few cases with him and he seems like a pretty straight-up guy to me," I say.

Richmond snorts. "Yeah, like you're an objective judge."

"What's that supposed to mean?"

"Oh, come on, Mattie. Everyone knows there's something going on between you two. Even I've heard the rumors, and I'm hardly in the regular loop."

"There is nothing going on between me and Hurley." I try to look offended by the suggestion but I can tell from Richmond's amused expression that he isn't buying it. Can't say I blame him. But while my denial isn't exactly the truth, it isn't an all-out lie, either. Sure, Hurley and I have had a kiss or two, but that's as far as things have gone.

"That's not what I've heard," Richmond says. "Rumor has it your attraction to Hurley couldn't be more obvious if you were humping his leg every time you're together."

Great. The last thing I need is to be the topic of more rumors in this town. It's not bad enough that I'm already the object of pity, thanks to David's indiscretions. Now I'm being labeled as the town hound dog as well. And given my current situation with Hurley, it couldn't have come at a worse time.

"I don't give a hoot what you've heard," I tell Richmond. "I swear there is nothing going on between me and Hurley."

"Whatever," he says with a dismissive shrug. "Like I said, I don't see this property line dispute as much of a motive anyway. I need to dig a little deeper into Minniver's life, see what other motives and suspects pop up."

Jonas turns off his vacuum, sets it aside, and dons some shoe covers. Then he gets his fingerprint kit and settles into the front seat of Callie's car. He sits there a moment, frowning, and then he calls Richmond over.

"Do me a favor," he says, offering Richmond the fingerprint powder and brush. "Check the seat lever down there for prints. I need to move the seat back but I don't want to smudge anything that might be there and I can't quite reach it from here."

Richmond takes the kit, and when he bends over to brush the powder on the lever, his shirt rides up along his back, exposing a wide expanse of derriere and a butt crack that rivals the Grand Canyon.

Izzy, who is watching along with me, quickly turns away and says, "That's my cue to leave. Need a ride back to your car?"

"Sure. Thanks."

As soon as Izzy drops me off, I take out my cell phone and call Hurley to give him a heads-up. He doesn't answer, so I leave a message letting him know about the car and what Patricia told us. Knowing I have a long drive ahead of me tomorrow, I stop off on my way home and top off my gas tank at the Kwik-E-Mart, which just happens to be located right next to the strip mall that serves as home to Mancini's Pizzeria.

Ten minutes later, I'm sitting at home eating my takeout pizza and wondering if Richmond is being equally bad. In an effort to mitigate my sin, I drop the end crusts onto the floor so Hoover can do the thing that earned him his name. After sucking up every last crumb, he goes to the door and whines to be let out. That's when it hits me. Tomorrow's trip to Chicago is likely to be an all-day event. And Hoover, though he has done remarkably well thus far, hasn't had his bladder tested for more than an eight-hour span.

The responsibilities of dog ownership weren't uppermost in my mind when I found him, especially since I wasn't sure I'd be keeping him. I ran a lost-and-found ad in the local paper, but got no response. I've had him for nearly a month now and with each passing day he steals a little more of my heart. Even Rubbish adores him. It's easy to see why, because as companions go, Hoover is damned near perfect. He senses when my mood needs lifting, listens patiently to everything I say, keeps me warm in bed at night, and shares my taste in ice cream. If only I could find all those traits in a man.

While I'm overjoyed to have Hoover, his presence does leave me with certain scheduling issues I didn't have before. As I let him outside and watch him wander about sniffing until he finds the perfect place to piddle, I consider taking him along tomorrow. But we'll be riding in Hurley's car to who knows where and for how long, so I quickly dismiss that idea. I then think about asking Izzy and Dom to take care of him but I'm hesitant to impose on Izzy any more than I already have, and besides, the less I have to face Izzy while I'm withholding information from him, the better.

I would ask my sister, Desi, but she, Lucien, and the kids all left town early this morning to drive to Arizona to spend Thanksgiving with Lucien's parents.

That leaves my mother. The obvious problem with this idea is that my mother is a serious germaphobe and I suspect a puppy will look like a giant agar plate to her. But she is also a hypochondriac, and that aspect of her personality gives me an idea.

"Come on, Hoover," I say. "Let's go for a ride."

Thanks to today's rising temperature, a good deal of the snow that fell Thursday night has melted. As a result, a lot of what was white and pristine yesterday is now gray and slushy, turning Hoover's tootsies into mud magnets. I'm not too worried about him muddying up the back of the hearse. I was told when I bought it that the rear carpeting was some industrial-strength commercial stuff that would resist the most insistent of stains. Given the cargo that was typically carried back there before I bought it, I shudder to think what tests the carpet company ran to be able to make that claim. But because my mother would probably go screaming in terror at the site of mud-caked paws, I grab an old towel from the house and clean off Hoover's feet the best I can.

There's no need to call ahead to see if Mother will be home because the woman rarely ventures out of the house. According to her, the outside world is full of horrible threats: germs, radiation, cancer-inducing sun rays, skin-wrinkling poisons, secondhand smoke, airborne pesticides . . . and that's before she starts thinking up the more bizarre dangers, like getting your head split open by "turdites"—her word for those frozen, blue meteorites that are created when crap gets jettisoned from airliner toilets. I've always thought Mother could score big in Hollywood—the makers of disaster movies could learn a thing or two from her when it comes to thinking up ways for people to be annihilated.

Mother's long-term paranoia and hypochondria have definitely shaped my psyche and may have been why I chose to be a nurse. As a young child I kept expecting her to turn up dead any time, either from one her many supposed ailments, or some uncanny and unfortunate accident. As a result, I was always choosing alternative caregivers from among my friends' parents and imagining what a more normal life might be like. Over the years Mom dragged me along with her to hundreds of doctor appointments, an experience that always proved terrifying. But my fright didn't stem from a fear of Mom's illnesses or possible death—by the age of ten I began to suspect that her only real sickness was a mental one. Instead I was scared to death of being mortified by her behavior.

Because of her fear of germs and her belief that doctors' offices are giant petri dishes, incubating all the horrific diseases of every patient ever seen there—a fear that unfortunately has some foundation in truth—she would always refuse to sit in the waiting room. Instead she would insist on being taken back to an exam room immediately upon her arrival. If she wasn't, she would raise a fuss until she got her way, something that typically happened pretty quickly since the front desk people were always anxious to shut her up and get her in the back so she would quit scaring the other patients.

Unfortunately, getting past the waiting room was only half the battle. Once Mom got to an exam room, she would make the nurses go through a rigorous cleaning procedure that she had to personally supervise, an exhausting process that often took fifteen minutes or more and plucked the last nerve on the most patient of nurses.

As a result of all these idiosyncrasies, Mom knows every generalist and specialist in town because she has seen and made herself persona non grata with most of them. Nowadays she travels nearly an hour to see her doctor and she has toned down her behavior quite a bit. I think she finally realized she was running out of options and would soon be forced to weigh her fear of flying against her fear of death because the only doctors left who would be willing to see her would be too far away to drive to.

My marrying a doctor certainly helped things, and in my mother's eyes it's the one thing in life I did right. When I started dating David, she was ecstatic; when we became engaged, she nearly had an orgasm. She can't understand why I now want to divorce him over something as mundane as infidelity. I have to admit that David, despite his many faults, has always been a veritable font of patience when it comes to my mother. And she definitely pushes the limits, calling him often and at all hours of the day and night. If I had a dollar for every house call David ever made to my mother, I'd be pulling into her driveway right now in something a whole lot nicer than a hearse.

Today there is another car in Mom's drive and it's one I recognize. It belongs to William-not-Bill Hanover, a nerdy, germaphobic accountant with a bad case of OCD and an even worse comb-over. William was my blind date for a Halloween party a few weeks ago and the results were nothing short of catastrophic. However, he proved to be a perfect, albeit younger match for my mother. Apparently the sharing of a common mental illness is a powerful aphrodisiac.

I leash Hoover and head for the front door, trying to sidestep the slush piles to keep his paws as clean as possible. Apparently Mother either saw or heard me pull up because the door whips open before I reach the porch. She looks at Hoover with a horrified expression and claps a hand to her chest. Her normally pale skin is whiter than usual; she looks like one of those pale, see-through creatures you might see on a *National Geographic* special about the denizens of the Mariana Trench.

"What is *that?*" she says, pointing at Hoover and curling her lip in repugnance.

"It's a dog, Mom. I'm pretty sure you've seen one before."

She gives me a disgusted look. "I *know* it's a dog. I meant why do you have it? And what is it doing here?"

"*It* is a he," I say. "And he's mine. I found him a few weeks ago starving and abandoned, so I took him in."

"Dogs are filthy creatures," she says, wrinkling her face. "They harbor fleas and worms and that mange stuff where their skin sloughs off like someone with Hansen's disease."

Hansen's disease is better known to the non-medical public as leprosy, but my mother's hypochondria has given her a better than average knowledge of medical information and terminology. She has four bookshelves filled with nothing but medical resources and texts, and I'd bet every bookmark on her computer is a Web MD knockoff.

"Hoover doesn't have fleas, mange, or worms," I assure her. Actually, I'm not sure of the latter since I haven't taken him to a vet yet, but the fact that I gave him a store-bought deworming agent and he hasn't been walking around scooting his butt on the ground makes me think he's okay. I wisely decide to withhold the fact that Hoover has a fascination with the crotches on my worn underwear and the deposits my cat, Rubbish, leaves in his litter box.

"Why are you here?" Mom asks. She is staring at Hoover like she wishes she had a crucifix and a garlic necklace to ward him off.

"What?" I say, all innocence. "I can't drop in for a visit with my loving mother?"

Mom narrows her glacial-blue eyes and gives me The Look. It's an expression she mastered years ago, one that can cut through the thickest bullshit like a laser scalpel through soft fat. The first time I remember her using it on me was some thirty years ago when I tried to convince her I wasn't the one who had scraped off and rearranged the frosting on the German chocolate cake she had baked for the company coming that night. At first I tried to deny that the cake had been tampered with at all, despite the fact that, by then, the frosting consisted of a thin, sugary glaze dotted with a few scattered strands of coconut and a handful of nut pieces. When that didn't fly, I tried to blame the tampering on my sister, Desi, ignoring the fact that she was still in diapers and confined to a playpen. Then I offered up the theory that the frosting had simply melted and been absorbed into the cake. It was an insane defense but I was naive enough at the time not to let the laws of physics get in my way. It was at that point that Mother gave me The Look. It left me shaking and trembling with fear. I not only confessed immediately, I cried for hours afterward, begging the whole time for forgiveness.

I haven't touched another German chocolate cake since then, though I have been known to buy cans of the frosting and eat it with a spoon.

Mom's Look now has nearly the same effect on me it had during the cake debacle, minus the blubbering part. I confess. "I admit I have an ulterior motive. I want to spend the day in Chicago tomorrow and I need someone to dogsit for me."

"Chicago? What are you going to do in Chicago?"

"Shop. I want to get my holiday stuff done early this year."

I look away, knowing Mom will likely smell a rat. She knows I love shopping about as much as I love getting what Desi calls the annual spread-'em-and-let-'em exam. Hoping to distract Mom from sniffing out the truth, I stomp my feet and blow into my hands. "It's cold out here," I say.

Mom chews on one side of her cheek, eyeing Hoover warily. Worried that she's about to say no, I play my trump card.

"By the way," I say, "Hoover here is part Lab. Did you know that Labs have such an exquisite sense of smell they can actually sniff out cancer in its earliest stages? Or predict when someone is going to have a seizure?"

Mom's eyebrows arch at this. "Really?" she says with newfound curiosity. Hoover thumps his tail and grins at her, as if he understands she's softening toward him. A shadow materializes behind Mom and Hoover's tail thumps even faster as the shadow morphs into William-not-Bill.

"Hi, William," I say with genuine warmth. Even though my date with him was an unmitigated disaster, deep down he seems to be a nice, decent guy. I like him and, more important, Mom seems to like him, though given her track record with men, I'm not sure this is a point in his favor.

"Hi, Mattie," William says, his eyes focused on Hoover. "Who have you got here?"

"This is Hoover," I say, and then I stiffen, recalling that

William is deathly allergic to cats—one of the things that contributed to our first date disaster—and wondering if he might have a problem with dogs, too. I'm ready to pull Hoover back when William squeezes past my mother, squats down, and gives Hoover a little scratch beneath his chin.

"Hey, boy," he says. "You're a cutie, aren't you?"

Hoover inches closer. Seconds later his nose is nestled in William's crotch and he's so happy his whole butt is wagging—Hoover's that is, though William looks pretty content, too.

"Is he yours?" William asks me.

"He is," I tell him. "I found him by a gar—" I catch myself before letting it slip that I found the dog next to a Dumpster. To my mother and William, that would be akin to saying the dog had rolled in toxic nuclear waste. "I found him behind a grocery store, begging for food," I say. "I ran an ad in the lost-and-founds but no one answered. So I guess he's mine for now."

"He's very cute," William says.

Mother is frowning at the two of us as if we're plotting against her. "Mattie wants to leave that creature here with us tomorrow," she says, practically spitting the words out. "But I don't need some dirty mongrel shedding and drooling all over my house."

"I'll bathe him tonight to make sure he's extra clean," I tell her. "And he's quite healthy."

"Come on, Jane," William says, staring at Hoover with a smitten look. "It's only for one day."

Mother's frown deepens. "Is he housebroken?"

"Absolutely," I assure her. "He'll let you know if he has to go and I promise I'll poop-scoop anything he leaves in your yard when I pick him up tomorrow."

"Fine, but just this once," Mom says, acquiescing at last. William claps his hands together like a little kid.

"Thanks, Mom." I lean over and give her a kiss on the cheek, which she promptly wipes off with the cuff of her blouse. Though she looks guilty for making the gesture, I know she can't help herself. Sometimes I wonder how she ever managed to conceive Desi and me. Sex is about as messy an activity as there is between two humans, and when one of them can't stand the thought of having someone else's spittle on her cheek, it's hard to imagine how any of her four husbands ever managed to score a home run. Despite my efforts to stop it, my brain makes the leap to wondering if William and Mom are doing it, and if so, how these two germaphobes deal with all the wonderful messiness that is sex. An image of the two of them outfitted in giant head-to-toe condoms that have a few strategic openings makes me smile. Then the ick factor of thinking about my mother and sex in any form hits me, and I quickly shift gears.

After leaving Mom's house, I head back home and haul Hoover into the bathroom. Half an hour later he is thoroughly sudsed, scrubbed, and rinsed within an inch of his life. Hoping to further enhance his foo-fooiness, I work a bunch of hair conditioner into his fur and let it sit for a bit before rinsing that out, too. Rubbish sits on the side of the bathroom sink watching the entire affair with an air of disdain, though he briefly gets into the flow of things by licking his paw a few times and smoothing down his facial hair.

By the time I'm done, Hoover smells divine, feels soft and fluffy, and looks utterly humiliated. I'm pretty pleased with the results until he goes to the door and whines to be let out. As soon as the door's open, he runs off to a patch of dead leaves, melted snow, and mud, flops onto his back, and starts doing the doggie version of the Macarena. By the time he's done, he bears a strong resemblance to Swamp Thing but he looks much, much happier.

I decide to let him have his dignity for tonight, knowing

As we leave the main part of the airport, I notice video cameras mounted on the roof of the overhang fronting the terminal. "This place has cameras everywhere," I tell Hurley. "It wouldn't be that hard for someone to verify that we met here."

"True, but hopefully they won't have any reason to suspect that we met up at all. And if they do, the airport isn't exactly the most logical place to look." He shrugs. "I know it's not perfect, but it was the best I could come up with for now."

"So where are we headed exactly?"

"Did you bring the items I told you to?"

I fish in my purse and pull out a steno notebook and pen. "Okay?" I say, and he nods. "Good. Now would you please answer my question?"

"The first place we're going is the TV station where Callie worked. I want you to talk to her coworkers there and see if you can find out what it was she was doing up in our neck of the woods. See if anyone knows what story she was working on."

"Okay, but Richmond said he already did that and no one knows anything."

"That's because Richmond's a cop and TV people are funny when it comes to cops. They tend to get tight-lipped around us because we have a history of ruining their stories. They might tell you things they wouldn't tell a cop, especially more personal stuff, like whether or not Callie was dating anyone."

His tone as he utters this last bit sounds irritated and I look over at him, studying his expression. The muscles in his cheek are twitching and his brows are drawn down into a frown.

"How long were the two of you together?" I ask. Part of me shudders at the thought of having to listen to him talk

that come morning I'll have to bathe and humiliate him all over again. But I make him spend the night on the floor on a towel rather than in bed with me.

"Might as well get used to it," I tell him as he tries to soften me up with his big, soulful, woeful, puppy-dog eyes. "If I ever get lucky again, this bed won't be big enough for all of us."

Chapter 15

Bright and early the following morning I let Hoover out before I throw him back into the tub. One wash and blow-dry later, I drive him over to Mom's and drop him off, leaving a bag of food and his bowls since I know Mom would never let an animal drink or eat out of any dish she owns. I'm amused to see William's car is still there, and given the hour, I suspect he spent the night, especially since I don't see any sign of him inside the main part of the house.

I stay long enough to set up Hoover's food and water in the kitchen, where the surfaces and floor are cleaner than the operating rooms I used to work in. Out the window I can see that Mom's backyard is a slushy, muddy mess and I grimace, knowing that Hoover will be tracking it in anytime he's let out. Before Mom has a chance to realize the same thing, I thank her and hurry off.

After nearly an hour and a half on the road, I arrive at the airport ten minutes before the appointed time and pull into the long-term parking lot. I'm not sure why Hurley wanted

me to park here rather than in the short-term area, but he was pretty specific about it. As I drive up and down the aisles looking for a spot, I catch several people staring at me and realize Hurley was right; my car is not the most inconspicuous one in the world. I can't help but wonder what's going through these people's minds as they watch a hearse cruise up and down the long-term parking lot.

I finally find an empty space, pull in, and shut the engine off. Per Hurley's instructions, I get out, lock the car, and head for the Southwest Airlines terminal. Before I can cross the road where everyone is loading and unloading, Hurley's car glides up in front of me and his window slides down. "Get in," he says.

I run around the front of the car and settle in on the passenger side. As we pull away, I buckle my seat belt and glance over at Hurley's chest, then at his lap.

When he catches my gaze, he flashes me a salacious grin and cocks one eyebrow.

"Don't flatter yourself," I tell him. "I was checking to make sure you had your seat belt on."

"I do."

"Well, sort of. I don't think having the chest strap behind you like that works very well."

"I'm sorry. Did I miss something?" he says, his voice rife with sarcasm. "Did someone promote you to seat belt compliance officer and forget to tell me?"

"Ha-ha, very funny, smartass. I'm a nurse, remember? And I've seen what happens to people who are too stupid to wear their seat belts. Besides, it's the law, you know."

Hurley pulls aside his jacket to show me that he's wearing his gun in a shoulder holster. "The shoulder strap interferes with this," he says, gesturing toward the gun with his chin. "Okay?"

I shrug. "Whatever."

about a woman he once cared for and presumably slept with. But another twisted, masochistic part of me wants to know every gory, painful detail.

"About a year," he says, staring straight ahead.

I wait, hoping he'll offer more but his reticence outlasts my curiosity. "Why did you break up?"

He hesitates, taking one hand from the wheel and running it through his hair. "I don't know," he says finally. "She was the one who ended it, and to be honest, I never saw it coming. One day she just called up out of the blue, said the relationship wasn't working for her anymore, and she wanted to part ways." His hand goes back to the steering wheel and his knuckles turn white with his grip. "I tried to get her to talk to me about it but she refused. She kept saying it would be best if we cut things off quickly and fully. That way we wouldn't stain all our good memories with the petty and hurtful detritus"—he lets go of the wheel long enough to make little finger quotes in the air—"that so often accompanies a breakup."

The hand gesture, along with the sarcastic, singsongy tone in his voice suggests he is quoting this last line from memory, and not a happy one.

"Detritus?" I echo. "She actually said detritus?"

"Yeah," he says with a laugh, though it sounds bitter. "She loved words—the bigger and fancier, the better."

Clearly Callie's cavalier dismissal of him and their relationship pissed him off, a slight I'm beginning to think he never got over. The thought of him still aching and pining for Callie triggers a little stab of pain to my heart, but masochistic Mattie can't resist one more question and I brace myself for the answer. "Were you in love with her?"

He hesitates a few seconds and then shrugs. "I don't know. Maybe," he admits. "But it happened a long time ago and it's all in the past now. Besides, it hardly matters anymore, does it?"

It matters to me more than I like and I sense Hurley knows it. So I say nothing, gazing out my side window at the passing scenery instead. We ride that way for several minutes, the awkward silence a wobbly rope bridge gapping the rift between us. When Hurley speaks again it's on a new subject.

"So our first stop today is the TV station where they film *Behind the Scenes*. I want you to talk to Callie's coworkers to see what you can dig up," he says again.

"Except that degree of investigation is a bit outside my job description," I say. "All that interviewing and investigative stuff falls more into your territory or, in this case, Bob Richmond's. And he's already spoken to them. What happens if Richmond talks to them again and they mention the fact that I've been there? Isn't that going to look a bit . . . fishy?"

"It will," he concedes, "which is why you're going to use a fake ID and say that you're a private investigator hired to look into Callie's murder."

I shoot him a look of incredulity. "You want me to lie to them?"

"Yeah."

I continue staring at him, slack-jawed and disbelieving.

"What?" he asks.

"I can't believe you want me to lie to a team of investigative journalists. Sniffing out the truth is what they do best."

He dismisses my concerns with a little *pfft*. "You'll do fine," he says.

"Yeah, right." I punctuate my skepticism with a roll of my eyes.

"Trust me, Mattie. You can do this. Based on my past experience, I have every confidence that you can lie quite convincingly."

He's referring to the first case we ever worked together,

one that involved the murder of my husband's paramour. When I realized David and I were both at the top of the suspect list, I withheld certain information until I could sort things out on my own. When Hurley figured it out, he was rather ticked.

"I never out-and-out lied to you, Hurley. I simply didn't tell you everything right away."

"Sorry, but I fail to see the distinction."

"You're just angry that I didn't share everything with you immediately."

"And you're doing it again."

"What do you mean?"

"This thing you did, sneaking one of my hairs out of my house so you could compare it."

Oh, that. "Come on, Hurley. I have a right to be cautious. We've only known each other for a few weeks and given what you're asking me to do, I think it's smart of me to be careful. Besides, if I didn't trust you, would I be sneaking around like this, leaving no trail of where I've gone and who I'm with? If you wanted to do me in, now would be the perfect time."

"Don't tempt me," he grumbles.

I fold my arms over my chest and turn back to view the scenery, letting him sulk. After a long period of stony silence, Hurley says, "I'm sorry. I seem to be edgier than usual lately what with everything that's happened."

"Apology accepted." I let my arms fall to my sides. "And I suppose it's understandable, given the circumstances. I'm sure Callie's death has hit you particularly hard."

He nods but says nothing, and just as I'm starting to relax, thinking a détente has been reestablished, he blindsides me.

"So as long as we're discussing exes, mind if I ask where things are with you and David?"

"They're progressing," I say vaguely.

"Progressing how?"

"I have a lawyer. She drew up separation papers and is prepping for the divorce filing."

"Did David sign anything?"

"Not yet. But it doesn't matter," I say with more conviction than I feel. "I'm going ahead with things no matter what he does."

Hurley nods slowly and I hope it means he's ready to let the subject drop, but then he asks, "Is he still making overtures toward reconciliation?"

I start to squirm. David has been frustratingly reticent to move ahead with this divorce thing and I've been a bit ambivalent myself at times. "I don't want to talk about David," I say firmly, hoping to eliminate any doubt in his mind that I am done with the topic. "The way the two of you keep pressuring me makes me want to turn tail and run before one of you whips it out and pees on me to mark your territory."

Hurley shoots me a glance and says, "Sorry. I didn't realize I was hitting such a sensitive nerve."

"Let's focus on the task at hand, okay? I'm nervous about these upcoming interviews and since you're the ace investigator, how about giving me some guidelines on what questions I should be asking?"

"There's no need. I trust your instincts." His compliment has me preening for a moment, but then he adjusts his sights and blows all my feathers off. "You seem to do very well when you stick your nose into things. So just do what you usually do. Be nosy and persistent."

Chapter 16

The TV station where Callie Dunkirk worked is located in a rectangular brick building situated on the edges of a suburban neighborhood filled with small, older homes. There is a definite institutional look about the place and given that the word GYMNASIUM is stained into the brick above a door at one end, I'm guessing it was once a school. Its current use is equally as obvious, not only from the station logo emblazoned above the front entrance, but from the giant radio tower looming behind the building and the two satellite trucks in the front lot.

Hurley parks a ways down the street, shuts the engine off, and turns to face me. "Here," he says, pulling a thin billfold and a cell phone from his jacket pocket and handing them to me. I flip open the billfold and find an Illinois private investigator's license in one side pocket, and an Illinois driver's license in the other. Though the driver's license has my picture and stats on it, both it and the PI license bear the name Rebecca Taylor. "Just in case they ask you for some ID."

"Who is Rebecca Taylor?" I ask. "And how did you get her PI license?"

"The license is mine," Hurley explains. "When I left the Chicago police force I needed a way to make some quick money. So I got a PI license."

"But this license has the name Rebecca Taylor on it," I say. "Is there some big secret about your private plumbing you haven't told me yet?"

"No, I haven't had a sex change," he assures me. "Rebecca Taylor is a name I made up for you. I didn't use my PI license very long because I got hired by the Sorenson PD pretty quickly. So I figured we could use it now to give you an in with the folks down here. I just had it altered a bit."

I peer down at both licenses, trying to discern the changes, but the documents look pristine. "Impressive work," I say. "How is it you know how to do something like this?"

He flashes an enigmatic smile. "I was with the Chicago PD for fifteen years and met a lot of talented lawbreakers during that time." He shrugs. "I still have a few connections."

"How'd you come up with the name Rebecca Taylor?"

"There is a database of licensed PIs in the state that anyone can check so I wanted to give you a name that would pass muster if someone gets curious. Turns out there is an R. Taylor registered and Taylor happens to be the last name of one of my all-time favorite Victoria's Secret models: Niki Taylor. I chose Rebecca because it's the first name of my other favorite Victoria's Secret model: Rebecca Romijn."

I'm not sure if I should be worried or flattered—worried because I'm coming to realize Hurley's standards in women are frighteningly high, or flattered because he thought of those women while trying to come up with a name for me. I suspect it's only the former given that one of my thighs is probably bigger around than the waist on either of the models. But we do share a couple of traits: they are tall like me and all of us are blondes, so who knows? It's definite fodder for later analysis, not to mention a nudge for me to consider another underwear upgrade.

"What about this cell phone?" I ask him, proffering the one he handed me.

Hurley leans over and opens up the glove box—giving me a peek at the very sexy nape of his neck and a whiff of that wonderful spicy scent he always seems to have—and pulls out a small manila envelope and a charger for the phone.

"It's a throwaway phone," he says, opening the envelope. "I already charged it up but you can recharge it with this." He hands me the cord and I stuff it in my purse. "The number for it is on these." He removes a handful of business cards from the envelope and hands them to me. "Give these out to anyone you talk to so they can reach you again later, in case they think of something more. Plus, it makes you look more legit."

As I tuck the cards, phone, and billfold into my purse, Hurley says, "Lift up your sweater for me."

"Say what?"

"Lift up your sweater."

"Why?"

He tips the envelope up and slides the remaining contents out into his hand. Then he shows me what he's holding—some pull-off sticky tabs, some wires, and a small round device. "I'm going to give you a wire," he explains.

"You want me to wear a wire? What do you think this is, a Mafia bust?"

"It's for my ears only. I want to be able to hear exactly what everyone says and, more important, how they say it."

"Isn't that illegal?"

"It doesn't matter," he says, slickly avoiding an answer. "It won't be used for anything official."

I hold my hand out. "Give it to me and I'll put it on myself."

"You don't know how."

"Well, can't you tell me?" I shoot back, exasperated. For some reason, the thought of Hurley touching my bare skin there makes me extremely nervous.

He gives me a wicked smile. "What's wrong?" he asks. "You haven't developed a strong sense of modesty all of a sudden, have you? Because I've seen it all before, remember. You've been photographed half naked in the oddest places several times recently."

This is true, but there were extenuating circumstances. What's more, Hurley wasn't touching me either time. "Fine," I say, resigned. I yank my sweater up, close my eyes, and try to imagine something as disgusting and unsexy as I can. The first thing that pops to mind is an image of Lucien.

Hurley puts the peel-and-sticks on me, connects the wires, and then threads the small circular device up under my bra. His fingers graze the insides of my breasts, making me gasp as my nipples stand up and say hello. "You better take it from here," he says, pulling his hand away. "I need you to stick the mike just under the cup of your bra."

I open my eyes and we gaze at one another for a moment, one of those long, innuendo-laden stares that says nothing and everything. He starts to close the gap between us and my heart steps up a notch in anticipation of a kiss. But when he's only inches away, a shadow descends over his face. He pulls back and turns away to stare out his side window instead.

I realize I'm holding my breath and slowly release it, giving myself a few seconds to come back to my senses. With fumbling fingers I position the mike the way he told me and then I stare at the back of his head, wanting to ask him a million questions but afraid to ask a single one. Finally I say, "Okay, the mike is in place."

He turns back from the window, but doesn't look at me right away. Instead he reaches into his jacket pocket and pulls out what appears to be a recording device with a pair of earplugs. He turns the device on, places one of the plugs in his left ear, and says, "Say something."

"What the hell just happened here?" I blurt out.

Hurley flinches slightly and bows his head. The muscles in his cheek twitch. Silence wraps around us like a dense fog. Finally he says, "Seems to be working fine. You're good to go."

I squeeze my eyes closed, clamp my jaws together, and shake my head. "I don't know why I let you talk me into this." I yank up on the door handle and just as I'm about to get out of the car, Hurley reaches over and gives my arm a little squeeze.

"You'll be fine," he says. "Just focus on the facts and take notes even if you don't think you need to. Dig in as far as you can and see what you turn up. I don't anticipate any problems, but if you need me for any reason, I'll be right here."

The idea of Hurley being there, waiting for me, calms me. As I get out of the car and cross the street I try to take on the persona of a private investigator, but I've never known a real one so I dig through my memory banks and come up with the only one I can remember: Jim Rockford.

I walk through the front door of the station with a cocky swagger and find myself in a wide lobby area. To my right is a staircase and located on either side of me just past the stairs are doors that I'm guessing open onto hallways that run the length of the building. Straight ahead is a reception desk positioned against the back wall, and the TV station logo is emblazoned across the wall above it.

There is a young woman seated behind the reception desk talking—or judging from all the eyelash batting, hair twirling, and coy looks—flirting with a young man in a security uniform. As I approach, they reluctantly tear their attention away from one another and turn it on me, both of them looking quite annoyed by the interruption.

"May I help you?" the girl asks with a weight-of-the-world sigh designed, no doubt, to let me know what a royal pain in the ass I am to her.

"Yes, my name is Rebecca Taylor and I'm an investigator for the state of Illinois," I say, snapping one of the business cards down on the desk and trying to sound as officious as possible. The duo looks unimpressed. "I'm looking into the murder of Callie Dunkirk and I'd like to talk to some of the people she worked with."

The mention of murder seems to earn me a bit of respect judging from the suddenly heightened expressions of interest.

"I heard about that," the girl says, her eyes wide. "Do they have any idea yet who did it?"

The security guard, who I'm guessing is in his mid-twenties, puffs his chest out and looks all serious. "It had to have been someone she knew, Misty," he says with a level of authority and conviction that make me peg him as a police academy dropout. "I heard she was stabbed in the heart, and a crime like that generally indicates intimacy and passion."

"Do you really think so?" Misty says, looking up at him with big doe eyes. He nods and puffs his chest out a little more until Misty shifts her focus to me. "Is that true?" she asks.

Security Boy's chest collapses a bit and he shoots me a quick side glance, like he's afraid I'll contradict him and make him look bad. I'm tempted, but I'm not here to crush blooming romances or make enemies. Besides, what the kid said is right.

"Yes, that's true," I say, and Security Boy's chest puffs

back up into pigeon mode. "Did you guys know Callie very well?"

Misty shakes her head. "I saw her when she came into work every day and she always said hi, but we never really talked or anything. She was one of the reporters." Judging from Misty's tone of awe, I gather that being a reporter is akin to being king, or in this case, queen.

"She was a real nice lady," Security Boy says. "Real pretty, too," he adds, making Misty pout.

"Was there anyone special in her life that you know of?"

Security Boy shakes his head. "Nah, she didn't date much. Between work and her kid, I don't think she had the time."

For a moment I'm dumbstruck. Then I blurt out, "Callie had a kid?"

Misty smiles and says, "Yep. His name is Jake. What a cutie-pie! He's like nine or ten months old and he's got these huge blue eyes and the most adorable little face." She smiles wistfully for a second before her expression turns suddenly grim. "Poor little Jakey. Losing his mom like that. It's not fair."

Security Boy proves he's not a total incompetent when he narrows his eyes at me and says, "As a cop, I would have thought you knew that Callie had a kid."

I mutter a curse under my breath and think fast. "Cop? I'm not a cop," I say with an incredulous smile, saying a silent prayer that I'm reading him right. I dig out my fake licenses and show them to him. "I'm a private investigator." I emphasize the last two words as if they're some sort of elite award. "Cops are so limited in what they can do what with all the restrictions the law puts on you, and I don't have the patience for that crap. Besides, I like doing things my own way, you know?" Security Boy nods eagerly. "I mean, if you know your stuff and have the wits to do the investigative end of things, why settle for a job that makes you work with restrictive laws and pathetic pay?"

"Oh, man, that is *so* true," Security Boy says. Judging from the distant, dreamy-eyed look he now has, I'm guessing I just steered him toward a new career path.

"Anyway," I say, hoping to get things back on track, "I was hired by someone to look into Callie's murder but I'm just starting my investigation. I'm afraid my new employer neglected to tell me that Callie had a child."

Though it is within the purview of the ME's office to notify the next of kin of someone's death, it's often doctors or the police who do it. In Callie's case, it was Bob Richmond who did the deed. It's easy enough to understand why Richmond wouldn't have mentioned that the woman had a kid, but I can't help but wonder why Hurley failed to share this bit of info. An ugly, dark suspicion starts to rise in my mind and apparently it's affecting my expression because both Security Boy and Misty back up a step or two.

"Who hired you?" Security Boy asks.

This is a question I anticipated. I give him a tolerant smile and using my most officious voice say, "I'm sorry, I can't reveal that. The PI Code of Ethics and all . . . you know." I wink at Security Boy hoping he'll see it as my acknowledgment of his inclusion in some mysterious inner circle.

Apparently it works because he says, "Oh, yeah, of course."

"Suffice to say, it's someone with a vested interest in the case."

"I'll bet it's Mike Ackerman," Misty says to Security Boy, her eyes growing big again.

"Who's Mike Ackerman?" I ask, digging out the notebook and pen from my purse. As I scribble down the name, Misty fills in the blanks for me.

"He's a big shot with the network, and everyone says he has a great eye for talent. He *did* discover both Carmen

Soledad and Dayton Wynn," she says pointedly, naming two young TV actresses whose recent surge in popularity has made them frequent fodder for the tabloids. "He's the executive producer for *Behind the Scenes* and the person responsible for bringing Callie on board. Everyone thought she was destined to be his next big find."

"Is this Mr. Ackerman here today?" I ask.

"Sure is," Misty says. She picks up the phone but I stop her.

"Actually, I'd like to talk to some of the other people here first, if that's okay. Anyone Callie worked with. Are her other coworkers here?"

"Sure are," Misty says, all helpful again. "In fact, I'd say most of them are here today. Sundays are always busy because it's the day our show airs." She turns and looks at Security Boy. "Gary, why don't you take Ms. Taylor back into the studio with you and see who might be free to talk with her."

Gary frowns and looks doubtful. "I don't know," he says. "Shouldn't we run it by Sheila first?"

"Who's Sheila?" I ask.

"Sheila Rabinsky. She's our station and production manager," Misty explains.

"And she doesn't care to have a lot of extra people hanging around," Gary adds.

I'm beginning to think Sheila has the potential to become a huge wrench in my planned works so I think fast and come up with an idea. "Tell you what," I say. "I don't want to risk you guys getting into trouble or losing your jobs. So why don't you let me talk to Sheila myself?"

The two of them look at one another, give simultaneous shrugs, and then Misty again picks up the phone. Many long minutes later, after I have paced the width of the lobby at least a dozen times pretending not to notice when Misty and

Gary make surreptitious grabs and gropes at one another, Sheila appears. She is tall, tanned, and anorexically thin, with huge brown eyes, pinched lips, and a cute, chin-length bob in anthracite black. Her makeup is applied with exquisite precision and while her pantsuit and shoes are stylish, the height on her heels and the material in her clothing are both workaday practical. I can tell from the skepticism in her expression and the wary way she is eyeing me that it won't be easy to pull a fast one on her.

"Hi," she says, extending a well-manicured hand. "I'm Sheila Rabinsky, the station manager. I understand you're here about Callie Dunkirk?"

I shake her hand, which is cold, dry, and surprisingly lifeless. "Yes, I am," I say, releasing my grip and handing her a business card. "I've been hired by a private party to investigate her death and was hoping I could talk with some of the people she worked with."

Sheila's eyes narrow as she scans the card. "You are a private investigator?"

"That's right."

"Do you have some other ID?"

"Sure." I take out the billfold Hurley gave me and hand it to her. She studies it closer than I like before handing it back to me.

"This may not be the best time," she says with a dismissive smile. "Sundays are very busy days for us."

"I realize that," I say, looking impatiently at my watch. "But it's rather important that I do it today since I have to catch a flight to Washington, D.C. this afternoon to investigate the connections Callie had there."

An expression of surprise flits across Sheila's face, but then disappears so quickly I wonder if I imagined it. "You think Callie's death is tied to someone in Washington?" she asks, feigning indifference.

I give her the same dismissive smile she gave me a moment ago and a mental kudos for cleverness since she asked about some*one* in Washington rather than something.

"I'm not at liberty to reveal that," I tell her, and watch as her eyes take on the look of a hungry predator. "It's a rather . . . delicate and potentially explosive situation. However, in exchange for your cooperation today I would be willing to promise you a preemptive exclusive on the story once we are ready to go public. Given the . . . um . . . stature of the people involved, I'm sure you can understand why things need to be kept very hush-hush for now, but I am certain my client won't mind having the truth come out once we can turn over enough evidence to ensure a conviction."

The corners of Sheila's mouth twitch as she anticipates the coup I'm offering her. "An exclusive that lets us break the story?" she asks.

"Absolutely. From what I understand of Callie, I'm sure she would have wanted it that way."

"Yes," Sheila says, nodding. "Yes, she would have." She proffers that dry, dead hand again and we shake on it, making me feel like I've just made a deal with the devil.

Chapter 17

I hate cameras and not just because of the extra poundage they add, though that's reason enough. I hate cameras because they hate me. Some people are very photogenic and even when they are caught with some goofy-assed expression on their face, or in some spastic pose, their pictures still manage to be captivating. My pictures are often captivating, too, but it's usually because I look like the accompaniment to a *Weekly World News* headline, or lately, because I'm half naked.

So when Sheila escorts me into what used to be the school gymnasium but is now the studio for *Behind the Scenes*, I'm instantly on edge. It's basically a large open room filled with cameras. I start to sweat, which makes the little stickies Hurley used for the wire itch like mad.

On the far side of the room, beyond the cameras and against the back wall, are the two sets used for the show. The one on the left is a basic conversation arrangement with three uncomfortable-looking, modern-design, molded plastic chairs in shades of plum and turquoise. Fronting them is a coffee table with slanting legs and a trapezoid shaped top, constructed with what appears to be the same plastic turquoise material. The wall behind all this is a geometric sculpture comprised of two gigantic triangular-shaped pieces of who-knows-what hanging at right angles to one another. One has been painted the same color as the coffee table; the other has been done in the plum.

The set on the right side of the room is a desk arrangement that looks like most TV broadcast newsrooms. There are modernistic touches here, too, in the angles and overall design, but its effect is less extreme than the conversational set. The real attention getter for the desk set is the giant blue screen on the wall behind it.

Clearly any design sense stops with the sets because the rest of the room is all business: towering ceilings, overhead catwalks, cords snaking every which way across the floor, klieg lights hanging and standing everywhere, and of course, the cameras.

About a dozen or so people are milling about the room, some wearing headphones, some carrying clipboards, some just standing around watching. At the news desk set there is a perfectly coiffed brunette who looks to be about a size zero getting some final makeup touches while she practices reading from a teleprompter. So far every woman I've met here is tiny, petite, and attractive. I'm starting to feel like an ostrich in the songbird cage at the zoo.

"Doesn't anyone in this business ever eat?" I mutter under my breath, though Sheila hears me.

She looks up at me with a patient, patronizing smile and eyes me from head to toe. "We can't all afford the luxury of daily indulgence," she says.

"Trust me, I don't indulge daily," I tell her. And it's true. I manage to miss a few days here and there. "If I did, I'd be huge."

The exaggeratedly embarrassed look she gives me suggests that I've already reached that plateau and just don't know it yet. "Our viewing public demands the very best when it comes to beauty and fitness," she says. "We try to maintain the highest of standards. Plus, those cameras do add a few pounds, you know."

Based on the pictures I've seen of myself recently, I'm hoping it's more than a few.

Sheila nods toward the skinny anchorwoman and says, "That's Tasha Lansing, Callie's replacement. She probably knew Callie as well as anyone since she worked both as her assistant and her relief anchor."

"Was there any competition between them?" I ask, scribbling notes in my pad.

Sheila doesn't answer right away. Instead she narrows her eyes at Tasha while brandishing a tight, thin smile. "I suppose there was a little," she says finally. "Tasha has always been a very ambitious person. But it wasn't cutthroat or anything like that. Everyone here knew that Callie was Ackerman's pet project."

"Ackerman," I repeat. "He's the executive producer, right?"

Sheila nods.

"Is he here?"

"I think he's in his office," she says. She is still watching Tasha but I notice a subtle shift in both her expression and her tone with the mention of Ackerman.

"Do you know what story Callie was working on when she was killed?"

Sheila finally tears her gaze away from Tasha and stares at me instead, looking as if she is surprised by the question. "I have no idea," she says. "No one here does. I've asked. In fact, I'm not even sure she *was* working on a story. For all I know she was traveling up north for personal reasons."

"Did she ever pursue stories on her own?"

Sheila shrugs. "Sometimes she would research things and then bring them to us, but Mike and I always have the final say on what does or doesn't get aired. The only stories we've had her working on recently was an investigation into a local daycare center that had some abuse complaints filed against it, and a follow-up with some of the survivors from that train accident last year."

"Did either of those stories have any connections in Wisconsin?"

"Not that I'm aware of."

Great, a dead end. Sensing that I'm not going to get anything more out of Sheila, I shift my focus. "I'd like to talk to Tasha for a couple of minutes if that's okay. Is she getting ready to go on the air?"

Sheila glances at her watch. "We have a segment we're about to tape but I can give you five minutes."

"That should be fine."

Sheila walks up to the desk and speaks to Tasha, who glances at me over Sheila's shoulder. Though I can't hear what's being said, Tasha nods, says something to Sheila, and then approaches me.

"Hi, I'm Tasha Lansing," she says, extending a hand and wearing her on-the-air, two-hundred-watt smile. "Sheila said you are looking into Callie's murder."

"I am, yes. Do you have any idea why Callie was up in Wisconsin?"

"No," she says, her eyes huge with innocence. "Frankly, it's pretty rare for her to go anywhere without Jake."

"Her son, you mean?"

She nods. "That boy is the love of her life."

I note that Tasha is referring to Callie in the present tense and wonder if it's significant. "So who did she leave him with when she headed up north?" I ask her, thinking perhaps this person might know more about Callie's plans.

She shrugs. "Family I suppose."

"By family do you mean a boyfriend, or husband? Was she living with anyone?"

"No, it's always been just her and Jake. She does have a sister in the area, and her mom, though I gather their relationship is strained at times."

"Is Jake's father in the picture at all?"

Tasha shakes her head but her gaze slips away and I get a strong sense that what she's about to say next will be something short of the truth. "Nobody knows who Jake's father is," she says. "Callie never talked about it."

I recall the dynamic duo at the front desk telling me Jake is less than a year old, so I do a quick calculation in my head. Hurley said he and Callie split up a year and a half ago, which would have been right around the time she found out she was pregnant. Was that why she broke it off? Did Hurley know she had a kid? And could he be the father? Misty did say the kid had huge blue eyes.

Hoping to appeal to Tasha's ego, I lean in close and whisper, "I've been told you worked very closely with Callie, that you were her protégée and main confidante."

She shrugs dismissively and says, "I guess." I can tell she is wary of my praise but also flattered by it so I pile it on a little more.

"I can see why they picked you to take over the main anchor role. You've got the beauty and the brains, and you seem to be a very keen observer. I'm guessing nothing much gets by you, does it?"

"I think I'm pretty perceptive," she says.

"So help me out. Who do you think Jake's father is?"

She starts to say something but then her gaze shifts over

my shoulder and the high-wattage smile turns on. "Mr. Ackerman," she says, practically cooing. "Have you met, um . . ." She hesitates and looks at me. "I'm sorry, what did you say your name was again?"

"M—" I catch myself just as I'm about to blurt out my real name. I cough to give myself a moment to recover and then, as I'm turning around to greet the wise and powerful Mr. Ackerman, I say, "Ms. Taylor."

It's all I can manage to get out because I am dumbstruck by the sight before me. Mike Ackerman is as stunning an example of the male species as I've seen in a long time: tall, broad shouldered, square jawed, and gorgeous. His eyes are the color of an October sky and rimmed with thick, dark lashes; his hair is a rich chestnut brown with gold highlights. There is an adorable cleft in his chin, a deep dimple in each cheek, and a pair of sexy, bite-me lips turned up into an inscrutable smile. It's a combination I imagine could easily melt the pants off most women.

"Nice to meet you, Ms. Taylor," he says. His voice is mellifluous and sexy, but there is a hint of humor in his tone when he repeats my name, suggesting that he is amused by my formality. His attire is casual: khaki slacks and a plain, white shirt unbuttoned at the collar with the sleeves rolled up. As he extends his hand toward me for a shake, I can't help but notice the tanned and muscular forearm it's attached to.

"Likewise," I manage. I take his hand and feel an electric volt of sexual energy race up my arm.

"I understand you're investigating Callie Dunkirk's death," he says, releasing me.

"Yes." I don't offer any more, thinking it's probably best to say as little as possible lest I start blabbering.

"Her death has been a terrible shock and loss for us all," Ackerman says, looking appropriately saddened, though something about it strikes me as false. "Not only was she a kind and very likable person, she was a rising star in the TV news world. Her death is a senseless, horrible thing."

"I'm sure it's been difficult for all of you," I say, noticing that both Sheila and Tasha are gaping at Ackerman, looking as starstruck as I feel. Clearly the man has some powerful charisma. "Any thoughts on who might have wanted her dead, or what she was doing in Wisconsin?"

Ackerman rubs his chin in thought for a moment and I notice that he's wearing a wedding band. "I'm sorry," he says, "but as I've already told the police, I have no idea."

I sense he is about to dismiss me so I blurt out one last question, hoping to keep his attention a little longer. "Any thoughts about who the father of Callie's son might be?"

The change in Ackerman's expression is subtle—there and gone in a blink—but it is echoed in the nervous movements of Sheila and Tasha, who both look away suddenly, as if they can't bear to watch. "Why would I know something like that?" Ackerman asks.

"I thought Callie might have talked about her private life."

"Not with me," Ackerman says. He turns and looks at the two women. Despite being unable to tear their gazes away from him a moment ago, they are now busy looking at everything but him. "Has she ever said anything to either of you?" he asks.

Sheila finally engages him and for a brief second she looks angry and bitter. But then she shifts her gaze to me, smiles, and shakes her head. "Callie kept to herself for the most part," she says.

Tasha, who is now studying her feet with heightened intensity, says, "That's true. She keeps—kept her professional and personal lives separate."

Ackerman glances at his watch and says, "I'm sorry, Ms.

Taylor, but that's about all I have time for today. We have a deadline to meet and we all need to get back to work."

Sheila takes the cue and gently nudges me toward the door with the flat of her hand on my arm. "Let me show you out."

I want to object but sense I'm not likely to get much more information out of anyone today anyway, so I let her steer me away. As we step out into the hallway she says, "So tell me something. Are you thinking Jake's father is someone in Washington?"

"I can't really say," I answer vaguely, knowing she'll be exploring that angle the minute I'm gone.

"But you think the identity of Jake's father might have something to do with Callie's murder." She isn't asking me; she's stating an opinion, no doubt hoping I'll confirm it. I decide to let her draw her own conclusions.

"I'm exploring every possibility at the moment," I tell her. "If you think of anything else, please call me."

Judging from the storm clouds I see on Hurley's face as I get in the car, I can tell that what he overheard isn't sitting well with him. As soon as I close the door, he starts the engine and pulls away from the curb, white-knuckling the steering wheel. I tolerate his stony silence for several blocks before caving in.

"Did you know Callie had a son?"

The muscles in his arms bulge with tension and his cheek twitches wildly. It's several seconds before he answers me. "No," he says through his teeth. "And I don't want to discuss it."

"That's not fair," I say, peeling off my wire.

He turns and glares at me, looking like he wants to toss me out of the car. Suddenly it's not hard to imagine him as a killer. "Not fair?" he says. "I'll tell you what's not fair. Lying to someone you profess to love, that's not fair. Keeping secrets from someone you should be able to trust, that's not fair." His voice rises in an angry crescendo and I pray that his ire is directed at someone other than me. "And manipulating other people's lives is definitely not fucking fair!" he yells.

His driving is getting erratic and too fast for the suburban streets we're on. "Maybe you should pull over and let me drive," I suggest as gently as I can.

"Yeah, maybe I should," he snaps irritably. With that he whips the steering wheel hard to the right and slams on the brakes as he hits the curb. Once the car is at a full stop, he jams the gearshift lever into park, leans back in his seat, and closes his eyes. "Son of a bitch," he mutters, shaking his head. "How could she do that to me?"

It's becoming clear to me that Hurley didn't know Callie had a child until now, and it's equally obvious the knowledge has hurt him deeply. The pain is etched on his face, but is it the simple fact that Callie withheld the information from him, or has he made the other leap by figuring out the timing and all the possible ramifications that go with it?

"I'm sorry you're hurting, Hurley." He grunts but says nothing. I let him stew for another minute or two before tossing caution aside and plunging headlong into dangerous waters by asking him, "Do you think Jake could be your son?"

Chapter 18

Hurley opens his eyes and stares out the windshield. "I'm sure you did the math, the same as I did," he says. He looks over at me. "But I can't bring myself to believe that Callie wouldn't have told me if she thought I was the father."

"Maybe she had her reasons."

"What reasons?" he shoots back, clearly irritated.

"I don't know. Maybe she didn't want to tie you down. Maybe she didn't know she was pregnant until after you two split up and she had already moved on to someone else."

He winces at that, and while it gives me pause, I know I have to push onward. One thing I've learned in my nursing career is that pain is sometimes a necessary part of healing.

"And maybe she didn't say anything because it had nothing to do with you," I suggest, offering a temporary balm. "If she broke up with you because she met someone else, maybe that someone else is the father."

A weighted silence fills the air and just when I think I can't stand it any longer, Hurley shifts the car into drive, looks over his shoulder to check for traffic, and pulls out onto the road.

"Change of plans," he says. "I need to get inside Callie's apartment."

The look of determination on his face worries me, but his driving is reasonably sane for now so I sit quietly and wait. I have no idea where Callie lived, but it's obvious Hurley does as he heads straight for downtown. Chicago is well-known for its traffic backups and bottlenecks, but at the moment traffic is relatively light so we manage to make pretty good time. Fifteen minutes later Hurley turns into a parking garage, grabs a ticket stub, and parks.

He undoes his seat belt and reaches for his door handle. "Stay here."

"Unh-unh, I'm going with you."

"No, you're not."

"Yes, I am." I open my door and get out of the car before he can object again.

He gives me a perturbed look, gets out on his side, and scans the surrounding area. Then he leans on the roof of the car, looks me straight in the eye, and says, "I'm about to break the law and I don't want you involved. I need you to wait in the car. I don't have time to argue about it."

"Then don't. Besides, it's a little late to be worrying about legalities and principles, don't you think? You dragged me into this and I've got a lot on the line at this point, so I'm coming along whether you like it or not." I fold my arms over my chest and set my jaw to show him I mean what I say.

He stares at me a moment, no doubt gauging the depth of my conviction. Apparently he decides I'm serious because he reaches into the car, pops the trunk, and then slams his door closed. "Christ, you are a stubborn woman," he mutters. He stomps around and opens the trunk, rummages inside it, and slips something into his jacket pocket. Then he hands me two pairs of latex gloves. "Stick these in your purse," he tells me. "We'll need them once we're inside but I don't want to put them on yet because it might attract attention."

I do as instructed and, once he has closed the trunk, follow him out onto the street. We walk several blocks until we reach one with a large four-storied brick apartment building. I follow Hurley up the stairs to the central door, which is locked. There is a number pad built into the wall next to it and after looking up and down the street, presumably to see if anyone is watching, Hurley says, "Give me one of the gloves."

I fish one out of my purse and hand it to him. He wraps it around one finger, palming the rest of it in his hand. Then he punches in a four-digit number. The door lock releases with a little click and, still using the glove, Hurley pulls it open.

"How do you know Callie still lives here?" I ask him as we step inside.

He doesn't answer me right away. Instead he walks over to a bank of mailboxes and scans the names on each one. "I didn't, but I do now," he says, pointing to a label bearing the name Dunkirk. Beneath the label is the number 401.

When Hurley turns away from the mailboxes I fall into step beside him, heading for the elevator. I pull one of the gloves out of my purse and palm it the way Hurley did in preparation for pushing the button but Hurley stops me with a hand on my shoulder and says, "No. We take the stairs."

"Why?"

"We're less likely to run into anyone."

He heads for the stairs and takes them two at a time, bounding up the first flight with ease. I follow along and do the same, determined to show him I can keep up. But midway up the second flight my thighs start burning like a grease fire and my heart feels like it's trying to claw its way out of my chest. I switch to taking the steps one at a time, wondering if this is Hurley's way of punishing me for insisting he bring me along.

By the time I reach the fourth floor, I'm sweating, red-faced, and puffing like a steam engine. Hurley, on the other hand, looks cool, calm, and utterly relaxed.

Apartments 401 and 402 are on one side of the stairwell, 403 and 404 are on the other. None of the doors appear to have peepholes, a lucky break for us. Another thing in our favor is the lack of police tape on Callie's apartment door. Though there is no way to know for sure if any police have been inside the place yet, I'm betting they have.

Hurley removes the item he had slipped into his pocket earlier, which I now see is a set of small tools. Their intended purpose becomes obvious when he slips two of the tools into the lock on Callie's door and starts jiggling them around. I expect him to get the door open inside of a few seconds, the way it always seems to go on TV. But he fiddles and cusses under his breath for a long time before we finally hear the faint click of success.

"Glove time," Hurley says.

After donning our respective gloves, Hurley opens the door to Callie's apartment and we enter a large open area that serves as living room, kitchen, and dining room space. The main décor is minimalist and distinctly modern, but there are children's items scattered about that clearly don't fit: a high chair in the kitchen, a playpen in the dining room, and a swing in one corner of the living room. There is also a laundry basket full of toys at one end of the couch, several of them spilled out onto the floor. The place appears very clean and well organized, yet there is evidence of disarray in the crooked couch cushions, drawers that aren't completely closed, and a pile of disorganized papers on the desk. Though I suppose these subtle bits of sloppiness might be attributable to

Callie's lack of housekeeping skills, there is a reckless, pitched-aside quality to it all that suggests the place has been searched.

"Are you looking for something specific?" I ask Hurley, who has zeroed in on a glass-topped desk in one corner of the dining room.

"Anything that might give me some answers."

"It looks like the place has been gone through already."

"It has. Callie was an extremely neat, organized person."

Score another point for the ex-girlfriend.

He continues looking through the papers on top of the desk and then opens up a side file drawer that looks jam-packed. Figuring it will take him a while to sort through the contents, I head for the doors at the other end of the living room, guessing correctly that they will lead to the bedrooms.

In the smaller of the two, which is obviously little Jake's room, there is a child's bed shaped like a sports car, a large toy box painted in bright primary colors, a dresser that doubles as a changing table, and a menagerie of stuffed animals in a bright red hammock strung up in one corner. It's a cute room but other than the changing table area, it has an empty, unused look to it.

As I enter the master bedroom, the initial impression is that it's Callie's room. There is a queen-sized bed covered with a white, down comforter that is slightly mussed as if it was pulled down and then carelessly tossed back into place. The pillowcases have lace tatting along the edges, and the curtains on the window, which overlooks the street, are also trimmed in a lacy pattern. The bed's headboard, the bedside table, and the dresser are all done in a French provincial design, painted white with small lines of gold trim. All that whiteness would feel cold and sterile were it not for several scattered splashes of color: a handful of throw pillows on the bed done in rich jewel colors, a royal blue throw draped over the foot of the bed, a large barn-red rocking chair in front of the window, two bright green hanging plants, and a bookcase filled with a wide assortment of colorful tomes—everything from writing manuals and a legal reference, to paperback novels.

Though the bulk of the room clearly belongs to Callie, in a corner near the bathroom there is a crib. It, like the other furnishings in the room, is painted white but this blandness is offset by a colorful baby quilt, bright blue sheets, and a multicolored mobile of birds attached to the headboard.

A tremendous sense of sadness fills me as I look at the crib and think about little Jake growing up without his mother—wondering about her, hearing stories about her, seeing pictures of her, but having no real memories of her, just an aching persistent hole in his heart that he'll never fully understand or be able to fill. I know because that's how I feel about my dad. And Jake has no second parent to step in since no one seems to know who his father is.

Could it be Hurley?

I head for the bedside table, a place where people often keep intimate things, and open the top drawer. It's filled with an eclectic mix of items: an eye mask, several paperback books, a bunch of loose change, a bottle containing an over-the-counter sleep aid, several notepads and pens, some lotion, some foot cream, and a pacifier.

After flipping through the notepads and discerning that all they contain are shopping lists and scribbled reminders, I close that drawer and open the bottom one, which sticks a bit. The only things it contains are dozens of pairs of socks. I rummage through them all, giving each pair a squeeze to make sure there isn't anything inside them. As I push them back down into the drawer so I can close it, something odd strikes me. I pull open the top drawer again, look inside, and then step back to look at it from more of a distance. Even though both of the drawer fronts appear to be the same size, the top drawer is much shallower than the bottom one. Curious, I go back to the top drawer and poke around inside it, pushing on its bottom. When that yields no results, I take the entire drawer out and flip it upside down on the bed, letting its contents spill out.

The wood panel that serves as the drawer's bottom is set into grooves along the front and sides of the drawer, but the back panel has no grooves and is shorter than the others, allowing the entire bottom piece to slide out. I do so and hit the jackpot. Hiding inside this secret space is Callie Dunkirk's diary.

Chapter 19

I start to holler to Hurley about my find but something holds me back. A quick scan of the diary's contents shows dates going back nearly two years and a last entry from just four days ago. After half a minute of self-debate, I decide to hold off until I have a chance to look through the book myself. For one thing, I'm dying to know what's in it and I'm not sure I can count on Hurley to share once he has his hands on it. For another, if there is anything in the diary related to Hurley, he might try to destroy it. I stuff the book inside the waist of my pants and pull my sweater down over it to hide it. Then I quickly reassemble the drawer, put the contents back, and replace it in the stand. I walk over to the bedroom door and look out into the main room to see what Hurley is up to. He is still seated at the desk going through files.

I do a quick search under Callie's bed and through her dresser drawers and closet. I get excited when I find a couple of storage boxes, but all they yield are story clippings from her newspaper days, some old tax returns, and a bunch of manila envelopes filled with business-related receipts.

Next I head into the bathroom, which is spotless. I do a quick survey of the medicine cabinet, vanity drawers, and towel closet, all of which have that slightly out-of-kilter look like the rest of the house, but I find nothing of interest.

Next I do a cursory inspection of Jake's room for the sake of being thorough. I don't find anything of significance, but the dresser drawers filled with little boy clothing give me pause. The sight of tiny OshKosh overalls, little button-down shirts, and baseball-themed pajamas triggers a painful lump in my throat, rousing some dormant maternal instinct within me.

I head back out to the main part of the apartment and find Hurley sorting through the kitchen drawers and cabinets. He is making no effort to be subtle in his search, stirring things around, tossing stuff aside, and banging doors and drawers closed when he's done.

"Shouldn't you try to be quieter?" I say to him. "We don't want to attract attention."

He whirls on me, looking angry, frustrated, and ready to tell me to mind my own business. But before any words leave his mouth, his expression saddens and his shoulders slump. In an instant the no-nonsense, tough-as-nails cop I know is gone and Hurley becomes the epitomic image of a man defeated.

"There's nothing," he says miserably, raking his fingers through his hair. "Not a frigging clue of any kind."

"Did she keep a date book of any sort?"

"If she did, it's not here," Hurley says. "She might have had one at work."

I glance over at the desk where some disconnected wires are snaking along the surface. "Did she have a computer?"

Hurley nods. "She had a laptop, but I suspect the local cops confiscated it as evidence."

"What about a file for important papers, you know, things like her passport, or a birth certificate?"

Hurley starts to shake his head but then he stops and his face lights up. "Of course!" he says, snapping his fingers. "How could I have forgotten?" He pushes past me and heads into Callie's bedroom. I follow and find him standing in front of the bookcase scanning the titles on the shelves. When he gets to the bottom-most shelf, he squats, pulls out a fat book with *War and Peace* running down the spine, and says, "Here we go."

As soon as he opens the cover I see that the book is just a façade. Inside is a small metal storage box. Hurley opens it, revealing a stack of papers. I stand and watch over his shoulder as he sorts through them and hold my breath when he comes across a birth certificate for Jake.

Callie's name is typed in the slot for the mother's name but where the father's name should be, all it says is "Unknown."

"Damn it!" Hurley says, tossing the certificate back into the box.

I place a hand on his shoulder and squeeze gently. "Maybe we can find out something by talking to her family," I suggest.

Hurley closes the box and the book cover, and puts it back on the bookcase shelf. "They won't know anything. Callie was a very private person. Plus, she didn't always get along that well with her mother and sister, so I'm pretty sure she didn't share much with them about her life, particularly something as significant as this." He sighs and stands, letting my hand fall from its spot. "I think we've discovered all we're going to here. Let's go."

I follow him out of the apartment and back to the car in silence, managing to slip Callie's diary into my purse along the way. There is a lonely sadness about Hurley—the slump of his shoulders, his shuffling walk, his hangdog expression—that touches me. I want to say something to him, to somehow reassure him, but I have no answers, no clever bon mot that will make it all better.

When we get into the car, I break the silence to tread into dangerous territory. "Did you know Mike Ackerman at all when you were dating Callie?"

"I knew of him. Hard not to if you live in the Chicago area. He's married to one of the richest women in the country, a pharmaceutical heiress. He's always been a mover and a shaker. I know Callie was pretty excited when he expressed an interest in her work and she hoped he might bring her over to *Behind the Scenes*. She got her wish, but by the time it happened she had already broken things off with me. Why do you ask?"

I shrug. "I don't know. There's something about him that bugs me."

"How so?"

"He's a little too good-looking."

Hurley shoots me a sidelong glance. "And that's a bad thing?" he asks, his voice rife with skepticism.

"Well, not in and of itself, but I get the feeling this Ackerman guy uses his looks. He exudes sex appeal like some gold-digging woman, and it's clear that the women he works with are blinded by it."

"But you weren't?"

I shrug and smile. "I have to admit, he's not hard on the eyes. But he came across as a little too slick for me." Hurley nods, but says nothing. "Don't you think the timing with him, you, and Callie is more than a little coincidental?"

Hurley's brow furrows. "What do you mean?"

"I mean you and Callie seemed to be doing fine and then all of a sudden Ackerman appears. Then Callie inexplicably dumps you, ends up pregnant, and the next thing you know, she has her dream job."

"Are you implying she slept her way into it?"

Hurley's face is a mass of thunderclouds so I choose my next words carefully. "Not exactly, but what if she fell for Ackerman's considerable charms in a weak moment, and then found herself pregnant? Ackerman is married. Maybe he offered her the job on *Behind the Scenes* as some sort of hush money."

Hurley's expression goes through a kaleidoscope of change: defensiveness, anger, thoughtfulness, denial, and then sadness.

"Maybe she broke up with you out of guilt," I go on, "because she was too embarrassed, or too ashamed to admit she strayed. And then later she realized she'd made a mistake, and that it was you she really loved."

With that Hurley looks so wounded, I want to lean over and hug him. Instead I try to appeal to his investigative instincts. "If you had the love of the woman he wanted, the woman who bore his child, it might have made Ackerman mad enough to want to get revenge on you. He strikes me as having the kind of massive ego that would fit that profile. And if he does, he might have killed Callie to shut her up and then framed you for it so he could exact his revenge on his chief competition."

Hurley ponders the idea for a minute, and then shakes his head. "I don't know. Maybe. Let me think about it."

We ride in silence for a bit and when I realize we're heading south of Chicago I ask, "Where are we going now?"

"To a town just outside of Joliet."

"Why?"

"Because that's where Stateville Prison is located. You and I are going to visit the one man who I know hates me more than anyone else: Quinton Dilles."

Chapter 20

Hurley gives me a primer on Stateville Prison as he's driving. The realization that we are going there spooks me a little, not only because I've never been to a prison before, but because I'm afraid I may end up in one by the time all is said and done. Stateville is a Level One facility, which means it serves as home to some of the worst criminals. Though no executions are performed there these days, there have been in the past—as recently as 1998—and the roster of murderous luminaries who have died there includes the likes of John Wayne Gacy and Richard Loeb of Leopold and Loeb fame, though Loeb was murdered by another inmate. As if the presence of thousands of hardened, vicious criminals isn't scary enough, the facility is also rumored to be haunted.

The building itself is quite daunting, with thirty-foot-high concrete walls topped with razor wire marking the perimeter. After driving through one set of guarded gates, we park in the visitor lot and head inside. Our entry requires us to show picture IDs—no fake identities this time—pass through two gates and a metal detector, and undergo a personal pat-down. Each time I hear a door clang shut behind me, it makes my heebie-jeebies worse.

Our first stop is in a wing of offices, where we are led into one occupied by a gentleman who is dressed in street clothes rather than a guard's uniform. Hurley makes the introductions, letting me know that the man before us, Maxwell Corning, is an assistant warden. Judging from the way Corning greets Hurley, I gather the two men know one another from the past. Though Hurley introduces me using my real name, he tells Corning I am his investigative assistant, leaving out mention of the fact that I work for the ME's office.

With the introductions out of the way, Hurley and I take seats across the desk from Corning.

"So, do you have my list?" Hurley asks Corning.

Corning shakes his head. "There isn't one. The only visitor Dilles has had since his incarceration here is his lawyer, Connor Smith."

Hurley frowns at the news and says, "I suppose any conversations they've had have been privileged?" Corning nods. "That doesn't help me much. Can you get me a list of his visitors from Cook County?"

Corning leans back in his chair and eyes Hurley with curiosity. "What is it you're hoping to find?"

"Just a hunch I have regarding an ongoing investigation," Hurley hedges.

"Okay, I should be able to get that for you before you leave today," Corning says, sitting up and scribbling a note.

"What about the other piece I asked you about?"

"Well, I do have better news on that front," Corning says. "Dilles agreed to having you on his approved visitor list so if you want to talk with him today, you can." Corning shifts his gaze to me and adds, "I'll have to ask him about your assistant here, though. If he doesn't okay her, she'll have to remain behind."

Hurley turns to me and says, "What are your feelings on the matter? Do you want to wait in the car or do you want to come with me if Dilles okays it?"

I'm not sure. On the one hand I'm curious to meet the man who has already caused Hurley so much grief. On the other hand, I'm spooked by the idea of coming face-to-face with a convicted killer.

Sensing my hesitation, Hurley says, "We'll have a Plexiglas barrier between us. The visitor area is completely isolated from the prisoners."

"Okay," I say, my curiosity winning out. "I'm game if Dilles is."

Corning gets up and says, "Let me check with him then. Wait here and I'll be right back."

As soon as Corning leaves, I turn to Hurley and ask, "What is it you hope to gain from this? Because if Dilles hasn't seen or spoken to anyone other than his lawyer, it's unlikely he's behind all this other stuff, isn't it?"

"Not necessarily. He was denied bail and has been behind bars ever since his arrest, but he was housed in Cook County Jail during his trial and wasn't moved here until after his conviction. So it's possible he could have talked with someone then."

"And you think he hates you enough to go to all this trouble just for revenge?"

"Hard to know. The fact that he's willing to meet with me makes me think he's still harboring a significant grudge." He pauses and shrugs. "Maybe all he wants is a chance to tell me off one more time. I can get a better feel for where his head is at if I talk to him face-to-face. And I'd like to get your take on him, too. You have a good sense when it comes to sizing people up."

Corning returns as I'm basking beneath the glory of Hurley's praise and says, "You're in luck. Dilles has agreed to meet with the both of you. If you'll follow me, I'll take you to the visitors' section."

Despite being behind bars, Quinton Dilles looks like money. His nails are well manicured, his hands are uncallused, and his body has a soft, spoiled look to it. His brown hair has grayed at the temples and though it is thinning on top, I can see plugs from a hair transplant. Despite being as tall as I am, he holds his head high, as if he needs to look down his nose at everyone. He's wearing prison scrubs but if he wasn't, I'm sure his clothing would be expensive tailored duds.

Greeting people in ankle irons and handcuffs should be a humbling experience, but judging from the smirk on Quinton Dilles's face, he wouldn't agree. There is a definite air of smarmy smugness about the man, one that befits someone who is used to the deference and privilege money can buy. Apparently prison hasn't been able to erase that from him yet, if it ever will. He strikes me as the type who will always have a sense of entitlement about him.

There are two seats on our side of the Plexiglas window. Dilles settles into his chair across from us and leans toward the speaker located in the center of the window. So far Dilles's eyes have been fixed on Hurley but as soon as Hurley and I settle into our chairs, Dilles shifts his gaze to me.

"So this is your . . . what did Corning call her . . . assistant?" Dilles says. "You do have a knack for attracting lovely women, Hurley." His eyes shift to my chest. "And I must say, you're good at picking ones with generous endowments."

"Knock it off, Dilles," Hurley snaps.

"But that reporter gal you were screwing had fake ones, didn't she?" Dilles says with a taunting smile. "How's she doing, by the way?" He looks back at Hurley, his eyes crinkling with amusement. He has admitted to knowing about Callie and that's a bit damning, but I can't tell if his inquiry about her is a casual taunt or a knowing one.

"She's dead," Hurley says.

I watch Dilles closely for a reaction, for any physical tell to let me know if this information is something new to him, but there is nothing. The two men stare at one another for what seems like forever until Hurley says, "Tell me, Quinton, how are they treating you here at Stateville? Are the accommodations up to your standards?"

A twitch starts up in Dilles's lower eyelid, the only indication that Hurley might have struck a nerve.

"I'm making do," he says with a wry smile. He turns his attention back to me. "Though I have to admit, I miss not having a nice piece of ass like her around whenever I want it."

Hurley starts to rise from his chair but before he can, I stop him with a hand to his leg. I get a sense that Dilles is used to being able to insult and boss around the women in his life so I decide to rattle his cage a little.

"Have you become anyone's piece of ass yet, Dilles?" I ask, smiling sweetly. " 'Cause I'm thinking they'll like a spoiled softie like you. Come on, tell us," I goad. "Don't keep us in suspense. Has anyone made you their bitch yet?"

Dilles's arrogant façade shows its first real crack as his smile turns down a notch and his hands close into fists. "You may think you're in control because you're on that side of this wall," he seethes, "but my reach is far greater than you'll ever know. You better watch your back."

Though I'm trying to maintain a calm, unaffected front, Dilles's threat frightens me. My hands start to tremble and I shove them down between my thighs to hide them. Like prey to a predator, I know that showing any sign of weakness to Dilles will only make him strengthen his attack.

"Why do you harbor so much venom toward Detective Hurley?" I ask Dilles. "I heard it was another cop who put you behind bars."

"Only because Hurley fabricated evidence against me," Dilles shoots back. "The other cops were just too stupid to see that."

"Are you saying you didn't kill your wife?" I ask him.

He smiles at me in a way that makes me want to get up and run. "I'm not sad the stupid bitch is dead," he says, avoiding a direct answer. "She was a smart-assed know-it-all, kind of like you." His gaze takes on an intensity that makes it easy for me to imagine him wishing me as dead as his wife.

"That's enough," Hurley says. "Come on." He grabs my arm and pulls me up out of my chair. "We're out of here."

The sound of Dilles's maniacal cackle behind us sends chills down my spine. As we head back to Corning's office, I can't resist the urge to keep looking over my shoulder, fearful the man has somehow breached the walls between us.

When we arrive in Corning's office the man's expression is grim. "I have a feeling you aren't going to like what I have to tell you, Steve," he says, handing him a fax. "From what the guys up in Cook County Jail told me, Dilles has been disowned by his family. It looks like the only visitor he had there was his lawyer, same as here."

Hurley takes the fax and scans it, sighing heavily when he's done.

"Sorry," Corning says. "How did the visit with Dilles go?"

"About how I expected," Hurley says. "It looks like this lead is a dead end but thanks for your help."

"No problem," Corning says. And then much to my relief, he escorts us out of the building.

Chapter 21

"I'm sorry that didn't pan out," I tell Hurley when we're back in the car and leaving the prison grounds.

He shrugs. "I'm sorry I put you through it. Dilles is a total scumbag."

"I keep thinking back to this Ackerman guy. There was something about him that struck me as slimy."

"Slimy? You were practically drooling over him."

"He *is* quite good-looking. But looks aren't everything."

"I don't think this lover's revenge theory of yours makes sense." Hurley's tone borders on the irritable but since I'm pretty sure it isn't directed at me, I let it slide.

"You're right. It is kind of flimsy," I admit. "So try this one on for size. What if he's the father of Callie's child? And what if she was asking him for more than he was willing to give? It sounds like his money is all from his wife so a divorce based on his infidelities would likely result in him getting cut off from the purse strings. That gives him motive to kill Callie."

"Maybe," Hurley says with a shrug. "But we never actually met or spent any time together. What I know of the man I know from hearing and reading about him in the news."

"He works with a bunch of investigative reporters so it wouldn't be that hard for him to research you. And you're the perfect patsy when it comes to Callie's murder since you're the ex-boyfriend. By framing you for her murder as well as Minniver's, it deflects suspicion away from both Ackerman and his motive."

"I don't know. It seems kind of far-fetched," Hurley says thoughtfully. "And how the hell could we prove it even if it was true?"

"Maybe one of his coworkers knows something," I suggest, but even as I say it I wonder if it will help. I suspect all the women Ackerman works with are too starstruck by his natural charisma and good looks to think anything bad about him, and even if they did, I'm not sure they'd roll on him. "Or maybe his wife," I toss out, thinking it might be the better angle.

"Let me think on it," Hurley says, and with that our discussion ends.

The remainder of our ride back to the Milwaukee airport is quiet but not awkward. I sense Hurley is deep in thought and struggling with his own emotions, so I keep mine to myself and let him be, grateful we have reached a level of comfort with one another that allows for long periods of silence without a compulsion to fill the void. I spend the rest of the ride gazing out my window and thinking. I make a mental note to do some research on Ackerman's wife and to try to meet and speak with her.

By the time we arrive in front of the Southwest Airlines terminal it's after three o'clock. I'm starving and briefly consider asking Hurley if we can stop somewhere for lunch, but I sense his need to be alone with his thoughts.

He pulls up to the curb, shifts the car into park, and turns to look at me. His eyes have darkened into deep blue pools of angst and I resist an urge to lean across the seat and hug him. "You okay to drive back home?" he asks.

"I'm fine. What about you?"

"I'll survive."

"Are you headed straight home?"

He shakes his head. "I've got some things I want to do first and I'm thinking I'll need to make myself scarce in case Richmond comes looking for me. I'll give you a call later."

I nod and open my door to get out, but before I can, Hurley reaches over and grabs my arm. "Thanks for helping me, Mattie," he says.

"You're welcome."

"I mean it. It means a lot to me."

I don't know what to say to that, so I simply smile.

"I'll be in touch," he says, and I take that as my cue to get out of the car. As I shut the door and watch him pull away, I have a strong premonition that neither of our lives will ever be the same again.

Since it's still early in the day, I decide to head to a nearby mall and do some shopping in order to justify my cover story. But before heading in to the stores, I park, take Callie's diary out of my purse, and start reading it. Unlike what I would expect to find in most diaries—thoughts, feelings, and long flowing passages of information on daily life— Callie's diary is all about her work. The entries are short and highly abbreviated, and the latest one, which is dated four days ago—two days before her death—sends chills down my spine.

Anon call, male, truth behind SH & why he left— police corruption? graft?

The initials, I'm certain, stand for Steve Hurley. That would explain what Callie was doing in our neck of the woods when she was killed. I quickly flip through some of the other entries and find similar notes for leads, tips, and story ideas. Others appear to be abandoned ideas or partially fleshed-out thoughts.

I'm curious to see what sorts of entries Callie might have made around the time she found out she was pregnant. Based on what I've seen so far, I doubt the book will contain any information about her personal life, but I still want to look. I don't want to do it here, though, not only because I want privacy when I read it, but because my stomach is rumbling a protest. So I slide the diary and the cell phone that Hurley gave me beneath my seat and head inside the mall.

My first stop is the food court, where I opt for a cheeseburger with all the trimmings and a side of fries. Sated and on a saturated fat high, I then cruise the mall, hitting up a handful of stores and finding several gifts: a pair of silver skull earrings for Erika, who loves all things dark and related to death; a nifty tome on the life cycles of insects for Ethan, who collects creepy-crawlies and has recently been asking me about forensic entomology; cookbooks for both my sister, Desi, and Izzy's partner, Dom, since they are both killer cooks; and a HEPA-rated air filter for my mother.

Feeling pretty proud of the fact that I survived several hours of shopping without having a mental breakdown and came out of it with actual gifts rather than gift cards, I drive home feeling rather chipper.

As soon as I'm back in Sorenson, I head straight to my mother's house. I half expect her to greet me at the door in an apoplectic state from her efforts to keep things clean while doggie sitting, but it's William who answers my knock, and when I come inside Mother is nowhere in sight.

"What did you tell your mother about dogs and cancer?" William asks me.

"That some dogs have the ability to sniff it out," I say warily, wondering where this is going.

"Ah, that explains it then," William says. "She has taken to her deathbed, convinced she has cervical cancer because Hoover stuck his nose in her crotch."

I look down at Hoover, who appears to be grinning. "Sorry, William," I say, grimacing. "I thought telling her that would help convince her to watch him for me. I should have realized she'd overreact."

"She wants me to ask you to join us for Thanksgiving dinner," William says. "Given that it will be her last one and all."

"I see." I can't help but smile. Mother has had several final holidays over the years and I long ago figured out it was her way of ensuring that her family would be there.

"She's upset that Desi won't be able to come but you should probably know that she's also invited David."

"Really?"

"Uh-huh," William says. "She wants to talk with him about her terminal condition."

"Of course she does. Did David accept?"

"He did."

"I don't know, William. It promises to be a pretty awkward meal if I'm here, too."

"It will be awkward whether you're here or not. So please come. I'm going to need someone to help me run interference. And I'll never hear the end of it if you're not there."

"What is she planning on making?" I ask. "The last time Mom made Thanksgiving dinner she served Tofurkey that was microwaved into a brick to make sure it was germ free. I'm not a picky eater by any means, but that was disgusting."

"I promise I'll make a real turkey," William says. "And I'm actually a pretty good cook." He bends down to give Hoover a pat on the head, and his comb-over flops down over his face. "You can bring this little guy," he adds. He tries to smooth his hair back with his free hand, but instead of lying flat, it sticks up along the middle of his head like a turkey comb. "Please?"

William looks so pathetically adorable that I can't bring myself to deny him. Besides, I feel kind of guilty given that the whole cancer snafu is my fault. "Fine," I say with resignation. "What do you want me to bring? Make it something I don't have to cook because I'm not much better in the kitchen than Mom is."

"Then why don't you bring some ice cream?"

"Ice cream I can definitely do," I tell him. *Assuming I don't eat it before I get here.*

After agreeing on a time for the upcoming dinner, I grab a handful of baggies and clean up Hoover's yard deposits. I try to be very thorough but despite my efforts, I suspect that my mother will slash and burn her entire lawn the first chance she gets.

Once I'm done and I've washed and alcohol-rubbed my hands into sterility, I reluctantly poke my head into Mother's bedroom to say hi, but to my relief she is asleep. So after giving William another apology, I bid him good-bye, load Hoover into the car, and head for home.

I'm glad I made the effort to do some actual shopping while I was gone because Izzy is outside when I arrive home and the packages I have to cart inside provide proof of my cover story.

"Did you drum up any business while I was gone?" I ask him, hoping to forestall any questions he might ask about my day. I still feel guilty about lying to him.

"Nope, it was a good day for the living," he says, petting

Hoover, who has jumped out of the car and is now groveling at Izzy's feet. "Want to join us for dinner? Dom has whipped up some eggplant Parmesan with crème brûlée for dessert. And I have some news to share with you."

Dom's cooking is exceptional and I rarely pass up an opportunity to indulge. Even Hoover seems to understand the importance of the invite because he has started whining and wagging his tail with great enthusiasm. Though I'm wary of spending too much time around Izzy until all this business with Hurley is resolved, I can't resist the lure of Dom's cooking and I'm curious about the news Izzy wants to share.

"You can bring this little guy along," Izzy adds, giving Hoover a scratch behind his ear.

Hoover looks at me with big, begging eyes, as if he understands.

Realizing I'm outnumbered, I relent. "Okay, just let me take these packages in and we'll be right over."

Fifteen minutes later, Hoover and I enter good-smell heaven, lured in by the enticing scents of warm bread, garlic, and butter. I find Izzy at the dining room table, which is already set for the meal.

"Have a seat," he says, gesturing toward an empty chair. "Dom said it will be another five minutes or so. Want some wine?"

I nod and let him pour me a glass of chardonnay from the open bottle on the table. I can hear Dom clanging and clinking out in the kitchen and my drool factor increases with anticipation.

"So what's the news?" I ask.

Izzy chews his lower lip for a second and I sense that his answer is going to be something touchy. "I sent Arnie to a meeting in Madison yesterday," he starts, "one of several they've had recently to discuss the state budget, which is looking rather grim. The primary purpose for yesterday's meeting was to announce some cuts that will be coming down the line."

My heart lurches as I realize this news may be far more serious than I thought. "Is my job at risk?"

"Not exactly," Izzy says cryptically. "You still have your job, but I had to make some compromises in order to assure that."

"Such as?"

"Your job description has been expanded. Basically it's been combined with another one in order to make your position more efficient."

"Okay," I say slowly, taking a bracing drink of wine. "What's the second job?"

"It's a newly created position, one that will incorporate the investigative duties our office already handles with more extensive evidence collection and processing, stuff that the police department mostly handled until now. That's why I sent Arnie. It seems there have been some recent problems, mostly in the Milwaukee area, with evidence disappearing, or not being labeled correctly, or not getting stored properly, as well as some hints of police misconduct."

Mention of police misconduct makes me flash on Callie's diary entry and my current situation with Hurley. I try hard not to look as guilty as I feel.

"As a result," Izzy continues, "several recent homicide cases had to be dismissed, which is not only a huge miscarriage of justice but more important, at least in the eyes of the government, a huge waste of money.

"So the Department of Justice and the governor got together and came up with a way to address both issues. They've decided to create a joint oversight arrangement between the coroners' offices and the police departments whenever a suspicious death occurs. Instead of being called a deputy coroner, you will now be known as a medicolegal death investigator. Along with the title are some education requirements—several of which you don't have, but they are willing to train existing personnel who can meet the requirements within a specified time frame."

"Okay," I say, thinking it doesn't sound too terrible. "So how will this impact our day-to-day functions?"

"Well, for one thing it will mean a change in the way we do things. We will be collecting, processing, and storing more of our own evidence, which turns out to be a good thing for us. I managed to convince the number crunchers that it will be timelier and less expensive in the long run to add a few key analyzers to our lab and train our personnel on how to use them than it will be to continue packaging and sending so much of our evidence to the Madison crime lab."

I shrug. "That doesn't sound so bad."

"No, it's not."

I sense there's something more, something he's keeping back, something I'm not going to like. "I can tell you're holding out on me, Izzy. So, give me the rest of it. What's the catch?"

"Well, with the new setup you will be working directly with the homicide detectives, not only in the collection of evidence, but with the subsequent investigation. All evidence must be collected, stored, and signed off on by both the detective on the case and someone from our office. Same thing with any investigative reports."

Hmm, more time with Hurley. This doesn't seem like a bad thing at all. But before I can breathe a sigh of relief, Izzy drops the other shoe.

"But because of the corruption problems, it also means there can be no hint whatsoever of any conflict-of-interest issues. That means absolutely no fraternizing." He pauses and stares at me with a regretful look, waiting for me to make the connection. I do so, with a groan.

"Are you telling me that if I want to keep my job, I can't have a relationship with Hurley outside of our working one?"

"Yes. Sorry. It was dicey enough before this, but once the new system is in place, it will be imperative that everyone remain above suspicion."

"Damn!" I punctuate this comment by pounding my fist on the table and it startles Hoover, who sits up and looks around with a wary expression, a low growl emanating from his throat. "Sorry," I mutter. Then I give Hoover a reassuring pat on the head. "It's okay, boy. Settle down."

Hoover goes back into sentry mode as Dom enters the room wearing a full apron and carrying a baking dish full of eggplant Parmesan. The heat of cooking has curled the ends of his auburn hair and put a rosy flush in his cheeks. He looks very feminine and utterly adorable.

"Hey, Mattie," he says with a smile. He sets the baking dish atop a trivet in the center of the table and then pulls his hands away with great flourish. "Dig in. I'll be right back with the salad and bread."

"Let's eat and we can talk more about this at the office tomorrow," Izzy says.

I manage to get through both dinner and dessert without looking or acting as upset as I feel. And my emotional state isn't just because the government has put an unwitting damper on my future love life. I'm also more concerned than ever about my current situation with Hurley. The partnership, no fraternizing thing is bad enough. But if it's hoped that this new arrangement will somehow halt police misconduct, my clandestine activities with Hurley aren't going to look very good if anyone finds out. My job is more at risk now than ever.

I shove my concerns to the back of my mind and focus on the meal. Fortunately our dinner discussion centers on Dom and Izzy's Thanksgiving plans, which include an invitation to Dom's family's house, which is in Iowa and a four-hour drive away, and another dinner invite to the assisted-living facility where Izzy's mother, Sylvie, lives. Unfortunately Sylvie isn't too crazy about the fact that her son is gay and as a result, only Izzy is invited to this latter function. Dom wants to spend the day at home, ignoring both invitations, but Izzy feels obligated to spend some time with his mother. I spend most of the meal playing mediator as the two of them argue.

By the time dinner is finished, they have decided to drive down to Dom's family the night before, spend the night and have brunch there on Thanksgiving Day, then drive back to Sorenson so Izzy can have dinner with his mother. They will rejoin at home for dessert. Hints of a similar dilemma during the upcoming Christmas holiday are raised during dessert, but I manage to escape before it turns into a major skirmish.

Hoover and I head home, both of us well-sated. I caught Dom slipping treats to Hoover several times over the course of the evening, everything from garlic bread crusts to a chunk of eggplant Parmesan. I curl up on the couch and watch TV for an hour or so—Hoover seems quite intrigued by the tiny human creatures in the big black box—before deciding it's time for bed. Though I feel exhausted, it takes me well over an hour to fall asleep because my mind is so busy digesting the ramifications of my current situation and the upcoming job changes.

My stomach is pretty busy too, digesting the remnants of Dom's meal. The rumbles and gurgles emanating from my GI tract make Hoover go on growl alert several times, though he calms with my shushing. But just as I finally fall asleep, he starts barking and no amount of reassurance, chastising or shushing will stop him. In fact, the harder I try to make him be quiet, the louder and more incessant his barks become. When he starts running back and forth between the bedroom and the front door, I start to wonder if all the crap he ate over at Dom and Izzy's place has upset his bowels.

"Aw, come on, Hoover," I moan. "Can't you hold it until morning?"

Resigned to getting up, I throw back the covers and shuffle my way to the door. When I open it, he dashes out, still barking, and stops a few feet away, facing into the woods that lie between my old house and Izzy's. It's then I notice the fur along his back has raised itself into a ridge, making me wonder if there is some critter in the woods that has him riled up.

I walk out onto the porch and peer into the trees, expecting to see a dark void. Instead the woods are aglow and I realize there is a strong smell of smoke in the air. Barefoot, wearing only my flannel pajamas, I step off the porch and make my way closer to the woods. Hoover charges ahead of me, still barking like crazy. It only takes me a few steps to realize what the source of both the glow and the smell are.

My old house, the one David still lives in, is on fire.

Chapter 22

I run back into the cottage with Hoover barking excitedly at my heels, grab my cell phone, and dial 911. While waiting for the 911 operator to answer, I dash over to Izzy and Dom's house and pound on their back door.

"Dom! Izzy! There's a fire!"

When I see a light come on in their bedroom window, I set off running through the woods, still barefoot and dressed in my jammies. After four rings the 911 operator answers.

"911 operator, do you have an emergency?"

"My house is on fire!" I yell into the phone. I rattle off the address and then add, "I don't know if there's anyone inside or not. Please hurry!"

My foot catches on a tree root and I go sprawling head-long onto the ground. The phone flies from my hand and I'm momentarily stunned as all the wind is knocked out of me. By the time I pick myself up I can't see the phone anywhere, so I leave it behind and continue my run.

By the time Hoover and I reach the house, there are

flames licking out broken front windows and running up the side of the house to the roof on the side closest to me. I skirt them and dash over to the garage, peering inside the window.

David's car is there, which means he most likely is, too. I holler out his name several times but the only thing I hear back is the snap-crackle of the fire. There is steamy smoke coming off the wooden front door so I avoid it and dash around to the back of the house, Hoover at my heels barking out the alarm. Scrambling up the deck stairs, I glance in the kitchen window and see that this part of the house is untouched, though I can see the orange glow of the fire down the hallway. I try the back door, but it's locked and I curse the fact that I didn't think to bring my key. I still have one even though I haven't used it since I moved out, and I debate running back to the cottage to get it. But even as I consider this, the orange glow grows brighter, taunting me, and making me realize that time is of the utmost importance. The front stairs are probably inaccessible already, but there are back stairs off the kitchen and so far the fire hasn't reached this part of the house. By the time I can run back and get my key, it may be too late.

Given the hour and the fact that the house is darkened, I assume David is sleeping. After years of pulling on-call duty he tends to be a very light sleeper, and the fact that he isn't already awake and out of the house makes me wonder if he's taken one of the sleeping pills he uses on his off days to help him sleep better. Unfortunately, they also make it harder for him to wake up. If he isn't already unconscious from smoke inhalation, he soon will be.

Several thoughts race through my mind. Though the fire station isn't that far away, I can't hear any sirens approaching yet; our fire department is all volunteers, and the firefighters answer the night calls from their homes, slightly lengthening their response time. I pray the 911 operator got all the info I gave her before I lost the phone, but what if she didn't?

I envision myself standing by watching as the house burns, knowing David is inside, knowing I might mean the difference between life and death for him. Could I live with myself if he died because I didn't try to save him? I shake my head, answering my own mental question.

Desperate, I look around for something to use to break a window. I remember seeing a snow shovel on the front porch and head back that way to grab it, but as I'm running down the far side of the house, something catches my eye and I stop. One of the basement windows has been broken out. I bend down and peer inside and Hoover does the same. The basement is dark, dry, and free of both smoke and flame.

I drop down onto my stomach on the ground and stick my feet through the small window opening, wiggling backward until my butt hits the frame. I push back a little harder and feel a stinging sensation on my left hip as my butt goes through the opening, but I hit another stopgap when I get to my chest. After reaching down and shifting my boobs around a bit, I contort myself first one way, then another, but to no avail. For a few horrifying seconds I think I'm stuck in the opening but after several more desperate grunts and squirms, I manage to push through and drop down onto the basement floor.

I pick myself up and spare a glance at Hoover, who is outside the window looking in at me. After telling him to stay, I head for the basement stairs, pausing at the top to put my hand to the wood to feel for heat. The door to the basement is in the hallway near the kitchen and away from the main fire, and though it feels faintly warm, it's not dangerously so. I slowly ease it open.

Though the basement air wasn't bad, as soon as I get to the main floor, I'm assaulted by roiling clouds of thick black smoke that make it hard to breathe and nearly impossible to see. I'm having second thoughts, thinking David will just have to wait for the fire trucks to arrive when Hoover darts past me, barking like a fool and headed for the back stairs.

"Hoover, no!" I yell, but his barking rapidly grows more distant and I can tell he's on a mission. I hunker down to minimize my smoke exposure and feel my way along the wall to the stairs. The flames are frighteningly close but the fire hasn't reached the stairwell yet so I grab ahold of the railing and start pulling myself up. I hold my breath for as long as I can and by the time I reach the top, I'm feeling light-headed. When I'm finally forced to suck in a breath, it makes me cough so hard I see stars and nearly pass out.

Off in the distance I hear sirens, and once again I have second thoughts. But over the roar of the flames I hear Hoover barking a short way ahead of me and know I have to go on. With my eyes burning and watering, I guide myself along the rail in the upstairs foyer and into the bedroom. I can't see the bed, but I fling myself across the room to where I know it to be and fall on it. I can feel David's legs beneath me and I pull myself up along his body toward his head.

"David? David! Come on! We need to get out of here!"

Hoover is beside the bed barking his agreement.

David doesn't move or respond and I feel my heart seize up in agony, wondering if I'm too late and he's already dead. Summoning every bit of strength I have, I leap off the bed, grab David's feet, and pull.

He isn't a small man by any means and because he works out regularly, his body is a dense mass of heavy muscle. Grunting, groaning, and trying not to pass out, I manage to drag him off the bed. His head hits the floor with a frightening *thunk* but I have no time to worry about that now. I move up to his head, wrap my arms under his with my hands laced together over his chest, and pull with everything I have.

Inch by inch I drag him across the room, into the hallway, and to the top of the stairs. Hoover gets into the act by grabbing the sleeve of David's pajama top with his teeth and pulling along with me. When I look toward the bottom of the stairs I don't see any flames so I turn around and start backing down, dragging David with me. My breathing is so strained I sound like an accordion. Twice I nearly fall over backward and then, halfway down, blackness begins to close in on me. Frantic, I double my efforts and try to pull harder. It proves to be a fatal mistake because this time I do lose my balance. As I feel myself fall I tighten my grip on David and hang on for both our lives.

My last sentient thought is how ironic it would be for David and me to be joined in death even though we are no longer joined in life.

Chapter 23

"**M**attie? Can you hear me? Mattie?"
Though the voice is soothing to my ears, I panic, struggling to get my breath. I feel as if I'm swimming up to the surface from some great depth and I'm not going to make it before my air runs out. Then I gasp as memories of the fire flood my mind.

Oh, no, David!

I try to say his name but my throat is dry and raw and I can't seem to get any sound out. There is a bright light behind my closed eyelids, and for a second I think that maybe I'm dead and I've somehow managed to luck out and end up in heaven despite the fact that I never go to church and have committed a host of sins over the years. I mentally thank God for her magnanimity and kindness in letting me spend eternity with Hurley, for I recognize that it's his voice calling my name.

Logic kicks in when I remember Hurley isn't dead—at least as far as I know. I try to speak again, but my chest is on fire and I cough so hard it feels like I'm hacking up a lung. That's when I realize *I'm* not dead either, though given the pain I'm feeling, I'm not sure if that's cause for celebration.

I sense that I'm lying in a bed, and when I finally open my eyes I find myself staring into a too-bright ceiling light that momentarily blinds me. That first cough has multiplied into dozens, a prolonged spasm that makes me start to gag, and I push up from the bed into a sitting position.

"Whoa!" Hurley says, placing the palm of his hand against the front of my shoulder. "Easy there."

As my vision slowly returns I can just make out Hurley standing beside me. The wall behind him shifts and I'm not sure if it's the movement of my head created by the coughing jag that's creating the illusion, or if I'm hallucinating. When another face joins Hurley's, I recognize Phyllis "Syph" Malone and realize the wall is actually a curtain, and that I'm in the ER.

I continue to cough and my head feels like it's about to explode. Along the periphery of my vision I can see tiny, sparkling lights floating in the air. Syph shoves a paper cup of water under my nose and says, "Here. Drink. It will help."

I go for the cup like a drowning man gasping for air, but when I try to swallow I'm seized by another hacking spasm and spew water all over the bedsheet. After sputtering like a dying engine for a few seconds, I try again and finally manage to get some of the water down.

It hurts like hell at first, like I'm trying to swallow a handful of razor blades. But eventually it gets easier and by the time I empty the cup, the cool water has become a soothing balm. Even better, the coughing has ceased, at least for now, though I suspect it will return since I can feel my lungs desperately trying to squeeze out all the crap in them.

"Better?" Syph asks.

I say yes and the word comes out as a hoarse croak.

"Don't try to talk too much yet," Syph says. "You inhaled a ton of smoke and your throat probably looks like a very used chimney right about now."

Mention of the fire brings my memories back. "David?" I manage to rasp, watching Syph's expression closely.

Concern flits across her face, but it's there and gone in a blink, quickly replaced by her placid professional persona. It's an expression I know and understand all too well as I've worn it a few times myself. Delivering mixed or bad news is an unpleasant but necessary part of working in an ER.

"He's stable for now," Syph says, and I squeeze my eyes closed with relief. "But he's unconscious. He inhaled a lot of smoke and has a minor head injury. They're debating on whether or not to intubate him."

"Damn," I whisper. Despite the antagonistic nature of our relationship of late, I don't want David dead, even if I did secretly wish it a time or two a few months ago after catching my coworker playing his skin flute.

Syph grabs ahold of my hand and squeezes it. "He's alive and that's because of you. They said that if you hadn't dragged him down those stairs, he'd be dead for sure."

"You're a hero," Hurley says, and Syph nods. She gives my hand one last squeeze and then lets it go.

"Try to get some rest," Syph says. "They want to keep you here for a while to make sure your respiratory status is okay, but I suspect they'll spring you in a couple of hours. I'll be back in a bit. Holler if you need anything."

"I will. Thanks."

As soon as Syph disappears behind the curtain wall, Hurley leans down and rests his arms on the side rail of my stretcher. "That was a brave but stupid thing you did tonight, Winston. You should have waited for the fire department to get there. You could have been killed."

"I couldn't just stand there and let David burn to death," I protest, wincing with the pain in my throat. I sip more of the water and feel a little relief. "I thought you were making yourself scarce," I say. "What are you doing here?"

"I heard the call go out over my radio and recognized the address. I wanted to make sure you were okay."

I suppose I should be flattered but given that I've become Hurley's only secret ally of late, I can't help but wonder if his motive might have been something else. "Do they know how the fire started?"

Hurley frowns and hesitates a second before he answers, and I know the news won't be good. "It was arson. The firemen found an empty gas can in the kitchen and there is an obvious pour pattern in one of the front rooms of the house."

"Who? How? And why?" I ask as the questions whirl through my mind. Hurley's frown deepens and a blanket of dread settles over my shoulders.

"They're not sure yet," he says. "There were no obvious signs of a break-in other than the basement window where we assumed you went in."

I nod. "It was already broken when I got there. I tried the doors first but they were all locked."

"Yeah, they figured that was how you got in when they found Hoover in the basement barking like a maniac."

I can't help but smile at the thought of Hoover raising the alarm. Then it hits me. "Oh, no, where is Hoover?"

"He's fine. Dom took him."

"It's all because of Hoover that I even discovered the fire," I say. "He woke me up by barking like crazy, and when I let him out he practically pointed to the house. I could already see flames coming out the windows." I pause and swallow some more water. "How much damage is there?"

"It's a total loss. Part of the back section of the house is still standing but other than that, it's just ash and rubble."

My eyes start to burn and tear, and I'm not sure if it's because they're irritated or because I'm so upset thinking about all that's been lost in the fire. "Why?" I ask Hurley, knowing he can't give me an answer. "Why would anyone do something like this?"

"I don't know for sure but I have an idea."

My eyes probe his, questioning, demanding that he go on.

Hurley leans in closer to me. "There's something else I need to tell you," he says, dropping his voice to just above a whisper. Judging from the expression on his face I fear things are about to tank faster than a patient having a widowmaker MI. "David and I had a bit of an incident the other day."

I take a second to try to parse this but come up blank. "What do you mean, you had an incident?"

"I ran into him at the grocery store and we had a discussion that got a bit . . . how should I put it? It got rather heated." It's not the best choice of descriptor given the night's events but I keep my opinion to myself. "And there were a number of people who witnessed the whole thing."

"What happened?"

"David basically told me I'm the reason your marriage has fallen apart, that I keep interfering with his attempts to reconcile with you."

"That's ridiculous."

"Not according to him. He was quite angry and very determined. And it isn't the first time he's approached me. When I went to see him for my follow-up visit after my surgery, he laid a guilt trip on me, implying that since he saved my life the least I could do was back off so you two can patch things up."

"There's nothing to patch up. I'm done with him. He knows that."

"I don't think he does."

As I consider what Hurley has just told me, things that

have happened over the past few weeks start to make sense. "Is that why you've been kind of standoffish with me lately?"

Hurley shrugs. "The guy has a point. He did save my life."

I ball my hands into fists and grit my teeth. I want to be angry with David for trying to manipulate my life, for his inability to put the blame where it belongs, and for being so blasé about the severity of his transgressions. But given his current situation, I can't. Besides, after what Izzy told me at dinner last night, none of it matters anymore anyway.

"There's more," Hurley says, and I feel my heart do a little *uh-oh* beat. "When the firemen found the gas can in the kitchen of David's house, they assumed it was evidence and put it out on the deck to protect it from any further fire or water damage. I got a good look at it and I'm pretty sure it's mine."

"Yours?" My mind struggles to understand the implications of this revelation but I feel too muddled to sort it out. "Why do you think it's yours? And how can you tell? Don't most gas cans look alike?"

"Not if they're hand labeled like mine is to differentiate between the plain gas I use in the lawnmower and the oil and gas mix I use for the snowblower. I recognized the writing on the container. And mine is missing from my garage."

"Oh."

"Yeah, oh."

"What are you telling me, Hurley? That *you* tried to burn down my house?"

"Of course not," he says, clearly exasperated. "But someone obviously wants it to look like I did. I'm sure my fingerprints were all over that gas can when it was taken and with the way things have been going lately, I'm betting they still are. It's just a matter of time before someone finds and runs them. Add that to the thing with Minniver, and Callie's murder, and . . . well . . . the evidence says it all."

"What the hell is happening, Hurley?"

"I don't know," he says sounding exhausted. He looks haggard and frustrated. "Two people are dead and you and David nearly ended up that way. Whatever the hell is going on, I've got to figure it out and put a stop to it." He pauses and looks at his watch. "I need to get out of here. It's only a matter of time before Richmond figures out the evidence all points to me, and if I get arrested my hands will be tied. I can't let that happen."

"What are you going to do?"

Before Hurley can answer, the curtain is flung aside and Izzy enters. His forehead is creased with worry lines and his expression is the most panicked I've ever seen him. "How are you?" he asks, coming around to the other side of my stretcher.

"I feel like I've been huffing from the chimney of the crematorium, but I'll live."

Izzy shifts his worried gaze from me to Hurley. "You feeling better?" he asks.

Hurley frowns at Izzy, looking momentarily stymied by the question, apparently forgetting that he's been calling in sick the last few days. Then his expression relaxes as it dawns on him. "I'm fine," he says, then he looks at me. "But I do have some things I need to take care of so I'm going to leave you in Izzy's very capable hands. Call me if you need anything."

Before I can utter a word, he's gone.

"Was it something I said, or did you tell him about the nipple incident?" Izzy asks. "He lit out of here like his pants were on fire."

"Given the day's events, that might not have been the best choice of words," I tell him, deftly deflecting his curiosity.

Izzy looks confused for a second before his mental light-bulb flicks on. "Oh, yeah," he says with a guilty smile, looking chagrined. "Sorry."

"I hear Dom has Hoover?"

"He does. The two of them were getting on quite nicely the last I saw them. In fact, I think Dom might try to dognap Hoover if you're not careful." His expression turns serious. "I heard that the fire was arson."

I nod.

"Do they have any idea who or why?"

I shake my head. "Not that I'm aware of. The only person I know of who's ever wished David dead is me."

"I've heard that adage about a woman scorned, but burning down your house with your husband in it does seem rather extreme," Izzy teases. He reaches through my side rail and squeezes my arm. "They said you saved David's life."

"I did what anyone would have done under the circumstances. But I'm not sure it was enough. They said he's unresponsive."

"Not anymore," says a voice behind the curtain to my right. A second later Syph enters my cubicle with a big smile on her face. "David just woke up."

"Is he okay?"

"He's alert and oriented, though understandably groggy."

"Thank goodness." I breathe a sigh of relief.

"Don't relax too much," Syph says with a devious smile. "Despite the fact that he's physically okay, I think he suffered some serious brain damage because the first thing he asked for was you."

Chapter 24

Izzy instructs me to call him when I need a ride home and then disappears. As Syph helps me out of bed, I learn that I've broken two toes on my right foot, though I don't know if it happened when I tripped over the tree root running through the woods or when I fell down the stairs with David in tow. I also feel a painful pull in my left hip and when I reach down to touch the area, I feel a neat little row of stitches.

"You cut yourself," Syph explains. "The firemen said they thought you did it on a small glass shard that was stuck in the frame when you went through the basement window." I recall the stinging sensation I felt there when I was trying to squeeze my butt through. "It took a few stitches but it was a clean cut. It should heal up fine."

I settle into a wheelchair, sitting on my right side to favor the left hip, and let Syph steer me over to David's room.

"I just gave him some Ativan, so don't be surprised if he starts to fade on you," Syph warns.

As we push aside the curtain around David's bed, he manages a little finger wave. There is a fine dusting of soot on him that has him looking and smelling like a charcoal briquette.

"How are you feeling?" I ask.

"They tell me you saved my life," he says, a total non sequitur.

"Actually it was the firemen."

"Thass not what I heard," he says with a beatific smile, his speech slurring. He blinks his eyes very slowly, clearly struggling to reopen them. "Any i-dee it started?" he mumbles.

"I haven't heard," I lie, figuring there's still plenty of time to let him know someone might have wanted him dead. And as I watch his head loll to one side, I figure it's unlikely he'll remember anything I say to him now anyway.

"Is he going to be released?" I ask Syph.

"Not yet. They're going to admit him to ICU for a while to keep an eye on his respiratory and neuro status. But if all goes well, there's no reason he shouldn't be home in plenty of time for Thanksgiving."

Home. Based on what Hurley told me about the damage, David doesn't have one anymore. I suppose I should feel saddened by the loss given that it was once my home, too, but oddly enough I don't. Over the past few months, that house has served as a constant reminder to me of everything I've lost. The fact that it's now gone feels strangely freeing and purifying, as if a monument commemorating the disaster has been destroyed.

I leave David to his Ativan dreams and after hanging out for another hour in my own bed, I check myself out of the ER at eight in the morning and use the ER phone to call Izzy for a ride. He arrives ten minutes later, looking concerned.

"I'm worried about you, Mattie," he says as we settle into his car. It takes me a minute longer to get in because I have to contort myself like some rubber-jointed circus performer in order to squeeze into his front seat. The task is more difficult than usual thanks to the gigantic flat-footed shoe I'm wearing to protect my damaged toes, which makes walking less painful but gives me a Frankensteinish gait. By the time I'm in the car, my broken toes are throbbing like a toothache.

"You look pretty peaked," Izzy says.

"I'm okay. I'm just tired, and in pain."

"And no doubt a bit spooked as well. This arson thing is pretty scary."

"Yes, it is."

"Well, I want you to take today off and get some rest," he insists. "In fact, take a couple of days. Enjoy the Thanksgiving holiday and I'll see you in the office on Friday. Arnie can cover for you until then."

"Thanks. I'll take the time off, but I doubt I'll enjoy the holiday very much. I'm having dinner at my mother's house."

"I can relate," he says, and I know he's thinking about his own holiday meal plans. "If it's any consolation, I'd rather be doing your dinner."

"No, you wouldn't. David's been invited too."

"Oh. That should prove interesting." He pauses and then adds, "Okay, you win."

Izzy parks in the drive, not bothering to pull into his garage since he's heading for the office. The day has dawned crisp, clear, and cool—a beautiful November morning—but when I crawl out of Izzy's car, I detect the lingering stench of burnt wood and plastic in the air, a reminder of the devastation next door. I wave to Izzy as he leaves, then turn to find Hoover and Dom standing in the back doorway of Izzy's house. Hoover barks and runs over to greet me with his tail wagging happily, and he licks my hands when I reach down to pet him.

"Want some breakfast?" Dom offers.

Hoover yips his approval—apparently he's become as much a fan of Dom's cooking as I have—but my mind is muddled and weary, and all I want to do is go off by myself for a while so I can think. "Thanks, but I'm going to pass for now," I tell Dom. "I need some sleep."

Dom looks disappointed, but I note it's Hoover he's looking at. I'm starting to worry that people like my dog better than me.

As soon as I'm safely ensconced inside my cottage, I swallow some ibuprofen and curl up on the couch with my broken-toed foot propped on a pillow. Though I'm exhausted, I'm too pent up and in too much pain to sleep. As I ponder the whole incident with the fire and all the deaths that have occurred, my mind reels with trying to make sense of it all. I wonder where, when, and how it will all end and I feel like a captive, spellbound and helpless as I wait for the next catastrophe to strike. The nasty burnt smell outside has permeated the walls of the cottage and, between it and my sense of impending doom, I feel an overwhelming need to escape.

After an hour or so the ibuprofen has made the pain much better but it has also left my empty stomach feeling like someone is drilling a hole in it. I take a shower, dry my hair, put on some clothes, and then get into the hearse with Hoover. Making mental apologies to Dom, I head out to get myself some breakfast and a reward for Hoover for his heroic behavior. A quick turn at the drive-through at McDonald's earns me some curious stares when I get to the food window—no doubt because of the hearse and my request for "two orders of bacon for my friend in the back."

I park in the lot long enough for Hoover to snort down his bacon while I enjoy a sausage biscuit and some orange juice. As I munch, I again reflect on the events of the past few days, running all the facts over in my mind. I've got two dead bodies, both with close ties to Hurley, and an attempt on David's life. While I suppose it's possible that someone has a grudge against David and tried to burn him alive because of it, I find it unlikely. He's a highly respected and beloved surgeon in the community. Even though every one of these incidents points a finger squarely in Hurley's direction, I feel pretty certain he's innocent. The public argument between him and David seems a little too coincidental to me.

But if Hurley isn't guilty, and he's right in his assumption that someone is trying to frame him, how did they do it? The evidence suggests that someone broke into his house and stole his hair, the potassium cyanide, and the gas can. It also means that whoever stole the stuff would have had to break into my old house to start the fire and into Minniver's house to poison his food with the potassium cyanide. Hurley has already shown me how easy it is to bypass a door lock with the right tools and the know-how, and the fact that he possesses both makes him look even guiltier. He could have gotten into Minniver's house easily enough, even without the missing spare key. My old house would have been a bigger challenge since all the doors had dead bolts and I knew David was obsessive about locking them every night, which explains the broken basement window.

Killing Callie hadn't required any lock picking, and the knife that killed her is easy enough to explain given that it was outside in Hurley's boat and accessible to anyone who looked there. All someone had to do was lure Callie here.

With that thought I recall her diary, which is still beneath the seat in my car. When I reach down and drag it out, the cell phone I had stashed there comes with it. I'd forgotten all about the phone and when I flip it open it tells me that I've missed a call. I look at the displayed number but don't recognize it. Then I get the smart idea of comparing this number to the ones in my own cell phone, to see if it matches any of them. I go searching through my purse for my phone but can't find it. Puzzled, I stop and think back to when I left the house, certain I hadn't seen the phone in the charger. Then I remember grabbing it last night to call 911, and dropping it when I was running through the woods toward my old house.

"Dang it," I mutter, making a mental note to go back and look for it.

In the meantime, the cell Hurley gave me still has a slight charge left on it so I dial the number of the missed call. It rings several times and just as I become convinced no one is going to answer, someone does.

"Hello?" says a female voice.

"Hello. Who is this?"

There's a long silence and then the woman says, "You called me. Who is this?"

I almost slip and give my real name, but at the last second I remember who the phone is supposed to belong to. "This is Rebecca Taylor. I received a call from this number on my cell phone so I'm returning it."

"Are you the private investigator who is looking into Callie Dunkirk's death?" the woman asks.

"Yes, I am. Why? Do you have something for me?"

"I might."

"Can I ask who it is I'm speaking to?"

"My name is Andi, short for Andrea. I'm Callie's sister. When I went into the TV station to pick up some of her things yesterday afternoon, someone mentioned that you'd been there asking a bunch of questions. She gave me your card."

"Who was that?"

"The girl at the receptionist's desk."

"Ah, Misty."

"Yes. She seemed to think you were working for my mother and me."

Uh-oh.

"But you're not. So who are you working for?"

"I can't reveal that. Sorry."

"Is it that prick, Mike Ackerman?" Even without her colorful descriptor, the venom in her voice when she mentions his name makes it clear what she thinks of him.

"Why do you think he's a prick?" I ask, avoiding her question.

"Oh, no, you don't," she says. "I'm not sticking my neck out so he can chop it off. If you're working for him, you'll tell him what I said and then he'll be coming after me. Next thing you know, I'll be dead, too, just like my sister."

Her words hit me like a punch to the solar plexus. Clearly she thinks it was Ackerman who killed Callie.

"You tell that son of a bitch that I've already gone to the cops and if anything happens to me they'll be on him like flies on shit," she says. She's trying hard to pepper her words with lots of bravado but I detect an underlying shakiness in her voice that tells me her fear of Ackerman is very real.

Sensing that she is about to hang up, I say, "I'm not working for Mike Ackerman. I can't tell you who I am working for, but I *can* tell you it's not him." She doesn't say anything, but I can hear her breathing on the other end so I know she hasn't hung up yet. "Do you think Mike Ackerman killed your sister?" I ask her. The phone beeps three times just as I finish asking the question and I realize the battery is about to die. All I hear of Andi's answer is "—did."

"I'm sorry, you cut out and I didn't hear you."

"I said the bastard . . . *beep* . . . to keep her quiet . . . *beep* . . . tell his wife . . . *beep*." After her last comment is broken up by three more beeps, the phone goes dead.

"Damn it!" I throw the cell aside and hear Hoover whimper behind me. "Sorry, boy," I say.

I sit and think for a minute about Andi's final comment, trying to make some sense of the part I heard. The words *keep her quiet* and *tell his wife* make me wonder if my suspicions about the relationship between Ackerman and Callie are right.

I turn my attention back to the diary and flip it open to the page with the note about police corruption. As I read it again, something nags at the back of my mind and I struggle to figure out what it is. It isn't until I look at the dead cell phone that it hits me. Callie's diary entry mentions a phone call and if there was a phone call, there'd be a record of where it came from. I make a mental note of the time and date of the entry so I can later compare it to calls Callie got. Though the entry may have been written hours or even days after the call, I figure it's worth a shot. If I had my own cell phone, I could call Bob Richmond and ask him if he's run Callie's phone records yet, but since I don't, it'll have to wait.

Phone calls aside, it all comes back to Hurley. He is the one thing that is common and central to everything that has happened, though not everyone knows it yet. With that thought in mind, I finish my breakfast and drive over to his neighborhood. I cruise down the street slowly, studying the other houses, and then circle around the block to Harold Minniver's street. I do this several times, not sure what I'm looking for but feeling like there is something here, something that will help me put all the pieces together.

Eventually I park, leash Hoover, and walk up to Hurley's house. After several rings of the doorbell and a few knocks, I deduce he isn't home. Curious, I head off the porch and walk around the side of his house to the garage area where the boat is parked. Nothing looks much different than it did when I was here a couple of nights ago.

I peek through the side window into Hurley's workshop. Sunlight coming in through the window in the bay door creates several sparks of light within the room. I realize it's coming from bits of metal scattered about and I remember the metal fragments we found in Callie's hair. One more piece of damning evidence against Hurley.

I study the other doors in the garage and see that the one to the outside has a dead bolt on it, but the one leading from the workshop to the house has just a keyed knob lock. The dead bolt probably doesn't offer much of an obstacle to someone with Hurley's lock-picking talents, and once someone gained access to the workshop, getting into the house proper would be easy. Heck, even I could do that and, in fact, I have. I bypassed one of those knob locks once when I was a teenager and locked myself out of the house. All I had to do was slide my library card into the door crack and use it to push back the latch.

I wander out into Hurley's backyard, to the rear line of the fence where it butts up against Minniver's yard. There is police tape across Minniver's back door, which opens into his garage. Similar doors, similar locks—access to one would make it easy to access the other. And that's assuming that both Hurley and Minniver were religious about locking their doors. Here in small-town America, people often don't. Plus there's the missing key to Minniver's house.

I head back out to the street, Hoover sniffing the ground as we go. Just before we round the front corner of the house,

Hoover stops dead in his tracks and raises his nose to the air. Then he barks excitedly several times. Thinking it might be Hurley, I head for the front yard at a fast clip and nearly trip over a white blur that runs into my feet as I round the corner of the house.

"Oh, my, I'm sorry," says a female voice. "I didn't know you were there."

The white blur has materialized into a small dog—some type of poodle-looking thing—and I see that the female voice belongs to an older woman with brown eyes and a gray Joan of Arc hairdo.

Hoover sits dutifully at my feet at first, watching the white fuzzy dog approach him. Seconds later he is desperately trying to stick his nose in the little dog's butt, while the little dog yips and barks and bounces around like it's on meth.

"Antoinette!" the woman yells, tugging on her leash. Unfortunately, the efforts of the two dogs have resulted in their leashes becoming intertwined and wrapped around my legs, so I nearly fall when the woman keeps pulling.

"Could you please ease up?" I say, trying to hop on my one good foot. The woman finally seems to realize what's happening and she drops her leash completely. I do the same, hoping to make the untangling process a little easier. But the fuzzy white wonder keeps darting in and out between my legs, nipping at Hoover's heels and making a general pest of herself. As Hoover tries to avoid her bites and sniff her butt instead, he starts running between my legs, too. Finally, in desperation, I reach down and unhook him from the leash completely. Sensing his newfound freedom, he immediately takes off for a nearby bush. Antoinette follows and I manage to get her leash unwrapped from my ankle in the nick of time.

"What are you doing here?" the woman asks, narrowing her eyes at me.

"I'm sorry, who are you?"

"Helen Baxter."

The name rings no bells so I start to do my own introduction. "I'm Mattie Win—"

"I know who you are," Helen says, cutting me off. "You're that nurse who works at the ME's office now, right?"

I nod, not surprised she knows me. My face along with other more delicate parts of my anatomy recently appeared on the cover of a national tabloid thanks to a rather high-profile case our office handled. That, combined with the fact that I live in a small town where the only thing that moves faster than good news is bad news, has made it hard for me to remain anonymous.

"What are you doing here?" Helen asks again.

"I'm trying to investigate—"

"You're looking into Harold's death, aren't you?" she says. "I live over on the next block and I saw you there at Harold's house with that cop the other night, and now I see there's crime tape up on his door. Was Harold murdered, because it wouldn't surprise me if he was. There have been some very strange things going on in this neighborhood lately."

"What do you mean?" I ask, getting the distinct impression that Helen doesn't miss much of what goes on in the area.

But rather than answer me, she yells, "Stop it, you little slut!"

I'm about to be offended when I realize it's her dog she's yelling at, not me. Hoover is sitting next to a bush trembling, his eyes big and round. Mere inches in front of him, facing away from Hoover with her shoulders on the ground and her treet, we had a pact of sorts to watch out for one another, you know? When you get to be our age, things can happen."

"Did you see Mr. Minniver on the day he died?"

She nods. "I didn't speak to him, but I saw him fetch his mail that morning when Antoinette and I were out on our walk. I take her out twice a day every day and walk a circuit of several blocks. Keeps me young, you know. That's how I spotted that strange man."

"What strange man?"

"The one who kept parking a black sedan around the neighborhood, different time and place every day. Sometimes he was on this street, sometimes on our street, sometimes he was on a side street, but he was here every day for the better part of a week."

I frown.

"I know what you're thinking," Helen says with a sneer. "Crazy old woman gets paranoid about some guy parking on the street."

I don't respond because she's right; that's exactly what I'm thinking. "What did this guy look like?"

She shrugs. "I never got a good look at his face. He was always wearing one of those hooded things the kids like so much these days. I was going to call the police about him but then he disappeared. Do you think I still should?"

"I don't think it will do much good since he isn't here anymore," I tell her, wishing she had called them sooner. "Black sedans are a dime a dozen. They won't have any way of finding him."

"Even if I give them a license plate number?"

It takes me a couple of beats to register what she just said. "Do you *have* a license plate number?"

"I do. I wrote it down in the pad I carry with me whenever I walk, in case I need to leave a note for someone. Like the time I left a note for Mr. Abbott saying I needed a

butt stuck up in the air, is Antoinette. Her knobby littl
twitching back and forth, back and forth, as she whi
Helen walks over and scoops Antoinette off the groun
ing me an apologetic look. "I'm sorry, Antoinette is in
and I'm afraid she's rather desperate to compromise
self."

I think of Hurley and empathize with Antoinette. Hod
looks up at me with an expression of sad yearning while A
toinette squirms in Helen's arms, desperate to get dow
Helen tightens her grip and says to me, "I'm a nurse. I use
to work at Mercy."

"Really? I don't recall ever seeing you there."

"You wouldn't. I've been retired for nearly twenty years,
and I'd imagine that was before your time."

"What department did you work in?"

"I used to be the Director of Nurses, before that odd job
took over."

The odd job she is referring to is Nancy Molinaro, a
short, stout, hirsute woman who was recruited from outside
the hospital to head the nursing department. It's rumored she
used to be a former mob hit woman—though some think she
used to be a man—who entered the witness protection program. It's easy to see how the rumors got started. The woman
talks with a whispered lisp, has spies peppered throughout
the facility, and eliminates employees she doesn't like with
frightening efficiency. Plus there is the acronym derived from
the Director of Nursing title: DON.

"Anyway," Helen goes on, "ever since my husband, George,
died, it's just me and Antoinette here. I kind of keep an eye
on things in the neighborhood, especially during the day
when most of the other folks are gone."

"Did you know Mr. Minniver?"

"We chatted every week or so. As the two old folks on the

plumber and wondering if he'd give me the name and number of the one I'd seen coming to his house twice a week for the past two months." She gives me a wink. "The Abbotts don't live here anymore," she says drily. She bends over and sets Antoinette down, then fishes in her slacks pocket, pulling out a small spiral notebook. "Let's see," she says, flipping pages. "Here you go." She rips the page out of the notebook and hands it to me.

"It was an Illinois plate?" I say, reading what she wrote.

"Yep, one of them damned flatlanders. That alone was reason enough to find him suspicious if you ask me."

"Thanks, Helen. I'll have the police run this and see what we come up with." I tuck the slip of paper in my pocket and turn to look for Hoover. Antoinette has dashed back to the bushes and Hoover is there tentatively sniffing her nether regions. Antoinette drops herself down so that she is flat on her belly on the ground, her legs extended straight out behind her, her tail standing at attention. "I think your poodle has a crush on my dog," I tell Helen.

"Antoinette is not a poodle," Helen says, all indignant. "She's a purebred bichon frise."

"A bitch on what?"

Helen gives me a look that rivals my mother's. It must be one of those things that improves with age. "I think you and your mutt had better leave now," she says, making a face like she just tasted dog shit. "If he gets my Antoinette pregnant, there will be hell to pay."

"Well, if your furry slut would quit enticing him, it would help," I say. "Besides I don't think my dog is old enough to do anything yet."

"Judging from the fact that his red rocket is out and looks ready to launch, I'd say you're mistaken."

I walk over and hook Hoover up to his leash, pulling him off Antoinette. Just as Helen said, Hoover's winky-dink is primed and ready. As soon as I rein him in, Helen walks over and scoops the slut back into her arms.

"Thanks for the license number," I tell her, dragging a humiliated Hoover toward my car.

"You'll let me know if it leads to anything, won't you?" Helen asks.

"Sure." *When your bichon freezes over.*

Chapter 25

A few minutes later, I'm pulling into the police station parking lot. There's no sign of Hurley's car anywhere so I tell Hoover to stay and head inside with the slip of paper Helen gave me. The day dispatcher, Stephanie, greets me with a smile.

"Hi, Mattie. How are things?"

"They're good. How are you doing?"

"Fine. I was sorry to hear about the fire. Is David okay?"

"He seems to be, yes. Thanks for asking." Before she can pursue the topic of David, the fire, my old house, and my marriage, I add, "Listen, I wonder if you could do me a favor. I have a license plate number I'd like you to run for me." I hand her the slip of paper and she studies it for a second.

"Illinois, eh?"

"Yep. You can still run it, can't you?"

"I can. Just give me a sec."

Steph starts typing info into the computer and as I'm

waiting, the door behind her opens and Bob Richmond comes out. "Mattie! I was going to call you this morning to see if you wanted to go to the gym with me but when I heard about the fire, I figured I should wait."

"It wouldn't have mattered if you did call because I've temporarily misplaced my cell phone. Besides, considering that I feel like I smoked an entire carton of cigarettes last night, I'm thinking it might not be the best time to start an exercise program. And I have a couple of broken toes to deal with." I stick my foot out and show him my Frankenstein shoe.

"Here you go," Steph says, handing me a sheet of paper. I take it, fold it up, and stick it in my pocket, hoping Richmond won't start asking questions. But there's too much detective left in him.

"What's that?" he asks, gesturing toward my pocket. "Who are you running?"

"It's nothing," I say, but I can tell from the way he narrows his eyes at me that I've only heightened his interest. "It's just some asshole who tried to run me off the road yesterday when I was in Chicago. I want to call him up and give him a piece of my mind."

Richmond frowns at this explanation, no doubt because it isn't a legitimate use of the system. Then I see the scared look on Steph's face, who is no doubt worrying if she's about to get into trouble for helping me. "Look, Bob, I know it isn't exactly kosher, but this guy was one of those rich assholes driving some big fancy Cadillac Escalade and acting like he owned the whole damned road."

Bob looks sympathetic and mutters, "Assholes" under his breath. I'm about to breathe a sigh of relief when Steph says, "I think you're out of luck anyway, because that plate is registered to a rental car company at O'Hare Airport."

"Oh. Well, thanks anyway."

"Listen," Bob says, "if we go to the health club today, all they'll do is an orientation. They show you how to work the machines and then they develop an exercise plan for you. It won't be anything too strenuous and they have plenty of stuff you can do that won't involve your foot. I'm sure they can take that into consideration."

I'm starting to regret ever agreeing to Bob's harebrained proposal and I'm about to beg off when the pathetic hangdog look on his face stops me. "Tell you what, Bob. I'll make a deal with you. Have you pulled phone records for Callie Dunkirk yet?"

"Yeah," he says, clearly confused about where I'm going with this. "For her cell phone, anyway. Her work phone is part of a main trunk line going into the building so there's no way to know for sure what calls go where in that place."

"I want to take a look at them. Let me have a peek now and I'll go to the gym with you later."

"Why?"

"Because I'm trying to learn about this investigative stuff and I figure you probably know more about it than anyone, given your years of experience." I pray that a little flattery will help sway Richmond and keep him from questioning my motives too closely. And it appears to be working since he's pursing his lips as if he's considering my request. "I know it's not my job to look at stuff like that, but it helps me get a better grasp of the overall picture. If you could go over it with me and explain how stuff like that works, and how it all ties together when you make a case, it would really help me. I want to learn from the best," I say, laying it on thick.

Richmond considers my request for a few more seconds and then shrugs. "Sure, I don't see what it will hurt. Come on."

Steph buzzes me into the back and I follow Richmond into a large office that holds four desks. He walks over to one of them, flips through some files, and then says, "Here we go." He pulls the phone company paperwork from a manila folder and hands it to me. I see a list of dates with corresponding phone numbers lining the pages. I immediately zero in on the date of Callie's diary entry for the police corruption phone call and scan the numbers there.

"So how do you know who these numbers belong to?" I ask.

"We run them by the phone company if we see anything that looks interesting. For instance, we ran all the numbers that appear on the day she was killed and for a day or two before that."

"And did you find anything useful?"

"Nah, it was all work-related stuff, or calls to her family."

Most of the numbers I see appear more than once on the list and they are labeled with names of Callie's coworkers, the TV station, and her family. When I look at the numbers for calls made or received on the day of the diary entry, they are all family or work-related calls. Then I notice something peculiar. "Why does this Ackerman guy have, what, at least three different phone numbers?"

Richmond rolls his eyes. "Apparently the guy has a cell for work and another one for his personal use that is unlisted. Plus he called her from his office phone a number of times. That's this one here," he says, pointing to an oft-repeated number.

I hand the papers back to Richmond. "Thanks, Bob. That was very helpful." I turn and head back out front with him on my heels. When we reach the front desk Richmond says, "Want to go hit the gym now?"

"I can't," I say, and Richmond's face turns momentarily angry. "I need to run by the hospital and check on David first, but I'll meet you at the gym after that," I add hastily. I glance at my watch and see it's almost noon. "How about one o'clock?"

"One o'clock it is," Richmond says, looking appeased. "See you there."

He waddles out the door, leaving me alone with Steph. "I'm sorry if I did anything that might get you in trouble," I tell her.

She dismisses my apology with a wave of her hand. "It's okay. I don't think Richmond cares anyway. And speaking of Richmond, what's this about a health club?"

"When I made the mistake of lecturing him on his weight, he begged me to go to the gym with him so he wouldn't be the only fat person there."

"You're not fat," Steph says. "You're just a big girl . . . large boned."

I shrug, knowing she's being kind. Steph is a bit overweight herself and these types of shared euphemisms are the secret passwords for entry into the overweight women's glee club. "I can use the exercise and Richmond can use the support," I tell her. "Besides, I feel obligated to help him try. If he doesn't do something, he'll be dead soon."

"Ah," Steph says with a knowing smile. "You're channeling your inner nurse. Well, I'm sure it will prove interesting. I hope your CPR skills are up to par."

"Have you seen Hurley today?" I ask her.

She shakes her head. "Nope, and I don't expect to. He requested some time off for a medical leave. He's going to be out the rest of the week. Convenient, wouldn't you say?" At first I don't understand what she's getting at, but then she adds, "Given that it's Thanksgiving week."

"You think it's a ruse?"

"Who knows?" She looks over her shoulder and then leans forward conspiratorially. "Nobody here knows much about Hurley. He's rather tight-lipped. A bit of a mystery man, you know?"

Boy, do I.

"But I guess that if the chief approved it, Hurley must have had some kind of supportive information for this supposed emergency, or a helluva convincing story. I wish I knew. I wouldn't mind having the whole week off, too."

I thank Steph for risking her job for me and head for the hospital to check on David. I'm told he's still in ICU and I make my way up to the third floor where it's located. When I step into the elevator—I see no reason to start the exercise abuse early by taking the stairs—I'm joined by Nancy Molinaro. She's wearing a black skirt suit with thick, flesh-colored hose and a pair of serious orthopedic shoes. I can see dark hairs matted beneath the hose and consider suggesting that she cut some of it and try to transplant it to her head, where her scalp is shining through in spots. But I don't. I'm afraid that if I piss Molinaro off, she'll come knocking at my door carrying a fish wrapped in newspaper.

"Mattie," she says, giving me a nod of acknowledgment. "Are you here on personal or official business today?"

"Personal," I tell her. "I'm here to check on David."

"Yes, I heard about the fire. Any idea yet how it started?"

"Not yet," I lie.

"Well, I hope David is back on his feet soon. We need our best surgeon."

That's Molinaro for you, all about the bottom line.

"I must say, it does seem as if tragedy is following you around these days," she says, looking faintly amused by the concept. "Ever since you left here and took that job at the ME's office. Although come to think of it, you did get called in during your on-call time more than any of the other OR nurses. And I seem to recall your cohorts in the ER saying you were quite the shit magnet. I guess some people just attract trouble. I mean look at what happened with you and that nipple incident thing. Who would of thought that—"

"Yeah, yeah, I know." I say quickly, hoping to cut her off. But she has a point. I did receive the Black Cloud Award four years running when I worked in the ER. Fortunately the elevator arrives on the third floor and I am able to make my escape.

When I enter the ICU, the nurse on duty recognizes me and waves me into Room Two. I tiptoe in, thinking David might be sleeping, but he's sitting up in bed wide-awake, eating his lunch, though *dissecting* it might be a better term.

"Hi, David."

"Mattie! Good to see you. You're just in time to run out and get me some real food to eat."

"It doesn't look that bad," I tell him, eyeing the food on his plate. "Better stick with what the doctor ordered."

"Are you kidding me?" He pries the top slice of bread off his sandwich with his fork. "I mean, what is this stuff? The nurse said it's chicken salad but I swear there's stuff in here I removed from people in the OR. And then there's this crap." He moves his fork over and stabs it into a green square of gelatin on a side dish. When he lets go, the fork remains upright. "You know, we tried to nuke this stuff once and it wouldn't melt. That's not a good thing."

"Other than the food, how are you doing?"

He pushes the tray away in disgust. "I'm fine. They tell me I have you to thank for making it out alive."

"No big deal."

"That's not the way I heard it. So thank you." He smiles at me and there's a hint of the old David I once knew and loved in the glimmer I see in his eye. "I've always known you still care for me."

The way he says this makes me wince. "I would have done the same for anyone," I counter.

"They said the house is a total loss," he says, ignoring my

comment. "I can't believe how much we've lost. And now I have nowhere to stay." He stares at me long and hard, clearly waiting for me to offer up a suggestion.

"One of the hotels in town should do for now."

"I was thinking more along the lines of staying with you."

Over my dead body. Then I remember Molinaro's shit magnet comment in the elevator and take it back, thinking I might be tempting the gods a bit too much. "The cottage isn't big enough for two people," I argue. "Hell, it's barely big enough for me."

"Don't be ridiculous," he says. "There's plenty of room."

"There's only one bedroom," I say pointedly. I give him a look that dares him to suggest we share not just an abode, but a bed.

"I'll sleep on the couch," he counters. "And it's only a temporary arrangement, until I can get the house rebuilt. It's the perfect opportunity for us, Mattie. It will give us the chance we need to work on our marriage."

I roll my eyes at him and sigh heavily. "David, how many times do I have to tell you that I'm not interested in working on our marriage? You and I are done. Finished. I'm moving on."

He throws himself back against his pillow and pouts like a child. "You are such an unforgiving bitch," he hisses. "This is about that cop Hurley, isn't it?"

"No, it's about you and your inability to keep your pecker in your pants. And speaking of Hurley, what the hell gives you the right to ask him to back off?"

"Ha!" He shoots forward and points a finger at me. "See? If it wasn't about him, he wouldn't need to back off, would he?"

"There is nothing going on between me and Hurley," I seethe. "And even if there was, it's none of your damned business anymore, David. You lost the right to have a say in my life when you decided to bed someone else."

His expression turns smug and he folds his arms over his

chest, leaning back again. "Say what you want, but I'm not giving up, Mattie. I love you and I want you back. I want us back."

"You should have thought of that before you went humping around like a dog in heat," I say, borrowing a page from Hoover's playbook.

"Object all you want but I know better. And I'm not going to sign any divorce papers. Sooner or later you'll come to your senses."

I figure two can play this game of hardball, so I cross my arms over my chest and fire back. "Well, if I recall correctly, David, that house that burned down is in both of our names. So until *you* come to *your* senses, I won't be signing off on any insurance checks."

His eyes grow wide with disbelief. "You'd really be that cruel?" he says.

"Damn right."

"You *are* a bitch."

"With a capital B."

The nurse pops into the room, effectively shutting both of us up. "Is everything okay in here?" she asks. "His heart rate and blood pressure are through the roof right now."

"He'll be fine," I tell the nurse. "Besides, he's too stubborn to die." I turn and glare at David. "I'm glad you're feeling better. See ya around."

I turn and storm from his room, fuming over his insistent denial. But he manages to get the last word in.

"Yes, you will," he yells after me. "I'll see you at your mother's for Thanksgiving dinner."

Chapter 26

I drive by the cottage to drop Hoover off and to change into some sweats and a T-shirt. At this point I'm glad I let Richmond talk me into going to the gym with him. After dealing with David, I have a ton of pent-up energy to let loose.

I dig the charger Hurley gave me for the throwaway phone out of my purse, plug it in, and put the phone on it. Then, since I have about fifteen minutes to spare, I hobble out to the woods to look for my other phone. The stink of burned everything is still hanging in the air and the smell gives me an instant throbbing headache. As I get closer to the site, I can see just how devastating the fire actually was. The entire front of the house is burned down to the foundation. At the rear, the kitchen—or what's left of it—is fully exposed, though a good portion of the back wall is still standing. Most of the stairs I climbed last night are gone. Only the top four remain, hanging in midair, a giant pile of burned rubble beneath them. Everything is covered in water, ash, and soot—a soggy, blackened mess.

I thought I'd made my peace with the loss of the house when I moved out, and I truly didn't think the fire would make that loss any worse. Now I'm not so sure.

A ruined, blackened hull is all that is left of what I've come to think of as the years BC—Before Cheating. I've been trying to think of the years AD—After David—as a new beginning, but seeing the total destruction of the house this way makes everything seem so utterly, irrevocably final.

I feel wetness on my cheek and for a second I think it has started to rain. Then I realize I'm crying. I swipe at the tears, turn my back on the house, and try to focus on the task at hand. After several minutes of scouring the grounds beneath the trees, I finally find my cell phone. Remarkably it is still intact, though it's as dead as the throwaway phone. Praying that the battery is the reason, I carry it back to the house and put it on its charger. The tiny yellow light that comes on cheers me to a surprising degree. Maybe there is some hope left after all.

When I arrive at the health club, which is called Slim's Gym, I see a guy behind the door who looks like a giant muscle on steroids. There is a look of horror on his face and at first I think it's because of how out of shape I am. But that makes no sense because I remember seeing Richmond's car in the lot and surely I can't be viewed as any more of a challenge than he is. Can I? Or have I been totally deluding myself?

The reason behind Muscle Guy's horrified look becomes clear as soon as I walk through the door. "Do you work at a funeral home or something?" he asks, efficiently bypassing any normal greeting. I notice he's staring over my shoulder toward the parking lot.

"No," I sigh. "That's my personal vehicle."

"Are you serious?"

"As a heart attack," I say, smiling. He doesn't smile back.

"Do you think you could park it around back? Having a hearse in our lot doesn't give the type of first impression I'd like."

"Fine," I say in a way that lets him know how put out I am. I do an about-face, get back in the hearse, and drive it around to the back of the building, pulling onto a tiny, concrete pad that borders on a big cornfield. The space I have to park in is barely big enough for two cars.

When I head back inside, Muscle Guy is waiting for me. "Sorry about that," he says. "But we do have an image to uphold here."

Whatever.

"My name is Slim, as in Slim's Gym. Get it?"

He says it like I'm five years old, and I'm tempted to fire back with a comment about how just because I'm overweight, it doesn't mean I'm stupid. But instead I smile and say, "Cute."

"Well, welcome. You're new here, yes?"

"Obviously," I say, figuring my physique should make that clear, given that a glance at the other patrons reveals people who are frighteningly fit and slender. I don't see Richmond, however, and I wonder if they've managed to kill him already. Maybe that's why they wanted me to park in the rear, so they could load Richmond's body into my car without anyone seeing.

"Bob Richmond invited me as his guest," I tell him.

"Oh, okay," Muscle Guy says, nodding knowingly, as if this somehow explains everything. "Come into the office and we'll get you started. First we'll go over a questionnaire about your health and exercise habits, and then we'll discuss your goals. Once that's done, we'll put together a routine of circuit training designed to help you meet those goals and then orient you on how to use the equipment. We assign everyone a personal trainer for the first week or so, until we think you've got the routines down pat. After that it will depend on your motivation. Your trainer will be Helga. She's very good."

I follow Slim into a cubicle where he hands me a piece of paper with about a hundred questions and check boxes on it. It takes me a few minutes to fill out the first side, and by the time I'm done I'm feeling pretty good given that I don't have any major illnesses, don't smoke or drink regularly, and don't have to answer a question about weekly ice cream consumption. I do mention the broken toes, however. Then I flip it over. On the back side are places to fill in my weight, height, and a variety of body measurements, and below that there's a drawn body that looks like a chalk outline at a murder scene. I hope it's not a sign of things to come.

"Don't fill in the weight and height section," Slim says. "We'll measure you in just a bit."

Gulp.

"For now just circle the areas on the body outline that you want to focus on improving."

I draw one big circle around the entire body and hand him the form.

He smiles and says, "Okay, come with me."

I follow him out into the main part of the gym, which smells like old blood and sweaty socks. He leads me past several rows of machines that look like torture devices from a dungeon, to a closed room near the far end of the facility. When we enter the room, I finally see Richmond. He's standing in front of a tall, slender woman who has a measuring tape wrapped around his ample girth.

Richmond glances over at me and smiles, but he looks terrified. The woman with the tape lets it go and then writes something on a piece of paper. "Okay, Bob," she says. "That's all we need for now. If you'll go with Slim here, he'll take you out and introduce you to the exercise machines."

Slim hands my papers over to the woman and says, "This is Helga. Helga, this is Mattie."

Helga, who is dressed in tight-fitting shorts and a sports bra, looks like a blond goddess. Judging from the six-pack on her abdomen and the size of her deltoid and trapezius muscles, I'm guessing she's a body builder. We eye one another and acknowledge the introductions with a polite nod, but I'm not fooled. There is a distinct air of disdain in the arch of her left eyebrow and the pinched line of her lips.

Slim beckons Richmond to follow him out to the main floor area and Richmond does so, looking like he's headed for his execution. He's already sweating profusely and I can't help but worry that he might flood the place once he's actually done something.

Helga examines the paperwork I filled out, points to the scale, and says, "Step on."

I brace myself for the bad news. I don't have a scale in the cottage and haven't weighed myself in several stressful months, and food is my primary coping mechanism for stress. First Helga uses the height bar, which measures me at six feet even. Next she slides the big weight on the scale to the one-fifty notch, and then starts nudging the smaller weight. When the bar fails to tip, she sighs, moves the big weight to the two-hundred mark, and then goes back to the small weight. I close my eyes, not wanting to see where it ends up. I listen as the little weight slides along the bar, praying it will stop soon.

"Well," Helga says, and I detect a hint of a German accent in the way she applies a faint v sound to her w. "It looks like we have some work to do. Your BMI is firmly in the overweight category. In fact, you are just shy of obese."

"I'm large boned," I say, knowing it sounds pathetic. "And these clothes are heavy."

Helga, to her credit, says nothing. Instead she takes a tape measure and wraps it around my bosom. When she reads the number her eyebrows rise, but she makes no comment. After writing the number down, she does the same with my waist and hips. Then she measures my arms, thighs, and calves.

"How did you break your toes?" she asks, glancing at my health questionnaire.

I'm tempted to tell her I kicked the crap out of the last person who told me I was on the borderline of being classified as obese, but I don't. "I tripped over a tree root when I was running." I figure wording it this way might shine me in a better light with her since it makes it sound like running is something I do every day for exercise, as opposed to something I do only when my house is on fire.

"Okay," she says. "We'll have to modify your workout for now to accommodate the foot injury but there's plenty here for us to work on." Her eyes grow big as she gives me a quick head-to-toe scan, as if she's wondering if I'm more challenge than she can handle. "Let's head out to the main exercise area."

I follow her out to the floor, where I spy Richmond sitting on a machine rigged with weights and pulleys, doing repetitive arm pulls with a bar. His face is beet red and he's already sweating buckets, creating a huge dark stain on his T-shirt.

Helga leads me to a different section and directs me to a similar-looking machine, though this one has some kind of widespread leg thingies on it. "Have a seat and put your legs inside these," she says, pointing to the leg thingies.

I do so, feeling painfully awkward and exposed when I end up semireclined and with my legs spread-eagled. "I generally only get into this position once a year and then I'm naked for it," I say with a laugh to disguise my discomfort. A woman two machines over shoots me a disgusted look and I fire one back at her. *Skinny bitch.*

Helga finagles the weights behind me and then says, "Okay, now bring your thighs together and then let them fall apart. Keep doing that for ten repetitions."

I do as she says and the first four reps are a breeze, made easier by the fact that my legs meet in the middle faster than most. I've always been afraid to wear corduroy pants, fearful that the friction created by my thighs rubbing together might get hot enough to start a fire.

Just as I'm starting to think this exercise thing is a piece of cake, the reps get harder and my muscles start to balk. By the time I reach number ten, my thighs feel like someone has set them on fire—and that's without the benefit of corduroy.

Helga looks pleased. "Very good," she says. "Now let's do some upper body strengthening."

Forty minutes later, Helga, who I'm now convinced is a semiretired B&D/S&M mistress, hands me some papers containing information about a proper diet for weight loss and then takes me to the locker room. I limp along behind her on legs that feel like they're made out of gelatin—and not the sturdy green hospital kind, either. She gives me a tour of the showers, which I vow to never, ever use after watching two extremely slender, well manicured women sporting genital topiary—one has pubic hair that looks like a tiny landing strip, the other has pubes in the shape of a lightning bolt—parade around stark naked. There is also a hot tub, which I would love to use if I didn't have to get undressed, because my entire body is throbbing like a toothache. I thank Helga and promise to come tomorrow for my second round of torture. It's a promise I'm not sure I'll keep.

Richmond, whose torture I suspect rivaled mine considering that his face looked like it was about to explode the entire time, meets me by the door. He hasn't showered either and I'm pretty sure it's for the same reason I didn't. While I can sympathize with his embarrassment, I'm glad we're not going to be riding home in the same car. He smells like wet towels that have been tossed in the corner for a week.

"So how'd it go?" I ask him.

"That Slim guy tried to kill me. Hell, he might have succeeded and my heart is just too stunned to know it yet. I'm going to drop dead five steps into the parking lot, like Bill did in the movie *Kill Bill,* after Uma used that Five Finger Exploding Heart move on him."

"Are you going to come back?"

He hesitates and I can tell he doesn't want to. "I will if you will," he says with a sigh of resignation.

Damn. "Okay, let's give it a few more times. How about we meet here again tomorrow, say around four in the afternoon?"

"Yeah, okay." He sounds disappointed that I've agreed.

"You better not stand me up, Richmond, because if you don't give Slim another chance to kill you, I'll do the deed myself."

"Fine," he grumbles. "But I'm going to spend my time until then thinking up ways to torture him for revenge."

As I watch Richmond waddle to his car, I breathe a sigh of relief when he passes the five step mark. My neck and shoulder muscles feel tight, so I roll my head to try to get them to relax. I hobble out to my car, my leg muscles protesting with every step. I suspect Richmond and I will both be paying dearly for this tomorrow, and oddly enough, this gives me an idea.

Chapter 27

Though I'm eager to hop into the shower and wash the gym stink from my body, I first retrieve the printout Steph gave me at the police station—which is still in my pants pocket—and then I check the cell phones. The throwaway has more of a charge on it than my regular phone so I take it off the charger. First I call information to get the number of the car rental office by O'Hare Airport. The person who answers sounds young, bored, and robotic as he recites the name of the place and asks if he can help me.

"Hi. My name is Rebecca Taylor," I tell him, resurrecting my alter ego. "I'm working for the Worldwide Insurance Company and I'm investigating a personal injury claim involving someone who says they were driving one of your cars. I suspect the guy is trying to file a fraudulent claim and I'm wondering if I can get some information from you."

"What information?"

"Well, I'd like to know if there was any evidence of damage to the vehicle in question. If I give you the license plate number of the car, can you tell me if it was returned with any dings or dents?"

"Yeah, I guess," he says.

I read off the make and model of the car from the note Steph gave me and the license plate number. He tells me to hold on a second and I hear the tapping of computer keys in the background.

"That car was rented for a week and hasn't been returned yet," the guy says finally. "So I'm afraid I can't help you."

"Really? That's odd, because the guy said he returned the car two days ago. You rented it out to a David Winston, right?"

"Nope," the guys says. "The name on the contract is Leon Lindquist."

Bingo!

"Hmm, that's odd," I say. "I guess I better go back and check on a few things. Sorry I bothered you and thanks for your time." I hang up before he has a chance to ask any more questions. Then I try to call Hurley, but once again it flips over to his voice mail. I leave a message telling him I might have a lead for him and ask him to call as soon as he can.

Seconds after hanging up, my regular cell phone rings and I snatch it up from the charger and answer it without looking at the caller ID, assuming it's Hurley. "It's about time you called," I say.

"Were you waiting on me?" says a male voice that is not Hurley.

"David?"

"Were you expecting someone else?" He sounds suspicious and it irks me—he's lost the right to be proprietary with me.

"Yes, as a matter of fact I was," I tell him. I leave it at that; let him think what he wants. "How did you get my cell phone number?" I know I never gave it to him so I'm wondering who did.

"Some gal in your office," he says, and I give myself a mental slap for never telling Cass to withhold the information. "Though you should have given it to me yourself," he adds, sounding sulky.

"What do you want, David?"

"There's someone here who wants to talk to you."

Frowning, I hear him hand off the phone and then a whispery voice comes on the line. "Mattie?"

"Yes?"

"This is Nancy Molinaro."

Uh-oh. This can't be good.

"I'm calling to ask a favor of you."

"Okay," I say hesitantly.

"Your husband has been approved for discharge from the ICU but his doctors don't feel comfortable sending him home alone. Not to mention the fact that he doesn't have a home to go to at this point. And he is refusing to stay on the medical floor. So I'm wondering if you would be willing to let him stay with you for a day or two, to watch over him."

I'm stymied. I can't believe David has sunk so low as to pull Molinaro into this. Though I must admit it's quite brilliant of him since he knows how much I fear the woman. "I don't know if I can," I say, knowing Molinaro might be mentally fitting me for a pair of cement overshoes already. "I have my job and other obligations."

"What obligation can be more important than family?" she counters. It's a question loaded with double entendre when I consider that it's coming from a rumored ex mob boss. "Besides, your office already informed us that you are off duty for the next few days."

Damn Cass! "Fine," I say. "I'll be there to get him in an

hour. But he can only stay for a day or so. Then he has to find somewhere else to go."

"Tell him that, not me," she says. And then the line goes dead.

I throw the phone onto the couch in anger, making Hoover scuttle off to the other side of the room. Then I head across the drive and knock on Izzy's back door. Dom answers a few minutes later.

"Uh-oh," he says, eyeing me warily. "What got your panties in a wad?"

"It's my frigging ex," I grumble. "They're releasing him from the hospital and I've been coerced into letting him stay with me for a day or two, like I need that complication in my life right now."

"How can I help?"

"Do you have an extra set of sheets I can borrow? I want to make up the couch as his bed so it's crystal clear to him what kind of favor this is I'm doing for him."

"Sure, hold on a sec." I wait a minute or so until Dom returns carrying a stack of linens and a pillow. He hands them to me and says, "If you need to escape, you know we're here."

"Thanks." I head back to the cottage, move my cell phone to the end table, and pile the linens on one end of the couch. I grab the pillow and start stuffing it into the case when my phone rings. I start to grab my cell from the end table, but when I hear it ring again I realize it isn't my main phone, it's the throwaway. I walk over, snatch it out of the charger, and flip it open.

"Hello?"

"Mattie?"

It's Hurley, and I breathe a sigh of relief. "Where are you?" I ask, sounding more irritated than I mean to. "I've been trying to reach you."

"It's probably best if you don't know for now."

"Has Richmond talked to you yet?"

"He called me and ran the whole lawsuit thing with Minniver by me. I told him I'd already decided to move the fence to placate the old man."

"Is that true?"

"No, but with Minniver gone there isn't anyone to contradict me. It will placate Richmond for a while, but once he gets the fingerprints off that gas can and finds out about the altercation David and I had, I'm sure he'll come back to me."

"So where do we go from here?"

"Just stick as close to Richmond and the investigation as you can." Great, I think. Now I have even less of an excuse to escape further gym tortures from Helga. "And keep me posted on any new developments. I'm going to stay off the radar for now. I left my cell phone at home in case anyone tries to trace it so I'm calling you from a throwaway cell. For now I'd like us to communicate using the throwaways only. Did the number I called from show up on your caller ID?"

"Hold on," I say, taking the phone from my ear and looking at the display. "No number," I tell him. "It just says out of area."

"Good. Get a pen and I'll give you the number. You can store it in the caller ID but give it a phony name of some sort."

"Okay, hold on again." I rummage around in my purse until I find the pen and notebook Hurley had me bring along for our trip to Chicago. "Go ahead," I say when I'm ready. He gives me the number and I scribble it down.

"Anything new you can tell me?" he asks when I'm done.

"Yes, as a matter of fact." I fill him in on Helen's story about the car and the name of the person who rented it.

"Very clever," Hurley says when I reiterate my conversation with the car rental employee.

"Does the name Leon Lindquist mean anything to you?"

"No, but that doesn't surprise me. You'd be surprised how easy it is to come up with a fake ID and credit card. Anything else?"

"No."

"Okay, I'll give you a call tomorrow to see if anything else has come up."

I start to agree, but then remember my deal with David. "Um, why don't you let me call you instead?"

There's a pause and then he says, "Why? What's going on?"

I don't want to tell him, but I don't see any way around it. "David's going to be staying with me for a few days."

My pronouncement is met with silence.

"It's only for a day or two, just to keep an eye on him while he recovers."

"I see."

"I'm making up the couch for him to sleep on."

"You don't have to explain yourself to me."

He's right, I don't. So why do I feel compelled to do so?

"Call me when you can," he says. And then he disconnects.

Chapter 28

After hanging up, I look up the number for Callie's sister and hit redial. The phone rings a couple of times and then flips over to voice mail. Rather than leave a message, I hang up and make a mental note to try again later.

I stash the throwaway cell at the bottom of my purse after entering the number Hurley gave me into its memory. After a little debate, I assign the number to my nephew, Ethan.

When I arrive in the ICU to pick David up, he is sitting on the edge of his bed wearing scrubs and smiling. "I really appreciate you doing this," he says, climbing into the wheelchair the nurse has insisted he ride in.

When we get to the patient loading area out front, the nurse hesitates. "Which car is yours?" she asks.

"The hearse," I tell her.

David shakes his head. "I forgot you were driving that thing."

"Hey, it's in better shape than your car at the moment," I

tell him, knowing his was destroyed in the fire. "Take it or leave it."

After we get into the car and I pull away from the hospital, David says, "What did you do to your foot?"

"I tripped over a tree root when I was running to the house last night and broke a couple of toes."

"You ran to save me?"

"Don't go reading things into it that aren't there, David," I say, scowling. "It was adrenaline that made me run, nothing more."

He sighs heavily and an awkward silence fills the car for a couple of minutes. Then he says, "Look, I know you're not happy about this. I get that. And I know I'm a schmuck for what I did to you . . . to us. But can we try to put the past behind us for the next couple of days and just be civil? No relationship talk, no future talk, just two people who once cared a lot for one another spending a little time together?"

I consider his request. "Okay," I say finally. "But you have to stick to your promise. No relationship talk. Deal?"

"Deal. Have any plans for dinner?"

Now he's talking my language: food. "Not yet. What did you have in mind?"

"How about we go out somewhere? My treat, except you'll have to run me by the bank first since my wallet was lost in the fire. I need to go by there anyway so I can replace my credit cards. And I also need some clothes." He plucks at the neckline of his scrub top. "At the moment, this is all I have."

I realize then that this fire has been far more devastating a loss for him than for me and I feel a twinge of guilt for all the nasty thoughts I've been harboring against him. He has quite literally lost everything, including the shirt on his back.

"Okay, let's do the bank first and then I'll take you clothes shopping."

"Thanks, Mattie. I really do appreciate everything you're doing for me."

"No problem."

After a lengthy stop at the bank, David emerges with a wad of cash and gets back in the car. "Next stop, Nigel's," he says.

Nigel's is the name of the only men's clothier in town, owned by a pretentious fop who sports a fake British accent and charges twice what his clothes are worth for the privilege of shopping where the snobbish elite go. "Why don't we hit up the Super Wal-Mart?" I suggest. "It's only a half hour drive away and it will have better variety for a much more reasonable price."

"I've always shopped at Nigel's," David says, frowning. "Their suits are a better quality and I can get them tailored."

"But you don't need suits right now. What you need is day-to-day stuff: underwear, socks, jeans, shirts, shoes, and some toiletries. Plus you're going to need a coat of some sort. You can hit Nigel's up for your suits later."

David thinks about it and though I expect him to stick to his snobbish ways, he doesn't. "Okay, you're right. I'm starting from scratch here so I guess we should begin with the basics."

I change direction to head for the highway and Wal-Mart. "I should make a list," David says. "Do you have anything I can write on?"

"Look in my purse," I tell him.

He grabs my purse, rummages around, and comes up with a pen and the small spiral notepad from the Chicago trip. "What's all this?" he says, flipping the pages of the pad and reading my notes.

Panicked, I reach over and grab the pad from him. "Those are notes on the investigation I'm working on." I rip all the pages with writing on them out of the pad, including the one that has Hurley's number on it, cursing myself for not destroying it earlier. Then I hand the pad back to him.

"Why do you have two cell phones?" he asks, peering into my purse.

I think fast. "Um, I temporarily misplaced my regular phone and had to get one of those prepaid ones. It still has minutes on it so I haven't tossed it yet."

"I need a phone," he says, taking both of them out of my purse. "Can I use the prepaid one until I get mine replaced?"

"No!"

He gives me a shocked look. "Okay already. I was just asking." He drops the phones and tosses my purse aside.

"Sorry," I tell him. "It's just that I don't want to give up the other one in case someone who has that number tries to call me, not knowing I have my original back." The story sounds plausible to me and I pray it will for David, too. "We'll get you a new cell phone tonight. I'm pretty sure Wal-Mart has them now."

A little over four hours later, David and I arrive back at the cottage, both of us exhausted but happy and full. After a sweeping run through Wal-Mart, where I found I actually enjoyed dressing David like some adult version of a Ken doll, we had dinner at a Mexican restaurant in a nearby town before heading home. David stuck to his word about keeping the conversation neutral and I found myself actually enjoying his company as we reminisced about things in our past and had a civil but rousing discussion about health care reform. Several times during the evening things felt so much like the old days, I forgot that we were no longer a couple.

Now the resultant emotions are seriously screwing with my head.

We carry our packages inside, where Hoover greets me with a gentle *whuff* and a happily wagging tail. After giving David a cursory sniff, he dismisses him and comes back to me. I leave David to his unpacking and take Hoover outside to do his business.

While I'm standing outside watching Hoover sniff and circle to find the perfect spot, I hear a door open behind me. When I turn to look, I see Izzy approaching.

"Hey, Izzy."

"Hay is for horses," he says. "Dom told me the news about David."

"Yeah, I should probably have my head examined for agreeing to it, but he and Molinaro basically cornered and guilted me into it."

"Wow, he got Molinaro involved?" I nod. "Devious move on his part. He knows how much you fear that woman."

"I'm only going to let him stay for a couple of days. Just until Thanksgiving. We're already committed to the dinner with my mother and William so I might as well let him stay till then."

"Dom wants me to invite you both over for breakfast in the morning. That is, unless the two of you need some time alone together."

I shoot him a look that makes him back up a step and hold his fingers up in the sign of the cross. "It was a joke," he says.

"Tell Dom thanks and we'll be there, or at least I will. David may opt to do something else."

"Let me ask you something, Mattie."

Uh-oh, I know that tone. It means something serious is coming. Has Izzy figured out that I'm keeping secrets from him?

"Have you considered going for marriage counseling with David?"

"No."

"Why not?"

"Two reasons. One, I hate shrinks, particularly after our experience with Luke Nelson," I say, referring to a recent case. "And two, there's no need for counseling. I'm not confused about what I want at this point, or rather what I don't want. I don't want David and I don't want my marriage back."

"Are you sure the situation with Hurley isn't clouding your judgment?"

For a second I feel a frisson of panic, thinking he's discovered I'm in cahoots with Hurley on this latest investigation. But what he says next makes me realize his true meaning.

"I mean, there's an obvious attraction between you and Hurley. Anyone who's spent any time around the two of you can see that. And I can't help but wonder if that isn't clouding your judgment some. If you take him out of the equation, which you're going to have to do now, are you sure being on your own is what you really want?"

I watch Hoover squat and take a dump, his haunches quivering with his efforts. And I think about what Izzy is saying. Had anyone else asked me this, I would have dismissed it out of hand. But I've come to respect Izzy for his insight and wisdom about things, so I feel obligated to give what he's saying some serious consideration.

"I don't know, Izzy," I say finally. "My head is kind of muddled right now, what with everything that's happened. Let me think about it, okay?"

"Okay."

"See you in the morning."

And with that, I head inside toward a future that is more confusing than ever.

Chapter 29

David has left most of his clothes in the bags from the store and he's still dressed in his scrubs. "Mind if I use your shower?" he asks.

"Of course not. Help yourself."

I watch him as he carries his brand-new pajamas and the bag of just-bought toiletries into the bathroom with him. As he closes the door, my mind envisions him undressing on the other side. I know the first thing he'll do is shave, standing stark naked in front of the sink, running the razor over the right side of his face first, then the left, moving to his neck next, and then the mustache area, finishing with the side-burns. After that he'll brush his teeth for a full two minutes, finishing off with a Listerine rinse. Then he'll hop in the shower and wash his body before he shampoos his hair. I can see that body—tall, lithe, and fit—in my mind's eye. David is a well-built, attractive man and as I imagine him lathering himself up, I feel myself getting turned on.

What the hell? Maybe Izzy is right. Maybe I should consider marital counseling because clearly I'm still attracted to David on some level. Then again, I haven't had sex in months so at this point even Helga looks good to me.

I settle on the couch with Hoover at my feet, turn on the TV, and start flipping channels, cursing my fickle loins and trying to focus on anything besides David naked in the shower. By the time he comes out of the bathroom wearing his new pajamas, with his hair damp and his face flushed, I've successfully shifted my attention to my back and shoulders, which are stiffening up with each passing minute. I'm not sure if it's because of my workout at the gym, my efforts with David during the fire, or a combination of the two, but I have a feeling I won't be moving well in the morning. Rubbish has curled himself up in my lap and even the minimal movement I'm making to pet him is growing more painful with each stroke.

David fetches himself a glass of ice water from the kitchen and then walks over and plops down next to me on the couch, making Rubbish leap from my lap and dash into the bedroom. Most likely Rubbish will hide under the bed for a while. He doesn't take well to strangers in the house and the only person he's not run from is Hurley, which is ironic when you consider that Hurley harbors a strong dislike of cats and often wants to run from Rubbish.

David smells fantastic and my mind starts thinking evil thoughts again. "How are you feeling?" I ask, hoping to keep the conversation as far away from delicate personal territory as I can.

"I'm okay. I still have a bit of a headache and I coughed up some nasty-looking stuff in the shower, but at least I don't feel like I'm one step away from slipping into the grave." He looks down at my foot, still encased in its Frankenstein shoe. "What about you? Are you doing okay?"

"My toes are throbbing quite a bit," I admit. I shrug and

roll my neck to try to loosen things up. "And I made the mistake of working out at a gym today and now my muscles are stiffening up in protest."

"You worked out?" he says, looking as shocked as if I'd just told him I'm really a man.

"Yes, I did. Why are you looking at me like that?"

He laughs. "It's just not like you. In the past you've taken to exercise the way cats take to water. Plus I noticed your freezer is well stocked with Ben & Jerry's."

I roll my neck again and wince. "Well, based on how I feel at the moment, I think my aversion to exercise is justified. Though I suppose my pain could also be from my having to drag you out of bed and down the stairs to save your sorry ass," I add, unable to resist one small jab in my defense.

I get the satisfaction of seeing David look properly chastised. He gets up and goes back into the bathroom, returning a minute later with three ibuprofen tablets and a glass of water. "Here, take these," he says.

"Thanks." I chug the pills down with a couple of swallows of water.

"You're welcome. Now turn around and face toward the end of the couch."

I stare at him, confused by the request.

"Just do as I say," he says with a smile. "Trust me."

Those last two words are loaded ones, given our history. Trust is the one thing sorely lacking in our relationship, but I decide to take this baby step and see what happens. A second later his hands are on my shoulders, gently kneading the muscles there. "Wow, your muscles really are tight," he says, moving toward my neck. "Is this helping?"

"Yes, it is." It's not only helping, it feels utterly glorious. His hands work magic on my tired muscles; I can feel them unwinding already. For the next fifteen minutes, his hands rove over my shoulders, my neck, and my back. I'm so lost in the sensations that I end up lying on my stomach on the couch at one point with no memory of how I got there. By the time he's done I feel utterly relaxed . . . and completely confused.

He leans down and kisses me on the nape of my neck—a spot he knows is a sensitive one for me. It triggers a deep longing in my groin and it's all I can do not to flip over and kiss him back. I half expect him to try to go further but instead he retreats, pats my fanny, and says, "Now you need a hot shower to keep those muscles loose."

I get up from the couch and stumble into my bedroom to get a nightgown. When I come back out, David is making up the couch with the linens Dom gave me and Hoover is watching him curiously, his head cocked to one side. I hurry into the bathroom and as soon as I shut the door behind me, I lean against the wall and try to get a grip on my senses.

What the hell just happened?

But I know what happened. Somehow David managed to reawaken feelings in me that I thought were long dead and gone. Was Izzy right? Had my attraction to Hurley somehow enabled me to bury my true feelings for David?

I turn on the shower and get it as hot as I can stand, and then I strip myself naked and climb in. At first I just let the water beat on my neck and shoulders for a while, fighting the images in my head. But no matter how hard I try, my mind keeps playing mini scenarios where David enters the bathroom and climbs into the shower with me.

Frustrated, I wash up, get out, and dry off. Then I spend another twenty minutes lotioning up my skin and blow drying my hair. By the time I emerge from the bathroom I'm still mightily confused and afraid of what might happen next. But David is sound asleep on the couch with the TV still on and Hoover curled up on the floor beside him. I turn the TV off, half expecting David to awaken when the sound cuts out. But he doesn't and I realize that a small part of me is disappointed.

I stand there watching him sleep for several minutes, admiring his patrician features, the lean lines of his body, and the almost childlike expression he has on his face. A part of me wants to crawl in next to him and spoon the way we used to. Another part of me remembers his horrible betrayal, and with that remembrance comes the realization that what we once had will never be the same. But just because it can't be the same doesn't mean it can't work, does it? Maybe we can build a new relationship, one that's even stronger than what we had before because of the many obstacles we'll have to overcome to get there.

I'm irritated with myself for thinking about any of this. While I clearly have some heavy thinking to do about David and me, I don't want my marital issues to cloud my focus on Hurley's situation. Plus there is a part of me that feels like I'm selling out by even considering giving David another chance.

I turn off the one lamp in the room that's on but it makes it too dark and I'm afraid David might trip or stumble into something in this foreign environment if he can't see. So I turn on the bathroom fixture and pull the door partway closed, allowing a small trapezoid of light into the living room. Satisfied, I turn my back on David both physically and metaphorically and head for my bed. I briefly debate whether or not to shut my bedroom door, but in the end I decide to leave it open so I can hear David if he does awaken. As soon as I'm under the covers, Hoover, who has followed me, lays his chin on the edge of the mattress, looking at me with those wistful brown eyes. Happy to snuggle up to any warm body along about now, I give him the okay and let him hop up on the bed with me. A few minutes later Rubbish comes out from beneath the bed and curls up on my other side.

Just as I'm about to drift off to sleep, I remember that I didn't lock the door. Given everything that's happened around here lately, it would be foolish of me not to. Annoyed with myself for forgetting, I toss the covers back and climb out of bed. Both Hoover and Rubbish awaken and watch me, but neither of them leaves the warm comfort of the bed to follow, apparently sensing that I'll be back.

I tiptoe past the couch and David's sleeping form, making a concerted effort not to look at him again since I'm convinced my hormones are inclined to flame like a Molotov cocktail and I can't trust myself any longer. It only takes a second to flip the deadbolt, but the act doesn't imbue me with a sense of security because I remember how easily Hurley—and presumably someone else—has already managed to get past such locks. Then I remember the broken and opened basement window in my burned-down house and decide I should check to make sure all my windows are secure, too. There are two in the living room, one in the kitchen, and one in the bathroom, and I make quick work of checking them all, relieved to find each one firmly closed and locked. That leaves just my bedroom window, which is located on the back wall of the cottage. Since I sometimes find myself having to sleep during daytime hours after a night spent up answering calls, my bedroom doesn't often see the light of day. Unlike the other windows, this one is mostly concealed by drapes for both darkness and privacy, though I notice a small gap up the middle where the two sides don't quite meet. I walk over and push the drapes aside to check the lock. Instead I end up screaming because there is a face on the other side of the glass looking in.

Chapter 30

My scream is an instinctive one, brought on by the shock of my discovery. Unfortunately it precedes my awareness of who the face belongs to, so by the time I realize I don't have to scream, I already have. Hoover reacts instantly, leaping from the bed and barking like crazy, turning around in circles because he isn't sure exactly what it is he's barking at.

On the other side of my window, looking in, is Hurley. Though my scream was a short one, it was enough to make him wince and now he's holding a finger to his lips to shush me. But it's too late. All the hullaballoo has spooked Rubbish, who is no longer on top of the bed, though I have no idea where he disappeared to. David has awakened, too, and I can hear him out in the living room behind me, cussing and thrashing about as he tries to get up from the couch. I turn away from the window for a few seconds and holler out to him, "I'm sorry, David. I didn't mean to startle you. I had a bad dream. Go back to sleep."

When I turn back to the window, Hurley is gone. Letting the drapes fall back into place, I head out to the living room to make sure David is okay. I find him sitting on the edge of the couch, his elbows on his knees and his face in his hands.

"I'm so sorry," I say, walking over and putting a hand on his shoulder. "I had this nightmare and in it I was screaming, and then suddenly I was awake and I really *was* screaming. And of course that set Hoover off."

David looks up at me through sleepy eyes and he reaches up and takes the hand I have his shoulder. He sandwiches it in between both of his and says, "In all the years we were together I never heard you yell out like that in your sleep."

Not knowing what to say since technically I *still* haven't yelled out like that in my sleep, I simply shrug.

"I think it's this new job of yours," David says. "You're dealing with death every day, crimes half of the time, and I know from my med school experience that cutting on dead people isn't much fun. Plus what you're doing is dangerous. You've already been attacked by killers a couple of times and that's got to leave you feeling rattled."

"I like my new job," I tell him.

David shakes his head. "You shouldn't be working at all. You know my feelings on the matter."

I do indeed. We had several discussions during our marriage about whether or not I should continue working and often as not they ended up in a standoff. But how he felt about it then has no bearing on the here and now since he no longer has a say in what I do. I pull my hand away from his, suddenly uncomfortable with where this conversation is headed.

"At least then you were working because you wanted to," he says. "Now you're working because you have to."

"Well, I have rent to pay, and food to put on the table," I tell him. "They can be powerful motivators."

"You shouldn't have to work at a job that makes you miserable. Why don't you go back to the hospital? I hear there are a couple of positions open in the ER."

"I can't go back to the hospital because everyone there looks at me with pity and embarrassment, thanks to you," I tell him, growing irritated. "And my current job does *not* make me miserable."

"Bull."

"It doesn't," I insist.

"The true test of love for a vocation is whether or not you'd do it if you didn't have to. So are you telling me that if you had enough money that you didn't have to work, you'd still keep this stupid job?"

"Don't call my job stupid," I snap. "And yes, that's what I'm telling you."

"I don't believe you. You're just being arbitrary because you're mad at me. You didn't even give the question any serious thought."

He's right about one thing. I'm pretty pissed at him at the moment. And it couldn't be better timing. All of my earlier waning on the topic of our marriage had blinded me to the harsh realities of our relationship. No matter how attracted I might be to David physically, our incompatibilities are simply too big to overcome. Skirmishes like the one we are having now occurred off and on throughout our marriage, a series of passive-aggressive battles as each of us tried to bring the other around to our own point of view. Despite the fact that these skirmishes escalated considerably during the latter months of our marriage, that in and of itself might not have been enough to destroy our relationship. But David's affair and the fact that he got his girlfriend pregnant, definitely is. Yes, I still find David attractive physically and yes, I still care for him as a person. But that's where it ends. In a flash of clarity I know our marriage is over, as dead as any client on my autopsy table.

And with this realization comes a stroke of brilliance, an idea so perfect I can't believe it took me this long to think of it.

"I do love my job, David, and I'll prove it to you. As I recall, that house next door is worth close to a million in today's market, and that's just the house alone, not the contents that were in it. I also know what it and the contents were insured for. And I can guarantee you that I'm going to take my half of that insurance money and keep it for myself. That should give me enough to live off of for a good while if I don't have a job.

"But I will have a job, David, the same job I have now. And do you know why? Because I like it. I like the puzzle-solving aspects, I like the scientific aspects, and I like the people I work with."

Whereas before he looked amused by our conversation, he now looks mad as hell. "You're just being spiteful," he says.

"I think I'm being practical."

He shakes his head, his face tightening with anger. "I can't believe you've become such a vindictive bitch," he snarls. "I just don't get you anymore, Mattie."

"I know you don't, David. You never have."

I spin on my heel and march back to my bedroom, Hoover following close behind. As soon as we are both in the room, I slam the door closed. I walk over to the window and part the curtains again, but Hurley is no longer there. A small part of me wonders if he ever really was there, or if my mind just conjured up his image. But I don't really believe that. He was there, and I want to know why.

That's when I realize I could call him on the throwaway phone, but it's in my purse, which is out in the living room.

And after the very dramatic and emphatic exit I just made, I can't go back out there; it would undermine the entire performance. Besides, the walls of this cottage aren't that thick and I'm afraid David would be able to hear anything I say on the phone, even through a closed door. It's not that I care if David knows I'm talking to Hurley, I just don't want the aggravation I fear will come with it.

Resigned to waiting until morning, I crawl back in between the covers and I'm happily sandwiched between my furry partners minutes later. Apparently decisive anger is good for me because I'm asleep in no time.

When I awaken early the next morning to bright sunlight trying to slink its way around the corners of my drapes, it seems a good omen. At least until I try to get out of bed. That's when I discover that I can barely move. My back muscles feel tighter than the sphincters of Green Bay residents during a Packers-Vikings game, and my legs are achy, tremulous, and shaky. I roll onto my side and push myself into a sitting position, groaning the entire time. When I stand and try to walk, it feels like the year my mother made me wear my Halloween costume over my snowsuit because we got ten inches of snow the night before. I can hardly move.

I waddle my way to the bedroom door, open it with a grimace because reaching for the knob makes my upper back scream with pain, and look out at the couch. It's empty and the sheets have been folded up atop the pillow and left in a neat little pile at one end. I shuffle out and look in the kitchen and bathroom, but they are empty too. Apparently David is up and gone, and I wonder if he's already over at Izzy's for breakfast. Then I remember that I never told him about the invite. I look out the window and see the hearse is still parked outside so I know he couldn't have gone far.

I hobble over to the front door and let Hoover out for his morning ablutions, watching him from the porch and admiring his ability to squat and hunch. The warming trend we had is definitely gone and despite a bright, sunny sky, the air has a bitter bite to it. I glance through the trees toward my old house, wondering if David is over there, but all I can see are bits and pieces of the few charred parts of the structure that are still standing. When Hoover comes back inside, I head for the bathroom, hoping that a hot shower and a handful of ibuprofen will make things better.

They do, but only minimally.

When I arrive at Izzy and Dom's for breakfast, Dom is putting a delicious-smelling quiche on the table along with hot cinnamon bread and fresh coffee.

"Where's David?" Izzy asks.

"Don't know and don't care," I say, easing into a chair at the table.

Izzy raises his eyebrows. "I take it the night didn't go so well?"

"Actually it was quite enlightening," I tell him. "It made me realize two things: that David's and my differences go much deeper than I thought, and that I need to get laid soon." Dom, who is putting coffee mugs on the table, drops one with a clatter. I see him and Izzy exchange looks. "To be honest," I add as Dom carefully rights the dropped cup, "I'm surprised David and I lasted as long as we did. But we are definitely done and it's time for me to move on. Shall we eat?"

The two men stare at me for a moment, clearly surprised by my outburst, but they recover quickly. Dom takes his seat and says, "By all means, dig in."

I start to reach for the spatula in the quiche dish but my back muscles seize up with a ferocity that makes me gasp.

"Not that I'm aware of," I say, pretty sure this theory is wrong. Reminded of the secrets I'm keeping, I focus on the food on my plate and avoid looking at Izzy. Fortunately this task is made immeasurably easier when Izzy's cell phone rings and he gets up to answer it.

He stands in the doorway between the living room and kitchen, taking the call, and both Dom and I remain quiet, hoping to eavesdrop. Though Izzy says little beyond the occasional "No" and "Really?" I can tell from the expression on his face that the news isn't good. When he hangs up and returns to the table, he looks seriously troubled.

"That was Bob Richmond," he says. "He wanted to know if I'd seen or heard from Hurley recently. He's going to be calling you next."

"Why?" I ask with what I hope seems like innocent curiosity, even though I have a pretty good idea of the answer.

"Richmond says they processed the gas can that was found in your house and they got some fingerprints off it. They ran them through AFIS and got a match."

"That's great," I say, trying to look relieved even as my gut tries to tie itself into knots. I can tell from Izzy's scrutinizing stare that he isn't totally buying my feigned reaction.

"No, it's not so great," he says, "because the prints belong to Hurley."

"Hurley? That's odd," I say, frowning. Then I pretend to hit on an idea. "Or maybe not. He told me he was there the night of the fire, so maybe he handled the can then."

"Maybe," Izzy says, unconvinced. "But there's more. Richmond said he has several witnesses who overheard Hurley and David having a rather heated discussion at the grocery store the other day. The topic was you."

"Me?" I ask, all innocence.

"Yes, you. Apparently David gave Hurley an ultimatum,

"What's wrong with you this morning?" Izzy asks. "You moving like my mother."

Given that his mother is in her eighties and has sever spinal kyphosis and more artificial joints than a robot, his comment doesn't paint a very pretty picture.

"I worked out at a gym yesterday and I'm paying dearly for it now. I always knew exercise could kill you."

"You went to a gym?" Izzy says, clearly shocked. Dom quietly takes my plate and serves me up a huge slice of quiche and some cinnamon bread.

"Why does that fact surprise everyone so much?" I say, picking up my fork as Dom sets the plate down in front of me. "I'm not above trying to maintain a healthy lifestyle. Plus I figure if I'm going to get back into the dating scene, I need to get into better shape."

Izzy digests this answer for a few seconds and then says, "What's the real reason?"

"Bob Richmond basically blackmailed me into going with him." I stab a piece of quiche onto my fork and wince with pain as I raise it to my mouth, but my efforts are rewarded when it melts on my tongue with a delightful burst of flavors.

Dom, who is naturally slender—a trait that would make me hate him if he wasn't such a damned good cook—serves up Izzy's breakfast and says, "I think it's a great idea. You should go with them, Izzy."

Izzy gives Dom a look that makes it clear what he thinks of this suggestion.

We spend the rest of the breakfast discussing the recent murders and the burning of my old house.

"Here's what I'm thinking," Izzy says. "The most likely culprit for the arson is a past patient of David's who was unhappy with his surgical outcome. Has David had any malpractice incidents recently?"

saying that if he didn't stay away and give you and David a chance to save your marriage, there would be hell to pay."

"David had no business doing that," I say, irritated all over again by my ex's chutzpah. "He's assuming I want to save our marriage, and I don't."

"A minor point," Izzy says, still looking troubled, "because there's more. There's the fact that Hurley is a neighbor of Harold Minniver's and had this property dispute going on."

"Yes, but Hurley said he'd already decided to move the fence, making the whole thing a nonissue."

"How about the fact that Hurley used to date Callie Dunkirk?" Izzy spits this latest revelation out like a piece of used-up chewing gum.

"Oh, my," Dom says.

Shocked that this fact has been found out already, I say nothing because I'm pretty sure my surprise shows on my face. Better to stay quiet and let Izzy think I'm taken aback by the fact itself rather than because it's now common knowledge.

"No one knows where Hurley is and attempts to reach him have been unsuccessful," Izzy says. "Do you know where he is?"

"No," I say without a hint of hesitation or guile, glad that this, at least, is the truth.

"Well, Richmond has obtained a search warrant for Hurley's house and I've been invited to attend, in case they find any evidence to suggest that Callie was killed there."

"That's just ridiculous," I say, feeling my breakfast congeal in my stomach. "Hurley wouldn't hurt a fly."

"You seem awfully defensive."

"I'm just being realistic. I know Hurley and he wouldn't do something like this."

"Look, I know you like the guy, Mattie, but we have to

face the facts here. He has ties to two murders and one attempted murder. What's the likelihood that it's mere coincidence?"

I sigh, because I know it's not a coincidence. "I want to go with you," I tell him.

Izzy shakes his head and frowns. "I gave you some time off so you can recover from the fire incident," he says. "And you're obviously not moving very well this morning."

"I'll be fine as soon as my ibuprofen kicks in."

Izzy's frown deepens. "I'm not sure it's a good idea for you to be a part of this."

"Why?"

"Because you're personally involved on several levels and I'm not sure you can be objective enough."

"I can keep an open mind," I argue. "And I promise you that if Hurley is responsible for any of this, I will personally make sure that he gets what's coming to him." This much is true. If I find out Hurley has been playing me all this time, I'll kill him myself.

Izzy eyes me with a troubled expression. "I don't know, Mattie."

"Izzy, I promise you I'll be as objective as anyone else there. Please don't leave me out of this."

He sighs heavily and I know I've won. "Okay," he says, looking like he's not convinced it's the right decision. "But I want you to work solely as my assistant. Let me and Richmond direct the handling of any evidence. With all this police corruption paranoia that's floating around, the last thing we need is to have our evidence compromised in any way, particularly if a cop is involved."

I start to tell Izzy he has nothing to worry about because I'm certain Hurley is innocent. But I don't because I realize it would belie the very objectivity I just swore to. I realize that I've dug myself in about as deep as I can go at this point by lying to both Izzy and Richmond, and blindly committing myself to Hurley. I pray my faith in Hurley is justified and I'm not just some gullible girl in heat, as desperate as fluffy Antoinette. If it does turn out that Hurley's been lying to me all this time, I'm done for. I'll not only lose my job and my best friend, I'll probably end up in jail, convicted as Hurley's accomplice. And the last thing I need is to end up in jail. Those horizontal stripes on the jail outfits are extremely unflattering for a figure like mine.

I tell Izzy I need a few minutes to feed and water Hoover before we go, and then head back to the cottage. As soon as I'm inside, I grab my purse from the end table by the couch, dig out the throwaway phone, and dial Hurley's number. While waiting for his answer, a small warning niggles at the back of my mind, telling me something isn't right. But I don't have any time to figure it out because Hurley picks up on the second ring.

"Hurley?" I say before he has a chance to speak.

"Mattie, listen, about last night—"

"Never mind last night. We can talk about that later," I say, standing by the door and watching for Izzy in case he decides to come over and into the cottage while I'm talking to Hurley. "I don't have much time and I need to tell you something. Richmond knows about the connections to both Callie and Minniver, and they found the fingerprints on the gas can from my house. He's obtained a search warrant for your place and Izzy and I are headed there now."

"Izzy is with you right now?" he says, sounding panicked.

"No, I'm in my cottage but I'm supposed to meet him outside in a sec. I wanted to call you first to give you a heads-up, so I told him I had to feed Hoover."

That's when it hits me what's wrong. Whenever I come home, Hoover always greets me at the door and follows me throughout the house. But this time he didn't and when I whip around to look for him, I see why. Hoover is in the kitchen snacking on some kind of food. And standing beside him, looking shocked and mad as hell, is David.

Chapter 31

"I have to go," I say into the phone, and as I hear Hurley start to protest, I hang up.

David, who is smudged from head to toe with soot and ash, is staring at me like I'm evil reincarnated.

"I take it you've been over at the house?" I say, trying to act innocent.

"What the hell was that?" he asks, scowling.

"What was what?"

"That phone call."

"I was just talking to a friend," I say nonchalantly. After dropping the phone back into my purse, I turn to open the door, planning to leave before he can ask me anything else. The movement makes my back muscles scream in agony but I swallow down the pain, determined to escape.

"Mattie!" The stern tone in his voice freezes me to the spot. "Did I just hear you say they found fingerprints on the gas can that was in our house?"

"I don't want to discuss this with you, David. In fact, I

can't discuss it with you since it's part of an ongoing investigation," I add, thinking it a brilliant rejoinder. "And since you seem to be doing so much better, I'd appreciate it if you would find yourself somewhere else to stay from here on out. Don't let Hoover out when you leave."

Before he can say another word, I exit the cottage, closing the door firmly behind me. There's no sign of Izzy yet and I curse to myself, afraid that David will follow me outside and try to pursue the conversation. If he does so in front of Izzy, the resultant fallout could prove devastating for me.

Fortunately Izzy appears a second later and I wave him over to my car. "I don't think I can squeeze myself into yours this morning," I tell him. "So can we take mine instead?"

Izzy shrugs and climbs into the hearse. I get behind the wheel quicker than I thought myself capable of doing and hit the gas.

"Slow down," Izzy says, fastening his seat belt. Though I'm quite religious about wearing my own, I don't hook it up now for two reasons. One, I don't think I can reach it without causing myself undue agony, and two, I don't want to stay at the cottage a second longer than necessary with David there. As soon as I reach the street, I slow down to a more reasonable speed and Izzy relaxes a little.

It only takes us a few minutes to get to Hurley's house and when we arrive we find several police cars parked in the drive and on the street out front. To my horror, I see Helen Baxter and Antoinette on the sidewalk a couple of doors away, watching everything with keen interest.

Izzy and I get out of the hearse, and I retrieve my evidence kit from the back. Since Izzy is already headed inside, I look down the street at Helen and after making sure no one is watching me, I put my finger to my lips to indicate to her that she needs to stay away and quiet.

As I enter Hurley's house, memories of our aborted dinner from a few nights ago come back to me. I swear I can smell the lingering scents of oregano and garlic still hanging in the air.

Most of the activity seems to be in the kitchen and workshop area and I cringe, knowing that the connection to the metal fragments we found in Callie's hair will soon be made, if it hasn't been already. I follow Izzy to the workshop, where we find Richmond and a cadre of other police officers, including Junior Feller and Ron Colbert, searching through all the minutiae there.

Richmond sees us enter and gives us a nod. "Well, as you can see, Hurley is into metalwork and I'm betting that if we compare the metal bits found in Callie Dunkirk's hair to the ones here, we'll get a match." He walks over and picks up a plastic bag containing a photo. "And then there's this," he says, handing it to us.

I look at the photo which is of Hurley and another man standing behind a picnic table, both decked out in fishing gear. Hurley is holding up a large walleye and grinning from ear to ear. The other man is holding one up, too, though his is a bit smaller. Lying on the table in front of them is a knife: the same one with the carved ivory handle we found buried in Callie Dunkirk's chest.

Izzy gives me a look that's half apology, half I-told-you-so. I look at Richmond and say, "So you think Hurley killed Callie?"

Richmond bites his lip and looks skeptical but he says, "The evidence seems to say so."

"But why would he do that?"

"He dated her for nearly a year when he lived in Chicago. And Callie Dunkirk has a son who was born around eight months after she and Hurley split up." Richmond shrugs. "Do the math. If Hurley fathered a child by Miss Dunkirk it suggests all sorts of motives. And the fact that we found his prints on the gas can at your house certainly makes it look like he's the one who set the fire, presumably with the intent to kill your husband. Did Izzy tell you about the altercation David had with Hurley the other day?"

I nod.

"That would seem to suggest that Hurley has issues where the women in his life are concerned."

"I'm not a woman in Hurley's life," I say quickly. "At least not in that way."

Nobody in the room contradicts me, but the momentary pause in the action and the deafening silence that follows suggest that everyone who heard me is waiting for someone to do so.

"Okay, yes, there was an attraction in the beginning," I explain, feeling the pressure. "But we've moved beyond that. Hurley and I work together, nothing more."

Still no one moves, and it's as if everyone in the room is waiting for a cue.

Richmond, thank goodness, finally gives them one. "There's also evidence linking Hurley to Minniver's death," he continues, and with his words, the others in the room resume whatever they were doing. "We found this here in his garage." He holds up another evidence bag and I see a container of potassium cyanide inside. "We also found a loose key in a drawer over there."

He points to the same drawer that Hurley opened the other night when he pulled out the pair of earrings he gave me, earrings I realize I'm still wearing. It's all I can do to resist the sudden urge I have to reach up and remove them.

Had that key been inside that drawer the other night? I try to recall what I saw when I looked in there. I don't remember seeing a key but I can't be certain. It might have been hidden beneath the many envelopes of jewelry.

Richmond continues skewering Hurley. "Colbert told me

about the missing spare key Minniver kept inside his front porch light, so I had one of the officers take the key we found here over to Minniver's house and try it. Want to guess what we found?"

"It was Minniver's key," I say with a sickening feeling.

"Bingo," Richmond says. He shakes his head and frowns. "I don't know what to think. I've always found Hurley to be a pretty straight-up guy and he's a good cop as far as his abilities go, but I have to admit, all this evidence is pretty damning."

Doubt rears its ugly head and I feel my hopes sinking faster than Toyota stock after the stuck accelerator debacle.

One of the evidence techs on scene, who has just finished taping black paper over the windows in the room, says to Richmond, "I'm ready whenever you are."

Richmond nods his acknowledgment and then waves us back toward the kitchen. "Given the evidence we've found, we suspect that this might be the scene of Miss Dunkirk's murder," he explains. "So we're going to Luminol the room."

Izzy and I back into the kitchen doorway and Richmond flips the light switch for the garage, plunging the room into darkness. There is enough ambient light from the kitchen for us to see what's going on, however, and we watch as the evidence tech starts spraying his Luminol solution on the floor of the garage. If there is blood here, the Luminol will turn fluorescent blue for about thirty seconds and one of the cops is standing by with a camera to snap pictures in case that happens.

For the first couple of minutes, nothing happens as the tech backs his way across the garage, skirting the center worktable and sweeping the floor with the Luminol spray. As we watch, Izzy leans over to me and whispers, "Do you remember that hair you found in Callie's wound?"

I nod, but say nothing. My throat feels like someone has a stranglehold on it.

"It was short and black, like Hurley's," Izzy goes on.

I nod again, fighting back an unexpected sting of tears. Then everything goes to hell when the evidence tech sprays an area a few feet in front of us. The floor turns fluorescent blue in a few spots. The cop with the camera fires away and I'm momentarily blinded by the flash. My mind scrambles for an explanation, thinking that Hurley could have cut himself here in the shop and the blood could be his. I also seem to remember reading somewhere that copper can cause a false positive reading with Luminol and there's plenty of copper in the room. Bleach can also cause a positive test and maybe Hurley used some to clean up the floor as part of his routine maintenance.

But before I can voice these thoughts, the evidence tech sprays again and over the next minute or so, a narrow smear of blood is highlighted, trailing from the area of the first few drops over to the bay door. It doesn't take a rocket scientist to imagine a body creating that trail as it was being dragged across the floor.

My heart sinks, and as the bright flashes from the camera mark the findings, my last glimmer of hope fades faster than the blue fluorescence of the Luminol.

Chapter 32

I assist Izzy with his part of processing Hurley's house—the collection of possible blood evidence from cracks in the floor near the bay door—in a state of numb fog. Every part of me wants to believe in Hurley but Richmond is right; the evidence is both damning and overwhelming. And now, because David knows about my alliance with Hurley and the evidence I've shared with him, I fear my career is lost, for it's only a matter of time before Izzy finds out.

I know in my heart that Hurley didn't do this but I'm afraid to trust my heart. My mind is a different matter however, and when I analyze things as objectively as I can, my mind comes to the same conclusion my heart did.

I'm standing next to Hurley's workbench, labeling a sample, when I make my decision. I turn around and call out Richmond's name.

He stops what he's doing—writing out a narrative report—and looks at me.

"Listen," I say, "I know that when it comes to Hurley all

of you think I'm about as objective as the Ku Klux Klan is toward Obama. But I have to tell you, none of this makes any sense. I mean, think about it. Hurley is a good cop . . . you said so yourself, Richmond. He has good instincts and as far as we know, a good reputation. What's more, he's also pretty savvy when it comes to crime scene evidence. So why, if he committed all these crimes, would he be so sloppy about leaving evidence behind?"

Richmond shrugs and says, "Maybe he's had some sort of psychotic break and his mind is no longer thinking clearly. Maybe this medical problem he took leave for is a psychiatric issue of some sort."

"But if that were true, how is it he had the sense to hide Callie's car, and to move her body? Why wouldn't he just leave it all here?"

"Maybe he didn't fully snap until after Callie's murder. Maybe it was Minniver's that pushed him to the edge," Richmond says.

I turn and look at Izzy. "You saw Hurley yesterday morning at the hospital. Did he seem like a psycho to you?"

Izzy thinks about it for a minute and then says, "No, if anything he seemed nervous."

"Yes!" I say. "And if he'd had such a severe psychotic break at that point, do you think he'd look nervous?"

Several of the people in the room frown and look at one another, as if they hope to find the answers.

"I'm not buying it," I tell the room. "At least not yet. The Hurley I know isn't capable of something like this. And yes, I realize that I don't know him all that well, but I think he deserves the benefit of the doubt. He's a cop. He's one of you. If the situation was reversed and one of you was under suspicion, wouldn't you want your cohorts to do everything possible to make damned sure you were really guilty before throwing the book at you? Wouldn't you want them to give you some benefit of doubt?" I don't wait for any of them to answer. "I would." I look Richmond straight in the eye. "I would do it for you, Richmond. You know I would." I shift my gaze to Larry Johnson, one of the other cops in the room and someone who has harbored a small crush on me for years. "I would do it for you, too, Larry." Next I look at the uniforms, one at a time. "And I'd do it for you, and you, and you." They all look away from me wearing slightly embarrassed expressions.

"All I'm saying is that Hurley deserves nothing less than our best. He deserves the benefit of our doubt and a promise that we will look at all the evidence and consider it in every possible light. My gut tells me that Hurley is a very smart guy, too smart to leave behind evidence as obvious as his hair embedded in Callie's wound, or his father's one-of-a-kind, highly distinctive knife buried in her chest, or Minniver's key sitting in plain sight in his drawer here. I mean, do you really think he's stupid enough to leave behind a gas can with his handwriting and fingerprints on it if he set that fire at my house? Or stupid enough to use his personal gas can at all for that matter? Even a dumb kid would have enough sense to buy a cheap generic gas can and use that instead of one that has identifying information on it. And if he did commit these murders, why would he step back from the investigations? He left the scene where we found Callie's body almost as soon as he got there, and yet if he'd stayed and handled the investigation, he could have hidden and manipulated the evidence to hide his guilt. It just doesn't make sense. Maybe you guys are ready to hang him based on all of that, but I'm willing to give him the presumption of innocence until I'm one hundred percent sure he's guilty."

I've been talking so fast and with so much enthusiasm

that I'm nearly out of breath. I pause to catch it and study the faces of the others in the room. To my delight I see some wavering and doubt there, so I push on.

"Richmond, how much do you know about Hurley's past when he was on the force in Chicago?"

Richmond blinks several times very fast and then says, "Not much."

"Have you talked to any of his prior coworkers? Have you looked into what kind of cop he was down there? Were there any hints of mental instability, or corruption, or anything like that when he was there?"

Richmond arches his brows and sighs. "I don't know."

"Then don't you think we should look into that and try to find out what kind of person his coworkers thought he was before we convict him?"

"She's right," Larry says, and even though I don't know if he's agreeing with me because he actually believes what I'm saying or because he's merely trying to earn Brownie points from me, I'm grateful for his support. "I've worked with Hurley for a little over six months now and I have to confess, I don't see him doing something like this."

One of the uniforms pipes up. "I agree. The guy has always been kind, civil, and polite whenever I've worked with him. And I know some crazy and evil people are good at putting forth a very convincing façade, but Hurley seems real. Real enough that I think Mattie's right . . . he deserves the benefit of our doubt until we know otherwise."

Several of the guys nod and I know I've gotten my point across. Richmond says, "You raise some good points, Mattie. But it would certainly help the situation if Hurley was here to address some of these issues."

"Give him time," I say. "That's all I'm asking, that you give him time and a fair analysis of all the evidence."

Richmond nods thoughtfully and says, "Okay then. Back

to work, people." He takes out his cell phone, starts punching in a number, and heads into the house while the others in the room go back to what they were doing. I turn and look at Izzy, who's been standing quietly behind me the entire time. I'm not sure what I expect to see on his face, but the dark, thunderous expression he's wearing definitely isn't it.

"What?" I say to him. "You don't agree with me?"

"Oh, I agree with everything in your little pep speech," he says, his lips tight as he speaks. "But I think you and I need to have a little chat of our own. The sooner the better."

He turns away from me and focuses on the remaining evidence, but when I try to assist him, he pushes my hands away and won't let me touch anything. I can tell he's angry, but I'm not sure why. Is it because I broke the promise I made to him to be objective?

A little while later, after we've finished collecting the blood evidence, he says, "We're done here. Pack up your kit."

I do so while he does the same. He then turns to Larry Johnson and says, "You guys can finish up here. We're going to head back to the office and get started on this blood analysis."

I follow Izzy out to the car, puzzled by his cold shoulder reaction and trying to guess what has set him off. As soon as we have all our stuff loaded into the hearse and climb into the front seat, I ask him.

"What's wrong, Izzy? Are you mad because I spoke up about Hurley?"

"Drive us to the office," he says, staring out the front window. "We'll talk there."

I start the car and pull out while Izzy takes out his cell phone and calls Arnie. "Meet us in the garage," he says. "I need you to take charge of this evidence we've just collected and process it ASAP."

We make the journey wrapped in an awkward silence and when we pull into the garage, Arnie is waiting for us. Izzy instructs him on what the evidence is and what he wants done with it while I lean against the wall, feeling like I'm waiting for the head soldier to finish instructing the firing squad.

As soon as Izzy is done with Arnie, he looks at me all tight-lipped and says, "Let's go to the library."

I follow him inside, dread growing with every step. As soon as we enter, Izzy shuts the door behind us with a bit more force than is necessary. "Sit," he says, yanking out a chair.

I do so while Izzy walks around to the other side of the table. He leans forward, his hands on the tabletop, and says, "Do you want to tell me how it is you know that Hurley's knife is his father's, or how you know it's one of a kind? Or how you know there was writing on the gas can when you never saw it?"

Oh, crap. I realize too late to do myself any good that I got a bit carried away during my little speech in Hurley's garage. My mind scrambles to find some way to explain myself, but the look on Izzy's face freezes my brain. I've never seen him this angry before.

"You've been talking to Hurley, haven't you?" he says.

"We've chatted a couple of times. He—"

"You two have been in cahoots right from the start on all of this, haven't you?"

"I wouldn't call it cahoots," I argue, wondering what the hell a cahoot even is. "But I believe him when he says someone is framing him. It doesn't make any se—"

"Damn it, Mattie!" Izzy seethes, pounding a fist on the table and making me jump. "Do you realize what you've done?"

"He didn't kill anyone, Izzy," I fire back.

"You can't know that for sure," he yells.

I open my mouth to argue the point, even though my only supporting evidence is my gut feeling, but Izzy doesn't let me get a single word out.

"And whether or not you *think* Hurley did it isn't what matters. What matters is the fact that you did what you did behind my back. That is inexcusable, Mattie. Not only have you possibly compromised evidence and our investigation, you have undermined this office and betrayed my trust in you. I gave you this job because I thought you were someone with integrity, someone I could trust to be fair-minded and completely scientific in your judgments." He pauses, looks at me, and then shakes his head woefully. "I need to reconsider whether or not you are appropriate for this position."

All my blood sinks to my feet, leaving me feeling dazed, stunned, and frightened. "Izzy, I'm sorry. Please, don't take my job away from me. I did what I thought was right at the time."

He stares at me, and the disappointment I see on his face is crushing. "I need some time to think about all of this. Go home. I'll let you know when I've reached a decision."

Chapter 33

I drive home in a deep funk, wondering if I've just made the worst decision of my life other than the one I made when I married David. And speaking of David, he is still at the cottage when I get there, sitting on the couch watching TV.

As soon as I walk in he picks up the remote and flicks the TV off. "I've been waiting for you," he says.

"Whatever it is, I'm not in the mood, David," I say sullenly. I head for the kitchen, take a pint of Cherry Garcia out of the freezer, and rip the lid off. After digging a spoon out of the drawer, I stand next to the counter and start eating.

David comes out and raises his eyebrows at me, but to his credit all he says is, "Rough day?"

"Something like that."

"I've booked a suite at the Sorenson Motel and if you'll give me a ride over there, I'll be out of your hair and you can have the place back to yourself."

"Okay. Just let me finish this," I say, proffering the ice

cream container. I scoop out another spoonful and shove it in my mouth.

"I spoke with our insurance agent and she came out to look over what's left of the house with me this morning. Because of the holiday, we probably won't get anything done until the early part of next week, though she's working on getting me a rental car by morning. She said we should have a check for the house soon so we can tear down what's left and rebuild."

I look over at David feeling mad as hell, though I'm not sure if it's him I'm mad at or myself. I realize that the money from the insurance settlement is more important to me now than ever. If I get fired from my job, I'm going to need that money to live on, and probably to find a new place to live. Remaining here as Izzy's tenant will be too awkward.

"Half of that money is mine, David, and I have no intention of using my half to build you a new house."

"Yes, I realize that, which is why I also contacted an attorney today. I'm prepared to make you an offer. I'll sign your divorce papers as long as you don't ask for any type of alimony. I'm willing to split the house money sixty-forty, and I'll use my portion to rebuild something that will be in my name only. It will be smaller, but that house was too big for me anyway."

"I want half the money, David."

"I don't think you understand. I'm offering you the sixty percent," he says, making me nearly drop my spoon. "To compensate you for the value in the land the house stands on, which won't be included in the insurance settlement."

"Seriously?"

"Yes, seriously."

"Why the sudden change of heart?"

"Because I know now that you've had a change of heart

with regards to me so there isn't much sense in dragging things out any longer. It's time to cut my losses and move on."

I narrow my eyes at him, suspicious of his sudden acquiescence. But I can't afford to question his motives for too long. I need that money.

"Okay, you have a deal. But it has to be in writing, as a formal part of the divorce settlement."

"No problem. I'll have my attorney draw up the papers next week."

I turn my back to him to toss my spoon in the sink and recap my ice cream, hoping to hide the shock and suspicion I'm feeling. I'm tickled that things have been so easily resolved yet it all feels too easy. There's more to the story, I'm certain of it. The question is what.

"I'm going to load my stuff into your . . . car." He says this last word with obvious distaste. "Let me know when you're ready." He turns and walks back to the living room, grabs several of last night's shopping bags, and carries them outside to the hearse.

I head for the bathroom to pee, but also to have a private moment to think. If David carries through on his end of our bargain, it will eliminate some of the immediate financial pressure if I do lose my job. But it won't lessen my sense of loss. I truly like what I'm doing now. Oddly enough, the job suits me and I've been looking forward to learning more and expanding my duties. While the settlement David is offering is generous, it's hardly enough to allow me to live a lifetime of leisure. I'll still need some type of job, and while I could go back to the hospital to work, I don't want to.

Plus there's Izzy. Losing my job would be upsetting, but losing Izzy as my friend would be devastating. Somehow I have to make things right again.

By the time I come out of the bathroom, David has all his stuff loaded into the hearse. Our ride to the motel is a silent one and when we get there, our only utterances are a few polite "I got it" comments as I help him carry his stuff into his temporary new home. As I carry the last of the bags into his suite and drop them on the counter of his tiny kitchenette, there is an awkward moment where we both stand there staring at one another, trying to find the right thing to say. This is such a momentous juncture in our lives that I feel the need to say something meaningful and profound. But in the end all I come up with is "Gotta go," before hurrying back out to my car.

I've got an hour before I'm supposed to meet Richmond at Slim's Dungeon for our next torture session and I'm tempted to blow it off given that my body is still in agony from yesterday's session. Then I figure some physical exertion may help me get rid of some of the frustration and anger I have pent up inside, not to mention the ice cream I just ate.

After trying once more to call Callie's sister, Andi, and getting her voice mail again, I drive home to let Hoover out and to change into my loose-fitting dungeon clothes, momentarily imagining myself in some cute, tight-fitting little leotard like some of the other women at the gym had on. Since I have a little time, I decide to make a quick run to the store to see if I can find some more suitable gym wear.

Ten minutes later, I'm inside a dressing room trying to squeeze into the largest size leotard the store has. It's a struggle—the thing is at least two sizes too small—but I'm hoping that all that elastic material will not only stretch to accommodate my body, but that it might help hold certain parts of it in and keep them from jiggling.

When I finally get it all the way on, I look in the mirror. The forgiving Lycra isn't. Every seam is strained as tight as it can be and I can barely breathe. I fear that if I bump into something with the least little bit of force, my fat will burst out of the leotard like popping-fresh dough from the can.

Resigned to looking frumpy, I get back into my sweatpants and T-shirt and head out of the store with my head hung low.

When I arrive at the gym I park out back in my designated hiding spot behind the building. I'm a few minutes early and Richmond isn't here yet, so after a few brief warm-up exercises, I head for the birthing chair machine and begin my workout. Helga is there and after a brief greeting, she leaves me to my own devices. I make my way through the circuit the way she showed me the day before but my performance isn't the best because my muscles are protesting every move. I keep an eye out for Richmond the entire time, but he never shows up.

By the time I'm done with my workout, I've dreamed up a hundred different names I'm going to call Richmond the next time I see him, none of them very ladylike. I'm muttering to myself as I leave the gym, rehearsing what I'm going to say as I dial Richmond's number on my cell. He doesn't answer—not surprising since I'm sure he knows I'm going to rip him a new one—and it flips over to voice mail just as I get to my car. With my keys in one hand and my cell in the other, I give him a piece of my mind.

"Richmond, you lying piece of shit. I'm at the gym and you're not. Now you're a dead man for sure because if your fat doesn't kill you, I'm going to. You better call me."

I disconnect the call and put my key in the door of the hearse to unlock it when my phone rings. Thinking it's Richmond, I answer without bothering to look at the caller ID. "You better have a damned good excuse for not being here. That fat of yours isn't going to disappear on its own, you know."

"What about my fat?"

Shit. "I'm sorry, Izzy. I thought you were Bob Richmond." I grimace, knowing that I've probably just made it that much easier for him to fire me.

"Actually, Richmond is here with me. I've got some new evidence regarding Callie Dunkirk's murder," he says. "Can you come to the office?"

"Sure. I'll be there in five minutes. Does this mean you haven't fired me yet?"

I hear footsteps approaching behind me and I turn to see who it is. But before I can, I hear a strange crackling noise—like firecrackers going off in my left ear—and then the left side of my neck burns like someone just lit it on fire. My body is wracked with a sudden, searing pain and I hear myself scream as my brain explodes in a flash of blinding light.

Chapter 34

The next few minutes are a kaleidoscope of fractured sounds and images: my body colliding with the hard pavement; my left ankle screaming with pain; someone grabbing me beneath my arms; my body being slowly dragged across the parking lot; someone grunting; a man's voice yelling—*Hurley?*—and then another collision with the pavement; feet running off; and then, miraculously, Hurley's voice close to my ear.

"Can you stand?" he asks me, sounding breathless. He grabs my hands and tries to pull me up but my left ankle refuses to support much weight. Hurley drapes my right arm over his shoulders, grabs me around my waist, and hoists me across the small parking lot. "Come on, we need to get out of here," he says, and the urgency in his voice helps me to get past the pain.

Hurley drags me to his car, which is parked at the far end of the front lot, dumps me into the passenger side, slams my door closed, and runs around to hop behind the wheel. "Can you fasten your seat belt?" he asks as he starts the engine. He doesn't wait for an answer, whipping the steering wheel hard and hitting the gas. As the car lurches forward, I fumble with my belt, trying to clasp it in place. I manage to do it but it's a struggle, both because I'm being tossed around by Hurley's driving and because my fingers don't seem to want to work. My head feels as if it's been overstuffed with cotton—dull, thick, and like my skull wants to explode.

"What the hell just happened?" I manage to say once I get my belt secured.

"You were Tasered. I'm guessing that whoever is framing me just tried to kidnap you."

"Kidnap *me?*" I can't wrap my mind around the concept at all. "Why?"

"Most likely they were going to use you to try to flush me out, or kill you to frame me for yet another death."

Kill me? Someone just tried to kill me? A million questions fill my head and I start firing them at Hurley. "How did they find me? Who is doing this? And how did you know they'd be coming after me?"

"I didn't for sure," he says, answering only the last question. "But I figured my disappearance wasn't a part of their plans, and that they would escalate their efforts somehow to flush me out. You were the logical choice. That guy back there at the gym has been following you since yesterday and I've been following him, waiting for him to make a move."

"That's why you were outside my bedroom window last night."

"Yes."

"Who is he?"

"I don't know," Hurley says with a frustrated sigh. "I've never gotten a good look at him because he's always wearing a hoodie. About all I can tell you is that he was short and of average build. I think it may be the same guy Minniver's neighbor lady saw."

"Did you get the plate number on the car?"

"I did. I have it written down somewhere but I didn't want to go to or call the station to run it. I'm willing to bet it's the same number you got from the neighbor."

I shake my head, hoping to knock some of the cotton loose. "I still don't get it," I say, confused. "Why come after me? Why am I the logical choice? What did I do?"

He lets out a humorless laugh. "You met me."

"Huh?"

"They've been going after people who play a significant role in my life, people who mean something to me."

"I mean something to you?" I say, grabbing at the only part of his explanation that my mind can fully comprehend at the moment.

He looks over at me and smiles, but says nothing.

"Where are we going?"

"Over near Tomah. There's a cabin there we can stay in."

"You own a cabin?"

"No, it belongs to a friend I know who lets me use it. When my dad was alive, we used to go there to fish a lot."

"Your dad is dead?"

"Two years ago. Cancer."

"Is your mom still alive?"

He shakes his head. "She died in a car accident when I was two. I really don't remember her at all."

"Did your dad ever remarry?"

"Nope, it was just the two of us."

I digest this information, saddened by the fact that Hurley has no family. That explains why whoever is trying to frame him is going after friends and neighbors, and why they came after me. I suppose at this point, I'm the closest thing to family Hurley has.

My head is clearer now and thoughts of family make me think of Thanksgiving, which makes me think of my mother, Dom, and Izzy. Then I remember Izzy's phone call to me, right before I was attacked. I lean forward and look around inside the car. "Where's my purse, and my cell? I need to call Izzy and tell him what happened. He's expecting me."

"Your purse got left in the parking lot," Hurley says. "Your cell phone is there, too. It bounced under your car when you dropped it and broke into at least two pieces. I wanted to get you out of there in case your attacker had some kind of backup waiting in the wings, so I didn't take the time to grab anything."

"That's okay. I appreciate what you did. Can I use your phone?"

He shakes his head. "Cell phones can be traced, and until I can figure out who's behind all of this, I don't want my whereabouts—or yours—to be known."

Something about this bothers me but it takes me a minute to figure out what it is. "Wait," I say. "That throwaway phone you gave me is in my purse and it has your cell number in it. Won't they be able to trace it from that?"

"Did you save my number under a different name like I told you?"

"I did. I assigned it to Ethan."

"Then they won't know it's mine."

I wince. "They might," I tell him. "David overheard my last conversation with you. He was in my cottage and I didn't see him right away."

Hurley frowns. He reaches into his jacket pocket, takes out a cell phone, and hands it to me. "Turn it off. As long as it isn't on, no one can locate it. If they do get the number somehow and trace the calls made to or from the phone to see what towers it pinged on, they'll think I'm still in the Sorenson area."

I open the phone and start to turn it off, but hesitate. "Hurley, that guy at the gym came after me while I was on the phone with Izzy. He was with Richmond and they were expecting me to meet them at the morgue. Izzy must have heard me yell and when I don't show up, he'll be worried and send Richmond out looking for me. I should let him know I'm okay."

Hurley doesn't answer right away but I can tell he's thinking.

"Please?"

Hurley cusses under his breath and rakes a hand through his hair, leaving it tousled and messy looking. There's an exit coming up and he turns on his blinker to take it. "Let's stop here and grab a bite to eat," he says. "Turn the phone off for now. I need to think."

He steers into a McDonald's drive-through while I shut down the cell phone. I order a Quarter Pounder with cheese and some fries, effectively negating the workout I did earlier. I try to mitigate the damage by getting a diet Mountain Dew to go with it and the thought that I'm no better than Richmond comes to mind, but I shove it aside. Hurley orders a Big Mac, fries, and a regular soda. He parks in a distant space at the back of the lot and we sit inside the car eating in silence.

The food gives new life to my frazzled brain and as I watch Hurley stare out the window, his brow furrowed in thought, I remember that I have other things to tell him.

"Do you want to know about the search warrant they exercised on your house today?"

"I don't know. Do I?" he asks, looking pained. "Did they find anything?"

"Well, they found that potassium cyanide stuff in your workshop and they collected some metal fragments that I'm betting will match ones we found in Callie's hair. Plus Minniver apparently kept a spare key to his house hidden inside the light on his front porch, but it's missing. They found it in that drawer where you kept these earrings." I touch one of the delicate filigrees still hanging from my ears.

Hurley's face darkens. "Is that it?" he asks.

"Afraid not," I say, wincing. "They also sprayed Luminol in your workshop and they found a blood smear on the floor leading to the exterior door. We sampled some blood we found in the threshold to do a DNA comparison with Callie's blood."

Hurley squeezes his eyes closed. "I'm sure it will match," he says. "Smart bastards. I'll give them that."

After another period of silent eating, I say, "What about calling Izzy? I don't want him to worry and the last thing we need is a big manhunt focused on me."

Hurley nods. "I have an idea, but it means letting Izzy know you're with me and that you're going to stay hidden for now. It might put your job in jeopardy."

I let out a mirthless laugh. "Too late for that," I tell him. "Izzy already knows I've been keeping secrets from him regarding this case and he's contemplating firing me."

Hurley leans his head back against the headrest and sighs. "I'm sorry, Mattie. I never should have dragged you into this. I didn't know who else to turn to."

"It's okay. You didn't force me into it; I did it willingly. I knew what the consequences were."

"How did Izzy find out?"

"I got a bit profusive defending you during the search of your house and revealed some knowledge I shouldn't have had. Izzy picked up on it right away."

"He's a very smart man."

"Yes, he is. So, what's this plan of yours?"

Hurley sits up and leans forward, staring out the front windshield at the surrounding lot. "We're about half an hour from home now, so I'm going to turn around and head back."

"Back to Sorenson?" I ask with a have-you-lost-your-mind tone.

"Well, back *toward* Sorenson, but we won't go into town. Once we get close I'm going to head east and after we've traveled for a half hour or so, you can turn the phone on. Then I want you to make either one very long call or two calls, to make sure the phone pings off of at least two different towers heading in an easterly direction. Once we've made the calls, we turn the phone off, head north and west, and make our way back toward Tomah. That way we can give Izzy a heads-up while also giving the impression that we're heading east. Hopefully that will throw people off the trail."

"It's a start, but what are we going to do once we get to this cabin of yours?"

"I don't know," he says with a shrug. "I guess we lie low and wait for whoever's behind this to make their next move."

Chapter 35

Sometime later we're headed toward Milwaukee on back highways and Hurley gives me the go-ahead. I turn the cell phone on and start to dial Izzy's number when it hits me that I don't know what it is. The number was plugged into my phone's memory by Izzy himself and all I ever had to do to call him was hit two buttons.

"You don't happen to know Izzy's number, do you?" I ask Hurley.

"Not from memory," he says. "Don't you know it?"

"Nope. It was programmed into my phone as one of my speed numbers so I've never had to dial it."

Hurley thinks a minute and then says, "I suppose we could call information."

"It won't help. Izzy's cell phone is an unlisted number."

"Wait, didn't you say Izzy wanted you to meet him at the office when he called? Do you know that number?"

I shake my head. "I do, but I doubt he's still there. Even if he is, he doesn't usually answer the main office phone. He lets it flip over to voice mail."

Hurley white-knuckles the steering wheel and scowls. Then his face lights up. "You said the throwaway phone was in your purse, right?"

"Yes."

"That number we have. Call it."

"But if it's in my purse—" I see where he's going then and smile. "Ah, very smart, Hurley. You're thinking they might have found my car by now."

He nods. "Izzy knew you were at the gym when you were attacked, right?"

"Yes, I think so. I thought it was Richmond calling and since he was supposed to meet me there, I started cursing him as soon as I answered. Richmond should remember our gym appointment and figure out that that's where I was. Plus I left a message on Richmond's cell phone."

"And judging from the way things will look when they find your car, I'm sure they'll be treating it as a crime scene. They'll have your purse with that throwaway cell in it, and when it rings, they'll answer it."

"Yeah, but *who* will answer it?"

"Doesn't matter," Hurley says. "Just insist on talking to Izzy."

"Assuming he's there. What if he isn't?"

"I consider myself a pretty good judge of character and I'm willing to bet Izzy will be there."

I pull up the number of my cell—the only one stored in Hurley's phone—and dial it. It rings several times on the other end and just when I'm about to tell Hurley no one is answering, someone does.

"Hello?" I recognize the voice as Bob Richmond's.

"Bob? It's Mattie Winston."

"Mattie! Where the hell are you? Are you all right?"

"I'm fine, but things got a bit dicey earlier. Are you at the gym?"

"I am. I'm by your car. What the hell happened?"

"It's a long story."

"Give me the abbreviated version."

"Someone tried to kidnap me."

"Kidnap you? Who?"

"I don't know who it was. I take it you didn't find anyone with my car?"

"No, all we found was your purse lying on the ground, along with your keys and your broken cell phone. What's with this other phone? Where are you?"

"I'm okay."

"That's not what I asked. You need to come back here."

"That's not going to happen, Bob, at least not yet. Is Izzy with you by any chance?"

"He is."

"Can I talk to him please?"

I hear Richmond mutter a curse and then some muffled sounds that make me suspect he has his hand over the phone so he can talk without me hearing him. A moment later, Izzy comes on the line.

"Mattie, what the hell is going on? Are you okay?"

"I'm fine, Izzy. I had a white knight ride in at the last minute to save me." I see Hurley shoot me an amused look.

There's a moment of silence on the phone and then Izzy says, "Hold on a sec."

I wait, wondering what he's doing. Is he helping Richmond trace the call?

"Okay," Izzy says finally. "I wanted to step away from everyone else so I can talk to you without being overheard. Are you with Hurley?"

I hesitate, knowing the answer might seal my fate with regard to my job. "I am," I admit. "But he didn't do these killings, Izzy. There's someone else involved and that some-one tried to kidnap me. Hurley said the guy has been follow-ing me the past couple of days. He thinks they did it to get to him, to try to flush him out."

"Why would they think that would work?"

"Because I'm the closest thing to family Hurley has."

There is another pause and I hear Izzy sigh on the other end. "Okay," he says finally. "I'm not totally convinced Hur-ley isn't involved, but I did find something that points toward someone else being Callie Dunkirk's killer."

"What?"

"Well, when I looked at the X-rays again, I realized that the angle of the knife ran from left to right and more or less straight in, perpendicular to the body. So did the track for the other wound. That suggests both a left-handed killer and someone who is close to the victim in height, which is around five-foot-six. And if I remember correctly, Hurley is right-handed and about six-foot-four."

"Yes, he is. That's great news, Izzy." The excited tone in my voice makes Hurley look over at me with a questioning expression. "Did you share that information with Rich-mond?"

"I did, but he isn't completely swayed. He thinks the knife angle might have been affected by the positions of the peo-ple involved, or that Hurley could have hired someone to do the killings. He's going to look into Hurley's financial affairs next to see if there is any suspect activity. But I think the knife angles, along with that little speech you gave earlier, are enough to make both him and me want to dig a little deeper."

"Good. At least he's willing to give Hurley the benefit of a doubt."

"What are you and Hurley going to do?"

"I don't know. Hide out for now. Try to come up with something."

"He needs to come in, Mattie. If he's innocent, we'll find a way to prove it."

"But if he's in jail he won't be able to investigate things on his own. And whoever's behind this seems to have a pretty extensive reach."

Izzy sighs again. "Okay, but promise me you won't do anything stupid."

"Based on your earlier reaction, I think I already have."

"Yeah, about that . . . we'll talk some more. If it turns out Hurley has nothing to do with this, I'll find a way for you to keep your job."

"Thank you, Izzy. I owe you big."

"Yes, you do."

"So I guess it's rather presumptuous of me to ask you for one more favor?"

"What now?"

"I need someone to take care of Hoover and Rubbish for me until I can get back."

Izzy chuckles. "No problem. Just know that if Dom spends too much time with Hoover you might not get him back."

I hang up the phone, and while I'm turning it off I tell Hurley what Izzy told me about the angles of the knife wound and Richmond's plan to look into Hurley's finances. "It sounds like Richmond is at least keeping an open mind," I conclude.

"It's a start," Hurley says, turning the car around and heading back the way we came. "But if I don't come up with something else pretty soon, you and I may both end up behind bars."

Chapter 36

The remainder of our drive is done by the light of a full moon, a good thing because after stopping at a twenty-four-hour gas mart to pick up some staples, Hurley drives us deep into the woods along a rutted, dirt road. I'm feeling like Hansel and Gretel when we arrive at our little hidey-hole, which turns out to be more a shack than a cabin. The scary thing is I suspect it looks better now than it really is and once daylight arrives, all its flaws will be clearly visible—assuming we survive the night. It's basically a one-room, wooden structure with a front porch that's falling off and a roof that looks like it's sagging in the center and ready to cave in any moment.

"Is this place safe?" I ask Hurley, getting out of the car. The night air has turned bitterly cold and I wrap my arms around myself in an effort to get warm. I'm only feeling the cold because it's so early in the season. Eventually we Wisconsinites adjust to the frigid temps of winter and by February, when any normal person would think Hell is frozen over, we might open our schools an hour or two late. "And does it have heat?"

"It's a little rough," Hurley admits, eyeing the place. "I haven't been here for a while but it will have to do for now. Come on, where's your camping spirit?"

"Camping spirit? You got the wrong girl. My idea of roughing it is a hotel without room service."

Hurley grabs a flashlight from the car and uses it to examine some rocks beside the stairs. A moment later he lifts one of the rocks, produces a key, and unlocks the door.

From what I can see in the beam of the flashlight, the inside of the cabin isn't much better than the outside. The place is primarily furnished with cobwebs and the few pieces of human furniture look like something I might see at the estate sale of someone's great-grandmother. The air smells musty and damp, and I hear something scurrying about off in one corner.

"I think I should have let Parking Lot Guy grab me," I say. "I'm betting his accommodations would have been better."

"Assuming he let you live long enough to enjoy them," Hurley fired back.

Well, yeah, there is that.

"I need to go outside and start up the generator." He turns to leave, taking the only light source with him.

"I'm going with you," I say, falling into step behind him.

I'm relieved to discover that the generator, which is at the back of the house beside a huge pile of chopped wood, has a large fuel tank attached to it. Hurley checks the gauge and says, "Good, there's plenty." As soon as he gets the generator started, he loads us both up with wood from the pile and we head back inside.

A short while later we have lights, our packages have been hauled in, and Hurley is stacking wood in the fireplace, which fortunately comes equipped with matches and a basket filled with packets of firelighter stuff.

"This should help brighten the place up," Hurley says when he strikes a match and puts it to the firelighter. A few minutes later the kindling catches and the wood starts to crackle.

The fire is warm and reassuring, but a more pressing need comes to light. I turn around to look at the rest of the place and that's when it hits me. "Hurley, where are the facilities?"

"Facilities?"

"You know, the bathroom?"

He picks up the flashlight and hands it to me. "Outside and around to the left," he says.

I stare at him, dumbfounded. "You're kidding, right?"

"Afraid not. There's toilet paper on the shelf by the door over there. Want me to go with you and hold your hand?"

"No. But I wish you'd told me about this before I ordered a caffeinated drink with dinner." I take the flashlight, grab the toilet paper, and head back outside in the direction he mentioned. There, on the other side of the cabin in all its smelly, ramshackle glory, is the outhouse.

I walk over and open the door, shining the flashlight inside. "Great," I mutter as I look at the bench with two holes cut into it side by side. "A high-class outhouse." I step inside and shine the light down into one of the holes. Just a few inches below the seat is a tower of spiderwebs with a half dozen little spiders in it and one gigantic one that I swear is as big as the burger I ate for dinner. I shine the light into the second hole, relieved to see that this one doesn't have an arachnid condo built inside.

I don't think I've ever peed so fast in my entire life, and when I'm done, I use the flashlight to examine my crotch and the inside of my pants before I pull them back up, just to make sure nothing has tried to move in and homestead either spot.

Back inside, I'm delighted to see that the fire is now a roaring, crackling source of heat and reassurance. I return the toilet paper to the shelf and walk over to the fireplace, turning my back to it to warm up.

"Glad to see you didn't fall in," Hurley says.

"Or become some giant spider's bitch," I toss back. "Have you looked down those holes out there? It's the New York City of Spidervilles. And I'm pretty sure I saw a red hourglass on the belly of one of the residents." I shudder at the memory and edge a little closer to the fire.

"I use them for target practice," Hurley says with a grin.

With nature's call out of the way, my mind takes in the rest of the room. There's a couch facing the fireplace, a card table with two folding chairs, a utility sink in what I'm guessing is supposed to be the kitchen—though I notice it has no faucets—and a number of built-in shelves and cabinets.

After taking note of what is here, I then notice what isn't: a bed.

"Where are we going to sleep?" I ask Hurley, who is loading logs into a woodstove beside the sink.

"The couch is a sleeper sofa. This place isn't designed for winter living, so we'll have to tend to the fire through the night if we want to stay warm. Want to go fetch some more wood?"

Not particularly, but I suppose I need to pull my weight. Reluctantly I grab the wood carrier and the flashlight, and leave the warmth of the fire to head outside. When I get to the woodpile I lay the carrier out on the ground and start stacking logs into it one at a time while I contemplate the night's sleeping arrangements. Two people, one bed . . . it doesn't take a genius to do the math. Normally I'd be excited over the prospect of sharing a bed with Hurley, but with Izzy's revelations about the new working arrangements and the whole no fraternizing rule, things have gotten much more complicated. I wonder if Hurley has heard about the budget cuts and the proposed changes, and if he has, what he thinks about it.

A few logs later, I hear movement in the trees off to my left. I freeze, listening, and hear it again . . . footsteps crunching on the carpet of dead and fallen leaves. I shine the flashlight in the general direction of the noise but the woods are so thick all I can see is an endless expanse of tree trunks.

I consider hollering out and asking who's there, but it seems too much like those scenes you see in a horror movie just before the next horrendous murder. Then I realize that the flashlight marks my location like a bull's-eye. Quickly I turn it off and stand there, still holding a log and hoping it's enough of a weapon, waiting for my eyes to adjust to the moonlit darkness.

For a moment everything is quiet, but then I hear the footsteps again, moving even closer. As my eyes adapt to the nighttime light, I abandon my post and do a fast gimp back toward the cabin's entrance.

"Hurley, there's someone out there," I say, trying to swallow down my panic. "I heard footsteps in the woods and they were coming this way."

Hurley drops the log he was positioning in the woodstove, takes the flashlight from me, and then heads outside, taking his gun from his holster. I hover just inside the doorway, unsure if I should go out there with him. My instinct is to stay inside behind the security of the walls, but I feel an obligation to keep an eye on Hurley. Realizing I'll be about as useful as teats on a bull, I wield my log like a one-handed batter anyway, hoping Hurley will shoot whoever's out there before I have to use it.

He disappears behind the cabin and I wait, listening for any sounds of a skirmish, or for a shot to ring out. Instead, I hear Hurley call out my name.

Chapter 37

"Mattie, come here."

Reluctantly I step outside and make my way along the side wall of the cabin to the back. Hurley is standing there next to my abandoned wood carrier, shining a flashlight into the trees. "Look," he says, gesturing in the direction of the light. "There's your culprit."

It takes me a moment to see what he wants me to because at first all I can see are trees. Then something moves and my eyes focus on a deer—a magnificent-looking buck sporting an eight-point rack. He stands there, staring into the beam of Hurley's flashlight, making no attempt to run off.

"Wow," I say. "He's beautiful."

"That he is, and he's also probably scared out of his mind since we're smack in the middle of deer hunting season."

We stand there having our stare-down for a minute or two more before Hurley lowers the flashlight and focuses it on the log carrier. He returns his gun to its holster and then bends down to pick up a log. "I'll take the carrier in but let's load your arms up, too," he says, holding the log out.

I extend my arms and Hurley stacks five logs onto them before I tell him, "I think that's my limit." As he grabs the carrier and we both turn to head back inside, we hear the sound of crashing branches behind us as the buck dashes off deeper into the woods.

We make three more trips to the woodpile before Hurley deems our inside stock sufficient. I stir up the fire in the fireplace and toss another couple of logs onto it while Hurley finishes setting up the woodstove. Once he's done, he lights the wood inside it and then pours water from one of the gallon bottles we bought at the store into a saucepan that's so dented it looks like it's been used as a baseball bat.

"What are you doing?" I ask him.

"Heating up some water for hot cocoa," he says. Among the provisions we bought is a box of instant cocoa mix and he takes two envelopes out of it, stashing the rest in one of the overhead cupboards. In a different cupboard he finds a couple of mugs, which he examines and wipes with the tail of his shirt before emptying the contents of the envelopes into them. There is something oddly sexy about this little slice of domesticity and with the night's sleeping arrangement still an elephant in the room, I decide to talk about it.

"So, Hurley, did you hear about the restructuring that's coming because of budget cuts?"

"I've heard rumors," he says, staring into the pot on the stove as if he has Superman's X-ray vision and can make it heat faster. "But nothing definitive. Why? Have you heard something?"

"I have." I then proceed to tell him about the police corruption suspicions and the recent problems that have occurred with evidence collection. "According to Izzy, the solution for now is to increase oversight of the investigative and evidentiary process by creating a tighter working alliance between the police departments, the evidence labs, and our office."

"Meaning what exactly?"

"Meaning you and I will be working together more closely in the future whenever there's a suspicious death."

He looks over at me and there's a hint of a smile on his face.

"It means we will be working together as a team in the future, to ensure there are no improprieties going on," I add.

His face falls and I sense he's figured out the ramifications. "Improprieties," he repeats.

"Yes."

The water on the stove has begun to boil so he busies himself for a few minutes pouring it into the mugs and stirring them. Then he carries them over to the couch, hands me one of them, and settles in beside me. "I take it these improprieties include you and me—" He lets the implication hang there between us.

"Yes."

He nods and sips his cocoa, staring into the fire. After a moment of silence he says, "So in order for us to continue working together, David will get his wish."

"I guess that's one way of looking at it, though I think David has finally moved on."

"You've thought that before and it didn't prove to be true."

"I know, but there's something different about him this time. Something has happened to make him change his mind."

"We'll see. Not that it matters, given the change in our job situation."

"That's assuming I still have a job."

Hurley shoots me a troubled look. "I'm sorry I—"

"Don't," I say, holding up a hand to stop him. "As I said before, I walked into this knowing full well what the consequences might be. I did it willingly. You don't need to apologize."

We sit in companionable silence for a while, sipping our respective drinks and staring at the fire, each of us lost in our own thoughts. I keep reflecting back on what Izzy said to me about having unresolved feelings for David, and the unexpected urges I felt while he was staying at my house.

"Look, Hurley," I say finally, after I've drained my mug. "I like my job. Oddly enough it suits me. I like working with Izzy. I like the puzzle aspects of figuring out what really happened, and I enjoy trying to gauge people to figure out what they're really thinking."

"You should enjoy your job," Hurley says. "You're good at it."

"Thanks." I lean forward and turn to face him. "I also like working with you. And while I can't deny that I feel a certain . . . attraction to you, I'm pretty new at this singles stuff and I'm not sure I can trust my own emotions. I would hate to ruin a good working relationship by muddling it up with emotional baggage."

Hurley looks wounded for a second, but then he sighs and says, "Fair enough." He gets up from the couch and takes my empty mug, carrying it and his out to the kitchen. "Tell you what," he says. "Let's get some sleep. It's been a hard day for both of us. Tomorrow we can tackle this case again, reanalyze what we know, and try to figure out where to go from here."

"Sounds like a plan," I say. I look around the cabin and raise the next obvious question. "How do we work out the sleeping arrangements?"

"I'll sleep on the floor," Hurley says. "You can have the couch."

I frown at that, knowing the floor won't be very comfortable and worried about the occasional scurrying sounds I keep hearing in the darkened corners of the cabin. "You don't have to do that," I tell him. "We can share the bed."

Hurley looks at me, his eyes dark and dangerous. "I don't know if that's a wise idea," he says, arching a brow at me.

"We can put a roll of blankets or something between us in the bed," I suggest. "It will be fine. We can leave our clothes on. And frankly, I'm too tired and sore from working out at the gym to consider doing anything anyway. Not to mention that I haven't had a shower."

Hurley considers this and gives in. "Okay, we'll give it a try."

He goes to one of the cupboards and digs out a stack of pillows and blankets. After a few minutes we have the couch opened and the bed made up with a rolled-up quilt serving as a line of demarcation down the center.

When we're done, we stand on either side of the couch, eyeing the bed between us. "You okay with that side?" Hurley asks.

"I'm fine." I climb in and pull the blankets over me to prove it.

After adding a few more logs to the fire and stirring it up, Hurley climbs in on the other side. I catch a whiff of him as he adjusts the blankets—that clean, faintly spicy smell that seems to send my hormones into overdrive. I turn on my side facing away from him, wondering if this was such a smart idea after all, and doubtful that I'll ever be able to fall asleep with a fabulous-smelling, handsome-as-hell hunk of man meat next to me.

Chapter 38

Apparently I was more tired than I realized because the next thing I know, I'm waking up feeling warm and cozy, still lying on my side, staring at sunlight beaming in through the window across from me. Memories of the night before come flooding back to me, and when I become aware of something along the length of my backside, at first I think it's the barrier quilt. But as my mind clears its cobwebs, I realize it's too warm to be the quilt. Then I become aware of a weight on my chest and when I lift the covers and look down, I see an extra arm there.

That's when I realize that it's Hurley along my backside, spooning himself against me, his arm draped over my side. We fit together disturbingly well and a part of me wants to close my eyes and stay snuggled up against him this way forever. But I know how dangerous our situation could be and besides, my bladder is throbbing with urgency. I carefully lift Hurley's arm and slide out of the bed. It isn't easy; my body is stiffer than ever and the left side of my neck hurts like hell where the Taser bit me.

The cabin is freezing cold and I see that the fire has gone out and the woodpile is depleted. Clearly Hurley got up during the night to tend to it and the thought of him being awake and watching me while I slept is titillating . . . until I remember how David used to tell me I tend to fart in my sleep.

Hurley rolls onto his back and starts to snore lightly. I stand there a moment, admiring the outline of his body beneath the blankets and imagining the could-have-beens. But I realize it's a slippery slope and after a minute I shake it off and head for the outhouse.

The spiders don't seem quite as intimidating by the light of day and after relieving myself, I head around to the back of the house and grab a bunch of logs. When I come back inside, Hurley is still sleeping so I busy myself stacking the wood in the fireplace. A few minutes later I light one of the little starter packets and the wood starts to burn.

When I turn back toward the rest of the cabin, I'm startled to see Hurley awake and watching me.

"Good morning," I say. "How did you sleep?"

"Amazingly well," he says with a stretch and a smile. "You?"

"Like a baby."

Hurley flings back the covers and gets out of bed, and my eyes are irresistibly drawn to the front of his jeans, where his morning erection is obvious. Flushing hot from more than the fire, I quickly look away and busy myself removing the bed linens from the couch.

Hurley walks over to the door and grabs the toilet paper. "Be right back," he says.

By the time he returns, I have the bed stripped and folded back into the couch. A surreptitious glance at Hurley's jeans lets me know that things are back to normal and I breathe a sigh of relief.

Hurley heads for the woodstove, where he lights a fire and puts a pan of water on to boil. A few minutes later, he has taken the package of bacon we bought last night out of the tiny fridge and several strips are frying in a pan. I join him in the kitchen and measure out spoonfuls of instant coffee into a couple of mugs.

Since Hurley seems to have a handle on the cooking duties, I lean against the counter and watch him for a few minutes. The sight of him being so domestic triggers an emotional response in me, followed by sadness and a sense of loss when I recall our discussion from the night before.

"So I've been thinking about your situation," I say, hoping to redirect my thoughts. "And I keep coming back to Mike Ackerman. I think it would be worthwhile for me to meet and speak with his wife."

"To what end?" Hurley asks, turning the bacon.

"To get a better feel for what she knows. If Ackerman was having an affair with Callie, she might know about it. Even if she doesn't, if we can put a seed of doubt in her mind and make her look at her husband a little more closely, it might put more pressure on him and make him do something desperate. Hell hath no fury and all that."

"Maybe," Hurley says, sounding unconvinced. "But it could be dangerous. I don't want to involve you any more than I already have. If we do it, I should be the one to talk to her."

I shake my head. "You need to lay low. There are too many people looking for you. Besides, I think Ackerman's wife will be more likely to open up to another woman."

"Let me think about it," he says.

Half an hour later we are seated at the small folding table

finishing up a hearty breakfast of scrambled eggs, bacon, coffee, and toast that Hurley made by placing slices of bread inside a foldable grill with a long handle on it and holding the whole thing over the fire. The toast is unevenly browned and still soft in spots, but a little strawberry jam covers it up nicely. I discover I'm ravenously hungry and make quick work of the food, which tastes surprisingly good.

Feeling sated and full, I lean back in my chair and sip my coffee.

"How does a person shower around here?" I ask, worried I might be getting a bit ripe.

"There's soap, washcloths, and towels in the cabinet over there," Hurley says, gesturing over his shoulder. "Heat up some water on the stove and then do the best you can. You're a nurse, so I'm sure you know how to do a sponge bath. I've got some spare clothes in my bag you can wear if you want."

I look around the cabin with a skeptical eye. "And where, exactly, am I supposed to give myself this bath? The outhouse?"

"I'll go outside for a bit and you can have the cabin to yourself."

"You won't peek in the windows?"

"Tempting," Hurley says with a wink. "But I promise to be a good boy. I'll knock before I come back in."

"What are you going to do in the meantime?"

"I'm going to go outside and get ready for our hunting expedition."

"Hunting expedition?"

"Yep, since tomorrow is Thanksgiving, you and I are going to shoot us a turkey."

An hour later I am as clean as I'm going to get. I've used soap and water to wash out my undies, which are hanging from the mantel to dry, and I'm wearing a long-sleeved pullover shirt with a mock turtleneck and a pair of sweatpants from Hurley's bag. The shirt collar covers the Taser mark on my neck and the ribbing in it rubs against the spot, making it sting. But it's the only shirt Hurley had in his bag so it will have to do. After debating on how to brush my teeth, I borrow some of Hurley's toothpaste and scrub them with a washcloth, following it up with a mouthwash gargle.

I'd like to wash my hair, too, but I decide I can let it slide for another day. I'm curious about what Hurley's up to since he headed outside with a hammer, a couple of nails, some paper, and a Magic Marker. I'm not a hunter and have no desire to become one, but I know enough about it to know that the supplies Hurley took aren't the usual tools of the trade.

I put on my jacket and my Frankenstein shoe and hobble outside. The day has dawned cool but sunny and I take a moment to close my eyes and tip my face toward the sky. I can hear the sounds of the woods around me: tree limbs knocking together in the breeze, birds chirping, the occasional rustle of ground leaves . . . and hammering.

This last sound makes me look around in confusion. I follow it toward the back of the house until I see the source of the noise. There is a small clearing behind the house and along the edge of the woods on the other side of it, about fifteen feet from the house, I see Hurley hammering something onto a tree. When he steps away I see that it's the piece of paper he took from the cabin and he's drawn a turkey in the center of it.

He comes back to me and says, "Ever shoot a gun?"

"Nope, never. I don't much like guns. As a nurse I've seen what they do to people."

"Well, you're going to learn how to shoot one today."

I shake my head and back away from him. "I don't think so."

"You dislike guns because you don't understand them.

I'm going to teach you what you need to know to handle them safely."

"Why?"

"Because you may need to know it someday," he says, handing me a gun. "And because *I* may need you to know it someday."

"I don't know, Hurley," I say, looking at the gun he's offering. I realize it's a second one because he's wearing his usual gun in his shoulder holster. "I think I'd rather just leave the gun stuff up to you."

"Trust me on this, Mattie, would you? Please?"

Damn it. The man sure knows how to get past my best defenses: those big blue eyes, that sexy, pleading voice, and as a final touch, a hand set gently on my shoulder. "Fine," I say in a way that lets him know how annoyed I am. "But don't expect me to shoot at anything other than that tree."

"Hopefully you'll never have to."

For the next half hour, Hurley goes over the basics of the handgun, which I learn is a Glock 9mm. First he tells me that every gun is assumed to be loaded until proven otherwise and should be handled based on that assumption.

"Never, ever point a gun at anyone unless you want to shoot them," he says. "And for heaven's sake, ignore all that crap you see on TV when it comes to holding a gun. You hold it in front of you with the barrel pointed down to the ground or straight ahead if there's nothing there. Never hold it with the barrel pointed up." He holds it in both hands under his chin, fairly close to his chest with the barrel pointed toward the sky. "Hold it like this and you run the risk of turning yourself into a jack-o'-lantern."

Having seen someone who did just that, I shudder and freeze the image in my mind to remind me.

Next he points out the various parts of the gun and tells

me what they're called: the sights, the barrel, the slide, the hammer, the tang, the magazine release button, the slide stop, the trigger and trigger guard, and the disassembly latch. As he does this, he shows me how to remove the ammo clip, how to open the slide, and how to check to see if there is a bullet in the chamber.

Then he takes the gun apart, removing the slide, the recoil spring, and the barrel. Once he has it all put back together with the exception of the clip, he hands it to me with the slide open and helps me position my hand properly, with my palm on the grip and my index finger down the side of the barrel, taking care not to touch the trigger. Though I'm reluctant to take ahold of the gun, once I have it in hand it feels heavier than I thought it would, but also strangely reassuring.

Or maybe it's Hurley's hand touching mine that I find reassuring.

He lectures me on barrel and bullet sizes and the importance of using the right size bullet for any gun. "This number here," he says, pointing to the side of the barrel, "tells you the size of the gun. And bullets all have their size stamped on the rim around the primer here." He pops a bullet out of the clip and shows me the stamped number on the rim surrounding the primer. Then he proceeds to remove all the other bullets.

"Now I'm going to show you how to load the clip," he says. "You slide the bullets in this way, one at a time." He demonstrates by doing the first one, and then he hands me the clip and a bullet. "You try it."

I do so, and manage to drop the bullet four times before I finally get it in place. Several bullets and drops later, I finally load the last one in on the first try.

"Okay," Hurley says. "Hang on to that a second."

I hold the clip while he removes his other gun from his shoulder holster. "Watch closely," he says, "because there will be a test."

He drops the clip out, opens the slide, and checks to see if there is a bullet in the chamber. There is one, and he shows me how to pump the slide to eject it.

"Now I want you to follow me. Pick up the gun the way I showed you."

I do as instructed, holding it in my right hand with the grip in my palm and my index finger down the length of the barrel.

"Next I want you to pop the clip in." He inserts his and I mimic his actions on my gun. "Now I want you to grab the slide, pull it back, and let it go so it snaps into position like this."

Again I follow his lead, startling when the slide snaps into place with a rapid, loud *snick*.

"Okay," he says, "your gun is now ready to shoot. Normally you should wear eye and ear protection but since I don't have anything, we'll have to do without."

Hurley then shows me how to line up my sights and take a proper stance with my feet spread apart and my arms extended. "Now breathe in, then out and squeeze the trigger when you exhale."

"But what if I miss and the bullet goes flying off into the woods, hitting something . . . or someone else?"

"Don't worry. This is private land and there's about forty acres of it. Plus there's a high ridge back behind these trees that will stop any strays."

Dubious, I close one eye and line the sights up with the turkey target, breathe the way he told me, and pull the trigger. The loud explosion nearly deafens me and it startles me so much that I yelp. I hear the bullet *thunk* as it hits a tree and just when I'm starting to feel pleased, thinking I might have hit the target, I see bark disintegrate two trees over.

"Okay, not a bad start," Hurley lies. "Let's try it again."

"I suck."

Hurley laughs. "Most people suck the first time. You'll get better with practice."

For the next hour we aim and shoot, aim and shoot, aim and shoot. Hurley takes a turn at it to show me how it's supposed to be done and obliterates the turkey's head with a series of six shots.

"Show-off," I mutter.

He smiles and says, "I know you're competitive by nature. So beat me."

"You mean with a stick?"

He gives me a warning look but there's amusement behind it.

"Okay," I say, resigned to my humiliation. And humiliating it is. Over the course of the hour I slaughter every tree surrounding the one with the target but manage to miss the tree with the paper on it every time. My shots go left, right, high, and low. By the time we're done, my shoulders ache, my ears are ringing, and the woods are begging for mercy.

"I guess I need more practice," I say, unloading the clip. I then open the slide, check to make sure the chamber is empty, and set the gun down. I may not be able to hit the broad side of a barn but I am much more comfortable just handling the gun.

I help Hurley take the guns apart and he shows me how to clean them. Then we put them back together without the clips. "It's best if you're going to carry a gun to have a secure holster for it, like one of these," he says, handing me both of his. "Over time you'll figure out what kind of holster works best for you."

"You say that like you think I'm going to be carrying one of these on a regular basis," I say. "That's not going to happen."

"You never know. And until we get this mess straightened out, I want you to have a gun with you."

I frown, examining the holsters as I try to imagine myself packing.

"There are smaller guns, like little Derringers you could carry in your purse, though it's illegal to carry concealed in the state of Wisconsin," Hurley explains. "But that said, you'd be surprised how many people do it."

He has me put on his shoulder holster and practice pulling his gun from it, but it feels awkward and my boobs keep getting in the way. The second holster comes with loops to run a belt or strap through, but given the girth of my hips, I'm not too keen on adding anything there.

"You can also get an ankle holster," Hurley says.

I glance down at my feet, both of which are swollen—one because I sprained it when I was Tasered, and the other because of my broken toes and the Frankenstein shoe—and wonder if anyone makes a cankle holster.

"For now, just keep this one close at hand so you can grab it if you need to," Hurley says, handing me the second gun.

A cold blast of wind blows against us and, as I take the gun, I pray it isn't an omen.

"You hungry?" Hurley asks.

"Always."

"Then let's get some lunch. Shooting always gives me a ravenous appetite."

Chapter 39

Since Hurley handled the breakfast duties, I decide it's my turn to demonstrate my culinary talents by fixing us lunch. In honor of the upcoming holiday, I fix turkey sandwiches and top it off by ripping open a bag of chips and popping the lid on a soda. Ever wary of the spider contingent, I opt for a noncaffeinated beverage this time.

The weather outside has shifted, and dark, heavy clouds are rolling in, churning above us in an ominous meteorological dance. Once more I wonder if it's an omen of some sort. I'm starting to feel twitchy and useless sitting here doing nothing.

Hurley must sense my restlessness because he heads over to one of the shelves and returns to the card table with a Scrabble game.

"I hope you don't mind getting your ass kicked," he says. "I'm pretty good at this. Callie and I used to play all the time and she was a serious contender. She even played in tournaments."

"They have tournaments for Scrabble?" I say, thinking it sounds ridiculous.

"Go ahead and laugh," Hurley says. "But the woman won hundreds of dollars at it. And not only is there a national tournament, there's a world competition, too."

I guess I shouldn't be surprised given that the Trekkies of the world hold huge conventions all the time. It seems the nerds and geeks in our civilizations are quite adept at using their hobbies for networking and profitable gain.

We start out simply enough with mostly three- and four-letter words and a nearly tied score until Hurley plops down all seven of his tiles, hooking onto an *R* I just played and making the word ROUNDERS through a double word score.

"That's good for seventy points," he says, writing down his score. "Twenty for the play and a fifty-point bonus for using all my tiles."

"Great," I say, pouting and staring at a rack that includes the *Q*.

I study my letters for a moment and then plop them all down playing to his *S*. "Too bad proper nouns don't count," I say, looking at the word QUINTONS.

"Interesting," he says with a smile, "but not acceptable."

"I know, but it seemed so appropriate." I take back the *O* and *N*, and play the word QUINTS instead, again using his S and landing the letter *Q* on a triple letter score. "Thirty-six points," I say, jotting down my score and feeling pretty good about the fact that I managed to come up with just over half of what Hurley scored with his last play. If the scowl on Hurley's face is any indication, I still have a chance.

"Hold on a sec," he says.

I look at my play, wondering if I screwed something up. Then Hurley surprises me by reaching over and taking the other two tiles off my rack.

"Hey!" I protest. "What are you doing?"

He doesn't answer me. Instead he reaches over and takes my last play off the board, setting all the tiles on the table beside him. Then he plucks several more tiles from the board and adds them to the collection.

"Hurley, what the hell are you doing?"

"Bear with me a second," he says, and he starts shuffling the tiles around until he has them all in a line. "What's that say?" he asks me.

"Quinton Dilles," I answer, stating the obvious.

Hurley then rearranges the same letter tiles, forming a new name. When he's done, he leans back in his chair and gives me a pointed look.

"Coincidence?" I say, staring at the new name.

Hurley shakes his head. "Nothing with that man is a coincidence."

"But it can't be him," I say. "He's in prison."

"He may be in prison, but somehow or other he's the one pulling the strings. It makes perfect sense. He's a game player and this sort of thing is just his style. Trust me, it's no coincidence that our car renter is named Leon Lindquist, a pseudonym that just happens to use all the same letters as Quinton Dilles." He scrapes the letters up and dumps them back into the bag they came from. "Pack everything up," he says, clearing the Scrabble board and folding it up. "We're leaving."

Less than an hour later we're on the road, everything we brought with us—including my still-damp underwear and my sweaty, stinky gym clothes—loaded back into the car. Hurley is wearing his gun under his coat in his shoulder holster and the Glock is tucked beneath his seat.

- "Where are we going?" I ask.

"First we're going to stop at the house of my friend who owns the cabin. Then I'm going to Connor Smith's office."

"Connor Smith? You mean Dilles's lawyer?"

"Yes."

"But it's the day before Thanksgiving. What if he isn't there?"

"I suspect he'll be there. He's working on a pretty big case right now. But if he isn't, I'll go to his house."

When my mind registers his pronoun use, I say, "You mean *we'll* go to his house, right?"

He shakes his head. "I've involved you too much already. I'm doing this alone."

"Don't be stupid, Hurley. I'm already in this about as far as I can be. And what if you need backup?"

He looks over at me with a tolerant smile. "Well, if I was going to meet with a dangerous and deadly tree that might be a valid argument."

"Very funny," I say, pouting. "Make fun of my shooting all you want. It's not going to change my mind."

"I'm serious, Mattie. You're not coming with me."

"Then where am I supposed to go? I can't go back home yet. If I do, I'll probably be arrested, killed, or kidnapped again."

"I know. That's why you're going to stay at my friend's house."

"Oh, great, I get to stay with some stranger?"

"No, you'll have the place to yourself. He's in Florida for the winter."

"Then why didn't we stay there in the first place instead of bunking down with the spider community in hillbilly hunter's haven?"

"Because I don't have a key to his house and it isn't very

isolated. As long as you keep a low profile, you should be okay there alone. It's my face they're looking for."

"Wait. If you don't have a key to the house, how are we going to get in?" Then I remember how he picked the lock on Callie's apartment and say, "Never mind." I sit back against my seat with my arms folded over my chest and pout, sensing that Hurley isn't going to back down.

A little while later, Hurley parks on a street in the small town of Tomah. "Come on," he says, taking the gun from beneath the seat and sticking it in his jacket pocket. "We're going to make the rest of the trip on foot. I don't want to risk my car being seen near the house."

We walk several blocks through working-class residential neighborhoods until we come to a small ranch house. Hurley's eyes are busy checking out the surroundings, watching for anyone who may be watching us. He steers me through a privacy fence and into the backyard, and as soon as we're secluded, he takes out his lock toolkit and goes to work on the back door.

We're inside within minutes and the first thing Hurley does is close the blinds on the front windows. The house is neat and sparsely furnished, and the air smells faintly of burned wood. There is a woodstove in the living room but there's also a thermostat on the wall to regulate a furnace.

"Don't use the woodstove," Hurley cautions. "The smoke coming out of the chimney might attract attention."

Next we head to the kitchen where Hurley opens the refrigerator. It's on and cold inside, but the shelves are bare except for an open box of baking soda. Next he opens the freezer, which produces better results. Stacked neatly on the shelves are a dozen or so frozen, microwavable meals—my sort of cuisine. The pantry is well stocked, too, with canned soups, fruits, and instant oatmeal.

"I'll be back later tonight after it's dark and I'll bring some groceries with me," he says. "Make yourself at home in the meantime but stay inside and keep the blinds drawn and the doors locked. If you want to watch TV, use the one in the basement and keep the volume down. If anyone comes knocking, don't answer. I'll let myself in when I get back."

"Hurley, I don't think this is a good—"

"I don't want to discuss it anymore, Mattie." He walks off and enters a den, where there is a desk and a computer. He boots up the computer and when it's done loading, he launches the Internet browser and types in Connor Smith's name. One click later he's scribbling down Smith's office address and a couple clicks after that he has the man's home address.

"You'll be fine," he says, stuffing the sheet in his pocket. He takes out a wad of cash and peels off a handful of twenties. Then he takes the extra gun out of his pocket and hands it to me along with a full clip. "I don't think you'll need either of these, but just in case I don't get back for some reason, use them if you need to. I'll see you later."

Two minutes later I'm alone in the house, feeling frustrated, lonely, and bored. So I take the next most logical step and start snooping. Rummaging through the desk drawers, it doesn't take me long to find out the name of the person whose house I'm staying in: Carl Withers. When I get on the computer I see that he has Outlook for his e-mail server and though I feel a few seconds of guilt, it's not enough to stop me from browsing through his e-mails. On a whim, I search through his old saved ones looking for Hurley's name and come up with nearly a page full. From these I glean that Carl is a widower who was a longtime friend of Hurley's father. The e-mails are brief and nothing but chitchat.

Bored with my snooping, I decide to head out to the

kitchen and fix something to eat. I opt for an oriental Lean Cuisine dish and carry it over to the microwave, which is mounted beneath a cabinet not far from the back door. That's when I see the key rack.

There are two keys there, one that looks like it might be a spare house key and one that is obviously a car key with a fob. Curious, I leave the kitchen and explore the hallway that goes to the bedrooms. Halfway down it I find a small laundry room that also serves as a mudroom. There is a metal exterior door at the other end and when I open it, I discover the garage and a relatively new Lexus.

The discovery of the car seems like a good omen to me and without a second's thought I head back to the den, get back on the computer, and pull up the browser history. When I'm done I head back to the garage and climb into the Lexus. Apparently Carl Withers is a short man because I have to move the seat back as far as it will go just to get my knees to clear the steering wheel. And as I do so, I flash back on the discovery of Callie's car and how the lab tech had to move the seat back when he got in.

That's when it hits me. There's no way Hurley could have driven that car with the seat in the position it was found because of his height. And then I remember the basement window in my house, and the trouble I had squeezing through it, which resulted in a cut from leftover glass, a cut that required stitches. Granted my butt may be bigger than Hurley's, but my shoulders aren't, and they barely fit through. Hurley's shoulders are delightfully, appealingly broad, much wider than mine. He never would have fit through there. Combine these things with the apparent left-handedness of the person who stabbed Callie and it all points to someone other than Hurley.

Five minutes later I'm pulling out of Carl Withers's

garage with a picture of Connor Smith from a newspaper ar-
ticle about Dilles's trial, and the addresses for his home and
office on the seat beside me. Hurley's gun and its clip are
safely tucked beneath the seat, and Hurley's cash is safely
stuffed in my bra. I wish I had a way to call Hurley and tell
him what I've figured out but he has the cell phone with him
and I don't know the number for it. Without my own throwaway phone, I have no way to reach him.

The Lexus is equipped with GPS navigation and when I
plug in Smith's office address, it tells me that my estimated
arrival time will be well into the evening hours. His home
address isn't much better since it only shaves fifteen minutes
off my travel time, so I settle into the Lexus—easy to do
since the seats are quite plush and come equipped with a
butt warmer—and drive.

As soon as I hit the interstate I take my speed up to sixty-
nine, wanting to travel as fast as I can but unwilling to risk
getting pulled over, especially since I'm now guilty of operating without a license and car theft—though I'm hoping
Carl Withers will see it as more of a car borrowing kind of
thing. I know Hurley tends to be a bit of a lead foot but I suspect he'll be cautious too, given that he doesn't want to get
caught. Though I don't really expect to catch up to him, I
keep scanning the cars ahead of me, looking for Hurley's.

An hour into my drive, when I'm only half an hour or so
outside of Sorenson, I notice that the Lexus's gas gauge is
bordering on empty and I start looking for an exit that can
provide me with food, gas, and a toilet. Though stopping
somewhere this close to home makes me a little nervous, the
next exit has what I need, so I take it and prepare to pull into
a mini-mart gas station combo. But I get caught in a bottle-
neck almost as soon as I leave the freeway and as I inch my
way toward the end of the exit ramp, I see why. A blockade

of cop cars is positioned in front of the mini-mart and an officer is directing us to go around. I follow the rest of the drivers, rubbernecking like everyone else but also wary of being seen and recognized.

And that's when I see Hurley, handcuffed and standing beside a police cruiser in the mini-mart parking lot.

Chapter 40

My first impulse is to hide but I realize that with all the attention focused on Hurley, I'm not likely to attract any more attention than any of the other drivers. Besides, I don't even know if anyone is looking for me. My second impulse is to stop and tell the cops that I know Hurley and what's more, I know he's innocent. But I quickly realize how suicidal that move would be. While I may be able to prove Hurley's innocence eventually, he'll be locked up anyway and who knows what might happen. So I stay in line with all the other cars, drive past the mini-mart, take the first U-turn I see, and get back on the freeway.

My mind is a whirlwind of questions and worries, wondering what the hell I should do now that Hurley is in custody. I push the Lexus's gas supply to its limits by going another ten miles down the road before I exit. Once I have the tank filled and my bladder emptied, I get back on the road and start filling my own tank with my just purchased items: a package of shortbread cookies and a cup of coffee that tastes like it's been on the burner for a month, making me wonder if the person who made it got the coffee mixed up with the cleaning products.

I turn on the radio and scan the frequencies for local stations, hoping to hear some news about Hurley's arrest. After suffering through half an hour of a country station and being forced to listen to twangy male singers whine about the women that done them wrong, my head feels like it's going to explode.

I consider altering my plans and heading back home to Sorenson, but quickly discard the idea. I have a feeling it will be difficult to explain away my recent car theft, not to mention my aiding and abetting of a suspected murderer. Feeling trapped and frustrated, I eventually decide to stick to the original plan and continue on toward Smith's office, hoping it will lead to something.

It's nearing seven o'clock at night when I finally arrive in Chicago. I find the nearest parking garage I can to Smith's office, but it's still nearly seven blocks away. After a moment of debate, I leave the gun stashed under the seat before taking to the streets on foot. I'm not a fan of the early darkness that comes with Wisconsin winters—after a few weeks of it I start to feel like I'm living in a postapocalyptic world—but I'm grateful for it now for two reasons. One, it makes me feel less conspicuous as I skulk along the sidewalks. And two, it makes the people inside lighted buildings very easy to see.

Smith's building is a four-story office complex, and since his address includes a suite number of 101, I assume his office is on the first floor. This is confirmed when I see Smith—recognizable from the picture I printed—through one of the first-floor windows. He and a heavyset black woman are seated in an office facing one another, Smith talking, the woman writing on a legal pad. I head inside and discover that Smith's firm—which consists of three other lawyers—shares the floor with a dental office, which looks dark and deserted.

The outer door to Smith's office is closed and locked but it and the surrounding walls are made of glass and I can see that several lights are on. There is a receptionist's desk near the entrance but it's empty. Behind the desk are a half-dozen doors, most of which are closed. But two of them—an empty office straight ahead and the one I saw from outside—are open with the lights on.

I knock as loud as I can, first on the door, then on the window. After several attempts, the woman I saw from outside finally comes out and stares at me through the glass.

"I need to speak to Connor Smith," I yell through the glass when it becomes obvious she isn't going to just open the door. "It's urgent."

The woman turns around and heads back to the office. Thinking she is ignoring me, I pound on the glass again and she reappears a second later with Smith on her heels. This time he approaches and when he sees me, I get the distinct impression based on his expression that he is both wary and surprised by my appearance, though I can't be sure why. Then I realize that a strange woman pounding on your locked office door late on Thanksgiving Eve is reason enough, especially when you're in the business of defending criminals.

Smith, who I note disappointedly is nearly as tall as I am, making him as unlikely a suspect as Hurley, stares at me for a few seconds and then unlocks the door.

"Can I help you?" he asks with a slick, practiced smile that reminds me of Lucien.

"I need to speak with you about a very important matter," I say vaguely.

"I'm sorry, but the office is closed for the holiday," he

says. "If you like, my assistant, Trina, can schedule an appointment for you."

"I don't need an appointment," I tell him. "I need to speak with you."

He gives me a quizzical look and then says, "May I ask what this is in reference to?"

"Quinton Dilles."

If I'm hoping for some kind of reaction from Smith, I'm disappointed. Trina, however, shoots Smith a nervous look and starts chewing on the side of her thumb.

Smith issues forth an irritated sigh and says, "Very well, I'll give you five minutes but that's all I have time for. I'm prepping for a big case I'm working on."

Score one for Smith for communicating his importance to me and letting me know he considers me a peon barely worthy of his time and trouble.

He directs me into the reception area and points toward his office. "Go in and have a seat. I'll be right there." Then he turns to Trina and says, "Pull up the case law I've given you so far and leave it on your desk. You can go home once you're done."

Trina nods and goes into the other lit office, where she settles in behind a desk and starts working on a computer.

I make my way into Smith's office, which is as pretentious as his behavior and utterly lacking in any personal items. I'm surprised there aren't any family pictures—Smith is a reasonably attractive man with golden blond hair, a tall but otherwise average build, and handsome, well-proportioned features. I can't help but wonder if the lack of pictures is simply his way of distancing his business life from his personal one—a logical thing to do given his clientele—or if he's just a perpetual bachelor and player.

I settle into a leather chair—the same one Trina was in—

while Smith closes his office door and settles into his desk chair.

"If you'll excuse me one minute," he says, "I need to send a quick text message."

He picks up the cell phone on his desk and starts tapping in his note. When he's done, he sets the phone down and says, "There we go." He steeples his fingers and taps them against his lips, eying me closely. "So what is it you want to talk about?" he asks.

"I'm a deputy coroner in Wisconsin and I'm investigating a series of murders there that I think your client, Dilles, may be involved with."

Smith laughs dismissively. "I'm afraid you haven't done your homework, Ms. . . ." He trails off, leaving me to fill in the blanks.

"It's Winston. Mattie Winston."

Smith picks up a pen—with his right hand I note—and scribbles my name on a notepad on his desk. "Well, Ms. Winston," he says as he writes, "Quinton Dilles is behind bars, so I'm pretty sure he had nothing to do with your murders."

"Does the name Leon Lindquist mean anything to you?"

"No," he says with a shrug after a moment's thought. "I'm afraid not. Why do you ask?"

I study Smith closely as he answers, hoping to get a sense for the truth of his response. If he's lying, he hides it well. The only nervous tic I notice is the way he's waggling the pen in his hand. "What about the name Steve Hurley?" I ask, ignoring his question.

His eyebrows arch and he shifts in his seat. "That name I do know," he admits, setting down the pen. "If I remember correctly, he's the detective who initially worked on Dilles's case. Is that relevant somehow?"

"At the moment he's being framed for these murders I'm investigating and Dilles seems like a likely culprit."

He gives me another of his tolerant but dismissive laughs, as if he's dealing with an ignorant child. "That seems a rather ambitious goal for a man who currently resides in a maximum security prison," he says.

"Dilles is rich and that kind of money makes anything possible."

My statement hovers between us for a moment while we stare one another down. Then Smith says, "Well, perhaps, but I'm not sure what you expect to get from me. Yes, Dilles was, and still is my client since we're waging an appeal of his conviction. And because of that, I'm not really at liberty to discuss him with you or anyone else."

Sensing that he's about to dismiss me, I decide to toss out one last taunt. "That's a nice cop-out."

Smith refuses to take the bait. "Call it what you want, Ms. Winston. I think we're done here. I wish you the best of luck on figuring out your murders but I'm afraid I can't help you." He gets up and walks over to the door, opening it and standing there in a clear invitation for me to leave.

Frustrated but realizing I've got no options left, I get up. Smith manages to patronize me one last time by placing his hand on my shoulder and steering me out of his office toward the main door. As we walk, I see Trina inside the other office. She has donned her coat and appears to be shutting down the computer, though her eyes keep darting nervously in our direction. As Smith opens the door to the hallway and gestures for me to exit, I hesitate. I want one last stab at him, if for no other reason than because his smug attitude has irritated me.

"If you have anything to do with this, Mr. Smith, I *will* find out."

He smiles to let me know my threat doesn't faze him in the least. "You have yourself a nice holiday, Ms. Winston," he says. "Good evening."

I leave, mumbling curses at Smith, and head back out to the street, wondering what to do next. A couple of blocks into my walk, I become aware of hurried footsteps following close behind me. Resisting the urge to turn around and look, I speed up my pace a bit. The footsteps do the same. The streets, though fairly well lit, are relatively empty, most likely because of the holiday. Still, I feel reasonably safe until I get close to the garage. Realizing how dark and isolated it is, I make the decision to turn and confront my follower. But before I can, a hand clamps down on my shoulder, making me yell out with fright.

Chapter 41

My follower yelps as well, a distinctly feminine sound. When I whirl around I find myself face-to-face with Smith's assistant.

"Trina," I say, stating the obvious and breathing a small sigh of relief. Then I put my guard back up, wondering if she could be involved somehow.

She claps a hand to her chest. "Lord, you scared the crap out of me," she says, rolling her eyes.

"Likewise. Were you following me?"

She nods. "I'm sorry," she says, glancing nervously over her shoulder. "But I couldn't help overhearing your conversation with Connor and I wanted to talk to you."

That she couldn't help overhearing us seems a bit of a stretch, given that the door to Smith's office was closed, but I let that slide.

"What about?" I ask her.

She reaches into a shoulder satchel she's carrying and for a second I'm certain she's going to pull out a knife or a gun.

I flinch and prepare to run but all she pulls out is a sheaf of papers. "Here," she says, thrusting them at me. "I've been planning on leaving Connor's firm for some time now but it took me a while to find another job and I'm a single mom with two boys to support. I just got an offer from Stern and Hageman and I haven't told Connor yet that I'm leaving. Your arrival tonight made me realize I can't ignore what's going on any longer."

"What do you mean? And what are these papers?" I ask her, struggling to read them in the dim light of the street-lamps.

"They're copies of e-mails between Connor and a private investigator he has used, and between Connor and a man named Mike Ackerman, who works—"

"I know who Mike Ackerman is," I tell her, instantly intrigued. "What's so important about the e-mails? And how did you get them?"

Trina grimaces and looks embarrassed. "I had some late-night work to do a while back and my regular babysitter was sick, so I brought my boys up to the office with me. They're both big into online gaming stuff so I let my oldest boy use the computer in my office and set the youngest up on the reception desk computer. Then I went into Connor's office and used his computer to get my work done. I discovered that Connor had minimized his e-mail account but hadn't logged out of it. So I expanded it with the intention of closing it out, but my curiosity got the better of me. I started reading and that's how I found those," she says, gesturing toward the e-mails I'm holding.

"They contain a lot of information about this Steve Hurley guy you were asking about. Connor uses private investigators a lot and based on these e-mails, he hired someone to look into Hurley's life. At first I thought it might be related to Dilles's appeal since I knew Hurley was a detective here in Chicago not long ago and was involved in the murder investigation at one point. But the information Connor got on Hurley seemed too personal to be of any use in that regard, stuff about his love life and all. Your name is mentioned in there," she says, pointing to the e-mails. "And stuff about his hobbies."

I suppress a shiver at the thought of Connor Smith's private investigator spying on me.

"I still might not have thought much about it if it wasn't for the fact that Connor's been acting kind of strange lately, all nervous and edgy."

"Are you saying you think Connor might be responsible for these murders?"

She shakes her head and looks over her shoulder again. "Not directly. Connor wouldn't get his hands dirty that way. He'd hire someone else to do it."

"How does Ackerman figure into it?"

"My best guess is that there was something going on between Ackerman and that reporter woman named Callie Dunkirk who was killed. Ackerman never refers to her by name but if you read the e-mails, you'll see references to a CD, and Ackerman claiming that this CD person is a problem."

"Do you think Ackerman killed Callie Dunkirk?" As soon as I ask the question, I try to recall if Ackerman gave any indication to his handedness, but I can't remember. However I do recall his height and overall size and that rules him out for driving Callie's car, though I can't be sure if he could have fit through the basement window. His lean runner's build might have enabled him to slip through.

"I don't know," Trina says, frowning. "But I'm pretty sure Connor is up to something and all of this seems a little too coincidental."

She's right, it does. And it makes sense. My gut has been

pointing me toward Ackerman all along and the fact that Dilles's lawyer is involved is likely nothing more than coincidence. But just as I'm convincing myself of that fact, Trina gives me one more startling tidbit of information.

"I know you were asking about Quinton Dilles, and even though he's in prison, I can't help but think that he may be involved somehow, too."

"Why?"

"Because Connor was having an affair with Dilles's wife right before she was killed."

I stare at her, stunned. "Are you sure?" I ask finally.

"Oh, yeah," she says. "I caught them kissing one evening when I came back to the office because I forgot something. At first I just thought it was some woman Connor was dating but when she turned up murdered a couple of months later and I saw her picture in the paper, I recognized her. Connor was kind of cagey about the whole thing, bringing the topic of her murder up in discussions with me all the time to see if I mentioned anything about recognizing her. But I played dumb because I thought for a while that he might have been the one who killed her. Then her husband was arrested for it and when I found out Connor was going to be defending him, I about had a stroke. That's why I couldn't resist taking a peek at his e-mails."

"Do you think Dilles knew about the affair?"

"I do. I think that's why he killed her. He wasn't about to let her cheat on him and then give her half his money in a divorce. But I don't think he knew Connor was involved." She glances at her watch and then looks over her shoulder again. "Look, I need to get home to my kids. But if you want to talk with me some more, call me." She hands me a business card for Connor Smith with her own name and number written on the back of it.

"Thanks, Trina. I appreciate this."

We part company and I make my way to my car, or rather Carl Withers's car. I climb in and take a moment to think about my next step. With Hurley arrested and most likely in jail, I feel the need to move quickly so I decide to try to call Bob Richmond. Then I remember that I don't have a phone and curse for not remembering sooner. I could have borrowed Trina's, assuming she had one. A pay phone is my next best option, so I head out of the garage, pay the man in the booth, and pull out onto a one-way street.

I creep along the street, looking for a pay phone, which in this day and age is like looking for a Sasquatch. I've only gone a few blocks when a white SUV a couple cars ahead of me suddenly revs up and veers sharply toward the sidewalk. In a split second I realize what's about to happen and I'm helpless to do anything about it. The car jumps the curb and plows into a pedestrian, knocking the person several feet into the air before it veers into the street again and takes off.

As I pull up next to the crumpled body of the pedestrian lying on the sidewalk, I engage in a few seconds of mental debate. My first thought is to keep on going. No doubt there will be cops here soon and the presence of cops means I might be recognized. Then I reason that anyone who arrives on the scene will be too preoccupied with the injured person to care or notice. Besides, the nurse in me won't let me go on.

I pull up past the pedestrian, park near the curb, and get out of the car.

A couple of other cars have stopped and two young men get out of one of them and hurry over to the victim. One of them, I'm relieved to see, is already on a cell phone, presumably calling 911. I hurriedly join them and do a quick assessment of the victim on the sidewalk.

That's when my heart nearly stops. I recognize the coat first, then the face.

It's Trina.

Chapter 42

I'm pretty certain that Trina getting hit was no accident and every nerve in my body is screaming at me to turn tail and run. But I can't leave Trina lying here on the sidewalk like this, so I shift into nurse mode and do a quick triage. I'm instantly drawn to her left leg, which is bent midthigh at an impossible angle. Her femur is broken and one jagged end of it has ruptured through her skin and her pants, leaving a large, gaping wound. It's hard not to gawk at the injury but I don't see any major bleeding so I remember my nurse's training and focus on my ABCs instead.

Trina is unresponsive but breathing, though her breaths have a ragged gagging sound to them. I kneel down at the top of her head, place my hands below her jaw on either side, and push it up to better open her airway. Almost instantly her breathing quiets and improves.

"Are you a doctor or something?" the guy talking on the phone asks me.

"I'm a nurse." I hear him relay this fact to the 911 operator. I look over at the second guy and say, "Can you take over here and hold her jaw like I am to keep her airway open?" The guy looks scared out of his mind but he kneels down beside me and lets me instruct him on what to do.

"Be careful that you don't move her head too much," I tell him as he positions his hands where mine were and thrusts Trina's jaw open. "She might have a neck injury." Next I feel along Trina's neck for her carotid pulse. It's there, but it's very fast and thready. Clearly she is in shock and I'm relieved to hear the distant approach of sirens.

"Oh, shit," the guy on the phone says. "Look at her leg. That can't be good." I assume he's talking about the gaping wound until he says, "Is it supposed to be pumping like that?"

Quickly I look down at the leg. Sure enough, a small geyser of bright red blood is now rhythmically squirting out of the wound. Oftentimes when an artery is ripped traumatically it will spasm for a period of time and clamp down on itself—a potentially lifesaving reaction that can temporarily contain bleeding. But as shock sets in the vessel eventually goes flaccid, triggering a hemorrhage. I suspect that is what has happened here and the fact that it might be the femoral artery that's bleeding makes this a very deadly injury. Trina could bleed out in minutes.

Frantic, I move closer and rip her pants open to get a better look. The wound in her thigh is about three inches across and four inches long. I try to peer inside it but I can't see very well by the dim light of the streetlamps. After hesitating for a second or two, aware that I am ungloved and about to come into contact with someone's blood, I press my hand down on the wound to try and dampen the bleeding. But I might as well be the little Dutch boy with his finger in the dike because the blood just keeps coming.

Fortunately a cop car pulls up and two officers get out and hurry over to us. "What happened?" one of them asks.

"Somebody hit her with their car," I tell him. "I'm a nurse and she's bleeding very badly from her leg here. How long before an ambulance gets here?"

"Five minutes or so," the cop says.

"She'll be dead by then if I can't stop this bleeding," I tell him. "Do you have a flashlight?"

The cop nods, pulls a flashlight from his belt, and hands it to me. I lift my hand and blood gushes forth in a frightening flow. I shine the light into the wound and what I see makes my heart skip a beat. Based on the size of the vessel I see pumping out blood, it is indeed Trina's femoral artery that has been severed.

I plunge my free hand into the wound, making the people around me gasp. I feel around for the pumping ends of the artery and when I find it, I pinch my thumb and two fingers around it as tightly as I can. Trina's blood is warm and slick on my fingers and I have a hard time maintaining my hold. But at least the blood has stopped pumping. I look at the feet of the people standing around me and see that the guy who was on his cell phone is wearing sneakers. "Quick," I say to him. "Give me one of your shoelaces."

The guy looks momentarily puzzled, but he squats down and starts undoing the lace from his left shoe. Moments later he hands it to me and it's none too soon; the fingers I have clamped around the artery are starting to cramp like crazy.

"I can't let go," I say. "If I do, she'll bleed to death. Someone needs to help me."

"Tell me what to do," one of the cops says.

"Put on some gloves," I tell him.

He dashes back to his car and returns a moment later with gloves on. "Now what?" he asks.

"Loop the lace around my thumb and fingers here," I say, showing him where. "Then cross the ends over like you're tying the first step in a knot."

He does so, his hands shaking.

"Okay, now leave the loop a bit loose and slide it down over my fingers as far as you can. We're going to try to tie off the end of this artery the way you tie off a ribbon on a gift when someone has their finger on it. Understand?"

He nods and carefully slides the lace down my fingers, moving from one side to the other. My fingers are cramping so bad I can barely stand it and I want to tell him to hurry, but I don't because I'm afraid it will make him more nervous. When he gets the lace down just below the level of Trina's skin, or where her skin would be if her leg wasn't gaping open, I tell him to shove the lace down inside the wound along my fingers as far as he can. He grimaces but does what I ask, pushing the lace down my fingers a millimeter at a time, until I feel one side of it slide off my fingertip and onto the artery.

"That side's good," I tell him. "Now do the other one." He tries to push the lace in along my thumb—a much tighter fit than the finger side—but it keeps sticking to his gloved fingers whenever he tries to pull his hand away.

The ambulance finally arrives and the paramedics grab their gear, rush over to where we are, and stand there a second staring at us. Judging from the expressions on their faces, they are clearly puzzled. But to my great relief I see that one of them has a pair of scissors and a hemostat hanging from loops in his belt.

"Severed femoral artery," I tell them. Then I focus on the guy with the tools. "Give me your hemostat."

The paramedic hands me the hemostat and I take it in my free hand. "Get some large bore IVs going and check her pulse and airway again," I tell them. The paramedics go to work and I turn my attention back to my police assistant. "You can take the lace off."

The police officer does so and as soon as the lace is out of the way, I open the hemostat and shove it into the wound alongside my fingers. Summoning all of my OR skills, I feel blindly for the open tips of the hemostat until I have them in place around the vessel and just above my fingertips. Then I clamp the device closed.

I wait a few seconds, trying to see if I still feel the faint pulsing sensation in my thumb and fingers. I don't, and warily I let go of the vessel and remove my hand. The bleeding has stopped.

"I got it," I say, breathing a sigh of relief and several people in the crowd around me applaud. I realize the number of gawkers has grown considerably and then I see that one of them has a large TV-type camera propped on his shoulder. And it's aimed right at me.

"Nice work," one of the paramedics says. "You may have just saved her life."

"I hope so," I say. "But you need to get her to the nearest hospital right away or she's going to lose that leg. Be careful you don't jostle that hemostat when you move her."

The paramedics have made quick work of establishing IV lines and stabilizing Trina's neck with a cervical collar and they are almost ready to load her into the ambulance. I stand up and turn my back to the guy with the camera, looking around for something to use to clean the blood off my hands. An officer sees my dilemma and steers me over to his car, where he hands me a container of antiseptic wipes from his trunk.

The guy with the camera follows and I finally whirl on him and say, "Turn that damned thing off, you vulture."

"Are you kidding, lady? After what you just did back there, you're a hero. This is a huge story. I make my living as a stringer and I can sell this footage to one of the local stations for a bundle."

I want to rip the frigging camera from his shoulder and

smash it onto the ground, or better yet, rip his gonads from his body and smash those on the ground. But I realize that reacting too strongly will only attract more attention to myself and possibly make the cops a little too curious. Besides, I hope to be long gone before the asshole's footage ever gets aired.

As I try to wipe the blood from my hands, the cop says, "Nice work, lady."

"Thanks."

"Did you see what happened?"

I nod and give the camera guy a dirty look. The cop senses what I want and turns to the guy and says, "Give her a couple of minutes, Rod, okay?"

Rod shrugs, lowers his camera, and then makes his way over to the ambulance to get his drama shot.

When he's out of earshot, I tell the cop, "Somebody in a white SUV ran that woman down on purpose. He aimed straight for her."

"Are you sure?" he says, looking skeptical. "You don't think it was just a drunk who lost control or something like that?"

"I'm positive," I tell him. "Somebody tried to kill her."

The cop takes out a notepad and a pen and asks me, "What's your name? I'll need it for my report."

I hesitate just a second, remembering that I may be a fugitive on the run. "It's Rebecca Taylor," I tell him.

He scribbles it down and says, "Stay here, Ms. Taylor. I'll be right back to get a statement from you but I need to give the other guys a quick heads-up so they can follow the bus to the hospital."

He heads back to the crowd around the ambulance and as soon as I'm sure he isn't looking my way, I hurry back to my car, get in, and drive away.

Chapter 43

As I maneuver through the streets of Chicago, I keep a wary eye out for any police cars that may be on my tail. Fortunately I make it back onto the freeway and out of town without incident.

I head back into Wisconsin, frightened and unsure of where to go. I consider returning to Carl Withers's house; if nothing else it will at least give me a place to hide until things blow over. And I could call Richmond or Izzy from there using Withers's phone to let them know what I've found out. But then I realize that if I call them from the house phone, it will be easy for them to trace where the call came from and find me. And if they can find me, I'm afraid anyone else might be able to, too.

Finally I decide that the quicker I can clear Hurley's name, the quicker the investigation will move in the direction it needs to be headed. And if I'm looking for somewhere to be safe, sitting in a jail cell surrounded by police seems like a reasonable solution.

With my mind made up, I steer the car back toward Sorenson. It takes me nearly three hours of driving to get there and when I pull into town, I head straight for the police station. It's just shy of eleven o'clock when I park in the public lot. Feeling exhausted, I grab the e-mails that Trina gave me and stuff them into the pocket of my sweatpants. Then I head inside where I see Heidi Cronen, one of the evening dispatchers, seated at the desk behind the window.

She looks up at me with a smile in preparation for making her standard greeting but when she sees it's me, her smile disappears.

"Mattie!" She hits the buzzer that lets me open the door beside her window and enter the area behind it. "Oh my God, are you okay?" she asks.

"I'm fine, tired, but in one piece. Is Bob Richmond around by any chance?"

"He's not in the station at the moment, but I can call him."

"Is Hurley here?"

She makes a face and shakes her head. "I've heard he's in custody," she says. "But not here. Let me call Richmond for you. Maybe he can give you more information."

She makes the call, tells Richmond I'm at the station, and then disconnects. "He'll be here in a few minutes." She looks me over from head to toe and says, "I heard about everything that's been going on. It sounds like you've been through quite the shit storm."

"It's been interesting, that's for sure."

"Do you think Hurley is guilty?"

"No," I say without hesitation. "I'm certain he isn't. But knowing it and proving it are two different things."

We pass the next couple of minutes indulging in polite conversation, updating one another on family status and sharing some minor gossip. Then Richmond arrives, coming in from the back of the station.

"Mattie, are you okay?" he says when he sees me.

"I am, but I have a lot to tell you."

"Is that blood on your hands?" he asks, staring at my fingers.

I look down and see that I still have traces of Trina's blood in the crevices around my nails. "It is," I tell him. "But it's not mine. It belongs to a woman in Chicago who was run down by a car."

Richmond's eyebrows shoot up in surprise. "Let's go in the back and talk," he says.

I follow Richmond to a room that serves double duty as both a conference and interrogation room. It's a pretty comfy spot, bearing no resemblance to the sparsely furnished, bare interrogation rooms you see on TV, other than the fact that there is a camera mounted in the ceiling designed to record whatever takes place.

Richmond directs me to one of the chairs around the table and says, "Do you want something to drink? Or a snack?"

"A cup of coffee would be great," I tell him.

He nods, says, "Be right back," and disappears from the room. He returns a few minutes later carrying a plastic tray bearing two Styrofoam cups filled with coffee, a jar of Coffeemate, a couple packets of sugar, and some spoons.

I fix my coffee by adding a heaping spoonful of Coffeemate, hoping it will cut the acid taste I know our cop-house coffee usually has. Richmond does the same with his but he also adds three packs of sugar to his cup.

"You really need to learn to do without that sugar," I tell him. "Or at least switch to the artificial stuff."

He sighs, stirring his coffee. "Yeah, I know. Little steps," he says. He looks at me then with an apologetic expression. "I'm sorry I wasn't there at the gym yesterday. But Izzy called me to come up to your office and I kind of forgot about the whole gym thing."

I dismiss his apology with a wave of my hand. "Don't worry about it. What's done is done."

He takes a pad and pen out of his shirt pocket and says, "Okay, where do we start?"

"How about telling me where Hurley is?"

He shakes his head. "He's in a secure location for now. That's all I'm willing to tell you at this point."

I let out a sigh of exasperation.

"Why don't you start by telling me what happened at the gym yesterday?" Richmond prompts.

Resigned to having to give information if I have any hope of getting any, I tell him how Hurley and I hid out at the cabin, leaving out the part about how we sort of slept together. Next I tell him about our trip to Chicago, my interview of the people at *Behind the Scenes* and my suspicion that Ackerman may have been more than just a boss to Callie Dunkirk, and after a moment of thoughtful debate, I also tell him about our search of Callie's apartment. I watch Richmond's face carefully as I talk, looking for hints of any disapproval or surprise, not knowing how much of this Hurley may have already shared, but his expression remains placid and neutral. When I mention Callie's diary, he nods and says, "We found the diary under the seat of your car."

Next I tell him about Helen Baxter and the man she saw staking out Minniver's neighborhood. When I explain how I got the name of the person who rented the car, he gives me a look of grudging admiration, but says nothing. Then I tell him about our trip to Stateville Prison, our talk with Dilles, our discovery that the only visitor Dilles ever had was his lawyer, Connor Smith, and how Hurley figured out that the name Leon Lindquist is an anagram of Quinton Dilles.

My story is somewhat convoluted and I feel like I'm leaving a lot of loose ends hanging, but if Richmond is confused by any of it, he doesn't show it. He just keeps taking notes and listening.

I explain how Hurley dropped me off at his friend's house and then headed for Chicago to talk to Smith. Finally Richmond halts my story to ask questions.

"How did you leave there if Hurley took his car?"

Looking abashed, I explain how I took Carl Withers's car and watch as Richmond sighs and shakes his head.

"You stole the man's car?" he says, looking chagrined.

"I'd call it more of a borrow," I say, wincing.

He shakes his head again and says, "Continue."

I tell him how I saw the cops with Hurley and ask how they caught him.

"We had a BOLO out for him and his car," Richmond explains. "An alert statey saw the car, matched the plate to our BOLO, and pulled Hurley over."

"I see." I realize then that it might have been fortuitous that Hurley left me behind. Otherwise neither of us would have made it to Chicago and I never would have uncovered the information I did. Of course, it might also have meant that Trina would still be alive and well.

I move on to tell him about my meeting with Smith, and the subsequent discussion I had with Trina afterward. Then I tell him how the poor woman was run down.

"So you're wanted by the Chicago police at this point?" he asks, looking worried.

I shrug. "I suppose. But all I did was avoid making a statement. I'm pretty sure they don't think I had anything to do with her attack."

"These e-mails the woman gave you, what did they say?" he asks.

"I don't know. I never had a chance to read them." I dig the papers out of my pocket and hand them to him. "Trina said they contained evidence that Smith was communicating with Mike Ackerman. I know Hurley seems pretty convinced that Dilles is behind all this, but I like Mike Ackerman for it. Though there is one other mitigating factor."

"What's that?"

"Trina said Smith was having an affair with Dilles's wife right before she was killed."

Richmond sets his pen down and runs his fingers through his hair. "So I'm confused. You're saying that both Dilles and Ackerman have connections to this lawyer . . ." He pauses and flips through his notebook but I fill the blank in for him.

"Connor Smith."

"Yeah, okay. But you don't think any of them committed the murders."

"No, for the same reason Hurley couldn't have done it. They're all too tall. I believe Izzy shared his findings with you, that the person who stabbed Callie was most likely short and left-handed."

"Yeah, but that's theory, not conclusive evidence."

"But there's more." I then explain to him my theory about the size of the murderer, mentioning the position of the seat in Callie's car, the size of the window in my basement and how much trouble I had getting through it, Hurley's description of the height of the man who tried to abduct me. Then I realize that the burns from the Taser are on the left side of my neck, which would make sense if the person who came up behind me was left-handed.

I start to add this fact to my litany but Richmond gets up from his chair and says, "Stay here. I need to make some phone calls."

Chapter 44

While I'm waiting, Heidi pops her head in and asks me if I'd like something to eat while I'm waiting, stating that there is some leftover pizza in the break room. I thank her and accept the offer, and a few minutes later she brings me two slices of nuked pizza. After scrubbing the blood remnants from my hands, I scarf the pizza down in near record time, surprised at how hungry I am.

Once I'm done eating, exhaustion sets in. It's as if my body has completely shut down, drained of all energy by the many doses of adrenaline that have coursed through it in the past few days.

When Richmond finally returns nearly an hour later, it's all I can do to keep my eyes open.

"You look tired," he says.

"I am."

"I read those e-mails you had and unfortunately they aren't what I hoped."

"What do you mean?"

"Well, Smith and his cohorts are always very careful to word things in a way that leaves the meaning very ambiguous and open to interpretation. Though they are suggestive of something going on between Ackerman and Smith, they don't point a finger at anyone or anything specific."

"Great," I say, dejected.

"Don't give up all hope. The fact that the two men exchanged e-mails at all is suspicious, given that they both have ties to Hurley. So I talked to some cops down in Chicago and they're going to bring both men in for questioning."

"Thank you for that."

He shrugs it off. "It's a start, but if what you're telling me is true, we still have a perpetrator out there somewhere who committed these crimes. And until we can figure out who that is, I think you should be in protective custody."

"Is that a nice way of telling me you're going to put me in jail?" Though I should probably be upset by the idea, I'm not. All I care about at the moment is having somewhere to lie down so I can sleep.

"No, I'm not going to arrest you. But I'm not letting you go home, either. If someone tried to abduct you once they may try again, so for now we're going to put you up in a room at the Sorenson Motel with a twenty-four-hour police guard."

"That's fine." As long as I can have access to a shower and a bed, I don't care where he puts me. "Did the cops say anything about Trina?" I ask, saying a silent prayer that she's doing okay.

"They did," Richmond says. "She's still in surgery but they said it looks like she's going to survive. And thanks to you, they think she'll still have her leg."

"Thank God," I say. "Can I drive myself over to the motel?" I ask him.

"No, I'm going to have an officer take you."

"What about Carl Withers's car?"

"You can leave it here for now," he says. "We'll figure out how to get it back where it belongs later. Sit tight for a few more minutes and I'll get someone to drive you to the motel."

Richmond leaves the room and as I'm sitting there, I remember that I have Hurley's gun stashed under the seat in Withers's car. I don't want to leave it there for two reasons: one, if it's found, it may get me into more trouble, and two, I don't want it to mysteriously disappear. I get up and head to the front of the station. Heidi smiles at me and says, "Ron Colbert will be here in a few minutes to take you to the motel."

"That's great," I say. "I'm going to run out front real quick and lock up my car," I tell her. "Be right back."

Though I'm afraid she might try to stop me, she doesn't; she simply nods. I hurry out to the car before Richmond can figure out what I'm doing, unlock it, and reach under the seat for the gun and the clip. I pull them out, then stand there a minute, stymied about where to put them. The holster makes the gun much more bulky so I remove it and stuff it back under the seat. Then I put the gun and the clip in my jacket pocket.

No sooner am I done than I hear Richmond's voice behind me. "Mattie, what the hell are you doing out here?"

"Sorry," I say, shutting the car door and then whirling around, trying not to look guilty. "I wanted to make sure the car was locked. Turns out it wasn't, so it's a good thing I checked." I take the key fob and aim it at the car, hearing the locks snap down into place. Then I hand him the key.

"I thought you might be making a run for it," Richmond says. He is holding a purse. My purse, I realize.

"What do you mean? I thought you said I wasn't under arrest."

"You're not, yet. But until I can do some more investigating, I don't want you running around loose. You have too great a penchant for getting into trouble."

I start to argue this point, but then I realize that history won't bear me out.

"Come on," Richmond says, handing me my purse and waving me toward the door to the building. "Ron Colbert is inside waiting to take you to the motel. He'll stay outside your door tonight and someone will relieve him in the morning."

Ron greets me with a smile and starts to lead me out back to his squad car. But I hesitate and ask Richmond one more thing. "Can Ron drive me by my place first so I can get some clean clothes?"

Richmond considers my request a moment and then shrugs. "Yeah, I suppose so." He gives Colbert a pointed look. "Just be careful, okay?"

"Will do," Colbert says.

As soon as I'm settled in the front seat of the squad car, I look through my purse to see if either of my cell phones is inside. They are not and I curse Richmond.

A few minutes later Colbert pulls up in front of my cottage, the squad car's headlights aimed at the front door. Izzy's house is dark and at first I assume that he and Dom are asleep. Then I remember their plans to visit Dom's family for Thanksgiving and figure they must have taken Hoover along with them.

Colbert shifts into park but leaves the engine running. "Is Izzy home?" he asks, looking over at the darkened house.

"I don't think so. He and Dom were going to drive down to Iowa to spend Thanksgiving morning with Dom's family."

"Wait here a minute," he says. "Just to be safe, I want to go in ahead of you to check things out. Do you have a key?"

I dig through my purse, find my keys, and hand them to him. I watch as he goes up, unlocks the door, and disappears inside. Lights come on and I can see him in there scouting out the place. It doesn't take long since the cottage isn't very big, and a moment later he is standing in the doorway, waving for me to come in.

I get out of the car and head inside. On the floor of the kitchen I see two huge bowls: one filled with water and the other filled with cat food, no doubt the work of Dom and Izzy. That means Rubbish is here somewhere and I start calling for him.

"If you're looking for a cat, I think it ran into the bedroom when I came in," Ron says. "I saw something furry run that way so unless you have rats, I'm guessing it was your cat."

I walk into the bedroom and get down on all fours to look under the bed. There, staring back at me, are two glowing eyes.

"Rubbish, come on out of there," I coo. But he doesn't budge. After a few more attempts at coaxing him out, the muscles in my neck near where I was Tasered start to cramp so I give up. I stand and see Ron in the bedroom doorway watching me. "I think he's spooked from being alone," I tell him. "He doesn't seem to want to come out."

I roll my neck and massage the area beneath the collar of my borrowed shirt to try to get my muscles to relax.

"That Taser must have got you good," Ron says. "It will be sore for a couple of days but then it should be fine."

"You say that like you've been Tasered before."

"I have. We had to get hit with one as part of our police training."

"Yikes. That couldn't have been much fun."

Colbert shrugs off my concern. "It was quick, at least," he says.

I walk over to the closet and drag my one suitcase out. After tossing it on the bed, I open it and then head for the dresser.

That's when it hits me. How does Ron Colbert know I was stung with a Taser? He can't see the mark; it's hidden beneath the mock turtleneck collar on my shirt. I think back to my talk with Richmond and to my phone conversations with both him and Izzy back when Hurley and I were making our getaway. Though I can't be sure, I don't recall mentioning the Taser to anyone. The only person who knew was Hurley . . . and the person who tried to abduct me.

All of a sudden, my mind starts making connections: the fact that Colbert has a small build, the fact that he's new to the force, the fact that he insinuated himself into every part of the investigation, and the fact that it was he who discovered Callie's body.

My heart starts to pound, racing along at a frightening clip. As I open my dresser drawer to take out some clean underwear, my hand starts to shake. Could Colbert be the killer?

Then I remember what Izzy said about Callie's wounds and look at Colbert's gun belt. His gun is holstered on his left side, though that in and of itself isn't conclusive. When Hurley was talking about holsters he said some people prefer to cross draw rather than pull from the same side. Maybe Colbert is one of those. To find out, I walk over and dump my undies in the suitcase and then open the top drawer of my nightstand. Inside is a pad and pen I use to write down information whenever I get called out in the middle of the night. I take them out and hand them to Colbert.

"Do me a favor while I finish packing, would you? I want to leave a note for Izzy since he's been taking care of my cat.

Can you just scribble something down for me that says I'm okay and I'll be in touch?"

"Sure," Colbert says with a shrug, and after anchoring the pad with his right hand, he starts writing the note with his left.

Chapter 45

I watch Colbert scribble out the note, trying to figure out what to do next. I don't want to jump to any wrong conclusions and convict the man just yet, because everything could be coincidental. But I don't want to put myself in jeopardy either.

I walk over to the dresser to grab some jeans from a drawer. "Where are you from originally, Colbert?" I ask, trying to keep my tone relaxed and friendly.

"I grew up in Chicago."

"Do you have family there?"

He shakes his head but offers no further explanation.

"Do you have any family here in Sorenson?"

"I'm pretty much on my own," he says, sounding a bit terse.

"How did you end up in Sorenson?"

"Are you about done?" he asks, clearly irritated. "We need to get going."

"Sorry," I say, giving him an apologetic smile and carrying my jeans back to the suitcase. "I didn't mean to be nosy."

He makes no response and when I look over at him I find him studying me with an intense, curious expression.

"Where do you want me to put this note?" he asks.

"There are some magnets on the door of my fridge. Go ahead and stick it there. That's where I always leave notes for Izzy." This is an out-and-out lie since I have no reason to leave notes in here for Izzy, but I want to get Colbert out of the room. As soon as he leaves, I remove the gun from my jacket pocket and load the clip into it. Knowing how loud the slide is, and how small the cottage is, I sit on the edge of the bed, grab the slide and pull it back, holding it there. Then I lift one foot up and kick my lamp off the bedside stand. As soon as the lamp crashes to the floor, I let go of the slide, which snaps into place. With the gun loaded and ready to fire, I'm afraid to put it back in my pocket lest I accidentally shoot myself in the leg or foot. After looking around frantically, I slide it under the pillow on my bed with the barrel pointing toward the headboard.

"What the hell?" I whip around and see Colbert standing in the doorway of the room with a suspicious look on his face and his gun drawn. Had he seen me shove the gun under the pillow?

Thinking fast, I hold my hand to my forehead like some swooning damsel in distress. "Sorry, I just got very dizzy all of a sudden and nearly fell. I knocked the lamp over trying to catch myself."

Colbert stares at me with cold, calculating eyes and an utter lack of concern for my condition. His gun is still in his hand, though it's pointed at the floor. "You know, don't you?" he says, moving closer. "Somehow you figured it out."

Though there is no doubt in my mind what he's referring

to, I opt for playing dumb, hoping it might settle him down or at least buy me some time.

"What do you mean?"

For a few seconds I dare to hope because I see doubt in Colbert's expression. But then his eyes narrow with decisive resignation and I know I'm done for. A second later I find myself staring down the barrel of his 9mm.

"Colbert, what are you doing? Please don't point your gun at me like that. It scares me." I make a move as if I'm trying to lean out of his line of fire and slide my hand closer to the pillow in the process. But Colbert stops me cold by closing the distance between us and shoving the barrel of his gun against my forehead. "Move again and I pull the trigger."

I squeeze my eyes closed and hold my breath, keenly aware that his finger is inside the trigger guard of the gun at my head and one false move on my part—or his—will leave my brains splattered all over the comforter.

"How'd you figure it out?" Colbert asks.

I don't say a word. My mind is incapable of answering his question; it's too busy envisioning my body spread out on Izzy's autopsy table.

Sensing that my fear has paralyzed me, Colbert takes the gun barrel away from my head. I slowly open my eyes, only to find that the gun is still aimed in my direction, but at my chest instead of my head. And Colbert's finger is still on the trigger.

"Tell me how you figured it out!" Colbert yells.

Every nerve in my body wants to flinch at his tone but miraculously I don't. I briefly consider trying to play dumb a little longer but I realize it's futile. Colbert has gone too far and there's no way to fix things at this point.

"I never told anyone about the Taser," I tell him. "Yet you

knew. And you're left-handed and short, two traits that Izzy identified for the person who stabbed Callie." I know I've managed to prick his ego a little when he straightens up and stands taller. It's a bittersweet victory.

"Clever girl, aren't you?" he says with a grudging nod.

I shrug.

"But not as clever as you think. I admit I was worried when you got away from me the other night and then disappeared. But then I got a text from Smith a few hours ago letting me know you were in Chicago." He shakes his head and *tsks* at me. "Not a smart move on your part. He planted a bug on you so we could track you."

I'm shocked by this tidbit of information and at first I don't believe it. But then I remember how Smith put his hand on my shoulder as I was leaving the office. I reach up and feel underneath the collar of my jacket and sure enough, there's a tiny disc of some sort stuck to the underside of it. I peel it off and toss it on the floor.

Colbert watches me and smiles. "We don't need it anymore anyway," he says. "You were dumb enough to come back to me."

I glare at him, angry that he so successfully duped me, and angry with myself for playing into his hands. "So what's next, Colbert?"

"The plan is to kidnap you and stash you somewhere until we can figure out a way to kill you that will point to Hurley. Having you show up in Smith's office threw him a bit. His text said he was going to plant the bug on you and follow you when you left. He didn't want to do anything in his office because Trina was there. He got in his car and started tracking you, but when he found you, he saw Trina handing you some papers and knew the dumb bitch was betraying him. He's been suspicious about her for a while now. He drove around the block and by the time he came back, you were gone. When he saw Trina walking along the sidewalk, he did what he had to do to silence her, figuring we could find you later with the tracking device."

"She's still alive," I tell him, but if I'm hoping this news will rattle him, I'm sorely mistaken.

"Doesn't matter," he says. "Smith will find a way to dispatch her while she's in the hospital. He has a lot of connections."

"Who hired you? Dilles or Ackerman?"

"What difference does it make?" he says with a shrug. "You're going to be dead either way."

Tears burn at my eyes and I struggle to keep them at bay. "Why are you doing this?"

"*I'm* doing it for the money," he says. Then he shrugs. "As for Dilles and Ackerman, they each have their own motives, not that I care."

This news comes as a shock. I was convinced one of the men had to be behind all this but I had no idea it was both of them. "What motives?" I ask.

Colbert considers my question a moment before answering. I can only guess that he's debating the wisdom of revealing this information.

"Come on," I coax. "What harm can it do to tell me if you're going to kill me anyway?"

Colbert considers this and apparently agrees—not a good sign for me.

"Good point," he says. "The way I understand it, Ackerman wanted to get rid of that Dunkirk woman and make sure he wouldn't be implicated in any way. Apparently she got pregnant by him and was pressuring him about child support. He paid it for a while but he has no money of his own to speak of. It all comes from his wife. He was having trouble hiding the payments and he couldn't afford to have his wife find out about his affair for fear she'd divorce him and cut him off. He knew about Dunkirk's history with Hurley, so he did a little investigative work and uncovered the history between Dilles and Hurley. Once he learned how much Dilles hated Hurley, he came up with a plan that would take care of his little problem and also give Dilles a chance to get revenge."

."How did you get involved?"

"I've known Connor Smith since I was a kid. Both of my parents were drug dealers and they had more than a few dealings with Smith because they got caught several times. Smith managed to get them off with light sentences the first few times, but eventually justice caught up to them. When I was thirteen they both ended up with convictions that led to twenty-year sentences. My father was killed by another inmate a year later, and my mother died of cancer two years after that. I ended up a ward of the state and did the foster home parade for a number of years, and got involved with a gang. After I got nailed and did time in juvie for a couple of robberies, Smith found me and made me an offer. He needed someone to carry out a plan for him and the men behind it had enough money to make it well worth my while. So he had one of his past clients create a new identity for me, pulled some strings, and got me into the police academy. Fortunately the Sorenson Police Department isn't high on anyone's list when it comes to job opportunities, and they always have openings. So it was pretty easy to get hired."

"But why would Smith do that? Why risk his reputation and his freedom to help the likes of Ackerman and Dilles?"

"Two reasons. One, the same motivation I had: money. While Ackerman's purse strings are tightly controlled, Dilles's aren't. The man has shitloads of money that's of little use to him now, so he's willing to use it to get the revenge he wants on Hurley. The other reason is that Ackerman somehow figured out that Smith was the man Dilles's wife was having an affair with before she was killed. So he basically threatened to reveal that fact if Smith didn't do what he wanted. The fact that Smith defended Dilles—unsuccessfully, no less—after boffing the man's wife is an egregious violation of ethics. If it became known, Smith would lose his license, his community standing, his money, everything. Not only that, it might make him look like an alternative suspect and give Dilles cause for a new trial. And I think Smith knows that if Dilles found out the truth, he'd kill him."

"A very clever plan," I say.

"Yes, it is. Or at least it was until you screwed things up." To my relief, Colbert takes his finger off the trigger, though the gun is still aimed in my direction. "Tell me something," he says. "How did you know Hurley wasn't behind these killings?"

"I know him well enough to know he wouldn't murder someone in cold blood."

"I see," he says with a smirk. "And judging from what I've seen and heard, you'd like to know him a lot better. Not exactly an objective judgment but fortunately what you think won't make any difference. By the time they find your body, there will be enough evidence to clearly implicate Hurley in three murders, one attempted murder, and the arson."

It doesn't take me long to do the calculations and figure out that the third murder will be mine. "What possible motive would Hurley have for killing me?"

Colbert looks irritated by the question and he waves the gun toward the bedroom door. "Enough with your twenty questions," he says. "Let's go."

Reluctantly I get up from the bed and walk toward the living room. "What about my clothes?" I ask, knowing it's a stupid question. But it's the only way I can think of to try to get my hands on the gun again.

Colbert confirms my stupidity by jabbing me in the back with his gun and saying, "You won't be needing them, so quit stalling and head out to the car."

I continue toward the door, feeling like a red-shirted Star Trek character that just got beamed down to the planet. My mind is scrambling for a way out, for any solution that might save my life. But I'm doomed. As far as anyone knows, I'm at the motel being guarded by one of Sorenson's finest.

I open the door, step outside, and head for the passenger side of Colbert's squad car utterly terrified and fighting back tears. Off to my side I hear a twig snap and at first I think it's Colbert who made the noise. Then I realize he's directly behind me. In the next second I hear Bob Richmond's voice holler out.

"Stop right there, Colbert."

I turn and look in the direction Richmond's voice came from, and out of the corner of my eye I see Colbert do the same. He instinctively points the gun that way and the second I realize its muzzle is no longer pointed at me, I know my time is now or never. I fling my entire body back and to the side, colliding with Colbert as hard as I can. The two of us go down like fallen trees and I hear all the air leave Colbert's lungs in a giant *whuff* as my weight lands hard on his chest.

Then I hear the best thing of all: Hurley's voice.

"Colbert, drop your weapon!"

I can tell Colbert is momentarily stunned, but he still has his gun in his hand. Not wanting to waste the opportunity, I roll off him and scramble the ten feet or so to the still open door of my cottage. As soon as I cross the threshold I dash across the living room and into my bedroom, running low and hunched over to make a less obvious target. I half expect to feel the sting of a bullet in my back any second but I manage to make it to the bed without incident. I throw myself on top of it, grab the gun from beneath the pillow, and then roll off the other side, ducking down to use the bed as a barrier.

I hear shots outside: first one, then another, then a third. Instinct tells me to stay where I am, holding my gun at the ready in case Colbert comes back inside. I hear more shots exchanged outside and since this tells me Colbert is likely distracted, I scramble out of my hiding place over to the bedroom door and carefully peek around the corner. The front door is still wide open but I can't see much because the couch is blocking my view. As quick as I can, I leave the bedroom and crawl over to the couch. Staying close to the floor, I make my way to the end of the couch closest to the door, and peer around it.

Colbert is squatting down—tensed and ready to spring—on the passenger side of his squad car, using it as a barrier between him and the other men. Movement catches my eye out the window off to the right of the door, and when I look I see Richmond making a dash toward the squad car. In the next second Colbert pops up, sees Richmond coming toward him, and fires off a shot.

Richmond drops like a ton of bricks.

I duck back behind the couch and sit there a minute, panicked and trying to figure out what to do next. With Richmond down I know time is of the essence, and in my gut I know I have to do something.

I look down at the gun in my hands and squeeze my eyes closed for a second to brace myself and muster up some courage. Then I open my eyes, stand up, aim the gun at Colbert, and pull the trigger. A nanosecond later, the driver side headlight explodes.

I duck back down behind the couch, expecting to hear another exchange of gunfire, but there isn't any. Is Hurley shot too? If not, is he armed? Not being able to see what's going on terrifies me because I realize Colbert could pop up on me any second. Like a turtle on speed, I thrust my head around the corner to look and then pull back. What I see reassures me a little. Colbert has moved down the side of the car toward its rear, farther from the house. His attention is focused on the woods and as I see him peer around the back end of the car, I raise myself up and look out the window, searching for Hurley. I don't see him, but I do see Richmond lying on the ground, groaning. At least he's not dead. Yet.

When I look back toward Colbert, I see him start to rise in preparation for another shot over the roof of the car. Seconds later he fires and ducks back down. Once again I wait for Hurley to return fire, but nothing happens.

Emboldened by this lack of response, Colbert stands and steps around to the back of the car, his gun held in front of him. I run hunched over to the door, ducking down by the front grille of the car. When I look toward the woods I finally spy Hurley standing behind a tree, his side to the bark, facing me. He sees me and gives a little nod. I breathe a sigh of relief that he appears to be okay, but then he shows me his hands, which are empty.

Colbert fires a shot at the tree and the bullet bites into the bark, sending pieces of it flying. Hurley flinches and hugs himself in tighter to the tree. Richmond moans and tries to pick himself up from the ground. I see his gun lying in the dirt several feet in front of him. And then I watch in horror as Colbert raises his gun and takes aim at Richmond's massive form struggling helplessly on the ground.

Desperate, I rise up, take my stance again, and try to line the sights on my gun up with Colbert's chest. My hands and body are shaking like I'm in the spin cycle of a washer but I pull the trigger anyway, knowing it's now or never.

I see sparks fly up about ten feet to the front and left of Colbert and realize the bullet has struck a large decorative boulder in Izzy's yard. I line Colbert up in my sights again and prepare to pull the trigger a second time, figuring if nothing else I might be able to rattle him enough to distract him, but then the most amazing thing happens; Colbert slumps to the ground.

At first I think he's merely trying to avoid my shots, but he's lying very still, not moving at all. Not trusting him, I keep my gun pointed at him and step around the front of the car.

Hurley peers around the tree, takes in the scene, and steps away from his protection, too. Slowly the two of us approach Colbert, who remains utterly still. Then I see the blooming red stain on the right side of Colbert's shirt and realize that when my bullet ricocheted off the boulder, it hit him.

Hurley closes the final gap with a few long strides and kicks Colbert's gun off to the side. Then he looks over at me. "Take your finger off the trigger and lower the gun, Mattie," he says in a calm reassuring voice.

I do as he says and he walks over and takes the gun from my hand. "Are you okay?" he asks.

I nod, staring down at Colbert. "Is he dead?"

Hurley kneels down and places his fingers along Colbert's neck, feeling for the carotid. After a few seconds he looks up at me and says, "He's got a pulse." As if to confirm this fact, Colbert moans. "Good thing he's a reckless, stupid rookie and wasn't wearing his vest."

Off in the distance I hear sirens approaching, and though I should feel relieved that the craziness is over and help is on the way, all I can think about is the fact that I just shot a man.

I shake it off and shift my attention to Richmond, who is lying on his back looking up at us, blood seeping from his belly. Unfortunately, he wasn't wearing a vest either and I suspect it's because he couldn't find one that would fit. Kneeling beside him, I start to undo his jacket so I can look at his wound.

"Will this get me out of going to the gym for a while?" he asks with a grim smile.

I smile back at him. "A little while," I say, ripping his shirt apart. The bullet hole is in his right lower abdomen and though there is a fair amount of bleeding, it appears to be slowing. "But I'm not going to let you off the hook forever," I add.

Cop cars come screaming up the drive, parking willy-nilly wherever they can. Junior Feller is the first out of his car and after quickly taking in the scene, he radios for a couple of ambulances. I take off my jacket and push it against Richmond's wound to further dampen the bleeding. The night air is bitterly cold but when I shiver, I'm not sure if it's nerves or the chill that triggered it.

As Hurley briefs Junior on what happened, I have one of the other cops come over and take over Richmond's wound management. Then I shift my attention to Colbert.

I move over to him but Hurley stops me. "Let him lay there," he says.

"I can't, Hurley. I'm a nurse. I have to try."

He frowns and sighs heavily. "Fine," he says. "But let me cuff him first."

I wait as one of the cops puts Colbert in handcuffs and removes his utility belt. When I'm finally able to open Colbert's jacket and shirt, I find a sucking chest wound on his right side. But he's breathing and his pulse, though very fast, is strong.

The ambulances arrive and I turn Colbert's care over to the EMTs. They load Colbert first and take off, then with the help of several cops, they manage to get Richmond on a stretcher and loaded into the second rig.

Hurley walks back over to me as the ambulance prepares to leave. "Are you sure you're okay?" he asks, putting a hand on my shoulder.

I nod even though I'm trembling uncontrollably due to the cold, my nerves, and lots of excess adrenaline. Hurley takes my chin in his hand and turns my head, forcing me to look at him. "You did good, Mattie. You saved my life. You saved all our lives."

I nod again. Then I burst into sobbing, body-wracking tears and let Hurley hold me in his strong, very capable arms.

Chapter 46

William walks into my mother's dining room carrying his pride and joy: a perfectly browned, crisp-skinned turkey. Thanksgiving was yesterday and I have to admit I'm a little bummed that I wasn't able to celebrate on the only day of the year when big thighs are thought to be a good thing. But it couldn't be helped. I spent the entire holiday in debriefing sessions with detectives from the county sheriff's office, trying to fill in the blanks about the Ackerman-Dilles-Colbert debacle.

At least most of my favorite people are here with me: Hurley, Izzy, Dom, William, and my mother. Okay, my mother isn't really one of my favorite people but she is my mother and I'm kind of stuck with her.

Hoover is here too, and he's hovering at our feet beneath the table, knowing that Dom and I are likely to be good for a dropped scrap or two.

William sets his pièce de résistance in the center of the table, which is well laden with all kinds of other fattening goodies, and after we all ooh and aah over the turkey, we dig in like a horde of locusts. As William starts carving, the rest of us grab dishes full of food and begin the big pass-around until our plates are piled high.

Everyone, that is, except my mother, who clearly didn't pass her appetite on to me. She takes tiny dribs and drabs of each selection while eyeing the turkey with a worried eye. "Are you sure we can't get the Asian bird flu from eating that thing?" she asks.

"It's an American turkey, not an Asian one, Mom," I say, knowing I'm wasting my breath.

She sighs, shakes her head, and declines William's offering when he tries to put a slice of the meat on her plate. William gives us all an "Isn't she cute?" smile and continues his duties. Clearly the man is smitten.

As soon as we all have our plates loaded up, everyone but Mom digs in with gusto. She pushes her food around and eyes the rest of us with disdain.

"I don't know how you people can eat after everything that's happened," she says. She drops her fork with a clatter and puts the back of her hand to her forehead. "I'm not feeling very well. Why isn't David here?"

"He had a date," I tell her. "Apparently he and our insurance adjuster hit it off. He's moved on, Mom. Get used to it." I knew something was up when David suddenly capitulated on the divorce thing. I should have known there was another woman involved; some things never change.

My mother lets out a sound of disgust, no doubt to mourn the loss of her personal family physician.

William says, "Mattie has filled us in on most of what happened, but the one thing she didn't tell us is how Bob Richmond figured out Colbert was involved."

"The e-mails," Hurley explains. "There were a couple of them that seemed to reference the same material as the ones between Smith and Ackerman but they were between Smith and another, unknown e-mail address. So Richmond called the Internet provider to find out who that e-mail belonged to. Apparently Colbert wasn't smart enough to sign up for an e-mail account using a phony ID. I'm surprised he didn't use the Leon Lindquist name Dilles gave him like he did for the car rental."

"How did you end up at my house with Richmond?" I ask Hurley. "I thought you were under arrest."

"I was," Hurley says. "The sheriff's deputies brought me to Sorenson and turned me over to Richmond right after you and Colbert left. Richmond was about to lock me up when he got the information about the e-mail address. Once he knew Colbert was involved, it didn't take Richmond long to fit the pieces together. He sent Junior and another cop over to the motel while he and I went to your place."

"Thank goodness," I say, the memory of how close I came to death making me shudder.

"Of course," Hurley goes on, "the full extent of Dilles and Ackerman's involvement wasn't clear yet, but fortunately Colbert sang like the proverbial canary yesterday when they offered him a plea deal. Now he and Ackerman are likely to end up as Dilles's prison mates. And the cops have arrested Smith, too. Between the damage to his SUV and the e-mails, they can hit him with both conspiracy charges and the attempted murder of Trina."

"How is this Trina woman doing?" Izzy asks.

"She's stable and they were able to save her leg," I tell him. "Her recovery will be long and hard, but it looks like she'll be good as new eventually."

"Well," Izzy says, bestowing me with a smile, "it looks like your faith in Hurley was justified after all. Congratulations on solving a very complicated case."

"Thanks," I say, and then I look over at Hurley. "I told you Ackerman was involved," I say, feeling smug.

"And I told you Dilles was," Hurley counters.

"And you were both right," Izzy says quickly, playing mediator. "Sounds to me like the two of you are going to make a crackerjack investigative team."

Hurley and I exchange a momentary look before we both drop our gazes to our plates.

Dom says, "I'm still a little confused on the details. This rookie cop was the one who committed all these crimes?"

I nod and swallow the glob of mashed potatoes and gravy I have in my mouth. "He was. Smith used his criminal connections to come up with a fake ID and history for Colbert, whose real name is Jonathan Haney. Colbert applied for a job at the Sorenson PD, which apparently has several openings, did his academy training, and then went to work learning all he could about Hurley. One of Smith's prior clients taught Colbert how to pick locks and once he had that down, it was easy enough for him to break into Hurley's house and do what he needed to do."

I pause and give Hurley a questioning look, knowing that the next subject I want to address is a sensitive one for him. He gives me a subtle nod and then focuses on his plate of food.

"Callie was targeted right from the get-go," I continue. "And since Ackerman knew about her past with Hurley, he got the idea to frame him for her murder, thereby taking care of Ackerman's problem with Callie's threatened paternity suit. Callie's sister knew Ackerman and Callie were involved and I suspect Ackerman knew she knew. That's why he had to have other murders occur that had no connection to him but would point the finger at Hurley. It was Ackerman who suggested that Callie investigate the police corruption thing with Hurley, telling her that he got the anonymous call. And since it didn't raise any eyebrows for Ackerman to be calling one of his employees, the phone records for Callie's cell didn't raise any eyebrows, either. After killing Callie, Colbert made sure there was evidence pointing to Hurley with the hair we found in her wound, the metal fragments that were stuck in her hair, and the knife he discovered in Hurley's boat.

"After that, it was easy enough to discover the lawsuit Mr. Minniver had with Hurley since it's listed on the public circuit court site. Once Minniver was targeted, Colbert watched him for a few days and stole the spare key the man had stashed in his front porch light. Then he snuck in and poisoned Minniver's iced tea with the cyanide, knowing Hurley had potassium cyanide in his shop."

"Frighteningly clever," William says, looking both intrigued and appalled.

"I still don't understand why they went after David," my mother whines.

"They thought Hurley and Mattie had a thing going on," Izzy offers. Then he quickly adds, "Understandable, since that's what David thought, too, leading to a very public argument between him and Hurley at the grocery store, an argument that Colbert witnessed. It gave him one more thing to use to frame Hurley."

"*Is* there something going on between you two?" William asks, looking from me to Hurley.

"Nope," Hurley and I both say quickly.

"We're working partners, nothing more," I add.

"David may not be here," Izzy says to my mother, "but be thankful he's alive. The plan was for him to die in that fire but thanks to Mattie, he didn't. Your daughter has been a hero three times this week."

"Yes, I heard that you were the one who shot this Colbert guy," William says.

Hurley chuckles and says, "Well, technically she shot a rock, but fortunately the bullet ricocheted and hit Colbert."

I give him an exasperated look. "So I'm not an ace shot," I grumble. "Sue me."

Hurley holds his hands up in surrender. "Hey, your lousy shooting saved both me and Richmond. If you hadn't hit the headlight with that first shot, Colbert might have gone after us that much sooner. As it was he thought that shot came from me. He didn't know I wasn't armed."

"How is Richmond?" Dom asks.

"He's doing fine," I say. "Ironically his fat slowed the bullet enough that it didn't do any serious damage. It nicked his bowel and he's going to be pooping in a bag for a few months, but other than that, he should be okay."

"Matterhorn Marie Fjell Winston!" my mother admonishes. "We don't discuss bodily functions at the dinner table."

Everyone at the table turns to look at me. Izzy shrinks down like a turtle trying to duck back into its shell, William looks confused, and Dom looks apologetic.

Hurley, on the other hand, looks amused. "Matterhorn?" he repeats in a tone that makes it sound like he just tasted something horrid. "Your real name is Matterhorn?"

I shoot my mother a look that rivals one of her own and have the satisfaction of seeing her flinch and clutch at her chest. "Oh my God," she says. "My days are truly numbered."

Just as I start to preen, convinced that I've finally mastered the talent of The Look, she adds, "Your dog has his nose in my crotch again."

Keep reading for a special sneak peek at *Lucky Stiff*,
the newest Mattie Winston mystery,
available in paperback and as an e-book in March 2013!

Chapter 1

There are few things in life that smell as bad as a burnt human body. You'd think with all that flesh, which is really just another form of meat, it might smell like a pig roasting on a spit. But you'd be wrong. Your average roasting pig doesn't have hair, intact organs, and vessels filled with blood. Unfortunately, the person whose death I now have to investigate comes with all those things, and the stench is nauseating.

Adding to the biological odors are the various household items that have burned: plastics, Styrofoam, building materials, and a variety of fabrics. This is a smell I know well because I've been living next to another burnt-down building for the past couple of weeks: the house I used to share with my ex-husband, David Winston. The only person who was in my old house when the fire struck was my ex and despite the fact that I've imagined him being tortured or dying in hideous ways many times over the past few months, he escaped from the fire unharmed. David is healthy, alive, and if his recent behavior is any indication, well into manopause, unlike the person before me now, who is burnt so badly I can't tell if the body is that of a man or a woman.

My ex is a surgeon. He cuts people open in an effort to better, or save their lives. My name is Mattie Winston, I'm a nurse, and I used to do the same thing, working side-by-side with David in our local hospital's OR. But after catching David using his penis as a tongue depressor on one of my coworkers, I left my job, my home, and my marriage rather abruptly. Fortunately my best friend and neighbor, Izzy, threw me a lifesaver by offering me both a job and the mother-in-law cottage behind his house. Since Izzy is the county medical examiner, my new job still involves cutting people open but with two significant differences: all of my patients are a certain distance past their freshness dates, and rather than trying to save their lives, I'm trying to figure out how they lost them.

The ME's office is located in the small Wisconsin town of Sorenson and we cover deaths for a county-wide area. I grew up in Sorenson, and that makes my job very difficult at times since I know most of the people I have to autopsy. Today the death I'm investigating is right here in town, a body discovered in a home that is now little more than a burnt-out shell. As a result, I'm not sure yet if our victim is someone I know. Adding to the tragedy is the fact that it's Christmas day as evidenced by the empty tree stand and a dozen or so broken glass ornaments in one corner.

Very little in the room I'm standing in is recognizable. Heat from the flames melted the foot or so of snow that was on the roof, and the melt-off, combined with the fire damage and all the water from the fire hoses, brought down most of the modest rancher's upper structure, leaving the scene a soggy, exposed, piled-up mess. An early afternoon sun is shining down on us, and the outside temperature is already forty-eight degrees—very atypical for December here in Wisconsin. Fortunately there was plenty of snow on the ground before today, allowing us some semblance of a white Christmas.

Izzy is beside me as we carefully pick our way through the charred remains, which are still smoking in places despite the heroic efforts of the fire department. It's a bit easier for me to maneuver than it is for Izzy, because I'm six feet tall and have very long legs. Izzy, on the other hand, stands right around five feet tall and his legs aren't much longer in their entirety than my shinbones.

Several of the firefighters are still on site, spot-quenching little flare-ups and guiding us through the debris field. They were the ones who called us when they found the body. Also here are several cops, including Steve Hurley, the tall, dark-haired, blissfully blue-eyed homicide detective I lust after but can't have.

"Are you guys sure this is arson?" Hurley asks a woman firefighter standing nearby.

"Positive," she says. She is a cute blond with a large, fluorescent name label across the back of her fire coat that says KANE. Her cheeks are flushed and there are smudges of ash on her face, but they're not enough to hide her prettiness. If anything they enhance it, giving her an impish, pixie look. Even with all her fire gear on I can tell she has a trim, petite figure and I want to hate her on sight, especially when I see Hurley give her the once-over . . . twice. My figure has never been petite, not even in the womb. My mother once described giving birth to me as akin to crapping out bowling balls for twenty hours straight. I have what Izzy's life partner, Dom, calls a Rubenesque figure, a comment that makes me want to both hate Dom and ask him to make me a Reuben sandwich. Dom is a killer cook.

Speaking of cooking, Kane points over toward the couch

and says, "There's a pour pattern over there and if you look at the alligator pattern on the wall above it, you can tell that's where the fire started, even though someone tried to make it look like it started here by our victim. There's this other, smaller pour pattern next to the body leading from this over-turned drink glass. Judging from the empty vodka bottles we found in the trash, and the ashtray beside this glass, I'm guessing someone wanted us to think the victim caused the fire by reaching for a drink, spilling it, and tipping over in the wheelchair while holding a cigarette."

"Any idea who our victim is?" Hurley asks.

"For now we're assuming it's the man who lives here, a thirty-eight-year-old paraplegic by the name of Jack Allen."

"Oh, no," I mutter, looking aghast at the blackened mass.

"You know him?" Izzy asks.

"I do. I've taken care of him at the hospital several times. In fact, I took care of him when he had the car accident that paralyzed him. It was back when I was working in the ER, about seven, maybe eight years ago. I also saw him when we took his gallbladder out last year, and again more recently when he came in to have a bedsore debrided."

Kane cocks her head to one side. "I'm sorry, I thought you were with the ME's office," she says, eyeing me with a puzzled expression.

"I am. I've only had this job for a few months. Before that I worked at Mercy Hospital as an RN."

"Ah," Kane says, and I see a glimmer of recognition on her face. "You're that gal who was married to the surgeon, the doctor who was doing it with that OR nurse who ended up murdered."

"Yep, that's me."

"And you also worked in the OR?"

I nod.

"Now I know why you look so familiar." I'm thinking

she's going to mention some surgical procedure she had recently, but no such luck. "You were the one who was pictured on the front page of that tabloid, standing by the Heinrich car crash in your underwear."

My face grows hot. "Yes, that was also me," I say, my smile tight. Izzy and Hurley snort with laughter and I give them a threatening look as I silently curse my recent claim to fame. There are many perks to living in a small town like Sorenson. Unfortunately, anonymity isn't one of them. Infamy comes cheap and lasts a long, long time.

"I'm sorry, I don't remember your name," Candy says.

"I'm Mattie Winston. Nice to meet you," I lie.

"I'm Candy Kane. Today is my birthday and my parents had a warped sense of humor."

"Happy birthday," Hurley says with a smile that makes me want to step between him and Candy to block his view.

"Thanks," Candy says, smiling back. "After I'm done here I get to go home and open all those lovely happy-merry-birthday-Christmas presents. We holiday kids tend to get the short end of the stick when it comes to gifts."

This seems only fair to me since she clearly didn't get the short end of the genetic stick.

I look back at the floor and try to make sense of the fact that the burnt corpse lying there might be Jack Allen. The body is lying on its side in a fetal position, the blackened arms bent up like a boxer trying to block a punch. I know from my recent studies that this pugilistic positioning is characteristic of severe burn victims, caused by shortening of the muscles and tendons as they heat up. I can't see the victim's face because the head and shoulders are covered with a pile of debris—ceiling tiles and old vermiculite-type insulation. The only thing about the body that fits our tentative ID is the wheelchair that's tipped on its side and positioned behind the body.

Kane says, "The neighbors say he was a smoker as well as a drinker, though they fell short of describing him as an out-and-out drunk. One other interesting tidbit mentioned by the neighbors is the fact that our victim apparently won a very large jackpot at the North Woods casino a few months ago."

"How large is very large?" Hurley asks.

"Five hundred thousand and change," Kane says.

Izzy lets out a low whistle.

"Sounds like motive to me," Hurley says. "And it might help us narrow down the list of suspects. All we have to do is follow the money."

"First we need to verify that this is Jack Allen," Izzy says. He steps forward, reaches down, and lifts one corner of a ceiling tile that's covering the victim's head, exposing the face. I can only see one half of it as the other half is against the floor, but the entire head is relatively untouched by the ravages of the fire. Izzy turns and gives me a questioning look.

"That's Jack all right."

Izzy stares down at him. "Interesting how the debris protected his face from the flames."

"It would," Candy says. "That vermiculite insulation contains asbestos."

"Asbestos?" I echo, looking concerned.

"Don't worry," Candy says. "Right now everything is so saturated it would be nearly impossible for any fibers to become airborne. But it will require a special crew with the proper equipment to clean the place up."

Izzy nods solemnly. "Well at least we have a tentative ID. We can verify things later with his dental records." He cocks his head to one side and stares at the body with a puzzled expression.

"What is it?" I ask.

"Look at the position of his head. His chin is tucked in close to his chest. If the head had been exposed to the fire I might think it was because of tendon shrinkage from the heat. But the head was protected from the fire, and that makes me think it was forced into that position. The presence of the glass and the ashtray suggest there was a table of some sort here, like a coffee table."

"There probably was," Kane says. She points to several burnt pieces of wood that look like long, skinny cinders from a fireplace. "These look like the legs on a wooden structure of some sort."

"If so," Izzy says, "it's possible Jack died from positional asphyxiation. If he fell out of his chair and his head became wedged between it and a table, it could have blocked off his airway. I'll get a better idea of how feasible that theory is when I open him up."

Kane looks at Hurley and says, "There's one more thing I think you should see." We follow her through the debris into what appears to be the dining room. She stops in front of a charred piece of furniture and points to the melted, twisted remains of a stereo on top of it. As I look closer at the burnt mess I see what looks like a large stereo speaker, relatively intact despite evidence of intense heat and flames.

"There's only one speaker," Hurley says.

"And it didn't burn," I add.

"Good eye, both of you," Candy says, though she directs her smile at Hurley. She points to some melted plastic and wires. "It looks like there was another speaker here but it was destroyed in the fire. There's a reason this one survived." She reaches over and flicks her finger against the front of the intact speaker, eliciting a metallic ping. "This is a false front. It's constructed out of metal and made to look like a speaker, but it's actually a safe." She pulls on the speaker front and it opens, revealing an empty metal box. "There's a key lock on the back that operates a little spring device to open it."

"Was there anything in there?" Hurley asks.

"Nope, it was unlocked and empty when we got to it, and no sign of the key. But we did find this." Candy points down at the floor near the corner of the buffet and I see the edges of a hundred-dollar bill poking out from beneath some debris.

After snapping a picture, Hurley reaches down with his gloved hand and pulls the bill loose. Though its edges are singed, the main body of the bill is intact.

Candy says, "A lot of people don't know that paper money isn't really made out of paper, it's made out of cloth . . . linen and cotton to be precise. And that means it doesn't burn so easily, especially if it's wet."

"You're thinking there was more of this in there," Hurley says, gesturing toward the safe.

Candy shrugs, but she gives us a knowing smile that makes it clear she does think that.

Hurley sighs. "Well if our casino winner was stashing wads of cash in his house, our list of suspects is going to be a hell of a lot bigger than I thought."

"Sorry to make things more complicated for you," Candy says with a cutesy little grin.

Hurley holds her gaze a bit longer than I like. "No need to apologize. You did some great investigative work here. I appreciate it."

"You're welcome. And if there's anything else you need from me, don't hesitate to ask." She takes a card out of her jacket pocket and hands it to him. "That's my personal cell number on there. Call me anytime," she says with a suggestive tone. Then she gives Hurley a flirtatious wink and adds, "If you're nice to me, I just might give you a candy cane."

I have a few suggestions for what she can do with her candy cane, but I keep them to myself.

"Ahem," Izzy says, eyeing me with a worried expression. "I suppose we best get to wrapping up the body so we can get it back to the morgue before all this water destroys our evidence. What do you guys say to doing this autopsy today?"

"Fine by me," I say. After years of employment at the hospital I'm used to working on the holidays. "You'll be giving me the perfect excuse for avoiding the remainder of the celebration at my sister's house. My mother was already having a conniption about all the germs that might be lurking in my sister's live Christmas tree. When I left for this call, she was bleaching the tree ornaments." My mother has a few mental quirks, not the least of which are her hypochondria and her OCD. I'm pretty certain that by day's end she'll be at home consulting her impressive medical library in search of tree-borne diseases, imagining symptoms to fit.

"I'm fine with it, too," Hurley says. "I have no plans for the rest of the day and I'd like to get this wrapped up as quickly as possible."

"Wrapped up?" I echo. "Interesting choice of words, given the holiday."

Izzy rolls his eyes and heads back to the living room. I follow reluctantly, leaving Candy and Hurley alone in the dining room together. I force myself to focus on the immediate tasks at hand, but part of my mind imagines me holding a giant candy cane with the curved end looped around Hurley's waist, dragging him away from Candy vaudeville style.

Chapter 2

Izzy and I manage to scoop up the remains of Jack Allen's body and get it back to the morgue some two hours later. We spend most of that time photographing and documenting the scene as the arson investigators collect their evidence.

Also documenting the scene outside is Alison Miller, Sorenson's ace reporter and photographer, who is lurking about snapping shots and talking to anyone who's willing. I've known Alison for years and it was right after our high school graduation that she went to work for our local paper, which comes out twice a week. I once considered her a friend, but our relationship these days is somewhere between animosity and outright loathing. That's because she became my chief competition for Hurley's affections not long ago, until Hurley made it clear he wasn't interested. Alison didn't take the rejection well and blamed it on me. I'm probably the only person she won't try to get a quote from.

Candy, the person who seems to be my new competition,

doesn't stay long. While her absence relieves me a little, I can't help but notice that Hurley still has her card tucked safely inside his jacket pocket. I remind myself that I have no right to be jealous of what, or who, Hurley does because we don't have that kind of relationship. It's not from a lack of desire, however. There is a definite attraction between us that became evident early on during cases we worked together. But my lingering ambivalence over my marriage—and the tiny fact that I was still married—put a bit of a kibosh on things.

The marriage thing has recently been resolved. After rejecting David's repeated pleadings to give our marriage another chance, he finally got the message that I was done with him . . . right around the time he met up with Patty, the very attractive and single insurance agent who is handling the claim for our house fire. Now the two of them are an item. My divorce became final two days ago and along with my freedom I also received a tidy little settlement of nearly three hundred thousand bucks—my portion of the insurance claim on our house minus the amount David gave me for the car I totaled some time ago that was in his name. The settlement wasn't as much as I'd hoped because David, who handled all our financials, apparently neglected to update our homeowner's policy two years ago when we added on several hundred square feet of house in an addition off the back. While the house was once estimated to be worth close to a million bucks, in the current housing market, which stinks worse than what's left of Jack's house, that value has dropped to around seven hundred grand. And the insurance policy was for the original amount of the purchase, which was only five hundred grand plus another hundred thousand for the contents. David had at one time offered to let me have a larger portion of the settlement in order to make up for the value of the land, which is now in his name only, but after listening to him bitch about how much it was going to cost to rebuild and refurnish the place, I decided—in the spirit of idiocy—to settle for an even fifty-fifty split.

Still, my portion of the settlement has made for a nice early Christmas present, and for the first time in months my bank account is flush while I try to decide how to invest the funds. David is using his half to rebuild the house, albeit a smaller, scaled down version of the original.

Unfortunately my newfound freedom doesn't help my situation with Hurley. Thanks to cuts in the Wisconsin state budget, and a few shady dealings by some cops and evidence techs in Milwaukee, a lot of job titles and duties were eliminated, merged, and otherwise shuffled recently, mine included. Instead of being a deputy coroner, I now bear the hefty title of medicolegal death investigator. Though it sounds fancier, it's basically the same job I was doing before, except now our office works more closely with the police department, both with the collection and processing of evidence, and with the overall investigation. We each provide oversight to the other. In a way, this is a good thing for me because it means I get to spend more time with Hurley and I can legitimately do what I've always done—be nosy and get into everyone else's business. But because we're basically serving as watchdogs for one another, it also means there can't be any hints of fraternization, or situations that might cause conflicts of interest. Bottom line, in order to keep my job, I can't date Hurley. And despite my recent windfall, I want to keep my job. I enjoy it, I'm good at it, and the majority of my money from the divorce settlement needs to be earmarked for retirement.

While I can't date Hurley, there's nothing that says I can't continue to place myself in strategic positions for observation whenever he has to bend over. And I do so as often as I can during our scene processing, admiring the long, lean lines of his back and a pair of buns that look like they could crack open an oyster.

I know these musings aren't healthy and at some point I'll have to pick myself up, dust myself off, and get back into the dating scene. It's not something I look forward to. The one date I've had so far turned out to be an unmitigated disaster and the man is now living and sleeping with my mother.

Speaking of dusting off, I feel and look like a chimney-sweep by the time we get Jack's body back to the morgue, so I opt to take a quick shower before heading into the autopsy suite. Stripping down in the shower room, I make the mistake of glancing in the full-length mirror to check out my new tan lines.

In a few days, Hurley and I will be traveling to Daytona Beach to attend a two-day educational seminar on advances in forensics, one of the requirements of my new job description. Though I failed to inherit my mother's tiny, trim figure, I did get her fair coloring, blue eyes, and blond hair. My normal skin tone is quite pale. Along with my height and my size twelve feet, it earned me the nickname Yeti in high school. Given the warm weather and the sunny beach where we'll be staying for the seminar, I thought it might be prudent to spend a little time in a tanning bed getting some base color. I know the sun can be dangerous, but the idea of worshipping it a little is irresistible, especially since I'm in the midst of one of Wisconsin's infamously long, dark, snowy winters. Thanks to daylight savings time, I go to work in the dark and come home in the dark. Every day I check my canine teeth in the mirror, expecting to see that they've grown.

So an artificial sun is my only choice and I've had two sessions at the tanning bed so far. I got a bit impatient yesterday and set the timer for longer than I should have. As a result I burned a little, leaving me cherry red instead of tanned. Fortunately I kept my panties on and draped a small towel over my boobs so my more delicate parts didn't get hit. I'm not too worried about the red parts because I know from past experience that they'll fade to tan in a few days, giving me an approximate two-week window of looking sun-kissed and healthy before giant sheets of my skin start peeling off like a sloughing leper.

I planned it all out so that I'd look my best when we hit Florida, but as I glance into the mirror and examine my backside, I realize I've made a fatal miscalculation. The curved tanning bed cradles me pretty tightly, and as a result I have a series of red and white stripes down both of my sides—red where my skin was exposed to the tanning bed, white where rolls of back fat kept certain areas tucked away and hidden. The end result is laughably hideous. I look like a mutant, albino zebra.

Disgusted, I get into the shower and try to block the image from my mind, vowing to get back to the gym. A hugely overweight, semi-retired detective by the name of Bob Richmond conned me into doing workouts with him a few weeks ago, but I've slacked off a bit of late while he's been at home recuperating from a bullet wound. My idea of exercise is walking to the bakery rather than driving, and I'm convinced that the exercise machines at the gym were purloined from a medieval torture chamber.

Fifteen minutes later I am cleaned of ash and my stripes are safely hidden beneath a set of scrubs. When I arrive in the autopsy room, Izzy informs me that he and Arnie, our lab tech, have already X-rayed the body—including a set of dental films—drawn vitreous samples, and obtained blood from the carotid artery. Hurley and another local cop by the name of Junior Feller are standing against the wall by the door and, as I approach the table, the song "Bad Boys" from the TV show *Cops* starts to play. Looking a bit embarrassed,

Junior takes out his cell phone and answers it, stopping the music.

"Are you kidding me?" Hurley mutters with a roll of his eyes.

Junior says into the phone, "Not now, Monica. I'll call you later." He pauses and then says, "Yes, I can pick up some eggs on the way home. But it may be a while." He snaps the phone shut and drops it back in his pocket.

"Seriously, dude?" Hurley says, shaking his head. "You have the theme song for *Cops* as your ring tone?"

Junior looks sheepish and shrugs. "Monica likes it."

Monica is his new girlfriend and a committed badge chaser. I wouldn't be surprised to learn that she and Junior do it in the back of his cruiser while Junior keeps his uniform and gun belt on.

Izzy and I smile at one another but say nothing, turning our attention back to the task at hand. Jack's body is already laid out on the table and fully exposed. It's a bizarre sight. His limbs look like giant, burnt chicken wings, his torso like a charcoal briquette, and yet his face looks relatively normal.

Izzy starts his superficial exam at Jack's face while I take a comb to what's left of his hair, searching for trace evidence. All I find are chunks of the asbestos insulation, ash, and some bits of ceiling tile. I collect it all on clean white paper, and then bag and seal it as evidence.

Izzy steps up on the footstool he has to use in order to reach everything, and opens Jack's mouth to look inside. "There's no sign of soot in his nostrils or in his mouth," he says. "That tells me he was likely dead before the fire started. I'll be able to tell better once I get a look at his lungs, and after Arnie runs the lab tests on the blood he sampled. But I'm guessing Jack's carbon monoxide level will be zero."

"Maybe not zero," I say. "He was a smoker."

"Good point." Izzy then explains the situation to the cops. "Smokers tend to maintain a carbon monoxide level anywhere from zero to ten, depending on what they smoke, how long ago they smoked it, and how often they smoke. But if he inhaled smoke from the fire, his level will be much higher than that."

Izzy peels back Jack's upper lip, then the lower one. "Hmm, this is interesting," he says, and both Junior and Hurley step up to the table to take a look. "He has some bruising here on the inside of his lips, something we often see when someone's been smothered."

Hurley asks, "Can it be caused by something else?"

Izzy thinks a moment before answering. "Yes, I suppose it could. The weight of the ceiling debris falling on his face might have caused it, but considering the amount of the bruising, I suspect he was still alive with his heart pumping when it occurred, and if that had been the case he'd have soot in his mouth. So I can only assume the bruising occurred perimortem, before the fire started and the ceiling came down. It's also possible he hit his face against the floor or some other object when he fell out of his wheelchair."

After Izzy snaps some photos, we examine the remainder of Jack's body surface, both in the room's normal light and again using our ultraviolet light. Aside from more ceiling debris, we don't find anything of interest but we bag and tag what we do find, just in case.

Next Izzy hoses the body down and the resultant gray water runs along channels on the sides of the autopsy table into a special filter and drain. The filter will be examined later for any additional trace evidence.

Izzy steps down from his stool and looks over at Junior and Hurley. "This next part is going to be a bit grim," he warns. "I need to straighten out his arms and legs." Izzy instructs me to hold Jack's shoulder and torso down while he takes ahold of the lower part of the arm and pulls. He throws most of his weight into it, a considerable effort despite his height since Izzy is nearly as wide as he is tall. His face flushes red and his bushy, dark eyebrows draw together and form a V over his nose as he pulls. Finally the arm gives way with a distinct *crack*. After a short breather, we repeat the procedure on the other side and then move to the hips and legs. By the time we have the body as straight as we're going to get it bits of charred flesh have flaked off onto the table.

Izzy takes his scalpel and starts his Y-cut. He has to work at it; burnt flesh doesn't cut as easily as normal tissue. Once he has the torso exposed, he goes to work cutting the ribs and removing the breast plate. The underlying organs are in better shape than I expected. They appear shrunken to some degree, but they are still identifiable and those in the upper part of the torso appear almost normal. The stench, however, is anything but. It smells like roasted, rancid meat and at this point everyone in the room is mouth breathing. The stinky aspects of this job do take some getting used to and even Izzy, who I'd begun to think can't smell at all since nothing ever seems to bother him, is wrinkling his nose.

"The organs are often protected to some degree by the outer layers of the body," Izzy explains, reading my mind and once again slipping into teaching mode. "But if the fire burns hot enough, long enough, they'll eventually get thoroughly cooked and might even become charred."

When he dissects the lungs and trachea, the lack of soot verifies his theory that Jack died before the fire. Jack's stomach contents include some type of bread, bits of tomato, some soft, gooey white stuff, a thin, half-moon-shaped piece of what looks to be some type of meat, and a couple small chunks of something hard and white. I'm pretty sure I know what Jack's last meal was and my suspicion is confirmed when Izzy crushes one of the small white chunks and the aroma of garlic wafts into the air.

Izzy and I exchange a look across the table and both say, "Pesto Change-o."

"Huh?" Hurley says.

"It looks like Jack's last meal was a pepperoni pizza from Pesto Change-o," I say.

"How can you be that specific?" Junior asks.

"Pesto's is the only place in town that puts big chunks of garlic like this on their pizzas," I say.

I hold up the beaker with the stomach contents in it and point to one of the white chunks, which nearly makes Junior blow chunks. He clamps a hand over his mouth, prompting a muttered, "Wuss-ass" from Hurley. Izzy and I share a smile and then turn our attention back to the autopsy.

The fire burned much hotter near Jack's pelvis and the lower down in the body cavity we go, the more distorted and damaged the organs are. Despite being shrunken and discolored from the heat of the fire, his liver appears otherwise healthy and non-cirrhotic. Apparently his alcohol consumption hadn't been enough to destroy it yet.

By the time we're done removing and dissecting the organs, Arnie pops in with the results of the lab tests he's run. It's the first time I've seen him today and I have to do a double take.

"You cut off your ponytail."

He looks back at me through his thick glasses and rubs the top of his head, where skin is visible beneath the thinning brown strands. "It seemed a little too compensatory and pathetic," he says. "My hair is falling out and it's about time I manned up and faced the fact."

Izzy, who has a superb bullshit detector, says, "Uh-huh." He stares at Arnie for a beat and then adds, "When are you going to tell us the real reason?"

"What do you mean?" Arnie asks.

Izzy stares back at him over the top of his specs, his left eyebrow arched in skepticism.

"Fine," Arnie concedes after several more beats of silence. "I lost a bet and had to cut the ponytail off as payment."

"Ouch," Junior says. "That's a pretty stiff penalty."

"Yeah, I guess," Arnie says with a shrug. "I bet a friend of mine who works for a certain government agency that the new big screen TV he won in a company raffle had a hidden camera in it that allowed interested parties to spy on him."

This comes as no surprise to those of us who know Arnie. He's a conspiracy nut who believes homeless people are government spies, and all cell phones are secret monitoring devices created by aliens. "And there wasn't one?" I ask.

Arnie shakes his head. "We dismantled the entire TV and now we can't figure out how to put it back together." He shrugs again. "The ponytail seemed like a fair price to pay."

"The new do looks good on you," Izzy says. Then he quickly gets back to business. "What have you got for me?"

Arnie shows him the printouts he's carrying. "I didn't find anything too unusual aside from his blood alcohol level, which was 402."

"Wow," I say. "Impressive. That's more than five times the legal limit."

"Would it be enough to render him unconscious, or kill him?" Hurley asks.

"Depends," I say. "When I worked in the ER I once saw a couple of guys who were long-term practiced drinkers who were functioning quite well despite blood alcohol levels in the five hundreds. Over time you build up a tolerance."

"What was his carbon monoxide level?" Izzy asks Arnie.

"Six," Arnie says. "Typical for a smoker."

"Cyanide?" Izzy asks.

"Cyanide?" Hurley echoes. "Why would you test for that? Are you having flashbacks to that other case we had recently?"

Arnie explains. "Certain types of foam and plastic give off cyanide gas when they burn and the end effect is not unlike being in a gas chamber."

Junior winces, Hurley looks thoughtful, and Arnie adds, "But that didn't happen here. The cyanide test was negative. Also, Jack Allen's dentist is local so I sent over the X-rays we took and got a confirmation that the body is that of Jack Allen. The dentist said she'll send us over a copy of the corroborating X-rays later today."

"Thanks, Arnie," Izzy says. "And thanks for coming in today. I appreciate it."

"No problem." Arnie sets his printouts on a side counter. "I didn't have any big plans anyway." As Arnie leaves the room, I can't help but wonder how he spent his day. He's a transplant from L.A. and doesn't have any family here. I wouldn't be surprised to learn that he spent his time online in a chat room with like-minded conspiracy theorists, all of them wearing their protective tin foil hats and discussing how the emphasis on holiday spending is a government plot to subvert religion.

We move on to Jack's head and our examination of the brain reveals nothing more, ruling out any brain injury from Jack's fall as a cause of death.

When we're done, Izzy looks over at Hurley with an apologetic expression. "I can't give you a definite cause or manner at this point," he says. "Nor can I give you a time of death. Hopefully the stomach contents will help narrow that down if we have any witnesses to when he last ate, but if not, we might be able to get an estimate from the potassium level in the vitreous fluid. Though I know he died before the fire, there's no way to tell if his death was a homicide or an accident. As I said before, the alcohol level alone might have been enough, though if he was a practiced drinker that's less likely. He also might have succumbed to positional asphyxiation when he fell by landing in a position that blocked his airway. Or someone might have suffocated him."

"Well, whatever happened, we know arson was involved, and possibly robbery, too," Hurley says. "So for now we'll treat this as a homicide until we can prove otherwise."

"I think that's wise," Izzy says. "Those bruises inside the lips bother me. Based on the position of his body when we found it and the location of the nearby furniture, I find it hard to believe they were sustained in the fall, but I'll have to review the scene photos again to be sure."

Izzy has replaced the calvarium, or skull cap, and pulled Jack's scalp back into place. Then he pauses and stares at the body for a few seconds, his forehead furrowed with puzzlement.

"What is it, Izzy?" I ask.

He sighs and shakes his head. "There's something bugging me, something I feel I'm missing, but I can't put my finger on it at the moment."

"Well, if you figure out what it is, give me a call," Hurley says. "In the meantime, Junior talked with some of the neighbors and rounded up our first list of suspects." He nods at Junior, who takes out a small notebook and starts reading.

"It seems that Jack has a girlfriend, a woman named Catherine Albright who conveniently appeared on the scene right around the time Jack won his money. I'm going to do a little research on her and see what I can dig up. There's also a housekeeper who comes several times a week and a nurse who comes once a day. Jack never married, had no children of his own, and had only one sibling, an older sister named Megan Denver. The sister had one child—a son named Brian who's now twenty—and the sister and her husband were both killed in a car accident a couple of years ago. That leaves the nephew, Brian, as Allen's closest surviving family member."

Junior closes his notebook and Hurley looks over at me. "We'll need to talk with all of these people, and there are more neighbors I want to canvas, too. I have names I can run, and I'll set up some interviews for tomorrow if that's okay?"

I glance over at Izzy, who nods his approval. "That should be fine," I tell Hurley. "How about I meet you at the police station around eight?"

"That'll work," Hurley says. "In the meantime, do you have any plans for tonight?"

I'm puzzled by the question because it sounds suspiciously like a date request. But then Hurley adds, "I think we should visit the casino where Jack won his money and check out the employees who were on duty that night. Are you up for a little investigative gambling?"

"Tonight? It's Christmas. Are they even open?"

"You bet they are," Hurley says with a sly wink. He's very punny today.

"Okay, sure. I've never been to a casino before. It should be interesting."

"Never?" Hurley says, sounding skeptical. "You've never gambled?"

"Oh, I've gambled plenty, just not at a casino." I'm pretty familiar with most games of poker because one of my step-fathers—my mother's third husband—used to have a bunch of friends over once a week to play. I'd often sit in and watch, studying the facial expressions and body language of the players as they considered their cards, asking questions whenever I didn't understand the rules, and sneaking the occasional sip from my stepfather's alcoholic drinks.

"Well, then you're in for a treat. How about I pick you up at your place at six?"

"Sounds like a plan."

"See you then." He turns to leave but hesitates and looks over at me. Then, with a sly grin on his face, he walks over and whispers a parting shot in my ear: "Be sure you wear your lucky undies."